BORDER WAR

"We're ready," the sergeant said as he hefted his musket. Tucked into his waistband were a tomahawk and a knife. Flints, lead slugs, and wadding bounced in a leather pouch on his left hip. At his right swung a powder horn.

"Then get into position along the top of the ridge. Unless something's gone bad wrong, we're about ready for the fight of our lives," said Colonel Stand Watie. Mayes and the three men with h__ ____ ___ _____ _____, firing all their muskets a_____. A lot of whoops and hol_____ ___hink they had been cut o_____ an entire regiment, and th_____ up the hill to where Watie'_____.

"Hold your fir_____ ____. ____ them all time to start up the hill before you fire." In the distance he could hear Mayes firing. If he hadn't known better himself, he would have thought an entire regiment was attacking. The Jayhawkers began making their way out of the woods. "Fire, all fire! Give 'em hell!" Watie shouted.

The first volley tore through the Jayhawkers and brought down two. A second volley killed more.

"Fix bayonets. Charge, men, give them what for!"

The smell of gunpowder was in the air. The mounted company galloped forward, firing their pistols. When their hammers came down on empty, they used knife and tomahawk on the Jayhawkers. Watie's troops fought hard and well.

It proved enough to win the day.

FIRST CHEROKEE RIFLES

Karl Lassiter

PINNACLE BOOKS
Kensington Publishing Corp.
http://www.pinnaclebooks.com

PINNACLE BOOKS are published by

Kensington Publishing Corp.
850 Third Avenue
New York, NY 10022

Pinnacle and the P logo Reg. U.S. Pat. & TM Off.

First Printing: November, 1999
10 9 8 7 6 5 4 3 2 1

Printed in the United States of America

While based on actual events, this book is a work of fiction.

For Dale Goble

Death to Traitors!
June 21-22, 1839

"They must die," Otoomie said stiffly, his words knife-edged in the soft night. How great was the contrast between the menace in the Keetoowah Society leader's words and the humid night alive with winking lightning bugs and the thundering snap of distant summer lightning. Not far from their Takatoka meeting place bubbled the sweet water of Double Springs, promising only life amid the gently rolling, grass-carpeted hills. Everywhere nature belied the vengeance demanded so angrily by those huddled sullenly around the fires.

Trembling with pent-up emotion, Allen Ross stepped forward into the ring of light cast by the largest of the fires in the clearing. He felt the presence of so many others—could as many as two hundred warriors have assembled? Was the hatred for those who had signed the Treaty of New Echota this great? Allen felt heat from both the fire and from the communal anger. He shared some of that wrath, but not in such a great measure. His father always cautioned moderation, especially after the deaths of principal chiefs Charles Hicks and Pathkiller twelve years earlier had brought about so much division in the Cherokee Nation.

How filled those years had been, Allen reflected. The

Treaty of New Echota had allowed the Old Settlers like Boudinot, Ridge, and Watie to take the best land in the Western Cherokee Nation. Illegally, they had signed that treaty and then sold tribal land in Georgia to the white man in violation of Cherokee laws. Then they had preceded John Ross and the majority of the Cherokee westward, avoiding the travails along the Trail of Tears. The Keetoowah Society, formed mostly of full-blooded Cherokee, cried out with increasing venom about the inequity of their position. Their friends and kinsmen had died on the march to Indian Territory, and now they were forced to raise crops in a country totally different from their traditional lands. They were proud hunters, not farmers. Worse, they had to compete against the Old Settlers' farms, established years earlier and mostly run by Negro slaves skilled in agriculture. This was not the way a Cherokee ought to live.

"Elias Boudinot and all the others were wrong in signing away our land," Allen Ross said, his voice shaking with emotion. He rubbed his hands nervously on his pants legs, wondering what his father would say if he had known of this meeting and stood in front of the Keetoowah Society—the Pins. Everywhere he looked Allen saw the reflection of light off the sign of membership on the collars and on the fronts of vests. Pins—simple straight pins, mostly—in a cross pattern. They were a symbol for integrity and maintaining the old ways, the ways of the full-blooded Cherokee.

He closed his eyes and heard his father's voice as plainly as those of the Pins around him. John Ross had opposed the treaty requiring the Cherokee to leave their Southern homelands and move to the unknown far west, but he would never permit murder, even of his most bitter political opponents.

As if every word flashing through Allen's mind sprouted from his lips and raced to Otoomie's ear, the leader who whipped up the spirit of killing in these Keetoowah Society members answered his objections. Otoomie stepped to Allen's side, dark eyes flashing. His flat nose twitched slightly, and his nostrils flared. A scar on his cheek gleamed a dull pink in the firelight, giving him a fierce aspect that matched his words.

"The laws of our nation permit this killing," Otoomie said. "Major Ridge himself invoked it back in Georgia, and now we invoke it against him and the others who have sold tribal land. I have spoken with clan leaders, and have been assured there will be no reprisal. It is our way. It is the way of the Cherokee."

Allen knew Otoomie was a full-blood, unlike those he indicted and sentenced to death. He swallowed hard, realizing how fragile his own position was. His father was only one-eighth Cherokee, and might have been included with the Ridge-Boudinot faction had it not been for his forceful speeches against the treaty. John Ross had ironically ended up the leader of the majority of Cherokee, mostly full-bloods, while the minority, led by Elias Boudinot and Major Ridge, controlled the purse strings of the nation.

Was peace with the white man worth the loss of so much of their hereditary land? The Red Stick War had shown how dangerous the white man could be on the warpath, and Andrew Jackson had heaped scorn on them at every turn, but the treaty was a fact. Killing those who spoke loudest in favor of it—and those who profited most—was still wrong.

But not *too* wrong, Allen Ross thought.

"If our laws permit it, why do we sneak about in the night?" he countered.

"You know the reason. Chief Brown and John Ross have not been able to form a new government because Ridge and Boudinot are powerful men, intent only on their own fortunes. The might of their influence does not change how they have wronged our tribe. They must die." At Otoomie's words, a ripple of agreement passed through those assembled. Here and there unsheathed knives glinted and tomahawks whooshed through the air, as if seeking fleshy targets and being denied.

Then the silence that fell around the assembly wore on Allen until a collective sigh was let out and cheering began. With the shouts of resolve came whoops and dancing in a long, snake-like line that wound in and out around the smaller fires.

"Go to your father," Otoomie said to Allen. "We know how he might oppose us. Keep him from interfering in what must be done. They must die. They *will* die for what they have done to our proud nation."

Allen nodded and slipped from the clearing. The sound of moccasin and boot soles tapping hard on the ground as the Keetoowahs danced accompanied him until he reached his carriage. He whipped the horse and got it moving back toward his father's house outside Tahlequah, in Park Hill. The deaths would anger John Ross, but Allen did not think his father would mourn any of those who would die.

He couldn't pretend sorrow, because he had opposed Major Ridge and the others too fiercely and for so long. It was time to act now that words had failed. Allen Ross whipped his horse and got it trotting in the direction of Rose Cottage where John Ross slept, not knowing how the destiny of the Cherokee was to be changed this night.

Just before dawn twenty men crept closer to the neat, small Honey Creek home of John Ridge. Ten circled to the rear to cut off any escape. The others climbed softly up the steps to the front porch and arrayed themselves along the wall of the house. Their leader pushed back his hair from his eyes, drew a knife, and then banged loudly on the door.

"John Ridge!" he cried. "Come out, Ridge!"

From inside the house came gentle sounds, sounds of

a man awakened from a deep sleep. The Pins exchanged looks. Such was life with the Old Settlers. They slept away the day when others were already in the fields futilely trying to raise wheat and beans and timothy. Ridge wouldn't sully his hands with such work. His slaves would be out in his vast fields, toiling away for him.

"Who's there?"

"Ridge!" repeated the leader of the Pins, his fingers tight on the hilt of his knife. Impatience overtook him. He kicked open the door and burst into the house, brandishing his weapon. The bedroom off the larger common room showed where John Ridge still lay in his bed. With a whoop, the assassin leaped forward.

John Ridge's eyes widened when he saw the knife rise and then plunge downward into his chest. He gasped, then spat forth a torrent of blood as he fell from his bed to the floor. Ridge's wife sat up in bed and shrieked. Her cries brought her children running. They clung to her in fear for their own lives.

Those Pins who had watched now leaped to the attack, dragging the still moaning Ridge from his house into the yard. Tomahawks and knives ended Ridge's life as his horrified family watched helplessly.

Only when the mutilated body began drawing flies and ants did the killing frenzy subside and the twenty leave, proud of their mission and how they helped execute the traitor to the Cherokee Nation.

Major Ridge stretched old, tired muscles and went into the out building. Two of his slaves were still down with belly cramps from eating green apples. He considered getting the doctor out to look at them if they didn't improve by noon, but that decision could wait until after he had mended the harness. Bellyaches weren't usually too serious, but these had gone on for two days. Everything fell apart at the same time, or so it always seemed. He laid out the leather strips and matched them to the broken harness from his carriage.

Punching holes with a slender awl, he then held up ancient hands, studied his handiwork, and smiled. No one worked leather better. For fifty years, no one had been able to match his skill. Major Ridge began the easier part of the job, stitching the pieces together so he would get more service from the harness. Everything cost more here in Arkansas—especially just across the Mississippi in Indian Territory, where the entire Cherokee Nation was dependent on trade with the United States. The wily white traders always managed to work a deal to their own benefit.

He thought on this as he worked, and decided he would mention it to his son, John. They might put together a mercantile association and turn the tables, selling to the whites around Fort Gibson rather than always being on the wrong end of the trade. He could arrange for transport from other parts of Arkansas and even Louisiana—up the Mississippi and then to Fort Gibson by barge along the Arkansas River—cheaper than how the Yankee traders brought their wares overland from Kansas.

It was worth considering, but he had to drive to Vineyard. Then he could see about Jed and George and their bellyaches. He hitched up his horse to the carriage, using the mended harness, then climbed in. Ridge wasn't sure which was worse, cold winters that froze his joints so painfully or the hot summer which caused every muscle in his body to twitch and creak in protest. He snapped the reins and got the horse moving, drove to the road and, headed toward Vineyard.

He usually appreciated the quiet drive with the red rock bluffs on either side of the road and the greenery so much like that home back in Virginia. Today his mind wandered. Major Ridge never saw the glint of sunlight off the pistol, or the killers who waited impatiently for him to come into range.

Shots rang out. Major Ridge jerked about as the slugs ripped through his body. The horse reared at the sudden noise and kicked out before settling down, dutifully walking along the road toward its accustomed destination, its driver dead.

"Mr. Boudinot, please, we need your help," pleaded the shortest of the three.

"What can I do for you?" Elias Boudinot asked. The hot sun beat down on him. He wiped away sweat and then put his broad-brimmed black hat back on. He had never seen any of these men before.

"Our families are in sore need of medicine, sir," spoke the tallest, "And we don't have any money. Come with us to Dr. Worcester. He knows you. If you speak for us, he'll let us work off the debt."

"*I* don't know you, either," Boudinot said. He glanced at the sun. It was past ten, going on eleven o'clock, and he had work to do. Then he remembered how needy so many Cherokee had been after the Trail of Tears. Never had he turned his back on any in need, and he wasn't going to now. "You fellows have your own farms, or are you working for someone?" Boudinot frowned when they exchanged glances, as if not sure what he meant.

The one of middle height spoke for the trio. "We only do day work. We've just arrived from New Echota, and there's no land. Don't know anything about farming."

"I'd hire you, but there's not enough for my hands as it is," Elias Boudinot said. He heaved a sigh. "You get work in Tahlequah and I'll talk to Dr. Worcester on your behalf. More than that, I cannot do."

"Thank you, sir," said the short one. "Our families are real sick, and we need medicine. Can you come now to

Park Hill with us? I don't know if my wife's going to make it another day without medicine."

"Very well," Boudinot said, with a deep sigh. "I know what it's like to have a sick wife. Mine's been feeling poorly, too."

"We'll hitch your wagon for you," offered the middle one. He and his two companions rushed to prepare the wagon with its double team. Boudinot watched them hurry. It was a bother taking time right now when the entire nation needed a new government, and John Ross, Reverend Jesse Bushyhead, and even Sequyoah himself were unable to bring all the factions together. The disunity did not surprise Boudinot, who was no stranger to political maneuvering, but it did wear him down a mite. John Ross could be so pigheaded at times.

"Here—hurry. We need to go," urged the tallest, already in the driver's box. The other two helped Boudinot into the wagon bed, and they rattled off on the road to Park Hill.

"When did you arrive?" Boudinot asked.

"Not long ago," the driver said over his shoulder. "We've only been here a short time."

Boudinot frowned. Something did not seem right to him.

"What's wrong with your families?" he asked.

"Sick," said another. "We told you that."

"Sick how? There's been malaria in the lowlands, along the river."

"Not malaria," said the driver.

Elias Boudinot shifted his weight, ready to ask another, more pointed question. He never got the chance. Strong arms pinned his arms behind him. The knife flashing in the bright noonday sun quickly vanished—into his gut. Over and over the three men hacked and slashed at Boudinot with knife and tomahawk, then left him dead in his wagon.

* * *

"Such a fine house. We have nothing as good," said one of the fifteen Pins who had gone to kill Stand Watie. "We should burn it to the ground."

"No," said another. "The clan will allow us only to punish those who broke the law. Watie sold tribal land. For that he must be punished. But we will not harm his wife or children. Or burn his house."

Grumbling accompanied this decision. Dawn stroked the sky with a gray and pink rake, followed by a bright sun in a cloudless blue dome stretching from horizon to horizon. It would be a hot day.

The dozen who had come to kill Stand Watie proved patient. He would emerge from his fine house and then they would surround him and kill him. Two had pistols. The rest carried knives and tomahawks. Even a man with the fierce reputation Watie enjoyed could never stand against such an attack.

"Where is he? Does he sleep away the day? Look, he has slaves in his fields, but where is he?"

"They have water and food. We don't," complained another. "Let's find and kill him, so we can eat."

Resolve faded as the sun climbed into the sky and Stand Watie did not appear. The gang of assassins went down the hill toward the neat, two-story brick house. Silent hand motions sent out the men in a half-circle around the house to cut off any escape. Then the leader went onto the sawed plank porch and rapped on the door.

A young woman came to the door.

"Mrs. Watie?"

"Yes, I'm Sarah Watie."

"I need to speak to your husband."

Sarah Watie blinked, looked past the man to where others stood impatiently in the front yard. Chickens pecked at them, and they ignored it. She felt an uneasiness at the sight of so many men trying to look unconcerned.

"Mr. Watie's not here. He went to Fort Gibson."

"When will he return?"

Sarah Watie wiped her hands on her apron and stared boldly at her inquisitor. She came to an easy decision.

"Not for a week or longer. If you return then, I am sure he will be glad to meet with you." She edged to her right, where a shotgun leaned against the inside wall. Seeing the hesitation in her unknown visitor, she reached out and laid her hand on the cold metal. It could be brought to bear in a flash—if the need arose.

"You are not lying?" demanded the man on her doorstep.

"There is no need to be insulting," she said tartly. "If you like, help yourself to some of the water before you leave. You have the look of a man—of men—who need to cool off."

The Pin spun and stalked away. Sarah caught her breath when she saw the number of men with him. More came from behind her house, men she had not realized were in position to cut off any possible retreat.

"What have you gotten yourself into now, Stand Watie?" she said under her breath. Only when the would-be assassins vanished into the hills did she take her hand off the shotgun and send a slave into Tahlequah to fetch her husband.

A New Division
September 6, 1839

"Watie's men might be riding on Park Hill while we meet," cautioned Allen Ross. His father slumped in his desk chair and shook his prematurely graying head sadly. Nothing had gone well since Boudinot and the Ridges had been killed. The careful political alignments designed to bring Western and Eastern Cherokee together had failed at every turn.

"He is destroying everything," John Ross said tiredly. "Why can't he see how he is dividing us?"

"He sees, Father," said Allen. "Killing his uncle and the others in his family turned him against all you are trying to do."

"What was done was no worse than what Major Ridge did in eighteen twenty-one," grumbled John Ross, a spark of fire coming to both eye and word. "Still, Watie refuses to acknowledge that I knew nothing of the crime, and did not cooperate with those who did the killing. What a stubborn fool he can be! The letter from General Arbuckle shows how this breach in civility affects us all."

Allen picked up the letter from his father's desk. The commanding general at Fort Gibson had demanded that John Ross go to the fort and answer unseemly questions about the deaths of Boudinot and the others. Wisely, John Ross had refused, sending a reply detailing how Watie had raised an army of Ridge Party members with the intent of killing those responsible for the massacre, and how it was the general's responsibility to disband this outlaw army and protect the innocent. Harmony had to be preserved at any cost during the sensitive and delicate discussions over re-uniting the nation.

Stand Watie considered John Ross to be the prime mover in those deaths, in spite of Ross knowing nothing of the clan decision.

"A mere hundred thirty-two muskets Arbuckle asks for. Watie has more men in his pirate army than that," John Ross complained. "How does the general expect to protect anyone with such limited armament? And he sent to Arkansas for ammunition and never received it. Will he use the muskets as clubs?"

"Forget Stand Watie, Father," urged Allen. "Chief Brown and Chief Rogers refuse to meet with you. Their influence means much more. Make peace with them, and Watie will follow like a meek little lamb."

"I don't need them to form a government," John Ross said hotly. "Sequoyah has brought John Looney to our side. With his backing, we can put an end to this madness."

"Not after the Illinois Camp Ground meeting last month," Allen said. "They drove us away. They banished you, Father!"

"I don't need them. Here, Allen, here is our new constitution. The United States backs us. Arbuckle might be a fool and discount Watie too easily, but he has written to Secretary of War Poinsett for approval of our new union. Even President Van Buren supports us."

"They are far away, Father," cautioned Allen. "And no one has responded yet."

"They will. What else can they do? I have the new constitution, and outside are gathered representatives from both the Eastern and Western Cherokee. We *will* unite, by God, we will, Allen!"

"Yes, Father," he said, but his thoughts turned to Stand Watie and his armed force, riding about Indian Territory hunting for those who had slaughtered his relatives. There had been no reprisal from the clans, as had been promised to Otoomie and the Keetoowah Society, but Allen saw what his father did not—the Cherokee were divided more deeply than ever by the killings. Just or not, according to Cherokee law or not, the deaths had driven a wedge between the factions.

"We will vote immediately to revoke the Treaty of New Echota," John Ross went on. "If necessary, Coodey and I will go to Washington and petition for redress in this matter. Even Stokes backs us. We cannot fail."

Allen sniffed in contempt at Cherokee agent Montfort Stokes. The man had intervened on John Ross's behalf at the Illinois Camp Ground council and had been rebuffed soundly. His attempt at absolving John Ross of the murders had rung hollow, in spite of the glowing words and apparent belief in Ross's integrity. Allen wondered if Stokes secretly believed John Ross was responsible for the killings. Stokes and his father had known one another for over twenty-five years, yet Stokes seemed completely in the dark about matters swirling through the Cherokee Nation like some dark, deadly tornado.

"Let's meet with the real leaders and unite our nation," John Ross said with determination. He gathered copies of the new constitution and walked from his study in Rose Cottage, head high. Allen followed, less sure of their position than ever. It seemed his father lived in a dream world, while the real one had fanatics like Stand Watie riding about, screaming for blood to be spilled.

John Ross stepped onto the porch of his fine house and saw the scores of representatives from many Cherokee clans assembled. He held up his arms and got their attention.

"Today we forge a new bond between factions of our

people separated by—" John Ross broke off when Allen handed him a letter that had just arrived by courier.

In a whisper, John Ross tried to shake him off. "Not now. I need to have their approval to—"

"Father, please. This is a letter from Secretary Poinsett. On General Arbuckle's suggestion, he has appointed John Rogers first chief."

"But he is a Watie supporter!" protested John Ross.

"They went to Washington," spoke up a man in the front of the crowd. "My son heard of their trip."

"What is this?" demanded John Ross. "What are you talking about?"

"Stand Watie, John Bell, and William Rogers were greeted warmly by the President and those in the War Department. Watie ran up great bills for clothing, and they stayed at the Globe Hotel, the finest in Washington. They were treated as if they were our chiefs. The white men in Washington do not deal with full-bloods, but with half-breeds," the man went on, increasingly bitter.

John Ross wobbled and had to support himself against the whitewashed post on his porch.

"Washington recognizes Watie and his private army as sovereign. They ignore us, John. They thumb their noses at us while we make small talk about unity of east and west. What are we to do?" Others in the crowd began muttering among themselves. John Ross felt his influence slipping away like sand through his fingers.

"We must defend ourselves—and our nation," John Ross said, resolve coming into his bearing and words. "It is the only way to prevent eternal division of our people."

Allen Ross swallowed hard. His father had always fought with his wit, not with a musket or tomahawk. He should not abandon the ways that had worked before to meet Stand Watie with force of arms now. Along that path lay only disaster. For Stand Watie. For John Ross. For all Cherokee, both Eastern and Western.

Colonel Stand Watie
July 12, 1861

"Defy him, Uncle," urged Elias Cornelius Boudinot. "He killed so many of our family, including my father. For years John Ross has meddled and tried to make the Cherokee Nation less than it ought to be."

"I know, I know," grumbled Stand Watie. He chewed on a blade of grass and spat when the bitter sap touched his tongue. Staring across the muddy field near old Fort Wayne in the Delaware District, Indian Territory, where his small army had assembled, Watie could only wonder at Ross's staying power. In the years since the deaths of Boudinot and the Ridges—and his own attempted murder—John Ross had been pecking at the edges of the Cherokee Nation like some demented chicken hunting seed. The Federals had promised so much when Watie and the others went to Washington, and they had lied.

There had been no aid after recognizing John Rogers as principal chief. There had been nothing but trouble as North and South pranced about in strange political maneuvering over states rights and slavery and trade, and so many other issues that did not concern the Cherokee. This was the perfect climate for a man like John Ross. Ever the opportunist, he slipped in and out of power until it became obvious Watie had to reach some reconciliation with him and his faction or the entire Cherokee Nation would be split apart like a rotted melon.

John Ross, ever the slippery one, had never admitted his part in the 1839 deaths, always apologizing profusely for what he had not done and for that which was not his to apologize for. Nor had he seen fit to pursue the ones who had killed Boudinot and the others. Somehow, over the years, Watie's anger had never diminished, but now it was deflected by the white man's war.

"Why do you stay in Arkansas?" he asked his nephew, turning from Elias's insistence that he try to depose John Ross as chief. Watie knew he was no politician. He preferred being in the saddle, commanding his company of volunteers, to sitting behind a desk all day and trying to manipulate men with different ideas using only honeyed words. Still, Elias might be right. Over all the years, justice had not been delivered to John Ross. If anything, the reverse was true. Ross was more powerful today than when he had ordered the murders.

"It is closer to power," Elias said simply. He stretched out, arranged his broadcloth coat to avoid a patch of mud, and stared into the azure sky dotted with fleeing white clouds. The fierce, brief storm earlier had scrubbed the air and turned the day sultry.

"Being elected secretary of the secession convention was a feather in your cap," Watie said, "but you are sorely needed in Indian Territory. Ross works constantly behind the scenes. You know I am no politician."

"That's the kind of fighting I enjoy," Elias said with a laugh. "You should consider it, Uncle. The casualties are not often bloody, but they are just as sure." Elias sobered and looked intently at his uncle. "Are the Jayhawkers still raiding into our land?"

Watie did not answer. Elias knew they were. If it were only the Federal guerrillas plaguing the Cherokee, there would be scant problems. They were surrounded by forces tugging and pushing, pulling and shoving, in ways none wanted to go. Watie wished they could simply live their lives, growing their crops and families, and be done with the savagery. John Ross made sure that would never happen.

"Ross is not the source of *all* our problems," Elias said diplomatically. "He has nothing to do with the Quapaws and Senecas coming at us from Missouri, or the wild Indians on the western plains constantly raiding our settlements."

"The Indians who support the Confederacy are nearly as bad," said Watie. "The Creek and Choctaw are our brothers, but why must they make it so hard to support them with their bloody handed butchery?"

"Consider how much they have lost. The Federals have destroyed a great deal of their property. The Creeks' slaves run away because of abolitionist sedition, leaving them far worse off than we are. Can you blame them if they are more . . . motivated in battle?"

"No," Watie admitted reluctantly, but he saw all too clearly the real menace facing all the Five Civilized Tribes. Even in the Creek there was a powerful division occurring, one faction favoring the South and the other turning violently abolitionist. He knew the source of the wedge driving them apart, too. "Damn the Kansans! If it weren't for the Knights of the Golden Circle, they would run over us and steal all our land."

"Such a fine name for a secret society," Elias said, almost mockingly. "You cannot oppose the Keetoowahs—or the Kansans—with one of your own. Stay in the open, stay in the bright sunlight where all can see you and learn from your courage."

"What do you suggest?" Watie relied so much on Elias's counsel. He did not know what he would do without it. The distance between Tahlequah and the plantation in western Arkansas where Elias lived was not great, but Watie wished they could be closer geographically than a hard day's ride. He did not know how they could be closer in any other way.

"The Southern Rights Party," Elias said with some passion, as if making a speech before a convention. "It is plain, it says what you mean, and it tells everyone you will not skulk about in the night like the Keetoowahs."

"I thought we had broken their backs," Watie muttered. "If it hadn't been for Evan Jones and his son, they would never have reorganized."

"They oppose slavery more than they uphold Cherokee tradition," Elias admitted. "Even the Baptist Board could not stomach their activities, but chasing them from the Nation did nothing to stop the Pins. If anything, it has made them more aggressive."

"They oppose the Knights more than slavery," Watie said, his own passion mounting now. More than once he had fought the Pins. It had been those fierce, bloody skirmishes that had driven him to the Confederacy for arms and support—and it had been given after the Federals had refused because the Pins so openly supported the Northern cause.

"Albert Pike is coming today," Elias said suddenly.

"What? Why?" Watie sat up and stared at his nephew. "I should be sure the men are on their best behavior. It's not every day the Special Commissioner comes from Little Rock."

"Don't get your dander up," Elias said. "I have a wire from him and it is good news—for a change. He . . ." Elias's words trailed off when he pointed to a party of five Confederate soldiers riding along the road leading to Fort Wayne. "That must be him now. Come along, Uncle. Let's greet him."

They mounted and rode down the hillside to where Albert Pike and the confederate officers with him stopped just outside the fence surrounding the fort. Pike waved to Stand and Elias.

"Good afternoon, Commissioner," greeted Elias. "You made good time getting here."

"Seldom do I have good news anymore," Pike said, wiping his face with a big white handkerchief. "I swear, this weather is hotter than any I encountered in Mexico during that sorry war."

"But not hotter than the debate in Richmond," suggested Elias.

"No, not hotter than that," Pike said, grinning. He turned to Stand and said, "What do you hear from along the Kansas border, Captain?"

"The Jayhawkers are burning Cherokee homes and destroying our crops. Everywhere they go, they leave behind nothing but death and destruction. I'll need more ammunition, muskets, and supplies if I am to stop them."

"That's part of the good news," Pike said. "All that has been promised by General McCulloch. The Confederate War Department has appointed him our new district commander."

"Ben McCulloch?" asked Watie. "I know him. A good man, a good field commander. A former Texas Ranger, if I remember rightly."

"He's been promoted to brigadier general. I for one am glad he has been recognized," Pike said. Together with Watie and Elias, they entered Fort Wayne and the shade offered by the few tumbledown buildings inside the stockade walls. Many of Watie's command trailed along, talking with the confederate officers accompanying Albert Pike.

"Have some cool water," offered Watie, handing Pike a tin cup filled from a porcelain pitcher. "There's nothing fancy here, but it's good water."

"It's better than the finest Monopole Champagne," Pike said, drinking deeply. He took a second cup and downed it, too.

"You haven't come all this way for the water," Watie said. He glanced at his nephew with some irritation. Elias stood with a tiny smile curling his lips. He knew more, but played his cards close to his vest. Watie had work to do.

"Always the blunt one, eh?" said Pike. "That's why Elias is the diplomat. I wanted to tell you, Elias, the Confederacy has sent David Hubbard to talk to John Ross about the failure of the Federals to pay what has been owed you for so long. It amounts to more than the three million dollars I won for the Choctaw a few years ago."

"The real fight is over the eight hundred thousand acres in the Neutral Lands," Elias said. "The nation has tried to sell it to the United States, but they refused our offers. We need the money for the considerable spending spree John Ross has embarked on. All the Federals want is to let white squatters in—and provide refuge for the Jayhawkers' forays deeper into our land."

"The CSA is offering you five hundred thousand—with interest—for the land. Hubbard is presenting the offer to Ross, but he will refuse it. I am sure of it, because of his claim of complete neutrality of the Cherokee."

"Neutrality," scoffed Watie. "He deals daily with the Yankees. After all, that young wife of his is from Delaware, and her family lives in Philadelphia. If he didn't drag his feet so, the Jayhawkers would not have their way. It's not only those who sympathize with the Confederacy whose homes are burned, too."

"They steal from everyone," Pike said with some distaste but trying to maintain an equitable argument. "But certainly you are right about Ross. He plays both sides against the middle, hoping to come out ahead by not recognizing you, and so many others are now firmly Confederate. Such a policy can lead only to disaster for the Cherokee. Sides must be taken. I am glad you have chosen."

"I'm a captain in the cavalry," Watie said. "I only wish

I had more power to stop the Kansans. With the matériel you promised, perhaps I can do it."

"There's more," said a gold-braided officer who had listened near the door to the small shack. He stepped inside, snapped to attention, and drew forth a sheaf of folded papers from the front of his butternut uniform jacket. Making a great show of it, he read the proclamation. "On this day, it is with great pleasure that I announce the appointment of Stand Watie as colonel in the Army of the Confederate States of America."

"Congratulations, Uncle Stand. I'm sure your men will agree with this well-deserved promotion!" Elias clapped him on the shoulder, and Albert Pike shook his hand. The officer—a lieutenant colonel and now subordinate to him—snapped him a smart salute. Stand Watie stared at the communiqué that elevated him in rank, a rank that gave the authority he needed to raise an even larger company to stop incursions into the Neutral Lands by the Jayhawkers.

If John Ross would not stop those guerrillas killing their people, Stand Watie would!

Along the Border
July 14, 1861

"Captain Mayes," called Stand Watie to a thin man straddling an emaciated dun horse. When the rider didn't acknowledge, Watie stood in his stirrups and waved. "Joel!"

"Here, Stand." The scout caught sight of his commander from down in the draw and rode faster than the scrawny horse ought to have been galloped, reining back beside his new colonel. His horse was lathered, and Joel Mayes looked as if he had ridden a thousand miles on that sweltering afternoon. "I been lookin' things over a mile on the other side of that ridge." Mayes pointed to a grassy rise that had been trampled in places by dozens of horses passing by recently. The fresh scars looked like a mutilation to Stand Watie. He waited for Mayes to catch his breath and continue the report. "Like you thought, Stand. Jayhawkers. An entire company of them. Reckon them to be the ones what burned down Matthew Threekiller's house this morning."

Watie jumped to the ground and quickly sketched what he knew of the terrain. The area along the Arkansas-Cherokee border was well-known to him, but not this country farther north, not near Kansas where the Jayhawkers leaked across like some vile fluid poisoning everything it touched.

"Here's the ridge, here we are. Where'd they go when they got to the other side, Joel?" He looked up to the scout. Captain Mayes's scouting skills had proven invaluable before, tracking down guerrillas and abolitionists trying to sneak into the Cherokee Nation to do mischief. Those had been small battles. *Hardly battles,* Watie reflected. *More like skirmishes.* Now he felt the need to show the Confederate States of America had not invested in him the power and authority of a full colonel for naught. Rumors of the Jayhawkers coming down from Missouri like a plague of locusts had been passed along to the lieutenant colonel accompanying Albert Pike. Pike's expertise from the Mexican War had been invaluable as they had planned a quick sortie before the commissioner had returned to Little Rock.

"How many men kin you get uphill, Stand?" asked Mayes.

"I have three hundred. Twice that if we wait a few days, but I don't want to do that."

"Them boys'll be back over the border 'fore you know it if you tarry," agreed Mayes. He dismounted and took off his battered gray cavalry cap with the captain's insignia pinned crookedly to it. He wore an officer's jacket without insignia or ornamentation, no shirt under it, and buckskin britches fashioned by his wife. Uniforms were scarce, but if he had to choose, Watie was glad that Pike's promised shipment of muskets and ammunition had arrived only hours after the commissioner. For once, the Cherokee soldiers rode into a fight with enough firepower to do some good.

"They know we're after them?" asked Watie.

"Doubt it. If they did, they wouldn't be stoppin' to boil theyselves some coffee." Mayes sniffed hard. "I kin almost smell it from here. Been a while since I had any."

"If we capture any, it's yours," promised Watie, distracted. His mind raced as he considered the chances of circling the guerrillas. It didn't look good. They would be camped along a small stream that meandered northward. If he attacked from either of their flanks, the guerrillas still had an escape route right back into their own country following the small creek.

"How fast can you and one or two men get to the north of them?" asked Watie. "I'd want you to carry a half dozen muskets apiece."

"What you got in mind?"

Stand Watie explained. As he talked, a big grin spread across Captain Mayes's face, revealing a broken tooth in front that needed dentistry and a gold tooth to one side that gleamed like the sun itself.

"Yes, sir, Colonel Watie, we surely are glad you're our commander," said a sergeant, a mixed-blood hailing from Cowskin Prairie, where Watie had a home and several business ventures. "We'd've elected you, no matter you got a colonelcy and all, proper-like."

"Thanks for the vote of confidence," Watie said, meaning it. Unlike the Federals, CSA units voted on their officers. Being shorthanded and dealing with untrained soldiers was nothing new, not in either army, but voting in a popular man with no sense of strategy or tactic had brought disaster to many a battalion. He knew enough to get by, and with both General McCulloch and Albert Pike approving his commission, Watie felt as if he could whip his weight in wildcats.

"We're as ready as fresh churned butter," the sergeant said. He hefted his musket. Tucked into his waistband were a tomahawk and a knife. Flints, lead slugs, and wadding bounced in a leather pouch on his left hip. At his right swung a powder horn. For once the soldiers had enough to make the fight worth the effort.

"Then get into position along the top of the ridge. Unless something's gone bad wrong, we're about ready for the fight of our lives." Watie trotted along the line of men flopped on their bellies, sighting down the long barrels of their muskets. He had a corporal here and there quietly point out to a green recruit that taking out the ramrod before firing was a good idea. These were proud men, and most of them had no memory of hunting in the lands of the Cherokee back in Georgia and the Carolinas. Watie sighed. Since coming west they had turned into farmers, not hunters.

Today the ones who did not remember stalking game in the forests of Virginia would learn what it meant to be a hunter. Joel Mayes and the three men with him would make a powerful fuss, firing all their muskets and pistols as fast as they could. A lot of whoops and hollers would make the Jayhawkers think they had been cut off from escape to the north by an entire regiment. If they were as crafty as he hoped, they would believe their flanks would be covered, too, making it seem the only way out of the trap was back south along the stream—and up the hill where Watie's men fidgeted and sought blue-belly targets.

"There's one, Colonel!" cried a soldier from the end of the skirmish line.

"Hold your fire, men," called Watie. "Give them all time to start up the hill before you fire." In the distance he heard Mayes firing. If he hadn't known better himself, he would have thought an entire regiment was attacking. Captain Mayes was doing a fine job of flushing the guerrillas. Already Watie spotted a half dozen guerrillas making their way out of the woods, following the stream, but it was too soon to open on them. Watie wanted them in plain view for easy shooting.

That's what he wanted, but he didn't get it. Someone

got buck fever and fired too soon. The others along the line opened up in response. Watie shouted, "Fire, all fire! Give 'em hell!" when it was apparent he had lost the element of surprise.

The first volley tore through the Jayhawkers and brought down two. A second volley killed that many more. Then the Kansas killers swarmed up the slope, rushing past the first line of Cherokee fighters. Watie gave the command. His more experienced men lay ready in a second line. They fired with devastating effect.

"Fix bayonets. Charge, men, give them what for!" Watie cried. The smell of gunpowder in the air made his nose twitch and his pulse race. Those of his company still mounted galloped forward, firing their pistols. When their hammers came down on empty chambers, they used knife and tomahawk on the Jayhawkers.

The charge he had ordered never materialized. Too many were confused by the rush of battle, the sounds of bullets and death. Mostly it was the noise that continued to shock him—what did it do to those who had never fought before?—but enough of his men fought to make the guerrillas think they faced the entire Southern army.

"Surrender, damn your eyes!" bellowed Watie. "Surrender or die!"

Ragged fire continued as his men reloaded. From the dull *smack* of some discharges, Watie knew some of his untrained, frightened recruits had forgotten to load in shot. More than one sent his ramrod sailing through the air after leaving it in the barrel. Still others panicked and ran. But most of his troopers fought hard and well. That was all he could expect from a company of volunteers without formal military training.

It proved enough to win the day.

As the white clouds of gunsmoke drifted away from the hillside, Watie accepted the surrender of a man dressed in civilian clothing with a lieutenant's bars pinned to his floppy brimmed, black felt hat.

Putting those who had turned tail and run in charge of guarding the prisoners, Watie let the others in his command rest. He laughed loudly when he saw Joel Mayes riding up with a big burlap bag heavy with coffee.

"Coffee for the whole danged company, Stand. I want to share the booty."

"You're a good man, Joel. You all are!" cried Stand Watie, rejoicing in his first real victory. It amazed him what a difference it made riding out in command with eagles on his shoulders—and enough gunpowder and ammunition for his men's rifles.

A cheer went up from the victorious Cherokee. And it was for him—Colonel Stand Watie.

Rose Cottage Council
July 14, 1861

"I believe you have already met with Mr. Albert Pike earlier in the month," David Hubbard said, eyeing the old chief carefully. Pike had warned him how difficult it was to gain any concession from John Ross that the old man did not want to give. Pike had gone so far as to say, "He is so shrewd that if I fail with him it will not be my fault."

Albert Pike had failed, and—as he had promised Chief Ross—he had immediately gone to deal with the Southern Rights Party led by Stand Watie. Still, the politicians in the Confederate Congress felt Ross might be persuaded to speak for all Cherokee, winning a valuable buffer between Kansas and Texas—not to mention preventing the Federals making a strategic move, sweeping down from Kansas and Missouri through Indian Territory and then driving eastward into Arkansas, forcing the Confederates to fight on two fronts instead of defending only their northern borders.

"My answer to you is the same as it was to Mr. Pike. The Cherokee Nation will not take sides in this conflict. We remain neutral."

"That is difficult when the Creeks, Choctaws, and some of your own tribe have joined the Confederacy already,"

Hubbard pointed out. "I spoke with many of the chiefs who came here to Park Hill early last month. Your support rests almost entirely on the will of the full-blooded Cherokee, of whom there are few."

"Not so few. The mixed-bloods also recognize that getting involved in a war that is not our doing will destroy us."

"Tell this to the Jayhawkers burning your houses and stealing your livestock," Hubbard said with heat. "Tell the women and children left without husbands and fathers—or tell the men who have lost their women and children to those damned guerrillas. The Cherokee cannot remain neutral against such tyranny." Hubbard saw John Ross was not moved. Albert Pike had been right. The old chief played a hard game.

"Money," Hubbard said, changing his tactics. "The U.S. promised you interest on the money on the Neutral Lands from the eighteen thirty-five Treaty of New Echota. How much have you received?"

"Although sale of these lands—and collection of our due—is important, can it be the deciding factor in whether to take up arms against the Federals?" From his expression John Ross did not appear to believe that Washington would default, and that the unpaid money was safe, for the moment.

"The Confederacy will assume payment of all the annuities you are not receiving," Hubbard said relentlessly. He hammered point after point, trying to find John Ross's soft spot. "Further, you may select your own delegate to the Confederate House of Representatives. Have any in Washington spoken of representation for the Cherokee in their Congress? I think not. They seek to keep you poor and powerless, for their own ends. We will even allow a Confederate court for the Cherokee Nation. You have sought all this since eighteen forty-six. It will be yours tomorrow, in return for your pledge of allegiance today."

"Treaties have been signed," John Ross said, tenting his fingers and peering at Hubbard over the tips. "We must honor them."

"Even if the U.S. does not?" Hubbard thought he had played his trump, but he found out why Albert Pike had failed.

"Your distinguished history of dealing with Indians is hardly better than that of the Northerners. Few Indians now press their feet upon the banks of either the Ohio or Tennessee."

"An independent nation," Hubbard said, uneasy at John Ross's parry and trying not to show it. "We have no desire to keep you under our heel, as the United States does. Within a year, all the land around us can be an independent nation, ruled by your own people, doing as you see fit in a sovereign country."

"McCulloch has established a military district here."

"Chief Ross," Hubbard said, "General McCulloch fears an invasion from the North. It is no secret we do not want a Union stronghold in Indian Territory. We do what we must to prevent it. Do what is best for your people—and maintaining a neutrality that will be increasingly difficult to stomach is not the way. Pledge your allegiance to the Confederate States of America. Do it for your people, for your people's freedom. Get all you have been promised. Seize your own freedom with a bold move!"

"I must speak with my other chiefs."

"Of course, but be aware Mr. Pike has already secured treaties with the Creek, Chickasaw, Choctaw, and even the Seminole. Will the Cherokee be the only one of the Five Civilized Tribes to honor treaties that have been ignored by Washington?"

"The Cherokee Executive Council has declared a national conference on August twenty-first."

"I am sure you will receive wise counsel," Commissioner Hubbard said. "Please let me know as quickly as feasible of your decision." The man left, humming a tune, knowing John Ross found himself backed into a corner.

The principal chief of the Cherokee Nation sat at his desk and stared out a window into the misty distance. Insects whirred and buzzed, and sweat ran down his leathery, wrinkled face. None of it mattered to him; he noticed nothing. John Ross was consumed only by thought of what was best for his people, and how to achieve it honorably. Never in his seventy years had he felt as if events raced past him, just beyond his touch and control.

He heaved himself to his feet and made his way to the front porch of his beloved house. There had to be a way to keep the Cherokee from between the colliding forces of Union and Confederacy. If only he could find it.

Battle of Wilson's Creek
August 10, 1861

"Gentlemen, we can defeat them," General Ben McCulloch said forcefully. He leaned forward on the plank table in his command tent, causing the coal oil lamp at the corner to teeter dangerously. No one noticed. They were too intent on the map, and McCulloch's plans for the coming battle. "The Federals are not ready for war, and this foolish maneuver on their part shows it."

"They surely got their asses whupped at Manassas," Captain Joel Mayes said, picking his teeth with the point of a large-bladed knife. His gold tooth shone like a beacon in the dimness of the tent as he pulled back his lips in a feral grin. Stand Watie tried to hide his own grin when he saw how agitated McCulloch was at Mayes's comment. It stole some of his thunder. More than this, it pointed out the difference in leadership style between the Cherokee and the white man. Watie had seen the way the soldiers under McCulloch's command snapped to attention and threw him salutes when he rode past.

Stand Watie remembered how he had felt getting that salute from a lieutenant colonel—why hadn't he found out the man's name? He had been promoted by the CSA, and it had been a fine day, but which of his men saluted him? Watie couldn't think of a single one doing it, unless they were coaxed into it. The one who came closest was his adjutant and old friend, Tom Anderson. And Tom was the only white man in his command, still back in Tahlequah. The Cherokee regiment he had formed simply didn't behave that way. They were fighters. They had shown that last month, when they had captured or killed twenty-three Jayhawkers. True, many of the Northerners had slipped away because of sloppy military procedure on the part of Watie's men, but the Cherokee had shown they could fight and win against the better trained guerrillas.

"Do we go into Missouri after them, or do we wait for them to invade Arkansas?" Watie asked, diverting McCulloch's attention from Captain Mayes. He had no reason not to keep the peace between these different men. Both were outstanding in their own way. Hadn't McCulloch made Mayes his personal scout? And McCulloch thought in ways Stand Watie wanted to learn. McCulloch knew how to move troops and keep them supplied. More than this, he understood the need to learn everything possible about his opposition and then use the weaknesses against the enemy, rather than simply flinging his men at them.

"Captain Mayes tells me we are up against John Frémont and Franz Sigel. Frémont is a showboater and not likely to be a difficult opponent, but I know nothing of Sigel."

"He's got a powerful lot of big guns trailin' him," Mayes said.

"An artillery unit," McCulloch said, rubbing his chin. He moved around the table with a crude map of the area, studying every aspect of the terrain they knew from Mayes's personal scouting coupled with a bit of guessing at the parts they didn't.

"We go after them," he decided. "Frémont's the sort who could never believe his opponent would dare attack *him.* That would be an affront to his self-conceit. Colonel," McCulloch said. It took a second for Watie to realize he was being addressed.

"Sir?"

"This valley leading to Oak Hill. How many men can you move up to this point"—his finger stabbed down on the map—"by noon?"

"Noon today?" Watie's eyes widened. "All of them, sir. All four hundred."

McCulloch sucked on his teeth for a moment, then asked pointedly, "And how many will *fight*? I've heard of dissension in your ranks."

"The Pins, sir? They cause some trouble, but most of the men are loyal."

"That's not what the grapevine tells me," McCulloch said relentlessly. "You ran afoul of them a couple months ago at Webber's Falls. And many of those same men are now in your rank."

"We took care of them real good, General," Joel Mayes piped up. "They tried to keep the Confederate flag from flying, but they couldn't stop us."

"Sir, it was more a demonstration of support for John Ross than it was against the Southern Rights Party," Watie said. "John Drew spoke for Ross. Drew is a slaveholder, and a moderate when it comes to neutrality, but a man to be trusted."

Mayes snorted in contempt. "Trust John Drew? Not 'less I grow a couple eyes in the back of my head. He spouts all that nonsense about the nation bein' neutral, jist like John Ross does, but they's not his words. They come from Ross, and no one else. John Drew ain't no more 'n a puppet dancin' to John Ross's tugging on his strings."

"Assistant Chief Vann also spoke, and he is no John Ross lap-dog. There wasn't any bloodshed caused by the Pins."

"The damned Keetoowah Society ain't so much ag'in

slavery as they are for givin' the full-bloods control of ever'thing," Mayes said, spitting.

"The flag was never raised," McCulloch said harshly.

"No one was hurt, either," Watie said. His throat tightened as he wondered if McCulloch meant to strip him of his command. He had worked hard, and his men were getting better. Losing Mayes to the general's command was a blow, but another of his friends, William Penn Adair, was coming soon to be head of scouts. The unit was finally taking shape. To lose it now would be a terrible affront to his dignity and authority in the Cherokee Nation.

"I recruited half my men after we left Webber's Falls. It swung many who were undecided in our direction."

"Hmm, possibly true," McCulloch said. "But how many of your troops are loyal to this secret society?"

"Not many," Watie said hastily, knowing he was lying to his commanding officer. It seemed important to him to present a unified facade rather than let McCulloch know how truly divided the nation was. He had no idea how many of his men owed greater allegiance to the Keetoowah Society than to the Confederacy, or him.

Or to the Cherokee Nation.

"We'll find out when the battle begins," McCulloch said dourly. "Colonel, get your cavalry up to Wilson's Creek immediately. At high noon the attack commences. I will open with artillery barrage from these two ridges." He pointed out the positions of his cannon. "Then I'll sweep down on Frémont with a frontal assault. He hasn't had time to fortify his position. If his men scatter, the battle is over."

" 'Less this here Sigel's got his guns up on Oak Hill and trained on the long stretch leadin' to Frémont's camp," Mayes said. "If we don't silence Sigel's artillery, yo're gonna end up in a meat grinder, General."

"I'm glad you appreciate your significant role in the attack," said McCulloch, looking as if he had bitten into a persimmon. "Colonel, Captain, to your horses. It is four A.M. now. In eight hours, we will duplicate the Federal defeat at Manassas, this time on Missouri soil."

Watie saluted and herded Mayes from the tent before the scout could suggest they all sit down for a cup of coffee. They had a long distance to travel, much of it in the dark, if they wanted to be in Missouri and fighting the Federals at noon.

"Don't look good for us, Stand," Joel Mayes said, wiping his broad face. He silently accepted Watie's canteen and drank deeply, then poured some of the tepid water over his head and shook like a dog, sending water droplets flying in all directions. "Sigel's got his big guns entrenched on that hill. We come sloshin' along Wilson's Creek, we'll be targets. Ain't no other approach."

"If we get to the base of Oak Hill," Watie said, "can we attack up the slope and take the guns? Sigel won't be able to train the guns down at us, not if he wants to protect Frémont's camp."

"If 'n I was him, I'd worry more 'bout losin' my own scalp than protectin' that fool Frémont. The muzzles'd be lowered and turned on us in a flash."

Stand Watie paced, hands behind his back as he thought. They had reached a wooded area a half mile from the base of Oak Hill. and had remained unseen until now. Once they trotted out into the creek, Sigel's spotters would range in on them. Watie wished they could have arrived hours earlier under the cover of darkness, but too many of their horses had balked and broken down, forcing half his men to ride double with the other half. This had slowed them even more, and left only exhausted mounts.

"We can't retreat, Joel," he said. "The horses wouldn't trot a hundred yards before they died under us."

"Don't leave much choice but to do what McCulloch

sent us to do, now does it, Stand?" Mayes went to the spot where he had a clear view of Wilson's Creek and Oak Hill gently sloping away from it, some hundred yards on the far side.

"Think they would notice if we just marched out?" asked Watie.

"Depends on how alert they are. Might be more trouble from Frémont's troops camped o'er yonder." Mayes pointed out the pickets slowly patrolling the fringe of Frémont's bivouac. "They's lookin' this way, not toward McCulloch's main body."

"That's good. We might decoy them," Watie said, realizing what he was saying. If Sigel's artillery turned on them and Frémont's infantry attacked them, thinking they were the main force, not a Cherokee would escape. Mayes also understood.

"Don't want to spill my blood for McCulloch, much as I like the son of a buck," Mayes said.

"It's not just for McCulloch," Watie said. "It's for the nation."

"Most of the men are lookin' for more 'n that. They want spoils."

"Only arms and ammunition this time," Watie said, a daring plan forming in his head. He checked his pocket watch and saw they had less than an hour before noon and McCulloch's attack on Frémont. Getting from the wooded area, across the creek, across the grassy area, and then up the hill would take that long, if they had to fight every inch of the way.

Watie looked back at his men, now dismounted. Few wore Confederate uniforms because the regular units back East still had first call on them, for all the pictures of troops fresh from their decisive victories. He understood the need. If they didn't pose for the photographs in new uniforms now, there'd be no chance soon. The war would be over, and there'd be no need for soldiers or uniforms.

"Sergeant!" Watie called. "How good are the men at close arms drill?"

"What's that, Stand?"

"Marching," he explained patiently. "How well do they hoist their muskets to their shoulders and march in rank?"

"Tried it once," the sergeant said. "Didn't much like it. Neither did any of the boys."

"We're going to do it now," Watie said. "Get them formed into squads. Load their muskets and pistols."

"Git them knives and tomahawks ready, too," added Mayes. His eyes shone with a fanatical light that took Watie aback. He had never seen this blood lust in the man before.

"Do it, but keep the tomahawks hidden as much as possible. And no caps or uniform jackets. We're going to march right down their throats."

"If you say so, Stand. We trust you," said the sergeant. He hurried off to follow his orders. Watie felt a moment's loss when the non-com failed to salute him, but such minor things would not matter if his troops obeyed in the heat of battle.

"Joel, you command a company and get straight up the middle. I'll try to keep Frémont from cutting you down."

"I get to tangle with Sigel and his big guns?" Mayes grinned even more savagely. "Be a pleasure, Stand. Colonel." Joel Mayes did salute. He smeared dirt on his cheeks and chin and forehead as if applying war paint. Then he was off to stand at the front of his company as they struggled into ragged ranks.

Watie hoped he was doing the right thing. He couldn't stay here forever, and he couldn't retreat. All that was left was doing his duty. "Pathkiller!" he bellowed. The junior officer hurried over. He didn't bother saluting. For all that, he didn't seem pleased to even be in Watie's presence.

"Lieutenant Pathkiller, take command of the third company, protecting Mayes's left flank. I'll be on the right, between Mayes and Frémont. Be ready to give support to either of us, should the need arise. I don't think there will be any attack from the north, but I need to be sure by placing your company there."

"My company's only in reserve?"

"Something like that, but you'll see plenty of action today," Watie said. "If the artillery on the hill starts firing, Mayes's company will be in sore trouble. If Frémont sees what we're doing, he might launch a straight-on attack against my flank. If you have to choose, back up Mayes, then me. Do you understand?" Watie watched as Pathkiller's head moved once in a tentative nod. "Then assemble your command. We're going to march out there, just like we belong."

"March?"

"As if we are a training unit," Watie affirmed. His heart beat faster now. "Get the drummer to roll out a tattoo, to make it seem we are heading back to our campground."

Pathkiller nodded again, then left without saying another word. Watie felt a moment of worry over the young man. He had joined after Webber's Falls, and had been elected lieutenant of his company. Other than this, Watie knew nothing about him—there just hadn't been time to learn. He wished Tom wasn't back home. At least his adjutant could look after Sarah and their family a spell longer, protecting them from John Ross's backshooters.

"He'll do his duty," Watie said to himself, watching the young lieutenant, then turned to his own company. He was shy on officers, and held command of the company himself rather than relying on another lieutenant or captain borrowed from McCulloch's company of Texas Infantry. It was luck enough having Mayes back with him for this attack.

He lifted his sword in the air and got his men's attention.

"The time is right, men," he said loudly. "We will be bold, we will be brave, and we *will triumph this day!*" He smiled as his ragtag company took up a cheer. Watie motioned to the drummer to begin a marching beat. The sergeant worked to get the men walking along with their muskets on the proper shoulder, but they *were* marching. And Stand Watie was leading them out into the open.

As he stepped out of the woods and saw the gentle creek below, the mass of Frémont's troops in their camp to the right and Sigel's entrenched position atop Oak Hill ahead, he felt a surge of panic. He forced it back. This was no time to give his men the wrong message. What would Sarah think of him if she ever heard he had run like a dog before a battle? What his dear wife thought of him mattered more than anything else.

He would not disgrace her.

Stand Watie stepped lightly on the grassy slope going down to the creek. It added energy to his step feeling the springiness beneath his boots, and courage built as he realized all three companies of his men marched out behind him. They took a desperate risk, but if he had launched an all-out attack, complete with whoops and shouts, the Federals would have spotted them within fifty yards and cut them to bloody ribbons.

They reached the knee-deep, sluggishly flowing Wilson's Creek before Watie noticed any interest in them from lookouts up on Oak Hill. He saw one sentry nudge another. The men seemed to be arguing. That brought Watie's entire company across the creek. Mayes's company was already crossing the broad sward leading up the slope of the hill.

Watie realized the two sentries who had spotted them weren't arguing, but laughing and joking about the green recruits drilling on the grassy sward beneath their position. One bluecoat waved and shouted something Watie thought was probably derogatory. He waved back and shouted, "We're doing the best we can!"

This produced definite laughter from the guards watch-

ing, and from several over in Frémont's bivouac as well.
His men were spotted, but the enemy thought they were
simply recruits learning the elements of military discipline.
That gave him enough time for all his men to cross Wilson's Creek and start marching up the slope of the fortified
hill.

Watie glanced to his far left and saw how much Lieutenant Pathkiller's company lagged. That didn't bother
him unduly. It allowed Pathkiller to choose between reinforcing either of the other two companies, though Watie
wished Pathkiller moved more quickly. When Mayes
needed support he would need it fast.

Even as the criticism of Pathkiller's slowness crossed his
mind, Watie found himself spun around by a musket ball
ripping through his left sleeve. For a moment he simply
stood, stunned. He had not heard the musket report; he
only felt the nearness of the hot lead. It had not even
nicked him, but the heat from the lead left a blister on
his skin.

Joel Mayes roared his command to attack. His entire
company broke rank and fired uphill. Watie doubted any
of that musket fire amounted to a hill of beans. Shooting
uphill—or down—required practice none of his men had.
He wished Sigel's sentries had been similarly ill-trained.

They hadn't. They had finally realized that the men they
laughed at were not fellow soldiers, but the enemy. What
had given away the deception Watie couldn't say, but now
the time had come for real battle.

At first only a few rifle rounds sailed downward. Then
came a fusillade that cut through Mayes's men like a scythe
through ripe grain. Mayes's men dropped their rifles and
whipped out knives and tomahawks. Their progress into
the teeth of Sigel's guns increased. So did their casualties.

"Fire, men," shouted Watie. "Give supporting fire!"

His men responded well. The air filled with the thunder
of muskets and the cries of men being wounded and killed

by return fire, and then Watie's ears refused to hear anything more. Sigel's cannon opened on him. The ground
shook, and a heavy hand brushed him away. Stand Watie
staggered and went to his knees, then recovered. Whipping out his pistol he ordered his men to support Mayes's
company in frontal assault on the entrenched artillery
pieces.

Watie wondered at the silence, then realized he was deaf.
His nose wrinkled at the coppery smell of spilled Cherokee
blood, but his deafness provided a single bright spot. He
could not hear the piteous moans of the wounded. His
lips moved, and he felt his chest vibrate as he screamed
for attack, and he hoped his soldiers could hear.

Legs pistoning back and forth, he trudged up the hill
protecting Mayes's flank. Frémont's camp stirred, respond-
ing slowly to the attack. Then Watie understood the Union
soldiers' dilemma. If they attacked his flank to protect their
artillery, they left their rear exposed to McCulloch's attack.

In the distance came clouds of white smoke and dust
kicked up and the flash of Confederate artillery. McCulloch's assault had begun.

"Up, up!" Watie shouted. It felt as if his head had been
shoved into a tin pail. Pressure built in his ears, and he
tasted salt, dirt, and blood on his lips. "Up, forward, attack!"

He was aware that Pathkiller's company did not partici-
pate. Then his world collapsed to a small patch of grass
immediately in front of him as Sigel's gunners fired. Once
under their muzzles, Watie fought Federal sentries with
knife and fist. How long he fought he could not say. A
minute, or an hour? It didn't matter. He fought until he
realized the ground no longer shivered under his feet from
the repeated fire of Sigel's cannon.

He stumbled and fell to one knee, then pulled himself
up on a caisson. Watie moved forward to the edge of the
fortified hill and peered down into Frémont's camp. Con-

fusion reigned there. From two sides the Union general found himself under attack by McCulloch's forces. Watie whirled around and motioned to his sergeant and three others from his company.

"Fire these cannon," he shouted, not sure how to do it. "Swing them down. Down into Frémont!"

The men knew little about artillery, but they succeeded in hoisting the rear of the artillery piece off the ground and dropping the tongue onto a large boulder. They loaded and tamped and jerked the lanyard. Watie felt more than heard the report as the cannon belched out its heavy load downhill and into the rear of Frémont's army. Before they could reload and fire again, Frémont's men were in complete rout.

Stand Watie stood on the rock wall that had protected the cannon as he studied the creek below. It ran red with blood. Federal blood. Through the patches of blowing gunsmoke he saw General Ben McCulloch's troops approaching at a dead run, bayonets fixed and thirsty for Yankee blood.

The battle was over. The day was won.

Scalps
August 11, 1861

"Go on now. You boys just line up, some of you kneeling down in front so I can get the lot of you in," the photographer said, peering under the black curtain of his camera and sticking his head into its guts. He held up a long, thin tray filled with gunpowder. Stand Watie jumped when the small explosion went off. For a horrifying instant he was pulled back to the blood and furor of battle the day before.

His hearing had returned, but there had been a more permanent loss, more severe to him than not being able to hear the cicadas chirping in the sultry evening. Lieutenant Pathkiller's entire company had deserted in the heat of battle, leaving the field rather than offering support to Captain Mayes as he fought his way up the hill toward the artillery battery. Watie heard the rumor of all Pathkiller's men being in the Keetoowah Society and refusing to fight against fellow abolitionists. He was unsure what to believe, especially since the celebration, following the decisive Southern victory, swirled all around him.

"I want another plate, but I'm out of powder. You boys just stand there and not move for a minute or two," the photographer called. "This is going on the front page of the *Richmond Herald* for Jeff Davis and everyone to see. You are all genuine heroes of the Confederacy."

Watie did as he was told, though he grew tired of having his picture taken. He wore a new uniform jacket for the photograph, his colonel's rank gleaming prominently. Others in his company wore motley combinations of their regular clothing, articles of Confederate uniforms, and Federal gear taken from both prisoners and enemy dead. The expressions on their faces were all the same—proud. They had fought regular army units and brought them down. General Sigel had surrendered, and Frémont had been routed, leaving most of the territory south of Springfield, Missouri, under Confederate control.

"Colonel, I'd have a word with you." General McCulloch, three aides, and several civilians stood in a tight knot, looking grim. Watie wondered what the problem might be. They were heroes. Everyone said so.

"How can I help you, sir?" he asked.

"You've done far better than any commander under me ever has, Colonel Watie," McCulloch said. "You and your company proved resourceful, brave under fire, and tenacious in battle. Without your successful assault the day surely would have been lost."

"Get to the point, General," growled one of the civilians. "He did it. Him or some of his savages in his command."

"That remains to be seen," McCulloch said brusquely. To Watie, he said, "You know I am not one to mince words. There have been reports of enemy dead being scalped."

For a moment Watie didn't know what to say. That wasn't so bad, but he remembered how hard-fought the battle had been. None of his warriors—his *soldiers*—had time to scalp. They had been too busy fighting for their lives.

"He doesn't deny it. He did it," said the truculent civilian. "How are we going to tell the War Department we got savages running amok on the battlefield lifting the hair of Union men?"

"Might put the fear into them," said another, a small

smile curling the corner of his lips. The others with him glared at him until the smile faded.

"The Union papers are filled with this atrocity. We must punish those responsible, and make sure it never happens again."

"No one in my company scalped an enemy soldier," Watie said. He might have lost his hearing in the melee, but he had seen everything from the top of Oak Hill.

"How can you be so certain?" demanded the civilian from the War Department.

"I am. Who is accused of this scalping?"

"It might have been your other company commander."

"Pathkiller?" Watie thought poorly of the man for desertion. He wasn't sure it would make the situation any better knowing the man had also scalped helpless soldiers as he ran from the field.

"Mayes. Captain Joel Mayes," the civilian said.

Watie gestured to his sergeant to fetch Mayes. The scout sauntered up a few minutes later, a fried chicken leg in his hand.

"What kin I do for you gents?" Mayes asked, seeing trouble brewing.

"Did you or any of your men scalp yesterday?"

"Fine day," Mayes said, drawling the words. "Yesterday was a tad more hectic, but I don't remember seein' anyone without their hairpieces."

"You deny it?" demanded the civilian.

"He said he did," McCulloch cut in. "If Captain Mayes said he did not scalp any Union soldier, I believe him."

"Might be one or two of my men what got excited in the battle, but no more 'n that," Mayes said.

"This was widespread. It is costing us valuable support among the populace in the North. How we will ever be able to use such savages in battle again is beyond me."

"Am I missing something, General?" asked Watie. "No Cherokee took a scalp yesterday, but he's talking as if we did."

"Someone did. The bodies are proof. Twenty of them!"

"Ever see a scalp after it leaves a man's head?" asked Mayes.

"Are you going to show me one?" the man said belligerently. "Are you admitting to this heinous crime?"

"See that scout yonder? The one from General McCulloch's headquarters company?"

"The Texan? Yes, but—"

Watie held down a surge of anger when he saw what sharp-eyed Joel Mayes already had. Swinging at the Texan's belt were four scalps, undoubtedly taken from their heads recently. Matted, fresh gore was still evident.

"Seems them Texas boys have a hankerin' for hair a mite bigger than any Cherokee," Mayes said. "Got some serious eatin' to do. This is mighty fine chicken, General. Thank you kindly for it." Mayes didn't bother saluting as he turned and walked away.

The civilians sputtered and talked rapidly among themselves. McCulloch's aides huddled together, pointing angrily and arguing.

"Will there be anything else, General?" Watie asked.

"Only that you and your fine men will receive their due, Colonel. Dismissed." Watie saluted and McCulloch returned it.

In the middle of glory, Stand Watie found only indignation at the way the officials from the War Department had jumped to the conclusion that the taking of scalps had been done by Cherokee. Worse, the hollowness inside at Pathkiller's defection worried him the more. Which of his remaining men were likely to join the Pins and desert when he needed them most?

He joined the swirl of celebration, even drinking a few shots of whiskey. It did nothing to ease his apprehension—or ire.

Cherokee Council
August 21, 1861

Stand Watie rode from Tahlequah into Park Hill at the head of a sixty man company, all decked out in new Confederate uniforms. Some even sported flashy ribbons and medals they had won from other soldiers in card games. McCulloch had tightened his disciplinary grip on his troopers and had given regimental punishment to several officers for wearing medals and ribbons they had not earned, but Watie saw nothing wrong with allowing his men to sport the gaudy decorations. Other than their new wool uniforms, they had gotten precious little after their victory at Wilson's Creek.

Watie swelled with pride when he saw how the others assembled at Park Hill for the council watched his men ride through. There must have been four thousand Cherokee, and all admired what he had accomplished in such a short time. Newspapers throughout the South had run banner headlines and photographs of Watie detailing his bravery. Who in this council had not already read at least one of those stories?

The Southern Rights Party would prevail, Watie knew. They would vote for the Cherokee Nation to sign the treaty with the Confederacy. He signaled his men to a halt, and was pleased to see they obeyed in a military fashion.

"Sergeant, dismiss the men," he called to his non-com. The sergeant released the sixty from formation, permitting them to hurry out among the watching throng to greet friends and relatives.

"Influence friends and relatives," Watie said to himself. He fastened the reins to a post and then climbed the steps of the Rose Cottage to greet John Ross. The old man seemed a shrunken shadow of his former self, but Watie did not underestimate the chief. Ross had maintained his influence for long years, dodging all responsibility for the 1839 murders and dozens of lesser crimes.

"Chief Ross," he greeted in as neutral a voice as he could muster. Watie met John Ross's direct gaze without flinching. This was the man who had ordered the Ridges and his Uncle Elias killed, Watie had to remind himself. Behind the principal chief stood assistant chief Joseph Vann, Ross's son Allen, and John Drew.

"You look hot in that heavy gray wool uniform," John Ross said. "Come, take it off and sit so we can talk. Allen, find some lemonade for our loyal neighbor."

Watie's mouth almost watered at the thought of lemonade, but he was not going to shuck his uniform. John Ross would see that as a sign he was not dedicated to the Southern cause, and those in the crowd waiting to hear what their leaders said would take it as an indication Ross had struck a secret deal with Watie. He could never permit that.

"Why don't you have your houseboy fetch the lemonade?" asked Watie.

"I have manumitted him," John Ross said, taking delight in the explanation. "My dear wife Mary persuaded me to free both our slaves. Her Quaker upbringing has much to do with her abolitionist feelings, and she finally persuaded me it is wrong holding such power over another human being."

"Yet you hold such power, deciding for the entire nation rather than allowing us decide our fate for ourselves? Which is the greater slavery?" Watie asked, sitting rigidly on the edge of the chair. He sipped at the lemonade. It was better than any he had ever drunk, but it still left a bitter taste in his mouth when he realized John Ross was not going to budge.

"The Council of Chiefs has decided on neutrality," John Ross said. "That is what I will recommend to the entire gathering."

Stand Watie looked past the old chief to the thousands of Cherokee assembled around Rose Cottage and stretching all the way to Park Hill. He recognized friends and enemies among them—he thought he even saw Lieutenant Pathkiller moving through the throng. It was only a shadow, a hint of the man. Then it was gone, and Watie had to deal with John Ross directly.

"The Keetoowah Society proved their cowardice during the battle," Watie said. "Pathkiller abandoned his brothers and ran like a scalded dog when the battle began."

"He would not fight those who believe as he does," Allen Ross cut in.

"You've spoken with him? Tell him he is a deserter. If I find him, I'll arrest him and bring him up on charges at a court-martial. It would give me great pleasure to order a firing squad for him," Watie said, his words steel-edged.

"Did you have to make such an entrance with your armed bandits?" asked Joseph Vann, not attempting to keep the rancor from his words. "You might have removed your uniforms to maintain an air of impartiality."

"You might be confused about our proper path, Chief Vann. I am not."

"You let the publicity the whites give you swell your head," John Drew said. "Words in a newspaper are a cheap price to buy a man's allegiance."

"Words can never replace deeds, either," Watie countered. John Drew stiffened at the implied insult of possible cowardice at Webber's Falls, but John Ross forced himself to his feet and raised his arms to get the attention of the crowd. For almost a minute the buzz of whispered conversations continued but slowly, in deference to their chief, the assembled citizens of the Cherokee Nation fell silent.

"You have come this day to hear the arguments for a treaty with the Confederate States of America, but I urge you to permit me to maintain our neutral position. There is no reason to be drawn into a war that is not of our choosing. Cherokee can never win if we become embroiled in the white man's conflict."

John Ross spoke long and well, but Watie saw a white man he recognized moving slowly through the crowd, quietly countering every point John Ross raised with those most likely to be influenced by such personal attention. Joseph Crawford had been the Federal Cherokee agent until recently, when he resigned and threw his lot in with Jefferson Davis. Now he worked effectively to sway the Cherokee into signing the treaty Albert Pike and David Hubbard had advanced. Of all those men who had worked for the government in Indian Territory, every one had gone with the South. The government in Washington had done nothing to plead their case to those in the Cherokee Nation, making it seem as if they had dismissed everyone south of Kansas.

When John Ross finished his impassioned speech, Stand Watie rose to address the throng. He paused a moment behind the whitewashed railing, saw Cherokee eager for a change to be made in their lives, and reflected how different this battle was from the one he had fought only eleven days earlier. At Wilson's Creek he had dodged bullets and Yankee grapeshot. A mistake meant severe wounds or bloody death. Here the weapons were softer, gentler, but nonetheless carried the promise of life and death for so many of his brothers. No one would lie dead on the ground because of what he said and did this day. He offered the chance for real freedom, but at what cost? Stand Watie wished he knew the answer. He could only present the best argument for what he believed, and devil take the hindmost.

"The sentiment of those gathered today will go against that of the council," Stand Watie started. "Chief Ross has already decided the Cherokee Nation must remain neutral in a world where standing and watching will guarantee us only . . . sorrow. The Federals do not pay us the interest promised on the Neutral Lands. Although we do not want or need them, we cannot sell those lands, because white men gathered in a distant city prohibit it. Other promises from Washington have also been ignored, treaties violated, our honor besmirched."

"We *should* have scalped the lot of 'em!" one of Watie's soldiers called. This produced a round of cheers. He waited for quiet to settle again.

"I have spoken with the men of power in Washington," Watie went on. "They speak earnestly and think they are telling the truth as the honeyed words flow like an endless river from their lips, but the many miles between our countries—between our different worlds—alter their good intentions, and give us only repeated disappointment. The CSA promises us sovereignty. Accept their treaty, and we will be a nation among nations." Watie paused as this rippled through the crowd. Too many times Washington had promised and never delivered because the Cherokee Nation was powerless, lacking representation and the courts to sue for its due.

"We will be equal," Watie went on when the murmur died, "if we choose to align our nation with the Southern Confederacy. Do we continue to be ruled by a Congress in Washington with no interest in us, other than to delay or deny money owed us under their law, or do we find allies who will support our way of life and give us freedom to rule ourselves?"

A cheer went up. Watie saw Crawford nodding in approval. More than one man in the crowd went to those of Watie's company who wore their Confederate uniforms and spoke with them. The council led by John Ross might refuse to sign the treaty, but Stand Watie had done what he could. He turned and looked at John Ross. The old chief's face was impassive with its deep furrows and leathery skin, but his eyes betrayed his true thoughts.

How he hates me! Watie thought. It was a good thing he had brought with him sixty armed men for protection, or John Ross might have ordered his followers to kill again, this time not waiting for the cover of night for their murderous crimes.

John Ross moved slowly to the porch railing and leaned forward. He cleared his throat, paused a moment until attention focused on his frail form, and said in a strong voice that belied his years, "The council has voted on neutrality. We will not become the pecan placed between the jaws of the white man's nutcracker."

An angry buzz went up from the crowd, then it began to disperse. Watie saw that John Ross had lost his last battle. He dominated the council with his force of will and seniority, but the council no longer spoke for all Cherokee.

Stand Watie did. It was an awesome responsibility.

Watie hurried down the steps and was immediately surrounded by hundreds trying to touch him, to speak with him, to find out what he would do next. He gave what assurances he could, but he wanted only to go home to be with his family. It had been too long since he had seen Sarah. Too long by far.

A New Regiment
August 24, 1861

John Ross closed his eyes and listened to the buzz of flies around him. He swatted idly at them, but they didn't go away. Neither did Stand Watie. How alike the two were, but unlike the insects Watie could not be swatted. He had left the meeting to recruit more and more men to his company. Worse, Ross had to admit the council decision of neutrality in the War Between the States would be ignored by most Cherokee. Watie had meddled and forced his Southern Rights Party agenda on others concerned about the illegal guerrilla incursions from Kansas.

"What of Opothleyahola?" John Ross asked his son. "Can we count on his continued support?"

"The Creek are in an uproar, Father," Allen said. "They are split like we are. Opothleyahola and the full-blooded Creeks are not going to succeed in gaining power if they voice their abolitionist policies."

"I know that," John Ross said tiredly. "I mean, can we continue to count on Opothleyahola's support if we remain neutral? I know the Creek are going to sign a treaty with the Confederacy. The parade of Southern agents tells me everything is done except letting the ink dry on the signatures."

"Opothleyahola has been a strong ally, Father, but if you overturn the council resolution and align with the South, he will abandon you."

"I feared as much. How is it my staunchest ally, the one who agrees most with me, the one whose path I would gladly follow, now becomes my enemy? We agree, and yet we will fight. It's not right!"

"No, it's not," Allen said. "Opothleyahola is forging stronger ties with the Keetoowah Society."

"Damn them! I want nothing to do with such radicals! They caused this shambles with Stand Watie by killing his uncle and Major Ridge. I know they did it, and he blames me. Mark my words, Allen, I am not sorry to see the Ridge-Boudinot faction leaders gone. They were bullheaded fools. But will the dust ever settle on murders done more than two decades ago?"

"No, no they won't," John Ross's son said. He had his own secrets to bear concerning those deaths. Never had he told his father of his part in the killings.

Silence fell until the sound of horses clopping up the path to the side of the house disturbed Ross's meditations. He rocked forward and gained his feet, his old knees not moving well. John Ross peered out and saw John Drew and several others dismounting.

"Have him come to my study. John Drew and I have much to discuss."

"His regiment?"

"What else?" John Ross said bitterly. "Fight fire with fire, they say. If Stand Watie is riding about the Cherokee Nation with a pack of gray-suited bandits then I must look to my own safety, and that of those who do not agree with him."

John Drew stood in the doorway. "Am I early?"

"No, no, John, come in. We have so much to discuss." John Ross's eyes went wide when he saw who stood immediately behind John Drew. "What is the occasion, having Stand Watie's son in my home?"

Saladin Watie inclined his head slightly in the presence of the principal chief. In spite of his tender years—hardly a teenager, John Ross thought—Saladin Watie showed just enough deference to avoid criticism combined with the arrogance Ross had come to associate with his father.

"I understand John Drew is forming a regiment. My father thought it would be useful if I passed along some of his experiences in recruiting to aid Mr. Drew."

"How thoughtful," John Ross said, not bothering to hold down his sarcasm.

"There is also the rumor that you intend calling John Drew's organization the First Regiment of the Cherokee Mounted Rifles."

"That is so," John Ross said, frowning. "Colonel Drew will be a fine choice to lead—"

"The name is not acceptable. Since my father's regiment was formed first and has distinguished itself in battle, *it* will be known as the First Regiment."

"Distinguished? With so many desertions—" grumbled John Drew.

"They were Pins. Recruit them at your own risk, Mr. Drew. They will turn tail and run like cowards under your command, also."

"They will fight for a cause," John Ross said. "Maintaining slavery is not their conviction."

"On this point we agree. They should be convicted," Saladin Watie said. "With so much unrest among the slaves in Indian Territory, I would suggest you suppress the Keetoowah Society, to restore peace."

"How can there be peace with war swirling all around?" asked John Ross.

"There cannot. That is why my father will lead the First Regiment of the Cherokee Mounted Rifles. Mr. Drew can lead the Second Regiment, if that is your choice."

"No, I will lead the First!" protested John Drew, puffing himself up. He gripped the hilt of the sword sheathed at his left hip as if he would draw it on young Watie. John Ross motioned to John Drew to let him do the negotiation. Of all the items he had thought he would deal with this day, arguing over a name was not one. Saladin Watie raised a good point about the slaves, and how they increasingly escaped to go north. John Ross knew Opothleyahola helped them.

He wished he could help Opothleyahola.

Stand Watie's son appeared unperturbed at John Drew's outburst. The young man wore a Confederate uniform, stained in places with what might be blood. John Ross had not heard Watie had his son with him in battle, but it might be so. It was unusual to send such a stripling to deal with a chief, unless Stand Watie intended to show disrespect.

"What is your father's concern about a mere name?" John Ross asked.

"A name is everything. Cover it with disgrace, and all will know it. Wear it proudly and all will know that, too. Colonel Watie *will* command the First Regiment."

"Perhaps there is a way we can all agree. Can your father object if he leads Stand Watie's Cherokee Mounted Rifles and my faithful servant leads John Drew's Cherokee Mounted Rifles?"

"The regiments would be called by their commander's names?" Saladin Watie considered this. As he thought, John Ross watched and lamented. Stand Watie's son would be a ferocious fighter and dedicated, skilled diplomat as he matured—because he was now.

"Chief Ross, I protest!" John Drew puffed himself up even more, but John Ross ignored him, waiting for Saladin Watie's response.

"Agreed. I will inform my father of your wise decision," Saladin Watie said. "Good day, sir." Saladin Watie locked eyes with John Ross, then turned and left without acknowledging John Drew. This pushed Drew to the breaking point.

"You gave in to a . . . to a boy!"

"Young in years, wise in getting what he—what his father—wants. This is a small matter, John. Pick your battles. You did well at Webber's Falls. Watie was unable to raise the Confederate flag. But we have bigger fights ahead of us, and some just might be with Stand Watie."

John Ross clasped his hands behind his back and began pacing from side to side in his small study as he thought. Escaping slaves, the need to support the Creek chief Opothleyahola without losing his own power on the council, the rising tide of militarism—so many problems, so many.

Not the least was the need to reverse his decision on neutrality and sign the damned treaty with the Confederacy. Stand Watie had pushed him into that. How could he push back? What could he gain for the Cherokee Nation Watie so naively split apart?

"Let Watie think he has won a small victory. It might make him overconfident so he will play into our hands later. We can lose the small fight in order to win the war."

Those were fine words he spoke to placate John Drew. Ross wondered if he believed them himself.

Chosen Sides
October 1, 1861

The bullet whistled past Stand Watie's head. He ducked behind the fallen tree for the scant protection it afforded. His horse, abandoned a few yards behind him as he took to cover, reared, neighed, and bolted. He watched the horse gallop off, cursing his bad luck. He had not thought to bring along a dozen armed men to protect him from John Ross's newly formed regiment.

"John Drew," he said under his breath, the name more a curse than an answer to the question of who shot at him. Once he had considered the man beneath contempt. Now he counted him as a dangerous enemy. Watie rolled over and pulled his pistol from its holster. Infinitely cautious, he peered around the butt end of the fallen tree. Termites had begun gnawing at the wood, and might have contributed to its fall when it was struck by lightning during one of the fierce northern storms that had blown through in the past few weeks.

"Northern storms," Watie said to himself, wondering if he might be pinned down by Jayhawkers. He scanned the other side of the road where his ambusher lay and saw the merest flash of war paint. Creek war paint. He had been beset by some of Opothleyahola's band.

Wiggling along tore his fancy uniform jacket and dirtied up his belly. He had meant to present a dignified figure when Albert Pike negotiated the final details of the treaty with John Ross, but that grand entrance and overwhelming presence was out of the question now.

New bullets tore away chips of the rotting wood, telling Watie he had to stay alive before considering how he looked at a signing ceremony. Just getting to the ceremony might be a problem.

Staying alive might, also.

New slugs sought him from a different angle. Then came a war whoop, and he fired point-blank into a Creek brave who had quietly circled and come up on him from behind. His bullet caught the man in the belly, but didn't slow him down. Stand Watie saw the lifted knife gleaming with its promise of silver death, and then he was deafened by a sharp report.

The shotgun blast lifted the Creek from his feet and moved him a yard to his left. He was dead before he hit the ground. A second shotgun roar told Watie he had allies.

"Father, stay down. Don't fight. Tom Anderson will be along in a few minutes, if we can hold them off."

"Saladin!" he called to his young son. "Don't expose yourself."

The blare of the shotgun told him his son ignored his order. He propped the butt of his pistol atop the log and began firing, thinking to pin down the attackers and keep them from returning his son's fire.

Saladin Watie dashed from a ravine and rolled, coming to a stop beside his father. He grinned at the older man.

"Mother would be terribly put out with me if I let you get shot."

"Your mother's always worried about me, but if anything happened to you or the others—" Stand Watie ducked low when a half-dozen arrows whistled through the air, arching upward and coming down in an attempt to wound him.

"Creek," Saladin Watie told his father. "Opothleya-hola's own men, unless I miss my guess."

"You'll seldom do that, I suspect," Watie said. Then came an explosion of firearms that echoed like thunder through the gently rolling hills. As soon as Watie thought it would stop, new waves assaulted his ears. He lay behind the log and bided his time. Soon enough the gunfire ceased and he heard the slow, soft thudding of a horse walking along the dirt road. Peering over the top he saw Tom Anderson. His adjutant had a rope around a Creek's neck and was almost dragging him along.

"Careful with him, Captain," Watie called. "He's got a wounded leg."

"If he can't keep up, that's his worry," the tall, slender man with walrus mustaches said. "First off, I thought him to be one of John Drew's pissants. Turns out he and the others were on their way to Rose Cottage to palaver with John Ross."

Watie saw that Tom spoke only to draw out the captive. The man's hot glare told him information wasn't likely to be forthcoming—and that Tom might have stumbled on the truth. He was expert at getting people to say what was really on their minds. Opothleyahola had tried to organize a slave revolt, probably with John Ross's complicity. News that the Cherokee would ally with the South had stirred up the old Creek chief so much that Watie wasn't surprised when he had been attacked.

"You really ought to have brought along more 'n young Saladin as a bodyguard, Stand," Tom said. "These are sneaky bastards."

"He followed me," Watie said, glancing at his son with pride. Saladin had been elected lieutenant by his company, and it wasn't simply because of his father being regimental commander. War aged men fast—the young most of all.

"Good for you, Saladin," Tom said. "I'll be proud to listen to your counsel." He tugged at the rope around his captive's throat, bringing the man to his knees. "If you plan to get into Tahlequah to watch that sockdolagizing fool John Ross sign the treaty, you'd better pretty yourself up again and shake a leg."

"I'm afraid whatever appearance I make will be ludicrous," Watie said, staring at his ruined jacket.

"If you aren't there, what will people think?" asked Saladin.

"I'll leave it to Captain Anderson to spread the word of my valiant battle against half the Creek Nation led by Opothleyahola himself." Watie laughed, then went to run down his wayward horse. Albert Pike and John Ross would be finished with their negotiations at Park Hill now. The treaty was to be signed in Tahlequah—and Stand Watie would be there, grimy or not.

The capital of the Cherokee Nation was bedecked with fluttering canvas banners and brightly colored ribbon everywhere he looked. Stand Watie felt a certain pride that he had swayed so many of the others, getting them to realize John Ross's policy of neutrality was doomed to failure and that maintaining the treaties with the United States was a dead end for the Cherokee Nation. The men in Washington had been given plenty of opportunity to make good on their highfalutin' treaties and endless promises. The Old Settlers had done well—Watie was among them— but for the majority of Cherokee, prosperity was only something to dream of.

John Ross kept those dreams bottled and hidden from those he governed. It was time to uncork the bottle of sovereignty and seek freedom from the United States. Stand Watie wanted nothing more than for Tahlequah to become the capital of an independent country, one exchanging ambassadors with other nations around the world, one looked up to for the excellence and bravery of its citizens.

Some signs were in the rolling, twisting alphabet Sequoyah had invented. Watie read them with some difficulty, English being his preferred language. He frowned. Many of those banners were carried by the full-bloods who mistakenly followed John Ross and the abolitionists. The signs supporting the treaty with the CSA told Watie the Keetoowah Society—and John Ross's faction—were dwindling in number and influence.

This might be the last official act the old chief performed.

Good.

After brushing off what dirt he could from his colonel's uniform jacket, Stand Watie climbed to the stage and sat on a chair at the far end. He talked with a few people in the crowd who came up, but Watie's attention was fixed on the road to Park Hill and John Ross's Rose Cottage, where Albert Pike must have finished by now. Watie was anxious to see the ink drying on the treaty so he could get on with his business. Jayhawkers raided endlessly, Opothleyahola's men were growing bolder, and then there was the matter of John Drew's troops. A talk with Albert Pike might integrate them with his own regiment—with him in overall command and Drew reduced to a desk job, where he belonged.

"There!" went up the cry. "There they come!"

Watie stood and shielded his eyes with his beefy hand. A smile crept onto his lips. Albert Pike was in full Confederate uniform and rode at the head of a column of cavalry. John Ross and his advisors were relegated to an inferior position in carriages behind the soldiers.

Pike climbed the steps of the platform, eyed Watie's dirty jacket, and said nothing. He saluted, then thrust out his hand. Stand Watie shook it with his firm grip.

"Glad you could make it, Colonel," Albert Pike said. "Looks as if you had a spot of trouble along the way."

"Just a little. Nothing I couldn't handle. How'd the final negotiation go?"

From Pike's expression he knew it had gone well, and John Ross had capitulated on every detail. He looked past to where Allen Ross helped his father climb the steps. Behind came John Drew, looking uncomfortable in his new uniform. A half dozen assistant chiefs whispered among themselves, none looking happy.

When they were seated, Albert Pike stepped forward and addressed the crowd.

"This is a momentous time for the Cherokee people," he said. "From this day forward you will embark on a journey to freedom, freedom from want, and freedom from the yoke of Northern oppression!"

A cheer went up. Stand Watie saw the old chief shake his head slightly. Even in defeat he remained true to his principles. It was a shame they were not those that best suited the Cherokee people.

With bold strokes, Albert Pike signed the treaty. With a somewhat shakier hand, John Ross followed. It was officially decreed. Watie was not a signer, but that did not bother him. John Ross had capitulated.

The Cherokee Nation had severed all ties with the United States and was now an ally of the Confederate States of America.

Extending the Olive Branch
October 8, 1861

"Preposterous!" cried Stand Watie. He stared at Albert Pike in dismay. "Giving Opothleyahola a pardon for his crimes makes a mockery of every Cherokee law!"

"I understand your position, Stand," said Pike, leafing through a sheaf of papers in front of him. He looked up, his face impassive. "You must understand ours. The threat of a slave revolt is too real, and the Confederacy cannot send troops to put one down."

"We can handle our own affairs. Isn't that the point of the treaty John Ross signed?"

"Yes, Stand. Yes, of course it is. Ross is establishing courts as we speak. You'd best have representatives present at the council meeting when judges are chosen," Pike warned. He rubbed his thumb along the top page, the one with the fancy gold seal and red ribbon on it—Opothleyahola's official pardon, should he choose to stop all fighting and sign a treaty for the Creek with the Confederacy.

"The threat posed by a slave uprising outweighs the need to punish Opothleyahola for his beliefs," Pike went on. This worried him more than anything else, and it showed on his face.

"A Creek war party tried to kill me! They are no better than the Jayhawkers sweeping down from Kansas to burn out our settlers."

"General McCulloch is aware of that sorry situation, and there are other changes in the military district coming," Pike promised.

"Changes? What changes?" This was the first Watie had heard of any change in the chain of command. It bothered him that he got it from Albert Pike in such an offhand manner rather than through more official channels. It was as if Pike had not meant to even mention it, and the words simply slipped out.

"General McCulloch has done so well he is being promoted. I might be speaking out of turn, but a new commander will take over soon. I think you'll find Colonel Cooper an astute leader and one attentive to the needs of the Cherokee."

Watie said nothing. He had heard of Douglas Cooper. He preferred McCulloch as a superior officer, but he had to admit McCulloch's success in the field had attracted positive attention after he had punished those Texan irregulars in his command who had been responsible for scalping Sigel's artillerists. Discipline had improved throughout Arkansas, and Watie had hoped it would spread into Indian Territory, especially John Drew's command. He feared those men more than he did any Jayhawker or abolitionist Creek.

"I must hurry if I am going to meet Opothleyahola at sundown," Albert Pike said, checking his pocket watch.

"Let me accompany you. You can't trust the Creek."

"I know, I know, Stand. I wish it were possible for you and your company to come along. It would make me feel much more secure. In addition, you—and that clever son of yours—could learn a great deal watching the negotiations. After the war you'll both have fine futures as diplomats. I feel it in my bones. How'd you like to be ambassador to the Court of Saint James?"

"England?" Watie grinned at the thought of such a responsible position. There had been Indians at the court centuries earlier, but they had been nothing but curiosities brought by Raleigh for the amusement of British royalty. To be an ambassador dealing with the fate of his nation! This was a dream of greatness. Then he shook his head. "Better to train Saladin for that."

"A good choice, also," Albert Pike said, closing his paper case and tucking the folio under his arm. "Until we can do what we like and not what is expedient, we will need men like you and your young son backing us up."

"Drew will be no fit guard for you," Watie complained, seeing the lead element of John Drew's regiment trotting up. They looked far more military in bearing than Watie's men, but they were nothing but parade ground soldiers— just like their colonel.

"Expediency," Albert Pike repeated. "John Drew and Opothleyahola share similar views, and Drew's presence will put the Creek at ease. This will aid me in convincing them to join our cause. Seeing Drew and hearing of John Ross's reasons for signing the treaty with the CSA might also sway him."

Stand Watie watched Pike march forth and salute John Drew. Drew shot Watie a cold look, then ordered his column to wheel about. They looked good in drill, but could they fight? Watie doubted it, because of their leaders. John Drew was no soldier, and John Ross had forced the appointment of his nephew William Potter Ross as adjutant. Will Ross was nothing more than a spy at Fort Gibson for his uncle, Watie knew.

The column rode off, heading into Creek country to meet Opothleyahola. Watie doubted Albert Pike would succeed, not through lack of persuasiveness but because of John Drew's presence. Opothleyahola would see nothing but John Ross's supporters and think the Cherokee, no matter what the treaty with the CSA said or that Ross had signed it, favored abolition.

"There will be a campaign against the Creek," Watie said to himself. He climbed into the saddle, ready to rejoin his regiment. If they were to have a new commander in the district, he wanted his soldiers to be in top fighting form.

Two Fronts
November 10, 1861

Stand Watie looked anxiously at his new commander. Colonel Douglas Cooper was an imposing figure of a man, broad of shoulder and thick of chest with a huge gray-shot mustache and full beard he stroked constantly as he spoke. The bushy eyebrows rippled like caterpillars on a hot griddle, and his eyes were piercing and dark. He had been agent to both the Choctaw and Chickasaw before the war. Now he commanded their military units, the only non-Indian commander in the Territory.

"It's all come undone," Cooper said, his voice gravelly. "General Pike has returned to Richmond at a bad time." Cooper looked around the table at his officers. "Opothleyahola rejected John Ross's overtures for peace, and escaped slaves flock to his camp. The Creek menace is greater now than it has ever been."

Watie spoke up. "Opothleyahola has been raiding, but there are a thousand Jayhawkers on our border waiting to invade our country."

"You refer to the rumor that Colonel Jennison is going to attack?" asked John Drew's representative, Captain James McDaniel. "Pish! The real threat is within our own borders. I agree with Colonel Cooper. We must stop Opothleyahola."

"A strange comment from one whose loyalty lies with the Pins," Watie muttered to his old friend, William Penn Adair. The commander of Watie's scouts grunted, and glared at McDaniel.

"I don't know for sure, but I think he deals more fairly with Opothleyahola and his abolitionists than with us. Mark my words, Stand, watch out for that snake." William pulled out his knife and began stropping it slowly on a leather strip fastened to his belt.

"I know something of Charles Jennison," Cooper said, his mustache bobbing in greater agitation now. "His skills are not to be lightly dismissed. As unfortunate as it is, gentleman, we must fight on several fronts simultaneously. Captain McDaniel, inform Colonel Drew that he will patrol the northern frontier to counter any incursion made by Jennison and his 7th Kansas Cavalry Regiment. If they do not attack, you should sally forth into Kansas after their camps and destroy them. They have plundered enough."

"A moment, sir," said McDaniel. He cleared his throat and looked uncomfortable. "That's not possible, Colonel."

"How's that? Isn't Colonel Drew's Cherokee Mounted Rifles prepared for action? The report from your adjutant, Will Ross, said you were combat ready."

"Lieutenant Colonel Ross failed to tell you that we are only a defensive unit. Chief Ross will never permit our regiment to leave Indian Territory."

"Sir, my regiment will defend our nation," Watie spoke up. "Use John Drew's men elsewhere." Stand Watie felt his heart racing as he glared at McDaniel. What did it matter if the bullet in the back came from Opothleyahola's Creek or a Federal Jayhawker? Dead was dead. Burned out was as bad by Indian hand as by white. Both had to be stopped. Now.

"General McCulloch told me you were a staunch fighter and a good man, Colonel. Thank you for volunteering your services." Cooper spread out a map of Indian Territory and studied it. "Here is what we will do. Colonel Watie, take your regiment north along the border and engage any of Jennison's troops you find. Go into Kansas after the bastards, if you can do so with little risk to your own soldiers. The details I leave in your capable hands. I'll lead the Chickasaw and Choctaw brigades against Opothleyahola's main camp and you, Captain McDaniel, tell Colonel Drew to position his regiment in the northwestern section of the Cooweescowee District. Coody's Bluff, about where the California Road crosses the Verdigris River, is an excellent place to prevent any of Jennison's soldiers from penetrating into the Cherokee Nation as well as keeping Opothleyahola bottled up. After I attack his main camp, he will try to escape. You will prevent that from happening. Any questions?"

Colonel Cooper looked around the table at the gathered officers, his gaze cold and unyielding. Before any of the officers could speak, he said, "You have your orders. Dismissed. And good hunting." This was directed to Stand Watie.

Cooper quickly left them. McDaniel and several of his junior officers followed. William Adair rocked back in his chair and used the tip of his knife to pick at his teeth.

"You see what I saw, Stand?" he asked.

"Pins," Watie said in disgust. "All the officers with McDaniel wore crossed pins in their lapels. You reckon they'll obey Cooper's orders, or go over to Opothleyahola?"

"Whatever happens in John Drew's regiment, it doesn't look like we can ever trust 'em. I sure as hell don't trust that James McDaniel. He's got things going on in his head nobody knows about."

"He was editor of the *Cherokee Phoenix*. You know what that newspaper said."

"Not much good 'bout us. Strong John Ross supporters. Strong Keetoowah Society ties, too. If I were a bettin' man, Stand, I'd lay you odds that James McDaniel is a Pin, and we've been tellin' the enemy everything we're going to do."

"That's Colonel Cooper's problem, since he's relying on John Drew to back him up. We have obstacles of our own to climb over if we are going to stop a thousand Federals from swarming across the border like ants and eating our picnic." He jerked his head in the direction of the door. He left, William trailing after. Stand Watie wished he had a better feeling about the fighting that surely lay ahead of them.

Before he mustered his troops he wrote a short letter to Sarah and sent it to her by courier—their son Saladin. He wanted the boy out of harm's way. He was no seer, and the future was blocked to him as it was to any other man, but he felt in his bones that the fighting would be fierce.

Opothleyahola
November 20, 1861

"We can do it, Colonel," the Choctaw scout told Douglas Cooper, peering across the darkened tent. It was an hour before sunrise, and a storm brewed, promising more than simple cold. None of the men took notice of the weather because they were too intent on what their commander had to say. "We been movin' fast up the Deep Fork. Opothleyahola's not expectin' us to come a'callin'."

Cooper played with his mustaches, then stroked his bushy beard, wondering if he could strike quickly enough. Reconnaissance had told him Opothleyahola had gathered more than thirteen hundred warriors from the Seneca and Osage, as well as his own tribe. With them were a sizable number of escaped slaves fighting for their very lives. It would be a potent force, because they camped on their home ground and fought what they thought was a war for survival.

"He should have accepted John Ross's offer of a pardon," Cooper said, more to himself than to either of his captains huddled in the tent. Outside a cold wind blew from the north, carrying with it snapping arctic teeth. No snow fell. For that he was thankful. The ground had frozen and barely thawed, making the way both cold and muddy.

This would slow any cavalry attack on Opothleyahola—and it had to be a lightning thrust. No infantry attack would work against the wily old Creek chief.

"The river's not completely frozen over," Cooper said, again more to himself than to his captains. "The entire Canadian River is a deathtrap for anyone trying to cross it. If we attack thusly," he said, moving his hand in a broad sweeping motion along one bank of the river, "we force Opothleyahola to stand and fight or retreat—across the river."

"We'd have 'im for sure," a scout said. "He'd be runnin' smack into Captain McDaniel's reserve."

"Has John Drew's regiment left Fort Gibson yet?" Cooper asked.

"The order was sent a week back. No reply yet," Cooper's adjutant said, "other than confirmation by McDaniel. He's got a company at his homestead on Hominy Creek. No reason not to believe the rest of Drew's men aren't there, also."

"No reason to think they are, either," Cooper said. "We make the attack and try not to depend too heavily on Drew's forces. I wish Watie were here. We could make a concerted assault on the Creek and snuff them out like a candle in the wind."

As he spoke, a strong gust almost took down his tent. The door flap snapped like a garrison banner, and Cooper put his elbows down on his area map to keep it from flying off.

"No word that Colonel Watie's found them Jayhawkers," another officer, Captain Gaines, said. "A courier could reach him, and with a quick march he could be here in a few days."

"Too long," Cooper said. "Opothleyahola doesn't know we've gotten this close. He's no fool. He'll find out. We attack in one hour at dawn's first light."

"Gonna be some fancy marchin', Colonel," opined Gaines.

"Fancy riding. We attack on horseback. Move the infantry into battle behind us as quickly as possible." He knew the cavalry might find itself outnumbered, enveloped, and beyond redemption if the infantry didn't step along lightly enough to reinforce after the shock of the initial attack wore off. He had no choice. Running down Opothleyahola was like trying to grab a handful of the wind whistling through his beard. He had felt so close so many times, and always he came away with nothing but cold.

Not this time. This time he would strike hard and break the back of the Creek resistance in Indian Territory.

"Big risk, Colonel," said Captain Gaines.

"Since you know whose rear end is going to be hanging out in the wind, you appreciate the importance of getting the infantry into the fray as quickly as possible. You're in command of the foot soldiers, Captain Gaines."

"I don't have much ambition, Colonel," Gaines said slowly. "Reckon that means I gotta get there 'fore Opothleyahola scalps you, though. No way I'd want to command this whole danged district, even if the War Department would put a mixed-blood in charge. Too many weasels in it, if you catch my meaning."

"You understand my position exactly, sir," Cooper said. "Muster your men and get them moving right away, since it'll take longer for them to get to the battlefield." Gaines saluted and left. Cooper sighed, knowing he was committed to a fight today, weather against him or not. To his adjutant he said, "Get the troops mounted. I want to ride in fifteen minutes and attack in one hour." He snapped open the face of his watch. A thin layer of frost formed when it was exposed to the wind. Gently wiping off the face, he stared at the watch given him by his father. He made a silent promise to his long-dead father, closed the watch, and then tucked it back into his jacket. Settling his heavy wool gray uniform, now filthy from the days spent in the saddle chasing the Creek, he stepped out into the gathering storm. All around him raced his officers, shouting commands and preparing their men for the battle.

His orderly brought his horse and Colonel Cooper mounted, ready for the fight of his life.

"Is Quayle in position?" Cooper had six companies of men, almost fourteen hundred soldiers, ready for the attack. The lieutenant colonel in charge of the 9th Texas Cavalry Regiment had problems getting to his post for the first assault. Cooper suspected he might have been drunk, although he dared not ask because he might find out. Disciplining the wild Texas officer now was out of the question. After the battle, it might not be necessary, if one or the other died.

The private acting as runner between the officers of Cooper's force nodded repeatedly, making it appear as if his head had been put on a spring.

"Yes, sir, the lieutenant colonel sends his regards and says, uh, says we're gonna to whup their red butts good."

Cooper looked around. He was the only white man commanding an all Indian unit. Major Jumper was out of earshot, firing up his Creek and Seminole Battalion. If the fight went well, some of his soldiers would be reunited with others from their tribe—as captors over traitors. The Creek were as badly split as the Cherokee when it came to the matters of slavery and the question of republic or confederacy as a way of governing themselves. They would face their own people—and that could not be an easy thing.

Cooper sighed. It wasn't easy fighting men he had known most of his life, and with whom he had worked so long and with such admiration. Many had joined him in the Southern cause. The ones he regretted most were those who had not, and were now his sworn enemies.

"Tell Quayle to listen for my bugler. He is to attack along North Fork while I follow Deep Fork River. We will catch Opothleyahola between us. Colonel McIntosh's 1st Creek will follow Quayle, and my own Choctaw and Chickasaw will engage first."

"Yes, sir." The private saluted and tore off to rejoin the Texas regiment. It was difficult having whites fighting alongside Indians. Sometimes the Texans did not understand what they were saying about their companions in arms was derogatory. For all that, Cooper was glad he had Lieutenant Colonel Quayle's men in the attack. Even without them, the Indian forces would crush Opothleyahola. They were some of the best fighters he had ever seen, red or white.

"My regards to Colonel McIntosh," Cooper said to his own courier. "Tell him to act as reserve for Quayle's men. If they do not need assistance, he is to swing around in a wide arc to the north and catch any fleeing Creek or escaped slaves." His courier, a Choctaw who had been with him since his promotion, nodded silently and set off at a ground-devouring trot. Unlike the Texas courier, he did not salute. Cooper hardly noticed. What happened in battle was more important than a forgotten salute now and then.

His men were as disciplined in battle, if not more, than any of the Texas units. Never had he caught any of the Indians scalping fallen foes.

Cooper waited impatiently astride his horse. The wind had kicked up, making it feel as if razors sliced his face. A touch of snow pellets beat a tattoo against his hands, promising heavier snowfall soon. When he figured his courier had dispatched his orders to McIntosh and that Captain Gaines would be well on his way, he raised his arm. He clutched his cavalry saber, but used it only to signal his bugler. No one but a fool rode into battle swinging the heavy weapon.

The blade flashed in the weak dawn light; the bugler sounded attack. Colonel Cooper sheathed his sword and drew his pistol. With a loud whoop, he put his heels to his horse's flanks and rocketed forward into battle.

They caught Opothleyahola's forces as they were breaking camp. The Creek chief had decided to move on early in the day, possibly beating the storm as he sought a more protected bivouac. He now found himself surrounded by a storm of a different kind.

"Get 'em, men!" shouted Cooper as he galloped through the center of the Creek camp. He fired as he rode. Two shots brought down men trying to level rifles on him. The other four rounds missed entirely. Cooper got to the far end of the camp and surveyed the battlefield. He had caught Opothleyahola with his drawers down. Those Creek not eating a morning meal were packing their gear, and were totally unprepared to repulse an offensive. Nowhere did Cooper see a sentry. Opothleyahola had been too secure on his home ground, and had not thought he could be attacked.

The first wave of his attack washed through the camp and gathered behind him as he reloaded.

"Again! Once more, men!" Cooper led the cavalry attack back through the camp.

This time they met more resistance. Opothleyahola had thirteen hundred men spread out along the bank of the sluggishly flowing Canadian River, and many of them dropped their supplies and picked up rifles and bows and arrows. The latter proved the most deadly for Cooper's second attack. The Creek fired arrows as fast as Cooper could cock and fire his pistol.

Horses and men tumbled to the ground where warriors swarmed over them, brandishing knives and war clubs. The scene took on disorienting, fantastical aspects as he stared across the campground. Everywhere dead men provided barricades for the living. Knives glinted in the dawn, and dry, white, snow pellets whirled like dust through the camp, mixing with blood and filling the air with a curious sanguinary mist.

Cooper struggled to reload his pistol again. As he worked, he felt a sudden sharp pain in his right shoulder. Looking down, he saw the tip of an arrow protruding from the front of his jacket. He broke off the barbed tip with his left hand, reached around awkwardly, and dragged out the arrow. Only then did he turn. He had reloaded one chamber. He lifted his pistol against a gravity that seemed to grow stronger by the second. Hand shaking, he pulled the trigger. For a ghastly moment he thought nothing happened. The tiny *pop!* sounded distant, farther away than the breeding ground for the Canadian storm blowing across Indian Territory this morning. In a curious movement, as if the world had been dipped in syrup, Cooper saw his target clutch his chest and slump to the ground, all his leg bones turned to pudding.

In a detached fashion he realized he was still alive, that he had killed the warrior responsible for shooting him in the back, and he ought to reload. A battle still raged around him. He fumbled, his hands numb with cold and shock, but he reloaded and prepared for yet another charge through Opothleyahola's camp.

The tumult of battle grew until he wanted to scream. He tried to urge his horse forward, but it balked, refusing to budge. Then Douglas Cooper saw that the fight was over. The third wave rushing through the Creek camp was being led by Major Jumper, his soldiers fighting with utter abandon against their tribal brothers.

Of Chief Opothleyahola Cooper saw no trace. He wobbled in the saddle, but remained upright as he coaxed his horse to walk forward. The Choctaw he used as a courier came running up, sweat beading his forehead, betraying the extreme exertion required to run in such blustery weather.

"Colonel," the Choctaw called. "Lieutenant Colonel Quayle sends his regards. He's lost Opothleyahola after he ran northward."

"Opothleyahola got away?" Cooper felt weak from the shock of the arrow. Then resolve burned hot within him. "No! I will *not* let him escape. Major!" he shouted to John Jumper. "Secure the area. Get prisoners back to Fort Gibson using as few troops to guard them as you can. The rest of your battalion, get it ready. We're going after Opothleyahola, and this time we will not let him get away. If I have to track him to the ends of the earth, I will *not* let him escape!"

Round Mountain
November 22, 1861

Colonel Cooper's adjutant saluted smartly, then took off his gloves and warmed his hands by the small campfire struggling against the sharp wind blowing from the north. Snow drifted lightly on the rocks around the firepit, giving a curious cold-hot appearance. For all the leaping, dancing flames, there was scant heat.

"So?" Cooper demanded impatiently. "What's that damned fool John Drew done now?"

"He's not in position," the adjutant said. "It looks as if the Pins are aiding Opothleyahola, too."

"Are you implying Drew is involved?"

The adjutant shrugged. It wasn't his place to make such accusations. "Looks suspicious that Captain McDaniel is sending messengers out more 'n he needs. None reach this camp. So where's he sendin' them?"

"To Drew?" suggested Cooper. He glowered. Moving closer to the fire did nothing to warm his hands, either. Shoulder to shoulder with his adjutant, the wind robbing them of their heat, he wiggled his mustache enough to crack ice from it. He did not try to break free the ice caking his beard.

"Might be. If so, Drew knows more about Opothleyahola's movements than we do. McDaniel was in position to watch Opothleyahola and all his Creek go waltzin' past. Didn't do a danged thing to stop him."

Cooper rubbed his hands some more, then motioned for his adjutant and several officers to join him. Captain Gaines was the last to crowd into the tiny tent, which did nothing to prevent the winter from dampening their spirits further.

"What say the scouts, Captain?" he asked of Gaines.

"Opothleyahola was already out of the camp when we attacked. That's the only reason he got away scot-free."

"What of John Drew?" asked the adjutant. Gaines glanced toward his colonel, then pursed his lips, lost for a moment in consideration of how to phrase his reply.

He finally said, "John Drew's waitin' for supplies from Fort Gibson. Cain't blame him for holin' up the way he has in this weather. But Captain McDaniel, now, he's at home. There's no way Opothleyahola got past him at Hominy Creek without him twiggin' to it."

"Are you calling Captain McDaniel a traitor?"

"Thought I was clear on that, Colonel," Gaines said. "Don't think you ought to let on you know McDaniel had throwed in with the enemy, though."

Cooper considered his proper course of action. How he wished Watie were here! He needed the Cherokee's leadership so he could tend to capturing Opothleyahola without watching over his shoulder and waiting for more bad news about traitorous officers.

"There's no reason to suspect Colonel Drew of disloyalty, is there?"

"Well, Colonel, seems McDaniel furnishes him with a lot of information we never see."

"Is it going to him, or to the Pins in his regiment?" asked Cooper.

"Cain't speak to that point, Colonel," Gaines admitted. "John Ross is a reluctant man when it comes to declaring for slavery, but he has done everything he can to fulfill the terms of the treaty with the Confederacy and to bring other tribes under the same compact. Opothleyahola is stubborn, but John Ross is doing all he can to persuade him to surrender. And what John Ross wants, John Drew does." Cooper looked at the haggard, frost-nipped faces of his officers. They said nothing, but they agreed. John Drew was likely a sympathizer with the abolitionists, as was John Ross, but like the Cherokee chief he was not actively opposing the treaty voted on by the majority of the tribe.

McDaniel was another matter. The man had been a firebrand too long to change. Cooper remembered all too well the editorials McDaniel had written in support of the Keetoowah Society and against the Southern Rights Party.

"We will deal with the captain later," he said, coming to a conclusion. "Captain Gaines, can we overtake Opothleyahola?"

"More 'n that, Colonel," the officer said. "He's at Round Mountain and prob'ly isn't plannin' on doin' anything other than waitin' out this storm. We attack, we got him."

"Then prepare your units, gentlemen. That is exactly what we shall do." Cooper closed his eyes and let the pain wash through him. Ever since he had taken the arrow, movement caused more than a twinge of misery. He was unable to raise his right arm, so he had his orderly load two pistols for him, both of which he thrust into his belt before mounting. He winced at the movement, then settled down. It would not do to have his men think he was incapable of leading them into battle.

Riding slowly in the fitful snowstorm, he watched as his officers grouped their men, got them mounted on tired horses, and began moving west toward the junction of the Cimarron and Arkansas rivers. This part of the country was blessed with rolling hills, but in that lay a dual edged sword. Opothleyahola would not know he approached, but his force would also come on the Creek encampment un-expectedly. There was no good way of positioning his men for a proper attack.

"Surprise," he muttered. "We'll take them by surprise, Opothleyahola with his entire band this time."

The Arkansas River flowed briskly, fed upstream by run-off. To cross that river would be suicidal, Cooper saw. The unknown depth and the freezing temperature would kill any soldier—or his mount—within minutes. He hoped this would serve to box in Opothleyahola, but then he had hoped the same before their last fight.

"Be there, old man," Cooper said. "I want this done."

A dark ghost ahead in the storm waved to him. Gaines. The signal was relayed that the Creek camp was near.

"Bugler, sound the charge," Cooper ordered through chapped lips. He winced as he drew one pistol from his belt. He cocked it and then galloped toward Captain Gaines as the bugler mustered the regiments and moved them forward in attack.

Cooper rode alongside Gaines and immediately found himself lost in a welter of confusion. A Creek sentry had spotted them and passed along the warning, for all the good it did. The snow tore at his face and hands and slowed his horse, but occasional swirls cleared and showed a camp far larger than he had anticipated.

"To the fray, men. Fight, get them, get them all!" Colonel Cooper shouted. The wind ate his words and the rifle fire from the camp tore through his leading element.

Opothleyahola's camp was filled with women and chil-dren—and every Creek loyal to Opothleyahola. Cooper emptied one pistol and discarded it. Then he began firing the second. He found himself fought to a standstill, unable to advance. Looking left and right, he saw all his cavalry had been similarly halted by the intense fire.

"Colonel, there must be two thousand of 'em in that

camp. Thought it was jist Opothleyahola. Didn't know," apologized Gaines.

"Captain, get the bugler. Sound retreat. We will fall back eastward along the Arkansas River to Concharty, and regroup there. Damn the weather! Damn Opothleyahola!"

A bullet took off Cooper's broad-brimmed hat and made him duck involuntarily. From there the battle went downhill.

The small Creek community of Concharty had swelled when all of Cooper's force entered by squads and companies, by two and threes. The increasingly fierce storm had caused the retreat from Round Mountain to become a rout.

White-faced and barely able to sit up, Cooper assembled his officers.

"What of Opothleyahola?" he asked. Cooper read the answer in their faces. The old Creek warrior had again eluded them. "Casualties?"

"Hard to say yet, Colonel," his adjutant said. "Six killed, four wounded, one missing. Those we know for sure."

"How many casualties did Opothleyahola sustain?" Cooper asked, eyes closed as he pictured the snow-blown, white landscape that had turned bloody red so quickly.

"No way of tellin', sir," Gaines said. "We left the field so's they could tend their own wounded."

"One hundred," he said. "That's how many we killed or wounded." He weaved about as shock set in from exposure and his earlier wound. "No, not that. One hundred ten."

"I know we surprised 'em," Gaines said, "but not that much."

"I'll get to the report, sir," said the adjutant, giving Gaines and the others a cold look. "You see to getting

yourself patched up. Rest and we can go after Opothleyahola when the storm lifts."

"Yes, when the storm abates. A good time." Colonel
Cooper staggered to a hard mattress and collapsed on it,
mumbling to himself.

Judge Not
November 20, 1861

"Jayhawkers!"

John Drew looked up from the book he read. Outside the wind shrieked and snow blew along fitfully, snow pellets mixing in with wetter, larger flakes. His camp at Coody Bluff was secure enough against the storm, being on the lee side, and Lieutenant Colonel Ross had promised a supply train from Fort Gibson any day now to replenish their supplies. He had even been unaware of Douglas Cooper's movements, which suited John Drew. Let the other colonel go chasing after Opothleyahola. Drew would rather follow John Ross's lead and negotiate with the Creek chief.

"Where are they?" he asked as the sergeant dipped his head to shake off the snow as he came inside the building that had once housed the county government. The sergeant had given way to more traditional Cherokee garb, as had most of the regiment. Supply was spotty, and when it did come John Drew wanted food, ammunition, and even muskets to replace those lost more than he did the poorly stitched Confederate uniforms.

"Sir, a force of more 'n a hundred swooped down on the Caney River settlement early today."

"Are you sure they were Jayhawkers?" Drew asked. He closed his book and realized this might be his chance to get away from supporting Douglas Cooper in his insane pursuit of Opothleyahola. Everyone in the Cherokee Nation agreed the Kansas guerrillas were not to be tolerated, and it was yet another mark of his good fortune that Stand Watie had been sent to deal with them.

"We reckon they got past Colonel Watie and came a'raidin'," the sergeant said. He wiped his face clear of water from melted snow. "Either that, or he jist let 'em get by to bedevil us."

"He wouldn't do that," John Drew said sharply. He held no liking for Watie or any of those in his Southern Rights Party, but Watie was a persistent and diligent fighter. Whatever he did to correct what he considered historical injustice would not include trying to make John Ross—or Drew—look foolish by letting Jayhawkers raid his own people indiscriminately. Stand Watie would want to capture them to show his own military prowess. Glory, that was all he thought about, John Drew was certain.

"Whatever happened farther north don't matter here, Colonel," the sergeant said, "since them guerrillas upped and kidnapped Judge Keyes."

"Riley Keyes?" This brought John Drew around so that he seriously considered the incursion. Keyes was the Cooweescoowee District judge.

"Yes, sir, and a Negro boy belonging to Joel Bryan."

John Drew dismissed this. The Jayhawkers would not harm the boy—if anything, they would free him—but the Cherokee rancher would be fit to be tied having his property stolen, and so deep in the district, too. The Jayhawkers proved bolder than ever.

"Other bad news," John Drew asked, seeing the sergeant worked to spit out more.

"They stole two hundred head of cattle and sixty horses, all owned by Cherokee. They're punishin' us hard, sir."

John Drew scratched his chin as he thought, then reached out and pulled a map from his gear. He folded it carefully, then held it up so he could study it in the dim light cast by the coal oil lamp near his bedroll.

"Assuming Watie and his band of ruffians are where they are supposed to be along the Kansas border—or perhaps they actually did as Cooper suggested and are raiding deeper into United States territory—that means the Jayhawkers came down through the Cherokee Outlet."

"But Captain McDaniel's over on Hominy Creek. They couldn't git by him without him knowin', Colonel."

John Drew considered this. McDaniel's company of fifty men guarded the western approach. He had not heard from the captain in days, although horses came and went in the night. So many of his regiment had friends and family in the Cooweescoowee District he had not made a point of checking on the strange traffic. Now he wondered if some message from McDaniel had not been passed along to him, through carelessness or intent.

"Sergeant," he said, coming to a decision. "We'll march along the California Road and see if we can't put an end to these raiders' careers."

"When, sir?"

"Now, of course," John Drew said firmly, closing his book and carefully putting it into his gear. "Pass along the order. Send a messenger to Captain McDaniel to get him into the field, also. There must be *some* evidence of these Jayhawkers."

"All right," the sergeant said reluctantly. He fingered crossed pins in the lapel of his coat, then turned and left. John Drew silently packed his gear, then buttoned his heavy coat and stepped outside into the storm. The small warmth within the building had felt good as he read. Outside, the wind whipped around the knife-sharp bluffs and sucked away his bodily heat. He took a long, deep breath of the frigid air, then set about finding his orderly to get his gear stowed and the men into the saddle.

He had guerrillas to stop.

"There, Colonel, there's some more of them cows," shouted a private.

"Round up the strays," John Drew said. "We've got the Jayhawkers on the run if they are abandoning their captured beeves."

"Sir, we've been out for more than an hour, and there's no real sign of the Kansans," piped up a lieutenant whose name he could never remember. "Why not return to camp? We'll never overtake them."

"Duty, son, duty," John Drew said firmly. "We're supposed to protect the settlers from these brigands." He shoved his hand inside his uniform jacket to warm it as he stared across the snowy field, all chopped up by the passage of many horses.

"They got a head start, Colonel," the lieutenant protested. "We'd have to chase 'em danged near into Kansas. See the trail? They're hightailin' it north."

"They hold a judge hostage," Drew said. "We dare not allow them to make off with him, or they will become emboldened and try it again."

John Drew saw two riders approaching from the west, in the direction of Captain McDaniel's company—or where it ought to be patrolling. He studied the sky for a clue about the weather. It had cleared and turned colder, if that was possible. No snow, but the lead-heavy gray clouds threatening along the northern horizon over the hills promised more. Chasing down the Jayhawkers would be difficult if they had truly decided to run homeward to Kansas. Watie might intercept them if he dispatched a messenger to the other regimental commander. That would allow his own Cherokee Mounted Rifles to herd the beeves back to their owners without venturing closer to the Kansas border, where John Ross had cautioned only danger lay.

"Defend the Cherokee, but don't incite," John Drew said to himself. The riders trotted up. One he recognized as a scout from McDaniel's company. The other rider was a civilian.

"This is Albert Threekiller," the scout said without so much as a greeting salute. "He got away from the Jayhawkers."

"They let me go," Threekiller said. "They rode in and kidnapped me and six others, including—"

"Judge Keyes," John Drew finished for him. "We are on their trail to free him." He frowned, sensing something wrong with the setup. "Why are you coming from the west if the Jayhawkers captured you? This is their trail, and it goes north."

"They let us go, and we found refuge with Captain McDaniel's men. Judge Keyes is with 'em."

"There are no more captives? Is that correct?" asked John Drew.

"Only the Negro boy taken from Joel," Threekiller said. "That's Joel Byron."

"They travel so fast," John Drew mused. "They can travel even faster now that they have left behind their captives and are releasing the cattle. The stolen horses they can ride, of course."

"No reason to go after 'em," the private said. "You been out for more 'n an hour. Get on back to Coody Bluff and wait for the supplies."

John Drew's eyes narrowed as he studied the young man. "You know a powerful lot about my regiment's situation. How is that, when I know next to nothing about McDaniel's?"

The private sat impassively on his horse, saying nothing. Albert Threekiller spoke up.

"It's like he said, Colonel. The judge is all right. So are the others. We're all anxious to get back home."

"True, I can understand that," John Drew said, looking from the former captive to the broad trail left by the fleeing Jayhawkers. He could overtake them. He could capture the men responsible for taking a Cherokee judge prisoner. That would go a ways toward relieving the criticism of John Ross and his policies. Colonel Drew could show how dedicated to protecting the Cherokee Nation they were.

"Lieutenant!" he called to the officer leading the scouts. "See that a squad accompanies Mr. Threekiller back to Captain McDaniel's company and then escort all the released men to their homes. The rest of the regiment will pursue the Jayhawkers. By God, we will not allow them to do this to Cherokee citizens!"

With those orders, John Drew set off on the muddy trail leading north. A quick capture of the Jayhawkers would be a feather in his cap, and show everyone that there were other soldiers besides Stand Watie in the field to defend their best interests.

On the Border
November 23, 1861

"This does not sound good," Stand Watie said. He tugged his wool officer's jacket up so the collar covered the back of his neck. The wind had died down but he still felt a chill—and this one did not come from the north. He studied the courier Colonel Cooper had sent, and wondered how truly desperate the situation was.

"Any reply to the colonel?" asked the corporal almost wistfully. The man looked around Watie's camp. For all the lack of military structure, the soldiers were well-fed and content, with small fires blazing merrily throughout the camp. Guards patrolled the perimeters, on the lookout for Jayhawker scouts, and the men worked without being told to keep their weapons clean of oil and grease so as not to freeze up in the frigid weather. They relied on their own initiative rather than being told every detail. This obviously impressed the corporal, and made Watie suspicious of how much support he might get from Colonel Cooper's regiment, should the need arise.

Watie sighed deeply. He wanted to remain on patrol rather than return to Cooper's command. At first he had thought this was only an assignment to show up John Drew's lack of commitment, but now Watie knew it for what it was: a necessity to keep the Jayhawkers from plundering all of the Cherokee Nation.

Watie felt as if he read the corporal's mind. If true, Cooper had sustained a terrible loss. Taking ten casualties was not bad, but having Opothleyahola so decisively rout him was. Watie had heard the numbers of Creek supposedly killed in the attack, and knew they were wrong. He held back, not actually proclaiming them a lie, but he suspected an official report had been filed saying 110 Creek warriors had been killed or wounded. Cooper was not a man to take defeat lightly, but Watie could not countenance lying in an official report to make the defeat seem less abominable.

"All the colonel needs from my regiment is support along the northern border? Such as we are already giving?"

"That's right, sir," the corporal said. His eyes drifted to a pot of coffee boiling on a nearby fire. His nose twitched at the smell of food coming from another fire.

"Get yourself something to eat before you start back. It'll take me a spell to compose my message to Colonel Cooper," Watie said, although he had nothing to report. Cooper wanted nothing more from him than what he already did—hunting down Jayhawkers slipping from the north to bedevil settlers. The Federals wisely avoided direct fights, letting the turmoil between the tribes take its toll.

"Within the tribes," Watie muttered to himself. Many Creeks rode with their Cherokee brothers under the Stars and Bars to fight their old chief Opothleyahola. And many Cherokee fought to destroy the treaty with the Confederacy. Watie growled deep in his throat as he thought of men like John Ross. They did not openly oppose the treaty. Rather, they fought a different war, dragging their feet, suggesting alliances that would only weaken and never strengthen. Watie could never forget who had ordered his

family killed—so long ago—and John Ross had not changed one whit.

"A snake in the grass waiting to strike," he said.

"How's that, Father?" asked Saladin Watie.

"Ah, you're back. How is your mother?" he asked, glad his son had returned from Tahlequah so quickly. "You must tell me everything about her, your brothers and sisters."

Saladin glanced toward Cooper's courier. "Shouldn't you deal with him first? That seemed an important message."

Watie laughed. "He would stay here until Opothleyahola is in his grave. Colonel Cooper is running low on supplies and morale, it seems. Let the messenger eat his fill. We have enough to spare since we captured that Federal supply wagon last week."

Saladin Watie hunkered down by the fire and told his engrossed father all he could of Sarah Watie and the four children still at home.

"She has all she needs?" asked Watie. "I can get Elias to help, if she needs flour or bacon or—"

"Father, she is fine. The cold winter is getting to her bones, as I see it is to yours, but she is fine. Besides, Elias has gone back to Richmond."

"I remember," Watie said. In some ways Elias Boudinot reminded him of John Ross, and they weren't necessarily good ways. "So much has been on my mind. I remember him saying he was chosen as a delegate to the Congress. When will he come home?"

"He hopes to be back before summer," Saladin said. "He does not think the war can last much longer, not after Manassas and your victory at Wilson's Creek."

Watie laughed. "I wish the two battles, mine so small, could have determined the war. The Jayhawkers fight fiercely, and Cooper has failed again to stop Opothleyahola."

"John Ross offered a pardon, but Opothleyahola refused it," Saladin said. "Ross does all he can to bring peace to Indian Territory, but nothing works. The divisions are too deep." Saladin paused and looked at his father, reading the emotions playing on the older man's face. "He is not a well man, John Ross. He is old."

"Allen Ross thinks as he does, and his nephew is John Drew's adjutant. Their hands might not have blood on them, but the entire family opposes ours. Which reminds me." Watie dug into his gear and pulled out a stack of letters. "A week's worth of letters. For your mother, for your brothers Cumiskey and Watica, for Jacqueline and Ninnie and your Uncle Charles—"

"Father, please. I can read. Do you do nothing but write letters?"

"There are long stretches when I have only memory of your darling mother to keep me warm. You, you're becoming a man, an officer, and at only fifteen years old." Watie sighed. "What of your cousin Charles?"

Saladin laughed. "He looks forward to enlisting and riding with you as his commander."

"Are we talking of the same Charles Webber?" Watie laughed again. "He is a wild boy, so different from you. It is a wonder you are such close friends."

"Charles is not wild," Saladin denied. "We never get into trouble when we are together. Well, hardly," Saladin said, grinning. He and his father talked for an hour of home and family before the corporal returned reluctantly to shuffle his feet, waiting to be recognized.

"I reckon it's 'bout time for me to ride back, Colonel. What's your message?"

"Corporal, this is Captain Watie, my son. He will accompany you to Colonel Cooper's camp, and from there he will return to Fort Gibson with any dispatches your commander might have."

"So he's gonna tell Colonel Cooper what he wanted to know?"

"Rest easy, Corporal," Watie said. "The colonel can depend absolutely on my support. We have destroyed several wagon trains of supplies intended for the Federals and continue to bottle them up on their home soil. If there is anything more Colonel Cooper needs of the First Cherokee Mounted Rifles, have him dispatch Captain Watie with orders."

"Yes, sir," the corporal said, looking from Watie to his son.

"Saladin, be sure those letters get to your mother. And when you return, you and Charles will have your own company to command. You've earned it."

"Thank you, Father. Sir!" Saladin Watie saluted smartly, did an about-face, and marched off to saddle his horse. The corporal saluted and headed after the fifteen-year-old. Watie read it in his expression that he thought Saladin had been promoted because of his father's influence. He would discover differently. Saladin Watie was a better officer in battle than most of those riding with Douglas Cooper.

Watie would not have traded him for General Lee.

He brushed a few snowflakes from his uniform, bellowed for the first company to mount, and then led them himself on a scout to keep the Federals across the Kansas border, where they belonged. William Adair could catch up later, and let him know of any potential dangers.

The entire time he rode Stand Watie thought of his son and the rest of his family in Tahlequah. He hoped Elias Boudinot was right, and that the war would be over soon. How he missed his children—and, especially, Sarah.

Gathering Forces
November 27, 1861

"We caught him sneakin' 'round down on the California Road, Colonel," the corporal said. He looked at Saladin Watie, who stood quietly behind and watched the scene unfold. "Figured you might want to talk to him."

Their captive snarled like a wild beast, then fell quiet and simply glared. Saladin doubted anything would be learned from this Creek, short of torturing it out of him. He and the corporal had been riding south to Concharty with his father's best wishes when they had seen the Creek scuttling along, trying hard not to be seen. If he had been more open or had even greeted them boldly, Saladin doubted they would have paid him any mind. His trying to wiggle through a snowbank and into mud to avoid being sighted had alerted them. Capturing him had been easy enough because he had been weighed down by so much mud on his boots.

"He was coming from the direction of Coody Bluff," Saladin said to the colonel. Cooper looked up, as if seeing him for the first time. Saladin was startled at how pale and drawn the colonel looked. Being defeated in battle was hardly conducive to good health, but Cooper had the appearance of a man with one foot in the grave.

"To or from? He might have been spying on Captain McDaniel," Cooper said, eyes fixed on the captive. Saladin Watie also saw the flash of fear in the captive's eyes. That single start convinced him the Creek had been carrying a message from McDaniel to Opothleyahola. Damn the Pins!

"Are you a member of the Keetoowah Society?" asked Cooper, echoing Saladin's thoughts. It was so apparent it hardly counted as an original notion. "Never mind. He won't tell us anything. Corporal, you have done well. See that he is taken to Fort Gibson under guard and turned over to Lieutenant Colonel Ross for safekeeping."

"Me, sir? You want me to take him?"

"Why not?" Relief flooded the corporal as he grabbed the prisoner and dragged him out of the tent. Cooper looked up from where he sat. "You think I did wrong, Captain?"

"No, the corporal is loyal enough. He doesn't have the belly for fighting, though. Do you have many like him in your regiment?"

"Too many," Cooper said. "I ought to have recalled your father's regiment. I can certainly use him and his troops more here than up north. Opothleyahola caught me flat-footed. We should have swept him from the field, storm or no storm. He had too many fighters, and they were defending their families. I didn't know women and children would be in the camp." He heaved a sigh and closed his eyes. Saladin thought he might pass out, but Cooper brought himself around.

"You are under orders to ride on to the capital?"

"I can ride to Fort Gibson with the corporal before going on to Tahlequah," offered Saladin. "I know most of them at the fort are sick with the flu, but I could take a message asking for support of your position, should you leave my father—Colonel Watie—on patrol along the border."

"No need. I have a sack of mail for you to deliver. Getting the mail to my soldiers' relatives is more important than any single spy being jailed."

"Are you worried about Captain McDaniel?"

"I'm more worried about overtaking Opothleyahola and stopping him," Cooper said with a touch of his old fire and determination. He sat up. Saladin saw how the movement caused the colonel pain, but made no mention of it. "Drew is at Camp Coody. McDaniel is still at Hominy Creek. And Lieutenant Colonel Diamond, Third Texas Cavalry, is positioned east along Grand River near Lost Creek. If scouting reports are correct, and I have no reason to doubt Captain Mayes, Opothleyahola is heading slowly toward Tulsey Town. I can overtake him and engage there. This time I will *not* be denied!"

"Sir, it would be my honor to serve with you in the field," Saladin Watie said.

"Thank you, Captain I have a better understanding now of the caliber of the Watie family. Your father is a great officer, and I see the acorn has not fallen far from the tree." Cooper took a deep breath. "There is no need to come along. Carry out your orders, Captain. See my adjutant for the mail to be delivered to Tahlequah."

"Yes, sir," Saladin said. He saluted and left, wondering if this might be the last time he saw the colonel. Cooper had the look of a walking dead man, more ghost than flesh. He shrugged it off. His father had known Cooper for years and thought well of him, although he had preferred General McCulloch and his experience garnered in the Mexico War when it came to field action.

Colonel Cooper sagged when Saladin Watie left. Having the young officer commanding a company would have been a plus, but he saw the young Watie's presence as having a spy in his rank. He did not need yet another report being made about the way he commanded his troops in the field. Anything Saladin Watie said would be listened to eventually by his father, who had the ear of those higher up the chain of command. Stand Watie was a hero of the Confederacy, and held up as the sort of Cherokee everyone in Indian Territory ought to emulate.

Watie won his battles. Cooper didn't. He shivered, as much with cold as with dread. His information about Opothleyahola was good. It had to be if he wanted to capture the elusive Creek chief. Another failure to bring the renegade to Fort Gibson as a prisoner would not be viewed favorably by John Ross—or by General McCulloch. What would they say if they found out two of his men had been captured by the Creek and brutally tortured to death—and that he had been unable to respond because he couldn't find the murderers? Cooper shuddered as he pictured the two whose brains had been knocked out, using hominy pestles. That had been bloody, bad, the stuff of nightmares. Why had the torturing bastards also punched out the eyes with sharp sticks?

He had to stop Opothleyahola now before matters turned even worse. His own soldiers wanted to respond in kind, and that would never do.

"Orderly! Get me a messenger." Cooper rapidly scrawled out orders for Captain McDaniel, then dispatched them with a less than eager courier. He wrote out other orders, for Colonel Sims's 9th Texas Cavalry Regiment, also camping up on the Verdigris. With McDaniel, the two units would come together and block off Opothleyahola's retreat to the north. He would march with his 780 men and push Opothleyahola ahead of him so Sims and McDaniel could deal more effectively with the fleeing Creek chief from fortified positions—or if Opothleyahola stood and fought, Cooper would finish him in direct battle.

An hour later his troopers rode out in the direction of Tulsey Town, intent on battle.

* * *

"Colonel, lookee what we got," a scout said, shoving forward a bedraggled man who had swum the frigid river to reach this side. "He claims to be an escaped prisoner from Opothleyahola's camp on the other side of the Arkansas."

"Get him a blanket. The man is freezing," Cooper said. Only when the man's shivering had subsided a little and he clutched a tin cup of hot coffee did Cooper ask the questions that had to be answered if he wanted victory. "Why did Opothleyahola take you prisoner?"

"I am Southern Cherokee. He never trusted me. When I saw how he got information from the Pins in your command, he worried I would sneak off and tell you."

"In my command?"

The prisoner's eyes widened slightly. "You are not John Drew?"

"Colonel Douglas Cooper," the officer said. He was the only non-Indian commander. Did he look so much like one of them now that he had a full beard shot with gray? That confusion of identity might have been a compliment, or the prisoner might be playing him for a fool. The latter vanished as an explanation when the man shuffled forward and peered harder at Cooper. His face lit up when he finally realized Cooper was a white man.

"I do not always see, but I hear well," the man said.

"Tell me what you've heard."

The man bit his lip and fell silent, as if considering how much he could reveal. He sipped at the coffee and stared hard at the cup, as if this warm liquid might decide the matter in his mind.

"You won't be harmed. I promise, no matter what you tell me. My mission is to stop Opothleyahola, and that is all." Cooper grew impatient, although he sensed he needed patience now more than ever.

"Do not depend on James McDaniel," the Cherokee

said slowly. "He sends Pins to tell those in John Drew's force of his real movement."

"John Drew doesn't know?" This surprised Cooper, since he had thought Drew and McDaniel were cut from the same cloth.

"John Drew waits only for the liquor shipments from Fort Gibson," the man said with some disdain. "McDaniel and those of the Loyal League plot against him—and you."

"The Loyal League? The Keetoowah Society?"

"The Pins," the man said, nodding. "They would betray you. Do not trust them. Their loyalty lies with Opothleyahola, not with you. They fancy themselves pro-Union."

Cooper dismissed this with a wave of his hand. "I'm aware of the divisions in my own rank. What of Opothleyahola?"

"He has two thousand men with him. They camp near Tulsey Town. And a Union force is coming south to reinforce them."

"Jayhawkers?"

"Yes."

Cooper considered this for a moment. Stand Watie could never patrol the entire Kansas-Indian Territory border. Jayhawkers sneaked across all the time, but seldom in numbers large enough to give real support in a pitched battle. What worried him more was the large force riding with the Creek chief. Two thousand fighting men? If he attacked such a force, he risked losing everything, unless Colonel Sims and Captain McDaniel joined the battle. That would even the sides.

Although Drew was better kept in reserve, his regiment was needed. Opothleyahola could be caught between the three Confederate forces. Sims was a tiger. Cooper knew he could depend on his own troopers, and John Drew's once they joined forces. Only McDaniel was an unknown.

If he hesitated now, Opothleyahola would slip away. If

he engaged the Creek and any leg of the attack faltered, victory would again slip away.

Cooper reached his decision. The eyeless, bloody sockets of the two men captured by Opothleyahola's braves haunted him. How much humiliation could he endure before being replaced as commander of the District?

"Orderly!" he bellowed. "Get these orders to Colonel Drew immediately. Dispatch a courier to Colonel Sims with this note." He scribbled fast, then sealed the orders with his signet and wax. "The time has come to put an end to Opothleyahola's marauding."

The orders were given. The difficult part was at hand. Cooper had to wait for John Drew's Cherokee Mounted Rifles to join his force, and for Colonel Sims to start marching southward with Captain McDaniel along the Verdigris River. Then, *then*, they would squeeze Opothleyahola.

"To victory," he said softly, pouring himself and the still wet, shivering man they had rescued a finger of good Kentucky bourbon from his personal flask.

Desertion
December 6, 1861

"We are ordered to join Colonel Cooper's force at or near the crossing of the road leading from the Verdigris River to Captain James McDaniel's home," Colonel John Drew read. He looked up at his company commanders and saw only one nodding. Captains Scrapper, Benge, and Hildebrand huddled together, whispering among themselves, looking as if they had bitten into a particularly sour lemon. "Do you find fault with this, gentlemen?"

John Drew licked his lips, wishing he had some of the rye whiskey Will Ross had sent from Fort Gibson in the last supply train. His hands shook just a mite. He tried to hide that by crumpling the orders and throwing the paper ball into the corner of the room.

"We've had scouts out, Colonel," said Captain Smith, Cooper's chief of scouts who had brought the orders from the courier's hand, along with intelligence about the Creek force they were to meet in battle. "We're up ag'in more 'n we thought possible. Opothleyahola might have four thousand braves, all painted up for the warpath."

"Four thousand!" cried a young lieutenant. He turned pale at the notion of so many Creek warriors. "We cain't fight that many. Not if we 'spect to whup 'em."

"We have our orders." John Drew turned to Captain Smith. "How many men are under Colonel Cooper's command?"

"Upward of eight hundred," the man said reluctantly. "Thass why he wants you, Captain McDaniel, and Colonel Sims of the Ninth Texas to join up in this attack. If we get together at the right time, we can force Opothleyahola to surrender."

"Four thousand?" murmured John Drew. "Our force hardly matches such a large army of fierce and dedicated fighters."

"You got orders, Colonel," the captain said brusquely. "I've got to return to report to Colonel Cooper. You got anything to pass along to him?"

"Tell the colonel the First Cherokee Mounted Rifles will be at his command when he needs us," John Drew said.

"Very good, sir." Captain Smith saluted and left. John Drew looked at his stunned officers. They filed out, muttering to themselves. He sank to a small stool, staring at the map of the Cooweescoowee District, trying to guess what Cooper planned. He was no tactician and, unlike Cooper, had no information about movement of either ally and enemy. Captain Smith had been tight-lipped about Opothleyahola's disposition and armaments. All Drew could do was his duty, as soon as he figured out where that lay.

He looked up when John Ross's son Allen opened the door and came in.

"Sergeant Ross reporting, sir." Allen saluted smartly. John Drew waved the salute aside. Although military order was necessary, he was not one to stand on ceremony with the son of his principal chief.

"Sit, Allen, sit and tell me what you've found."

"First, a letter from your wife, sir," Allen said, passing over a sweat-stained envelope he had carried inside his uniform jacket. John Drew took it and pressed out the wrinkles. He would read it later in private, though her letters always made him sad. How he wanted to be with his family. Drew hoped John Ross was right—that a peaceful solution could be brought about with proper negotiation.

"There's something more," Allen said. "I took a message to Opothleyahola's camp for my father, asking for a truce. Opothleyahola refused quite pointedly to even speak of a treaty. They are planning to attack Cooper's force when he reaches Musgrove's Place on Caney River."

John Drew laughed. "And Cooper is planning to attack them at the same place, I suspect. This is rich. Two armies coming together, each thinking it has surprise on its side. With luck and some good weather we might reach Camp Melton, where we are to join the colonel's main body."

Allen Ross blinked. "That's close to Opothleyahola's camp—within ten miles, sir. Is that wise?"

John Drew blinked in surprise. Captain Smith had not mentioned this. "That's what Cooper wants of me. I am not privy to all his plans." John Drew shrugged. His thirst grew, so he reached for the jug of whiskey and poured himself a little. He silently offered some to Allen, who accepted. They drank in silence, each lost in thought.

Finally, Allen Ross said, "I need to return to Park Hill, sir. Is there anything I can do for you? Word to your family?"

"I have sent messages already," John Drew said. "My highest regards to your father, and a prayer he is successful in dealing with the Creek. They pose a greater threat than the Jayhawkers."

"Not to hear my father talk," Allen said glumly. "He still considers Stand Watie to be far worse than Opothleyahola. The Creek will at least accept messengers."

"Watie," John Drew said, more to himself than to Allen. He took another drink, then corked the jug when Allen indicated he would not drink further.

"I wish you nothing but good fortune, sir," Sergeant Ross said. He stood and saluted.

"To us all, to us all," John Drew said, returning the salute. Allen Ross left Drew to his dark thoughts. Then the commander of John Drew's Cherokee Mounted Rifles pushed to his feet and began issuing orders. Battle was imminent, and they had to be in position at Camp Melton as soon as possible.

"Your boys look all tuckered out," Lewis Melton said, eyeing John Drew's column. The cavalry had begun the twenty-five mile ride in good form, but stragglers were slowly left behind in Drew's need for haste reaching this point. "You going to pitch camp here?"

John Drew frowned. "Where's Colonel Cooper? He was supposed to meet us here."

"Cooper? Can't rightly say where he is." Melton scratched his head and looked around, as if guaranteeing a private conversation with John Drew. "I *can* say where the Creek are. Not ten miles down the road is a big encampment of them. You know that. All pro-Union, the lot of them."

"You sound a trifle bitter, sir. What's happened?" John Drew dropped to the ground and staggered slightly. His legs had gone numb riding so far that day. The weather had cooperated, but the road proved muddy and even impassable in places. This had further strung out his command as they struggled through knee-deep bogs.

"My house," Melton said, his anger mounting. "They burned it. Stole danged near everything I owned. And what they didn't steal, they ruined. Ripped open a perfectly good featherbed, just to keep me from using it again. Killed my dogs. And a clock that'd been in the family forty years? They used their tomahawks on it, laughing as they smashed it."

"What had you done to anger them?" asked John Drew. He peered down the road, pleased to see another unit of his cavalry making their way through the rugged spots. He would have his troop reassembled in another hour. By then Cooper ought to have shown up with his men.

"We had shelter from the winter, and they didn't. That was it, pure and simple. I had some sympathy for them be-

fore, if you must know the truth." Melton spoke aggres-
sively, as if daring John Drew to accuse him of disloyalty.
This was as far from Drew's mind as anything could be.

"Your family? They are safe?"

"We fled and hid out. That's all that saved us from being
killed."

"You are safe now, sir," John Drew said. He called to
Captain Scrapper. "George, take some men and scout the
perimeter. There might be some of those pro-Union Creek
still lurking about."

"Right away, sir," Captain Scrapper said, sounding put
out at having to do still more for his commander.

"What of us, sir?" asked Pickens Benge.

"You and Captain Hildebrand ride on down the road
and see what you can see. Report back quickly. If you spot
Colonel Cooper, ride back directly."

"Nobody's said anything about Colonel Cooper being
here, too," Lewis Melton said.

"There's a reason for that," John Drew explained gently.
"We don't want Opothleyahola to know we're gathering for
an attack. What of Captain McDaniel?"

"Don't know him," Melton said.

"Very well. You and your family have been through much
today. Come and dine with me. We'll camp here until the
others show up."

"Hope it's soon, Colonel," said Melton. "I want to see
them punished bad for what they did to me."

"They will be, Mr. Melton, they will. Now, tell me
about . . ." John Drew put his arm around Melton and
guided him to a spot where they might talk. It was pleasant
to get away from the need to command constantly, to talk
of farming for a short while.

In less than an hour John Drew saw Scrapper riding back,
followed by his squad of scouts. He counted ten prisoners
in their midst.

"Sir," reported Captain Scrapper, "we found them skulking about two miles away from Melton's Camp. There's not

been time to interrogate them proper-like, but the main body of Opothleyahola's men can't be far off. These ten weren't carrying any food, and living off the land at this time of year is hard enough."

"Be sure they are guarded well, Captain," Drew ordered. "I know where the camp is, thanks to Mr. Melton. We don't want your prisoners scampering off to tell Opothleyahola we are here."

"Where's Colonel Cooper, sir? Or Captain McDaniel?"

"Not here yet. Perhaps they encountered worse roads than we did." John Drew was beginning to worry at Cooper's absence. If Melton was right about Opothleyahola being so near, Drew's entire command was in dire jeopardy. His pitiful few hundred against four thousand could never stand long.

"What of McDaniel?" asked Scrapper. "He didn't have as far to travel."

"Perhaps he has already joined Cooper," John Drew said. "Tend to our prisoners."

Melton looked uneasily from the prisoners to Scrapper to John Drew. "If you don't mind, Colonel, me and the family are going to head south. My wife's relatives are there, and we can find shelter."

"It is very late in the day. You'll have to travel at night, and the way *is* treacherous. We just traversed that road."

"Don't matter," Melton said. "I don't want us to be around a battleground."

"I'll assign a few soldiers to accompany you to safety," Drew offered. Melton tried to refuse, but Drew would not hear of it. He was distracted when Captains Benge and Isaac Hildebrand galloped up.

"What's wrong?" Drew asked anxiously, seeing his officers' expressions.

"We were stopped down the road by six Negroes and a dozen Creek. They ast us which side we belonged to," blurted out Benge.

John Drew could not tell the color of the two officers'

uniforms in the twilight. They might have been gray or they might have been black. No fancy buttons or other insignia betrayed their allegiance. He had not noticed this before, but then so many of his men, as well as the officers, wore only makeshift uniforms. Hildebrand and Benge wore leather trousers, and neither had a cavalry cap, preferring their own floppy-brimmed hats which were more useful in the wheat field than on a cavalry patrol.

"We tole them we was Cherokee soldiers in the service of the South."

John Drew held his tongue. That might have been dangerous. Where *was* Cooper?

"We beat a hasty retreat, sir," Benge said. "We was outnumbered and outgunned. Them Creek carried fancy repeater rifles."

"Henrys," Hildebrand said. "Where'd they get 'em?"

"You did the right thing returning immediately," John Drew said. "Post double sentries and have your men bed down for the night. We must be ready when Colonel Cooper arrives to lead us against Opothleyahola."

"When's that, sir?" asked Pickens Benge.

"You have your orders," John Drew said gruffly. The two officers rode away, leaving him stewing. His thirst built again, but he refused to touch the whiskey jug. Not yet.

That night James McDaniel slipped into camp and spoke with the Keetoowahs in John Drew's company. The Pins took a quick vote, and McDaniel withdrew. Within an hour, half of John Drew's regiment stole into the night, taking their rifles and ammunition, and made their way to Opothleyahola's camp to join their Loyal League brothers.

Reunion
December 7, 1861

"They deserted?" John Drew's eyes went wide with shock. He took a quick gulp of his whiskey, then put down the jug, sloshing a little onto the ground. He took no notice of either the warmth in his belly or the wasted bourbon. His heart raced, and sweat broke out on his forehead in spite of the new gusts of frigid wind from the north. Hands shaking, he wiped away perspiration from his upper lip.

"Some that stayed say James McDaniel hisself came waltzin' into camp. The sentries talked to him, since they knew him. Most of the Pins were convinced they was bein' used, and that the only way the Cherokee Nation could ever be free was to fight for the Federals." Pickens Benge looked around, as if he might spot some of the deserters. He shoved his hands into the front of his coat and fell silent when he failed to locate any of the wayward soldiers.

John Drew swallowed hard. His mouth was dry, and a vein pulsed hard in his forehead as he stared at Captain Benge.

"How many of our men are left?"

"A couple hunnert, that's all," Benge said.

"And Colonel Cooper is nowhere to be seen," moaned

Drew. "We were supposed to join up with him by now. What are we going to do?"

"Sir, we jist might be facin' as many as four thousand Creek. There's not much we *can* do," Benge said.

"I know what Chief Ross would do," John Drew said, straightening. "Captain, you and Hildebrand will accompany me under a truce flag to meet with Opothleyahola. I shall offer a pardon to him, and present it in such a fashion to make it seem that we are here only for that purpose."

"That's not gonna work if he knows the Keetoowahs deserted."

"We have no other choice but to run like whipped dogs," Drew said. He settled his uniform jacket and shouted to his orderly to prepare his horse. "Get ready, Captain. From this desperate moment we might extract victory peaceably."

"And hell's gate is blowin' open," Benge said, shaking his head. They had fewer than two hundred men left in the camp. Bluffing now would never work with a shrewd chief like Opothleyahola. The only chance they had was for Cooper to arrive and absorb what few men remained into his larger force. It was now more than obvious they would never be joined by McDaniel's company this side of purgatory.

John Drew climbed into the saddle and glared at Benge. "Captain, accompany me. Try not to look so distraught." Drew glanced across the camp and saw Isaac Hildebrand trotting up. He motioned to the other officer and took off at a brisk gait, knowing time worked against him. Drew was not sure when McDaniel had subverted his men— damn the Keetoowah Society!—but it could not have been more than a few hours ago. As he rode, another thought occurred to him. If Opothleyahola had known of the desertions, the Creek chief would have attacked those remaining at Camp Melton immediately.

"Hurry, gentleman, we must make all haste." As he rode along the muddy track, John Drew was aware of eyes watching from all quarters. He lifted a white handkerchief and waved it. He slowed his horse to a walk but kept moving outward, wondering when Opothleyahola's sentries would stop them.

His heart almost exploded in his chest when he saw who stood in the path ahead. No sentry, this. Chief Opothleyahola himself crossed arms across his chest and waited.

"Greetings to my Creek brother," John Drew said. "We have come on a mission of peace."

"I know why you have come. Greetings to my brother Chief Ross."

John Drew was heartened by this. He knew they were surrounded, although he saw none of the hundreds of Creek warriors who must accompany their old chief. He had to make the most of the chance if he wanted to get away alive.

". . . so I offer a full pardon and a chance for reconciliation between our tribes," John Drew finished, not even sure what he had said.

Benge and Hildebrand eyed one another uneasily. Drew wanted to chastise them for such nervousness, but held his tongue. It was time for Opothleyahola to answer.

"We do not want war," Opothleyahola said carefully. "This has been brought on our heads by the South."

"By the Southern Rights Party," Drew said.

"Where is Stand Watie?" asked Opothleyahola. "You do not speak for him."

"No," John Drew said. "He is a difficult man to talk to. John Ross is the principal chief of the Cherokee, and is a man able to compromise."

"So you deal behind Watie's back?"

"I deal for the benefit of all our people in Indian Territory," John Drew said. "Watie is not chief. John Ross is."

"Very well. I will consider this and send word soon to your camp."

John Drew did not question that Opothleyahola knew where the Cherokee Mounted Rifles were bivouacked. He had won some time—and might have brought peace to the territory.

John Drew watched the Creek chief vanish into the woods. Only then did he wheel his horse around to head back to camp.

"We've done it, we've done it!" he cried. "There will be peace now."

Neither of the officers with him said a word until they reached Camp Melton. Only then did Benge and Hildebrand let out a whoop of relief.

A messenger from Colonel Cooper had arrived.

Peace Delegation
December 8, 1861

"You're bein' mighty optimistic, aren't you, Colonel?" asked Captain Benge. "We ought to go into this with eyes wide-open. What's to keep that Creek bastard from murderin' us?"

"That will be enough, Captain," John Drew said sharply. "Colonel Cooper has contacted us from his camp at Bird Creek. We can rely on him for aid should the peace negotiations fail. But they will not!"

"Why not?" asked Captain Hildebrand. "What's in it for the Creek and Opothleyahola?"

"He does not have to die fighting a white man's war," John Drew said. "That's in it for all of us. We can restore order to Indian Territory and hold the rest of the war at bay."

"Curious thing to say, you wearin' that Confederate colonel's uniform," Benge said.

"If I were not in such a good mood over the end of this madness being in sight, I would bring you up on charges, Captain." John Drew sweat from drinking a little too much of his whiskey—he had to contact Fort Gibson to have more sent. It was all that kept him going, through the pain of being in the field away from his family and simply being put in this untenable position. At least, it had been untenable until Opothleyahola agreed to accept a delegation.

Now John Drew—and by reflected glory, John Ross, also—would be the saviors. Let Stand Watie fight the Jayhawkers. United in the south, the rest of the Cherokee Nation would push away anyone trying to intrude on their daily lives. That was all John Ross wanted for his people: peace. Now Drew felt it within his grasp. There were no others fighting so fiercely to pull apart Indian Territory as Opothleyahola. Quelled, Opothleyahola would become a staunch ally.

"You're sendin' out all your officers," Benge complained. "You go, let us stay in camp."

"Are you a coward, Captain? No, I did not think so. You have your orders. Get the best terms possible for peace with Opothleyahola, but *get them*. We cannot continue this fighting among ourselves while the Federals burn out our farmers."

"So if we don't succeed, will Colonel Cooper be there to back us up? Even after half our regiment has deserted?" asked Hildebrand.

"You, too, have your orders. Get your delegation assembled and go. I will remain here, drafting the terms. A copy will be sent to Chief Ross, along with a request for a meeting of both chiefs."

"Yes, sir," Benge said, shaking his head to cut off Hildebrand's protest. The two officers exchanged glances, saluted, and left. John Drew heaved a sigh as the tent flap fluttered after them. Such dissension in the ranks had caused the Pins to leave. As much as he agreed with their abolitionist stands, the Keetoowah Society members ought not to have deserted. The ultimate fight was for peace in Indian Territory and unity among the Five Civilized Tribes.

He seated himself on a small stool and began drafting the peace treaty, his hand shaking a little until he took a swig of bourbon. Definitely, he would have to get Will Ross to send more. Since arriving at Camp Melton their supplies had dwindled. Of course, the Pins had stolen away with much of their equipment. Drew pushed this out of his head as he worked on the treaty.

John Drew spelled out how the Confederacy did not desire the shedding of blood among Indians, and offered an outline of choice for the issue of slavery. Many Creeks held slaves, and many did not. As he worked, Drew heard activity outside in the camp. He worked for a few more minutes, then threw down his pen to go and see what the furor was.

John Drew recoiled when he saw two of his men running past, cornhusks woven into their hair.

"Stop!" Drew shouted at them. "Explain why you are—" he sputtered. The two never slowed. They mounted their horses and rode away without a backward glance. Frowning, Drew stalked through Camp Melton trying to find someone in command. He realized most of his officers were away parlaying with Opothleyahola, but a sergeant had to remain. Somewhere.

He saw no one with stripes or authority in the deserted camp.

"Fall in!" Colonel Drew bellowed. To his surprise only a dozen men poked their heads out from odd places and timidly came forth to form a ragged line. He glared at them. All were privates.

"Where are your sergeants?" he asked. The privates looked frightened. "What's going on?"

"Colonel," said the bravest of the small knot of soldiers, "all the non-coms are gone."

"Gone? Where? What's wrong?"

"The Keetoowahs all upped and left, sir," the private said.

"The other night? I know that. What—?" John Drew had gone cold inside when he realized James McDaniel had seduced away only a fraction of the Pins in the camp. Now the rest were gone.

"Sir, there's not sixty men left in the whole danged camp," the private said. "If 'n we had any brains, we'd be a mile down the road, too."

"Sixty?" John Drew was stunned. He had less than fifteen percent of his force left. In only two days eighty-five percent of his soldiers had deserted to the enemy, nary a shot being fired.

"All of 'em went to join Opothleyahola. Said they was tired of fight in' their own people."

John Drew sputtered, not sure what to do. The pounding of hooves allowed him a chance to turn and put his thoughts into order. He saw a wild-eyed Pickens Benge astride a lathered horse.

"Colonel, Colonel!" Captain Benge shouted. "We got big problems. They deserted. The Keetoowahs deserted!"

John Drew's mind refused to grip the truth and turn out a solution.

"We'd better be off, Colonel," Benge said, "as the enemy are upon us! Opothleyahola's attacking! The peace palaver was a trick to separate our force."

"The Creek are attacking us? Here?"

"Colonel, we got less than fifteen minutes to clear out!"

"Men!" barked John Drew. "Mount up and ride for Colonel Cooper's camp!" The handful of soldiers remaining in Camp Melton obeyed with alacrity. John Drew ran to his tent, glanced longingly at the draft of the peace treaty, then swept it from the small writing table in an anger that knew no bounds. How could Opothleyahola double-cross him like this?

"Colonel, we got your horse. Git on out of here!" urged Benge.

John Drew rushed from his tent and jumped into the saddle. He put his spurs to the horse's flanks. The horse rocketed away from the camp, and Drew rode hellbent for leather for almost a mile down the road until a thought struck him.

"Captain Benge!" he shouted. His officer spun in the saddle, then trotted his mount back to where Drew had reined in. "What if we're riding into an ambush along the road to Bird Creek? We don't know where Opothleyahola is camped. We might be playing into his trap."

"We kin fight our way out," Benge said.

"How? We left all our ammunition back in camp!"

"What are we going to do?" asked Benge.

"Return for the ammunition. If we have to, we burn it to keep Opothleyahola from getting it! Get your men back right away!"

John Drew wheeled about and got some order into the frightened soldiers around him. All told, he and Benge formed a company of almost forty men—most of those who had been left when the Pins deserted. Convincing them to return to Camp Melton in the face of a Creek attack was difficult, but the men were so frightened they actually did what Drew told them. He was the only one who seemed to know what he was doing.

They returned to the camp as quickly as possible.

"Captain, get the wagons loaded. Hitch up teams. Colonel Cooper can use the ammunition, even if—"

"Colonel, it's Opothleyahola! He's leadin' his whole damn army of Creek!" Benge got a squad armed with muskets into a ragged defense line. They fired into the edge of a wooded area near the trail leading from the camp.

"Stop firing! Stop!" bellowed John Drew. "Cease fire! Those are our own men!"

Benge had opened fire on his own men. John Drew didn't see how his situation could get any worse, but it continued to do so.

And No Shot Fired
December 8, 1861

Colonel Douglas Cooper stared at John Drew in total disbelief. His mouth opened and his mustache quivered. Then he closed his mouth and worked to think of something to say. He tugged on his beard. His mind had gone utterly blank at the news Drew brought him.

"All your officers?" Cooper croaked out.

"No, not all of them. Some remained loyal," John Drew said stiffly. He stood at attention, although Cooper had specifically told him to stand at ease. There would never be any more easiness between them, Cooper knew. Not after this.

"Who might we be looking down the barrels of our muskets at, then?" he demanded. "I got the news Captain McDaniel has deserted. A scout saw him and Opothleyahola together. McDaniel had ripped off his insignia but still wore his Confederate uniform. That's why the scout took notice of him at all. Seemed he fit right into the Creek camp, otherwise."

"We retreated in an orderly fashion from Camp Melton after Captain Benge warned us."

"From the condition of the few men with you, it was not an orderly withdrawal," Cooper accused. His adjutant,

Roswell Lee, came over with his easy and almost boneless gliding step and whispered all he had discovered in his commander's ear. The adjutant finished, stepped back, stared at John Drew with something approaching pity in his eyes, then left Cooper and Drew alone again.

"You fired on your own officers!" cried Colonel Cooper. "Benge fired on the others in the peace delegation!"

"It was a mistake. Opothleyahola *was* moving his guerrillas toward our camp."

"He's moving on us, too. My scouts report more than four thousand Creek warriors out there." Cooper heaved a deep breath, then inhaled slowly, trying to keep his temper. It was hard. "Do you realize that Opothleyahola agreed to a peace meeting with you solely to get your officers out of camp so the Keetoowah Society members could desert without opposition?"

"I see that now. I had not realized the Pins were such a prominent factor in my company."

"How could you not? You are a colonel, dammit!" Cooper made no effort to hide his anger now. "You're John Ross's frog jumping whenever he tells you to go 'croak.' It's bad enough McDaniel deserted with his entire company. But all *your* officers?"

"Not all, sir. Only Captains Vann and Scraper, and Lieutenants White Catcher, Smith, Nate Fish, John Bear Meat and—"

"Who else?"

"Well, sir, that's hard to say. So many left. Some might have been killed trying to fight off the Creek."

"Opothleyahola did not fire a single shot," Cooper said hotly. "Noah Drowning Bear and Big Sky yah too kah from McDaniel's company have been spotted along the road leading back to Camp Melton. That means they are advancing on us, your camp already overrun."

"See, sir? Captain Benge was right."

"You fired on your own men because you forgot to take

ammunition with you when you retreated and had to go back for it." Colonel Cooper felt a vein in the side of his head throbbing. He tried to calm himself. John Drew ought to be court-martialed, but Cooper knew it would never happen. John Ross would not permit that, for one thing. Politics. How he hated it

"By God, I wish Watie were here now. We would march right into the teeth of Opothleyahola's guns and defeat him!"

"My teamsters can return to the camp and get what was left behind."

"Which is damned near everything. An entire supply train from Fort Gibson lost because of you, not to mention horses and all your camp equipment."

"Sir," came a brusque officer's report, "we got our camp on alert."

"Very good, Lieutenant Colonel Quayle. Now, see to it that Colonel Drew and his men return to Camp Melton. Secure all his equipment and see to it that his command is in good form. Do you understand me, Quayle?"

"Sir, the 9th Texas Cavalry Regiment will not fail you!"

"Sir, I protest. My men are exhausted."

"From panic, Colonel Drew, from being cowards. You *will* return to Camp Melton, you *will* hold that position after you have regained your equipment, and you *will* prepare that camp against Federal attack. Lieutenant Colonel Quayle will assist you."

"It seems you have placed him in command over me," Drew said intractably. "That is not a condition I can agree to."

"He will *assist* you. How many from your command remain?"

John Drew mumbled.

"How many, Colonel Drew?"

"Twenty-eight."

"Twenty-eight left of four hundred and eighty soldiers

who rode forth under your command. And Opothleyahola didn't fire a shot. Colonel, Quayle will *assist* you, and you will not utter one word against this order or him. Do you understand fully?"

"Sir!" John Drew snapped a salute and marched off, his lips set in a thin, angry line. Cooper watched him go, his hands clenched into tight fists. He forced himself to relax. As if by magic, Adjutant Lee appeared at his side.

"Sir, Major Pegg, along with a half-dozen other officers, have been spotted on the road heading toward Fort Gibson. Several of Drew's enlisted men are accompanying them."

"Deserting?"

"Running like scalded dogs, sir."

"Do you realize that tonight, because of Colonel Drew, I have lost one-third of my entire force?" Cooper said, more amazed than angry as he figured this out. "Worse than being casualties, many of Drew's men now *oppose* us. Not only have we lost soldiers, but they'll fight against us for a pro-Union guerrilla chief."

"Sir, I have doubled the patrols around our camp. Quayle ought to reach Camp Melton before sunrise and secure it—or report back that Opothleyahola has sacked it." Adjutant Lee had been just out of earshot, waiting for John Drew to be sent on his way.

Cooper considered the lay of the land and tried to imagine where the Creek chief might hide his main camp. "I think Opothleyahola is camped, as we are, on Bird Creek. He won't go after Camp Melton, especially considering that most of the soldiers once there now fight for him. All he can gain is equipment. If he wins against us, he can ransack the camp at his leisure, and during battle he won't need most of the equipment."

"You reckon he's going to attack us here?" asked Roswell Lee.

"Yes, yes, I do," Cooper told his adjutant. "I want you

to take a patrol out at dawn and find Opothleyahola's forces. We need to know where he is, and what he intends to do. We are sorely outnumbered, but we can still win if we retain the element of surprise."

Douglas Cooper rubbed the spot where the arrow had impaled him. He was recovering well from the physical wound, but the political and strategic wounds he had received from men like John Drew worried him more now. He had been beaten back once. To lose another battle would end his military career—and worse, leave pro-Union Opothleyahola in command of Cooweescoowee District, opening a road from the north into the heart of Texas. An expeditionary force of Kansans could sweep downward unopposed, gathering recruits from the Creek and Cherokee, and divide Texas, further hindering the Confederacy. Everything west of the Mississippi would quickly fall into Union hands.

That could not happen. Not as long as he drew breath.

"God, I wish Stand Watie were here," he said. "He knows how to win battles."

Caving Banks
December 9, 1861

"Sir," reported Adjutant Roswell Lee, "no sign of Opothleyahola around Camp Melton or on the prairie to the east. Colonel Drew is trying to fortify the area the best he can with so few men left in his command."

"What of Quayle?" Cooper asked, distracted. For two cents he would sell John Drew to Opothleyahola. Hell and damnation, he would *give* the worthless officer to him!

"He's still out on patrol. He's not as inclined to give support to Drew as he is to alert us about attack."

"What do you think will happen?" asked Cooper. He was feeling poorly again this morning, hands shaking a little as he traced along the curving length of Bird Creek back to his supply base at Coweta Mission.

"Opothleyahola is in the hills to the west. Send out patrols in the direction of Park's Store along the river, right about here," Lee said, indicating the spot on Cooper's map where a horseshoe bend formed in Bird Creek, "and attack only when the Creek start to move." The entire area was a convoluted maze of twisting, turning rivers and broad stretches of prairie cut with deep ravines. Any of those cuts could hide the Creek chief's pro-Union fighters, all four thousand of them. If Cooper blundered along the wrong ravine, he might find his entire force swallowed up in Federal gunfire.

He had to stay close to Bird Creek and engage Opothleyahola there, flushing him out of his hiding places and using the chilly, bluff-bounded stream as a barrier to prevent all-out attack—or Opothleyahola's retreat. Nothing less than victory would satisfy Cooper this day.

"I've got reinforcements coming from Tulsey Town," Cooper said, indicating the small town on the map. "You've got a good point about waiting for Opothleyahola to make the first move. If he is hiding anywhere along the stream around Caving Banks, where the creek makes this bend, we would have to attack uphill. That is a recipe for disaster."

"What are your orders, Colonel?" asked Lee.

"Break camp, move to the east side of Bird Creek. Maintain contact with the scouts. Who's out ranging in that area?"

"Captain Foster, with two of our Creek companies. He's protecting us from a sneak attack if Opothleyahola manages to bring his forces into that horseshoe bend." Lee pointed out the tangled area that worried Cooper the most.

"Good. I suspect we may have to reinforce him in a hurry. Will we be able to do so?"

Lee smiled crookedly, then said, "As long as you keep Colonel Drew out of my way."

Cooper had to laugh. "Colonel Drew will stay busy fortifying Camp Melton for some time with so few men in his command. It'll let him turn in a good report to Chief Ross about how important he was to our defense." Cooper snorted in disgust. "Defense," he said almost sadly, "when what we need most is a clear view of an enemy to attack."

Roswell Lee paused a moment, started to speak, then clamped his mouth shut.

"Go on, Roswell, spit it out."

"We could use the ammunition Drew is tying up. There's going to be a fight today. I feel it in my bones."

"Politics, Adjutant, politics. Never ignore it, especially when you depend on the politician's nephew to send you supplies from Fort Gibson. Don't forget John Drew is Chief Ross's personally selected commander."

"I understand, sir." Lee saluted and went to break camp and begin the troop movement. Douglas Cooper wiped sweat from his forehead. A sudden wave of weakness passed over him and forced him to sit down. He stared at the map, his mind racing as he wondered where Opothleyahola would attack.

"Caving Banks," he decided, staring at the horseshoe bend. Creek Indian strategy called for them to fortify such an area, using the water as protection on three sides and then defending strongly the fourth. "He's not going to come after us, not with his entire force. He'll make us go to him. Maybe try to lure us into that bend so he can attack with his full force." Cooper heaved a sigh. He wanted this campaign over, even as it seemed to stretch ahead of him endlessly. Folding his map, he barked orders to his striker to pack his gear. Then Cooper began preparing to cross Bird Creek. He had a battle to plan, and if it was fought at Chusto-Talash, as the Cherokee called Caving Banks, there would be blood flowing bank to bank in the water before the day was over.

"Sir, sir," gasped out a courier, stumbling along on foot. His moccasins were torn, and holes appeared in them. Either he had not taken the time to repair them or didn't have the material. He held out a torn scrap of paper. "This here's from Cap'n Foster."

Cooper took the ragged sheet and worked to decipher the cribbed, smeared writing. "How many men attacked Captain Foster?" he asked the courier.

"A large force. Danged near a million of 'em, I swear."

"Was Foster able to hold his position?"

"Captain Parks came up in support with two companies. The skirmish didn't last too long."

"What is Foster doing with his six prisoners?" Cooper asked, tapping the scrap of paper with his scout's report.

"He's fallin' back, I suspect," the courier said. "There wasn't much time to get 'em to tell what all they knew. And stayin' there is a sure cure for livin' much longer."

"Tell him we will advance to support him," Cooper said, coming to a quick decision. "Tell Captain Foster to skirmish as vigorously as possible."

"Yes, sir," the messenger said. He headed back in the direction he had come, still puffing and panting from exertion. Cooper called over another messenger.

"Get to Colonel Drew. Tell him to load his equipment on wagons and move across the prairie. Lieutenant Colonel Quayle will support him. I don't want him hanging out to dry with Opothleyahola's forces moving now. Do you understand?"

"On my way, Colonel," the messenger said. Before the man had wended his way through the gathered forces to his horse, Adjutant Lee rode over.

"Things are startin' to sizzle, Colonel," he said. "We are under attack at the bend in Bird Creek."

"The horseshoe bend?" It was as he had feared. That was not terrain for a decent fight. His entire force had crossed the creek to the west side. Better to have at Opothleyahola out on the open prairie, where superior discipline might win the battle.

"The rear guard is about two miles from it. There doesn't seem to be any danger at the moment. It's as if they're testing us with sniping and a lot of whoopin' and hollerin'."

"I ordered Colonel Drew back to rejoin our forces. You were right about his equipment being more valuable to us than to him. Get him into the center of our formation. Surround his command with the First Choctaw and Chickasaw Regiment on the right and the First Creek on his left flank. Keep Lieutenant Colonel Quayle moving—and if even one of Drew's command tries to desert or turn tail and run, kill the traitor on the spot. Is that understood?"

"No more desertions," Lee confirmed. Cooper's adjutant hesitated, then asked, "What if Drew—?"

"Drew, also," Cooper said grimly. He would not permit *anyone* to desert in the heat of battle, including John Ross's hand-picked commander.

"I understand, sir," said Lee.

"See to your orders, Roswell. Tell the bugler to sound assembly. We're moving out!"

Lee saluted and went to put the sluggish machinery of attack into position. Cooper felt a curious blend of exhilaration and dread at again meeting the Creek chief in battle. For every Cherokee defector from the Confederate forces, the pro-Union side gained one. That had to stop. Colonel Cooper rode to the head of the cavalry column moving out like a disjointed snake, then rode with a sharp eye on the countryside. Bird Creek had thawed, and the occasional ice floes were gone for the day. The wind had died, leaving a curious unnatural warmth in the usually sharp winter air The sun was well above the horizon when Cooper reached the front line, where Captain Foster battled the pro-Union Indians.

"It's Captain McDaniel we're facin'," Foster blurted out. "Him and the rest what deserted from Drew's regiment. I recognize a goodly number of them traitors."

"They have the same chance to die as they ever did," Cooper said. "Only now it'll be a Confederate bullet knocking them out of the saddles."

"And they're using *our* ammo to knock *us* out of the saddle," Foster said.

"Prepare your companies, sir," Cooper said, not wanting

to argue with him. "We'll form three lines and attack straight across the prairie."

"You're leavin' yourself open for a rear attack," Foster said. "I heard 'bout them already bein' ready to climb up our butt up there at the horseshoe bend."

"Then we shall have to advance faster than they can bite our rears," Cooper said. He sent the word along the line. Three lines formed and immediately launched the attack toward a huge ravine where Cooper saw Opothleyahola's troops milling about, as if in disorder. What was the size of the force he attacked? Was it Opothleyahola's main force? He doubted it. This was a diversion, one he dared not ignore. However many Creek—and Cherokee deserters—he faced, it was enough to cause woe if he tried marching around them and left them at his rear.

He pulled a pistol from his holster, cocked it awkwardly with his right thumb, then fired into the air and let out a rebel yell. "Get 'em, boys. Get 'em! Charge!" Cooper put his spurs to his horse and rocketed forward, at the front of the attack. Seeing their commander in the battle instilled a fearlessness in the soldiers that had been lacking after the report of defeat by John Drew.

The open prairie stretched in front of him, and the world seemed to expand endlessly to the far horizon. He fired left and right and kept his horse charging. For a moment he felt himself to be invincible. Nothing could touch him, nothing could stop him. Then he plunged down the slope of the ravine. Cooper shot wildly, not caring if he hit any of the scattering pro-Union Creek soldiers. Just being there inspired his men.

And they followed.

Opothleyahola's men were routed, dropping their muskets and running for the sanctuary offered by the woods along Bird Creek.

"Swing about, men," cried Cooper. "Maintain your battle lines and keep after them!" Cooper saw Roswell Lee galloping toward him. The man's hat had been shot to tatters, and blood ran down the side of the adjutant's face. None of this slowed him, though.

"Colonel, we got 'em retreating toward Caving Banks. All of Opothleyahola's men are gatherin' there after Drew and the rest with him blundered onto them along the east bank of Bird Creek."

"Drew is fighting? That's an improvement, even if he is on the wrong side of the river," Cooper said sarcastically. He knew what had really happened. Quayle and his Texas Regiment, along with the Confederate Choctaws and Chickasaws, were bearing the brunt of the battle.

"Opothleyahola's on the west side at Caving Banks in that twisted maze of steep riverbanks and fords. They know the lay of the land. We don't."

"Any of the Cherokee able to get in there?" Cooper doubted any of the men riding with Drew knew the land well, but he could use them to flush out Opothleyahola's soldiers and save his own for real combat.

"There's a small farm in the middle of the bend we didn't even know about. Opothleyahola's got it fortified, logs around a cabin, so we can't attack from the west on dry land. And then there's a gorge in the prairie in that direction that'd keep our cavalry from crossing to north of the bend if we wanted to ford the creek and attack from that direction."

"Go all out in the attack, Roswell," Cooper said. "We can't let Opothleyahola keep a stronghold."

"There's a series of shoals forty or fifty feet high, all sandstone," Roswell Lee said. "If we get to the top we can fire down on the Federals."

"Don't split the force. Getting to the top of a sandstone bluff would take too long, also. To be effective from that height, we'd need artillery we don't have. I'll lead the attack on the west bank straight into the horseshoe. I want to keep the Union Indians pushed out on the prairie so they can't reinforce Opothleyahola at the bend. That cabin must be destroyed."

"It's going to be bloody, sir."

"Order the attack," Cooper said. "Fight from horseback if possible, on foot if not. No one gets past. No one!"

It took the better part of an hour for him to assemble his forces and get them facing the log abutment. Bird Creek churned about them and sandstone cliffs rose up, making the area seem constricted, small, insignificant. Cooper knew better. Opothleyahola had most of his men waiting for the attack in and around the cabin and behind the log fences.

With Colonel Sims on his right flank and Lieutenant Colonel Quayle to his left, Cooper launched his attack right up the middle.

For a brief giddy instant, Cooper thought they would be able to jump the logs and get to the cabin. Then the mouth of hell opened. Arrows and bullets filled the air, forcing him to order a retreat. Panting and sweating hard, he wheeled his horse around and looked at the situation again. They had no choice if they wanted to maintain the attack but to come at the cabin from the west. That also meant Opothleyahola was trapped. He could not easily escape in any other direction without fording Bird Creek.

"Again!" cried Cooper. "Once more. Attack!"

Again he charged straight at Opothleyahola's forces—and again he was turned back. This time he had his horse shot out from under him as he retreated. He fell heavily and lay stunned for a moment.

"You all right, Colonel?" came Sims's worried query. "You took a mighty big tumble there."

"Reinforce the line, Sims," Cooper ordered. "I'm fine, and will lead an infantry charge on them. Use the cavalry, what there is left of it, as support. Have we enough men afoot to make the attack?"

"Colonel, I'll follow you into hell," called Quayle. "You want all my boys on foot?"

"Do it!"

Again they charged, this time with bayonets fixed and knives flashing. Cooper reached the first of the log barricades and swarmed over it, immediately finding himself entangled with a fiercely determined Creek brave. Cooper proved the more resolute and smashed his pistol barrel into the side of the man's head, buffaloing him. The brave sank to the ground without uttering a sound.

"Coming up, sir," called Quayle.

Men flooded over the logs and rushed past a gasping Douglas Cooper. He staggered along. Then they were forced back again.

Regrouping in a small wooded area out of musket range, Cooper wiped sweat and blood and dirt from his face and called Quayle and Sims over.

"What will it take to push through and capture the cabin?" he asked. "We hardly gained the first line of defense."

"He's a cagey one, that old Creek chief," Sims said in admiration. "We been at this an hour now, and he's no worse off than before it all started."

"We can flush him out," Quayle said forcefully. "Send Captain Young and a hundred of his Choctaw and Chickasaw in from the north side across Bird Creek as we attack. We reinforce from the west and get them in a cross fire. They either die on the spot or retreat east across the creek or north, where Young attacked."

"They can't get to the south easily, not with the maze of ravines and bluffs there. Or if they do, there's no way any officer can keep command. They'll be scattered." Cooper's head spun, and he had to wait for the 270 dizziness to pass. How he wished he had not taken that arrow!

"Well, sir?"

"Send orders to Young. He's to attack in twenty minutes. We'll launch another assault then, me at the head of infantry and you, Sims, and you, Quayle, on either flank with cavalry. We reach the cabin and take it this time. May Opothleyahola be there!"

This attack proved more difficult than any before for Colonel Cooper. He dodged bullets and arrows and again found himself wrestling with a brave half his age and twice his strength. His pistol thrust into a rock-hard belly and turned the fight to his advantage. When his pistol discharged into the Creek's stomach he set fire to his foe's hide shirt. Cooper kicked free and fired a second time, ending the man's life.

The tide of combat had flowed around him and broken over the log cabin in the center of the river's bend. Captain Young had rushed forward after crossing Bird Creek in the north, and Sims and Quayle had outpaced the plodding infantry. The brief fight at the cabin drove the defenders out, as Cooper had hoped it would.

What he had not counted on was the table being turned on him and his forces. He arrived at the cabin in time to see the Federals closing off the tongue of land and bottling them up on the small patch of land surrounded by Bird Creek.

"Attack!" he cried, seeing the trap. "Break through!"

And they did, after another half hour of vicious fighting. Cooper knew better than to ease back. He had not caught sight of the Creek chief during the fight, nor had any of his scouts reported seeing Opothleyahola fleeing.

"Colonel Sims!" Cooper waved to his cavalry commander. "The horses. Take two companies and go immediately to be sure the horses in the woods are still there."

Sims shot him a hasty salute and bellowed his orders. Cooper sank to a rock and waited until Sims returned ten minutes later.

"Colonel, you got eyes in the back of your head?"

"No, I just thought of what I'd do if I were a Federal."

"Good thing. We got there in time to chase a whole danged regiment of them away. They weren't in any shape to fight. Truth to tell, we weren't either, but we shouted louder and made 'em think we were. We saved all our horses."

"Get Quayle on fresh horses, if there are any left, and chase them across the prairie. Catch them if he can, keep them running to the Osage Hills if not. I want Opothleyahola's men scattered all over creation."

"Yes, sir. What about me?"

"Get our wounded loaded into wagons and take them to Vann's Place for immediate doctoring." Cooper looked up at the darkening sky. They had fought better than four hours, and it was turning cold with the setting of the sun. "See to it that Colonel Drew sends in a request to John Ross's nephew for more supplies, especially ammunition. In the morning I'll see what there is to see at the cabin."

"We whupped them good, sir," said Sims.

"Real good," he agreed.

The next morning he personally scouted the area and tallied the dead and wounded on each side. The Confederates had lost fifteen killed and thirty-seven wounded. As best as Cooper could tell—and it made his report look the better for it—they had killed 500 of Opothleyahola's warriors and wounded another 300, many of whom had escaped.

But Opothleyahola had also escaped. And where the hell *was* that supply train from Fort Gibson?

Support From Fort Gibson
December 10, 1861

"We don't know what we're gettin' into, Colonel Ross," complained Lieutenant Ah mer cher ner. "We shouldn't be leavin' Fort Gibson like this."

"Colonel Cooper needs reinforcements," William Potter Ross said, distracted. The lieutenant was right—he felt it deep in his belly—but he had no choice but to bring out a wagon train laden with supplies and munition. He thought Cooper was a fool stringing his men out all over the Cooweescoowee District like he was doing, and tangling with a seasoned chief like Opothleyahola anywhere near Chusto-Talash invited disaster. Worse, the flu epidemic that ravaged the troops at Fort Gibson ran unabated. Not one in five of his men was able to stand guard duty, much less fight.

So why was he on the road to Camp Melton? Ross knew the answer. Colonel Drew needed support, and he was the only one in a position to give it. The political strength of his uncle depended on maintaining John Drew's First Cherokee Mounted Rifles as a counter to Stand Watie's band of pirates. The reports from Drew about the Keetoowah Society defections were unsettling, but Ross doubted they were as serious as Drew thought. He had known the man most of his life and, his uncle's trust in John Drew notwithstanding, Drew partook of whiskey a bit too much and showed too little daring when occasion demanded.

"What's going on ahead?" asked Ross. He stood in the stirrups and shielded his eyes against the winter sun. A rider approached. "It looks like Lieutenant Little Bird."

"He was scouting on the road," Ah mer cher ner said uneasily. "He doesn't spook easily, and it looks like he's scared out of his wits."

"Get back to your men, Lieutenant," Ross said testily. He had no time for such craven comments. Better to see for certain what trouble Little Bird had found than to speculate wildly. Still, following his own advice proved hard. Little Bird *wasn't* prone to alarm.

"Colonel, Colonel," called Little Bird. He reined back. His eyes were wide, and he seemed pale.

"Calm yourself, man. Are you injured? What's happened? Report!"

"Colonel Ross, the survivors are down the road. On foot. They're tryin' to get back to Fort Gibson."

"Survivors? From what?"

"Colonel Drew's command, sir. They were attacked by Opothleyahola's men, and he overran the camp. Everyone but a handful of men was killed dead."

Will Ross halted the wagon train, then turned to his scout. "We'll ride ahead and speak with them. I want to find out for myself what happened."

"This way, sir," the lieutenant said. His horse was lathered and stumbling as it retraced his path. Ross trotted behind, thinking hard. He could hardly believe Drew had lost his command—and possibly his life. He had known John Drew all his life! What would his uncle say if this were true?

"There they are. Camped beside the road. Some weren't able to get any farther toward the fort."

Huddled in twos and threes were more than a dozen men. None wore a Confederate uniform, but Ross recognized several of the refugees as being in Drew's command. One he knew to be a lieutenant. Ross dismounted and went to the man, thinking he was in charge of the retreat.

"Report, Lieutenant," he said. The man looked around as if he wanted to run and hide.

"How'd you know I was an officer?"

"You aren't?"

"No, I am. Was, am, yes sir," he stammered. "We been through too much. The officers, they went out to a peace conference. Then Opothleyahola attacked Camp Melton."

"During the conference?" Ross was astounded. He had thought the old chief possessed greater honor than this.

"Yes, yes! They come ridin' in, and we fired on 'em. Colonel Drew ordered us to retreat and—"

"This is all that's left?"

"After the Pins deserted, it was," the lieutenant said. "Colonel Drew, he lost danged near all his soldiers. They deserted, them and Captain McDaniel, and joined up with the Federals."

It was Will Ross's turn to act as if he had been bludgeoned. He hardly believed this. The Keetoowahs had finally deserted! They were John Ross's biggest supporters. With the full-blooded Pins leaving, deserting, that split the Cherokee Nation down the middle. Stand Watie would not hesitate to take advantage of John Ross's lessened support.

"What of Colonel Cooper?"

"Don't know 'bout him," the lieutenant said. "Reckon he got wiped out, just like we did."

"The Keetoowahs fought against John Drew?"

"They killed any of us they could. And we were messmates not a day before!"

"How many Union soldiers were in Opothleyahola's regiment?"

"Thousands. They outnumbered us and Cooper combined."

"Lieutenant Little Bird!" Ross called. "Get a wagon up here for these men. They're the only survivors of John Drew's Regiment."

"Do you want them returned to the fort, sir?" asked Little Bird.

"I want the whole damned supply train turned around and back at Fort Gibson as quickly as possible. Opothleyahola is out there, and I don't want to ride into a trap." Under his breath he added, "And I surely will *not* fight my fellow Cherokee."

He herded the pitiful men into the back of a supply wagon and returned directly to the fort, formulating his report to John Ross as he rode. It wasn't going to be good, however he phrased it.

Called Into Battle
December 15, 1861

"How am I supposed to write this to my wife?" Stand Watie cried. He slammed his fist down on the small writing table. Pen and ink pot jumped, some of the fluid spilling onto the letter he had been drafting. "Cherokee fighting Cherokee? That's unthinkable!"

"That's what's happened, Colonel. John Drew's entire regiment upped and deserted, all of 'em going over to the pro-Unions." Adjutant Tom Anderson took no satisfaction in telling his colonel this bad news.

"I knew Drew was a fool, but to let all the Keetoowahs desert?" Watie shook his head. "While we're up here chasing down Jayhawkers by ones and twos, the real fight is down south."

"Cooper's chased Opothleyahola into the Osage Hills," Tom reported. "If he wants to do any more he's got to return to Fort Gibson and get some recruits."

"That's not going to happen any time soon," came Saladin Watie's higher pitched voice. The teenager pushed into his father's tent. "Sir," he greeted his father. "I rode up from Fort Gibson and the entire area's in great disarray."

"What's happened to Lieutenant Colonel Ross?" Watie asked, almost too exhausted in spirit to want to know. He felt as if he had wasted his time rushing about, skirmishing with a few guerrillas who managed to sneak back into Kansas. Now he was listening to how a real battle—an important one to the Cherokee Nation—had been waged so poorly. All because of John Ross and his political lap-dog, John Drew.

"Disease runs rampant in the fort," Saladin reported, "but Drew and the few of his men—not more than thirty, by my count—arrived ahead of Colonel Cooper, eager to fight flu rather than their fellow Cherokee. Lieutenant Colonel Ross had taken a supply train out, then turned back for no reason, leaving Cooper without supplies."

"Why didn't he—never mind," Watie said. He was past caring why William Potter Ross or any of those in the Ross faction did what they did. It was as if they sought out action designed to ruin Confederate chances of winning, without quite coming out against the CSA.

"Colonel Cooper has written to Colonel McIntosh in Arkansas for troops, since he is losing confidence in Indian soldiers."

"Well that he should," Watie said angrily, "when he has only officers of John Drew's and William Potter Ross's caliber to gauge us by."

"That's a bit extreme, now, Stand," opined Tom Anderson. "He's got some good officers ridin' with him."

"He depends too heavily on Sims and Quayle and other Texas cavalry officers," Saladin said. "He's had to, since Drew failed so miserably in maintaining his regiment. It's not easy having soldiers who ate your food now shooting your own bullets at you."

"Heard tell the Chusto-Talash fight was a success," Tom said.

"Colonel Cooper's report contained some . . . exaggerations," Saladin said carefully. He looked at his father, who pinned him with his intent, dark-eyed stare. "Cooper claimed more than five hundred Creek killed. I spoke with a few of the Choctaw in Sims's regiment, and he said they buried only twenty-seven. Still, they did rout Opothleya-hola and chevy him across the prairie."

"But Cooper needs reinforcements to put an end to Opothleyahola's raiding," Stand Watie said. "Does he ask me for help? No! He goes to Colonel McIntosh and the Military District Headquarters for troops, instead."

"You're doing needed work along the border, Father," Saladin protested. "Without our regiment, the Jayhawkers would sweep down into the center of our nation and split us."

"Aren't we split anyway, thanks to the Pins?" asked Wa-tie. "Don't we already fight brother against brother be-cause of John Ross's failures? I should never have allowed General Pike to sign the treaty with Ross. I should have forced a vote for principal chief and driven Ross out."

"Stand, playin' the 'I shoulda' game will only make you crazier than you are," said Tom Anderson. "We've got or-ders, and we need to keep after those guerrilla bastards."

"Tom," chided Watie. He glanced at his son.

"Stand, he's heard worse. He's a *captain* in this man's army, and he deserves it. I've seen him fight. And he's probably said worse himself. He's a man, and ought to be treated like any other in this man's army."

"Thank you, Adjutant Anderson," Saladin Watie said, not flustered by the argument flowing around him. "I am capable of defending myself, if needed. And it is not." Turning to Stand Watie, he said, "I think Colonel Cooper will realize how capable the First Cherokee Mounted Rifles is and call us down into the Osage Hills for the final fight with Opothleyahola. He is not a fool, even if he has officers like John Drew in positions of authority."

"Not his doing," agreed Watie. "Maybe I ought to write a letter to Colonel McIntosh, offering our aid."

"You do that, Stand. And me? I'll get after the Jayhawkers. William's heard tell there's a gaggle of them squawkers tryin' to sneak south before the storm hits."

"Go on, Tom," Watie said. "Give them hell."

Tom Anderson smirked, threw a salute, and slipped from the tent.

"What do you want me to do, Father?" asked Saladin. "Take the letter to Colonel McIntosh?"

"No, you've spent enough time on the road, wallowing in that den of thieves and traitors at Fort Gibson. You go find Charles Webber, and you get a company ready to ride and fight. If Tom can't find those Jayhawkers, you do it."

"Yes, sir!" Saladin Watie saluted and left, leaving his father to sit and mull over the disconcerting news he had heard from Fort Gibson, Cooper, and Tahlequah. He turned back to the letter he'd written to his darling Sarah, outlining his frustrations and praising Saladin.

With a dozen like him, the Cherokee Nation would be great and rise proud and independent, a nation among nations, he wrote. Then Stand Watie signed his name with a flourish and sealed it. He could find another courier to carry the letter to his wife in Tahlequah. If there was to be real battle, he wanted Saladin at his side.

The Real War
December 19, 1861

"We caught six more Jayhawkers trying to sneak back into Kansas, Colonel," reported Saladin Watie. "They were trying to smuggle three escaped slaves and a considerable amount of stolen grain."

"Where did they get the grain?" asked Stand Watie. His belly growled at the thought of Sarah's fine biscuits and Ninnie's flaky crust peach pies, or even Jacqueline's bread, which always carried a heavy salt taste he did not mention because she tried hard to equal her sister and mother and never quite succeeded.

"They raided a couple of farms. Most of the grain came from Seth Crawford's, fifteen miles southeast of here."

"Don't know him, but he must be a good farmer to have put up so much grain. Did the Jayhawkers have a wagon-load of it?"

"Five hundred pounds, all sacked," said Saladin. "We can return it or—"

"Return it with our good regards to Mr. Crawford. That does not mean you should not suggest to him that a portion of it could be put to good use by the First Cherokee Mounted Rifles." His belly growled again. Watie sipped at a tin cup filled with cold water from melted snow. The

blizzard had been quick and fierce, affording them a
chance to get fresh water by melting the snow. That same
blizzard had killed twelve horses. These had provided
some fresh meat to a hungry regiment, but a few corn
dodgers or freshly baked bread would go well with any
meal.

"I'll send my sergeant to see to it immediately."

"Thank you, Captain," Watie said, proud of his son.
Saladin performed well in a skirmish, and had developed
a sense of diplomacy lacking in John Ross. Saladin Watie
would make a worthy successor one day as principal chief
of the Cherokee Nation. Watie felt it in his bones, and it
had little to do with his being his son. Those with Saladin
felt more confident because he was sure of himself without
being arrogant.

"Rider comin' fast!" shouted a sentry. Watie pushed
away from his writing table and ducked outside. The sharp
wind cut at his face, but he still smiled. His old friend and
Congregational minister Stephen Foreman rode up.

"Reverend Foreman!" he called. Watie's words were
swallowed by the wind, but the gangly minister saw Watie
and waved. A soldier took Foreman's horse, and Watie ush-
ered him into his tent.

"It's not much against a real storm, but it shields us a
little," Watie apologized. He tapped the thin canvas walls,
now billowing against the rising wind.

"After my freezing ride from Tahlequah, this feels like
the Garden of Eden," Foreman said, brushing off snowflakes from his long coat. "Truthfully, being in the blizzard
is warmer than the reception I get in Tahlequah these
days."

Watie indicated a small, three-legged, camp stool for his
friend. He dropped onto his bedroll and propped himself
up on one elbow to keep his head from being slapped
constantly by the heaving tent wall.

"What news do you have? I hear such terrible things, things I can hardly believe," Watie said.

"They're all true," said Reverend Foreman, turning grim. "Ross actually offered a pardon to all those who deserted from Colonel Drew's regiment!"

Watie shrugged. He had heard this already. It did not surprise him, since John Ross's sympathies were much closer to those of the Keetoowah Society—and Opothleyahola—than to his own.

"Colonel Cooper has spoken eloquently to those remaining in Drew's regiment, urging them not to desert and to remain loyal to the Confederacy. I fear his words fell on deaf ears, or ones filled with hollow promises from John Ross that work at cross purpose to those of Cooper's."

"Has Drew's regiment been reformed?" asked Watie. "As it remained after most of the Pins went over to Opothleyahola, it was not a fit fighting force."

"I suppose they have, Stand. There were rumors of a few deserters returning to their homes, having no stomach for fighting either the Federals or Opothleyahola."

"What's the difference?" asked Watie. "Ross is not likely to punish any of the deserters." He held down a smoldering anger at this. Discipline was difficult to maintain at the best of times. He fought constantly to keep his men in line, to keep them from plundering and wantonly killing as the Jayhawkers and other Federals crossing the border did. Truth to tell, Watie had looked the other way in their brief skirmishes with Opothleyahola's men, letting his men kill their captives in retribution for all that had been done.

But John Drew went beyond the pale. Allowing the heart of a regiment to desert to the enemy or simply quit because they no longer had the fire and grit to fight undermined everything he tried to do with his regiment. And John Ross, as principal chief, was to blame as much as John Drew.

"Are you used well along the Kansas border?" asked Foreman.

"What are you suggesting? That I return to Tahlequah and seize power from Ross?" Watie let out a deep sigh. He had given this some thought. Cooper would never oppose him if he succeeded—and John Drew's regiment could never stop him. Watie's soldiers were both loyal and seasoned battle veterans, in sharp distinction to the other Cherokee officer's regiment.

"The Cherokee Nation needs you, Stand. It does not need John Ross dancing about like he has on toe shoes, trying to appease both pro-Union and Confederate factions. A strong hand is needed, Stand, and it is yours. Return to Tahlequah and take control of a foundering nation. You have more friends than you realize."

"I am flattered, Reverend," Watie said, "but I'm fighting one civil war already. There's no way I can start another, this one pitting Cherokee against Cherokee."

"Do you not already fight this battle?" asked the reverend. "Cherokee fights Cherokee now."

"Ross permits it," Watie said. Then he saw how Foreman had swung him around—remove John Ross, remove the problem—but it could never be that simple. "No," Watie said, holding up his hand to forestall the reverend's coming argument, "we are already fighting our own blood. It would become worse if I openly opposed Ross, especially doing it using military force."

"Sometimes a deeper cut has to be made to save the patient," said Foreman. "Cut off this arm, this so-called principal chief, Stand. Get rid of John Ross, who fears you, and let the healing begin."

"He fears me?" This pleased Watie. He had no love for John Ross, far from it, but he had no idea of the depth of the principal chief's feelings about him. If anything, Watie worried John Ross held him in contempt rather than fear because he championed the mixed-bloods in the tribe.

"Of course he does," Reverend Foreman said. "He quakes in his shoes thinking you might ride to Park Hill and seize power. Everything John Ross does is directed toward securing his own position and undermining yours. Never does he speak publicly that he does not denigrate you. Sometimes the words are subtle, but you are foremost in his mind every time he mentions the war."

"I know," Watie said. "My Sarah writes often of the meetings. It angers her more than it does me. I know how treacherous John Ross really is—and it extends far beyond words." Bitterness chilled him as remembered how his uncle and so many others had been murdered. Had it been twenty-two years ago? It seemed only yesterday to him.

"I know you feel your duty to the CSA strongly, Stand, but your own nation ought to come first."

"Many Cherokee troubles will be over when the Confederacy wins," Watie said. "We will be independent then, and free to manage our own affairs."

"Do it now, Stand," urged Foreman. "The Confederate Army can do without you for a few weeks, even days. That's all it will take to drive that snake Ross from Indian Territory."

Stand Watie considered this, but he had his orders. What Stephen Foreman said might be true, but Watie had assumed the title of colonel with great fanfare and it meant a considerable amount to him. Honor did not permit him to follow his heart in this matter, even if the opportunity looked golden.

"Sorry, Reverend," he said. "Your faith in me is touching, but I have sworn duties here."

Reverend Foreman sighed, reached into his jacket, and pulled out a letter sealed with a fancy wax signet.

"I was asked to convey Colonel McIntosh's regards to you, and to give you this." Foreman shoved the letter toward Watie, who took it and opened the seal.

He quickly scanned the sheet, then looked up at his friend.

"Do you know what this is?" he asked. Stand Watie could hardly contain his excitement.

"I know Colonel Cooper asked for support from Arkansas to fight Opothleyahola. Since this came from the hand of McIntosh's adjutant and carried his desire that I keep my mission confidential, I guess that they want you to join the fight against the Creek and do not want John Ross to know."

Stand Watie glowed with pride. More than Douglas Cooper recognized his skill in the field. Colonel McIntosh was the Arkansas Military District Commander, and he wanted support from Stand Watie's First Cherokee Mounted Rifles!

He would get it.

"Thank you, Stephen," Watie said. Then he got to his feet and began barking orders to strike camp. They were needed in the Osage Hills to the southwest to fight Opothleyahola.

Unlike John Drew, Watie knew his men would never desert—and they would ride the battlefield victorious at the end of the day!

No More
December 19, 1861

"Father, can we deal with them?" Allen Ross asked. He pushed back his garrison cap and then rubbed his hands over the stripes on his sleeves. Why had he ever agreed to join the army, even if he did have a decent post at Fort Gibson under Will Ross? "Perhaps going back to Rose Cottage is wiser than staying."

"Tahlequah is my capital," John Ross said. The old man's resolve hardened. "I will not be run out of *our* capital. This place is for all Cherokee." John Ross smiled a little as he added, "And these are our supporters. Think of the anger we would see if they were supporting the Ridge-Boudinot-Watie Party."

Allen shuffled his feet nervously as he went to the window and looked out into the broad, snow-caked yard to the east of the three-story brick courthouse. Dozens of Cherokee, many with cornhucks woven into their hair, milled about. These were Keetoowah Society members, and all worried about the same thing: the safety of their families. As long as Stand Watie roamed the territory with his band of murderous thieves, no one was secure.

"There must be several hundred gathered," John Ross said, looking past his son's shoulder. "Invite in a few to act as spokesmen. It will not do if we keep them outside in this cold. That will only incite them to act like Watie."

"We wouldn't want the town burned down," agreed Allen. He went to the double doors leading out the north side of the courthouse and beckoned over two men wearing crossed pins in their lapels.

"We demand to speak with Chief Ross!" The smaller of the pair was also the more strident. His larger companion stood with arms crossed and a glare that would melt ice—or freeze a heart.

"We understand the problems you face, and Chief Ross is willing to speak of them. Will you speak for those assembled?"

"There's more 'n three hundred of us," the smaller man said. "Not all of us are Pins, but every man of us is scared of Watie."

"Come in," Allen invited. The two crowded past him into the courthouse, making their way directly to the principal chief's office on the second floor. He did not follow. What his father said would be right. Protection had to be given to those worried most about their lives, and not only protection from the Jayhawkers marauding out of Kansas and stealing grain and livestock. Any Cherokee remaining loyal to John Ross—and the Cherokee Nation—was targeted by Watie's men for death. Allen himself feared every time he saw a squad from Stand Watie's Cherokee Mounted Rifles ride through town. He could not keep himself from wondering and worrying about who they were out to kill.

He waited as patiently as he could until the two Keetoowahs and his father came out to stand on the broad courthouse steps. With a voice stronger than his body ought to have allowed, John Ross spoke to the crowd.

"I have heard your concerns, and I agree wholeheartedly with them," he started. A murmur passed through the crowd. Allen noticed others coming down the main street, others not likely to be as friendly toward John Ross. He recognized several as Watie supporters. They took their place peaceably enough at the rear of the crowd, and he saw no hint they went to draw their too-well-used weapons.

But he watched and worried as John Ross spoke.

"There must be protection, not only from those who are pro-Union," John Ross said, "but from those criminals in our own midst. Toward this end, I have issued orders that any who have deserted from Colonel Drew's regiment be given full pardons."

This caused a ripple of comment to pass through the crowd. Allen saw how the wave broke against the back shore composed of Stand Watie's men. Some reached inside their heavy coats, undoubtedly intent on drawing pistols and causing more havoc. Firing into this crowd would guarantee dozens of deaths, just the kind of thing they relished. Allen touched the butt of the pistol jammed into his own holster, but knew he had no chance against so many. Why hadn't he contacted Will Ross and had him send a detachment from Fort Gibson?

"Those who have received pardons can honorably withdraw to their own homes and protect family and friends, or they can rejoin Colonel Drew's forces at Fort Gibson. I have instructed my nephew, Lieutenant Colonel William Potter Ross, to accept them without punishment of any kind, except forfeiture of pay for the time they were not in uniform."

"If yer lettin' 'em off scot-free, why not pay 'em for desertin', too? Pay 'em for supportin' Opothleyahola and his torturin' braves," bellowed one of Watie's followers. "They're traitors. They turned tail and ran in the face of the enemy—or worse! They ran when there wasn't any enemy at all 'cept their own shadows!"

This received mixed response. The Pins in the crowd began reaching for their knives and tomahawks, and Watie's supporters pulled out pistols.

"No violence!" cried John Ross. "We are all brothers, we are all Cherokee. We fight the enemy, not one another."

How hollow the words sounded to Allen. Of all men here, his father feared Stand Watie's reprisals the most—and of all those gathered, John Ross had the most to fear. He was Stand Watie's sworn enemy. That had been sealed with blood years earlier, with the Treaty of New Echota.

"We must protect our homes, our women and children," John Ross called in a strong, booming voice that carried echoes of his earlier firebrand ways. "I urge you to bury your animosities and fight for the *Nation*, not any individual."

Allen sighed when he saw Watie's followers thrust their weapons back under their coats and leave, grumbling about John Ross's leniency toward traitors. They left, but to perpetrate what horrors on their brothers?

Battle of Patriot Hills
December 26, 1861

"Are you sure of this?" Stand Watie asked his chief of scouts, William Penn Adair. William nodded solemnly.

"Colonel McIntosh has come from Arkansas and joined up with Cooper. From the way they are moving so fast along into the Osage Hills, they must know where Opothleyahola is, and intend to engage him quickly."

"And decisively," Watie said, frowning. He had been ordered to sweep along the northern side of the hills, cutting off any escape, but he had not been invited to join the main attack—if that was what this turned out to be.

"No, Stand, I don't think McIntosh intends driving the Creek into our guns," William said, his thin, dark mustache drooping. With a toss of his head, he shook his long hair from his eyes, smiled crookedly, and shook his head. "As highly as Colonel McIntosh thinks of our fighting, he wants to be at the battle personally."

"Why not let Cooper be the reserve unit instead of us?" groused Watie. Then he heaved a deep sigh that sent a long stream of frosty exhalation into the cold morning air. "I know why, I know," he said. "If I were in command, I would do the same. Taking away any glory from Colonel

Cooper would only embitter him, after so many weeks on Opothleyahola's trail."

"Cooper's men will probably form the major part of the attacking force," William said. "It's McIntosh who might act as backup. I tried to find Captain Mayes and see what reports he's giving Cooper, but he was in the field and unavailable."

Stand Watie unfurled a map of Indian Territory and held it against the fitful wind blowing across the land. Some snow pellets swirled, but mostly the day was only cold. From the look of the lead-gray sky, another storm was possible by night, but not now. That made today the perfect time to attack the pro-Union Creek forces. The battle would be in decent weather, and any escaping Creek would be caught in a storm.

"Sir, a messenger from Colonel McIntosh," barked Watie's striker. Watie looked up and saw his adjutant talking with a flustered looking corporal.

"Tom, get that message over here on the double," he called. Tom Anderson obeyed, the courier trailing behind as if the adjutant had him on a leash.

"Stand, we got new orders. Head for the post on the Grand River, sally forth from there and engage any and all enemy we find."

"Grand River," said Watie, circling the area on his map using his blunt fingertip. "If Opothleyahola is at Hominy Creek, as I suspect, that means any of his men trying to get away will head toward the Patriot Hills." He rolled his map and tucked it under his arm. "Tom, fresh horses, if we have enough, for a company to patrol that region. William, scout the road for us. The rest of the First Cherokee Mounted Rifles, on to Grand River and glory!"

"How is the battle progressing?" Watie asked his son, just returning from the front.

"Can't rightly say," Saladin reported. He brushed snow off his jacket. In the dim afternoon light his gold braid and captain's bars gleamed. "Opothleyahola is putting up quite a battle, but it looks as if McIntosh caught him unawares. McIntosh's main body overran the Creek camp and flushed them right away. There was a company of Cherokee with Opothleyahola—it looks likely they will be running head-long into the Patriot Hills, as Colonel McIntosh figured."

"Cherokee," muttered Watie. "Our brothers." Then re-solve hardened. "Better they lie dead on the prairie than sit in council with the like of John Ross and the rest of the damned abolitionists. We can remain at Grand River, or we can commit the entire regiment to pursuing them. What does Colonel McIntosh want us to do?"

"I know what you'd prefer, Father," Saladin said. "And that is what the colonel's orders are. After the fleeing Cherokee. Take as many prisoners as possible, but allow none to escape. There might be elements of Choctaw and Creek fighters with them, but no one is sure. The fight is confusing. Not even Lieutenant Colonel Adair is sure what is happening, and he's about the best scout in the field."

"So our orders are to do what is logical?" Stand Watie shook his head. "I'm beginning to like Colonel McIntosh."

"Sir, one other thing," Saladin Watie said. "None of Cooper's men was able to join the battle."

"What?" Watie's eyes grew wide as possibilities flashed through his mind, none of them good.

"Colonel Cooper's teamsters deserted, and stranded his brigade at McNair's Place."

"That makes our service all the more valuable," Watie said. He rushed off to get his horse. The rot from John Drew's regiment had penetrated deeply into Cooper's command. It was good that McIntosh had arrived quickly from Arkansas.

Stand Watie would show the colonel how real soldiers fought.

* * *

"They've broken into small bands," Tom Anderson told Watie. "We've captured a few, but they are mostly women and children. No soldiers. We did learn one thing. James McDaniel wasn't with Opothleyahola at Hominy Creek. He had already gone into Kansas asking for Federal aid."

"A pity," Watie said. "I would have enjoyed leading the firing squad at his execution." The darkness worked against him now more than Opothleyahola's scattered followers, with their Henry rifles and deadly bows and arrows. He scanned the flat area and the gentle rise beyond leading into the Patriot Hills. Once there, tracking down the refugees would be more difficult, if not impossible, even for an able tracker like William Adair. And the storm the chief of scouts had predicted that morning was gathering force. Within an hour it would be completely dark, and the teeth of the snowstorm would begin gnawing at Watie's exposed cavalry.

"Continue, or make camp?" asked Tom.

"Continue. Have a company remain behind to guard the prisoners and oversee a bivouac. We're not going to let any of them slip through our fingers, not when we are this close."

The words had hardly escaped his lips when a ragged volley sounded. He wheeled his horse about and trotted in the direction of the gunfire. As Watie rode, he heard return fire—softer *pops!*—as if the enemy had not put in a full load of gunpowder. Down a ravine and upslope he rode, Tom Anderson at his side.

"There, Colonel, there's our boys," his adjutant said.

Watie took in the desperate situation quickly. Then he was diving for cover as the enemy spotted him. Watie jumped to the ground and duck-walked along the bottom of a shallow ravine to a point of safety behind a pair of uprooted tree trunks.

"How many are there?" he asked a sergeant.

"Colonel, pleased to see ya," the non-com greeted, grinning broadly when he recognized his commander. "We blundered onto 'em 'fore we knowed what was happenin'. I reckon there's twenty, thirty, maybe more, out there. And all Cherokee."

Watie listened to the report as he studied the terrain. "How many men do you have, Sergeant?"

"Half what's shootin' at us," the non-com admitted. "But we got powder and shot. 'Less my ears deceive me, they're runnin' low, leastways on powder. Those are half loads, hardly enough to punch the bullet out the barrel."

"Mount your command. We're going to attack."

"Stand!" protested Tom Anderson. "They outnumber us!"

"And we are not going to let them know that until they've surrendered," Watie said calmly. He swung into his saddle and drew his pistol. Seeing the sergeant had his men on their exhausted mounts, Watie let out a rebel yell and led the attack. Tom tried to keep up, and the sergeant spurred his horse on in spite of the animal stumbling with every step.

The wind raced past Stand Watie's face and caught at his wavy hair as he rode. For a moment he thought he would take wing and soar into the gathering storm. Lightning flashed, and gave a curious unreal quality to the land—and to him. The power was upon him, and he could never die—not this day, not now at the hands of his own people.

To the pro-Union Cherokee he must have looked like an avenging angel, revealed by crashing lightning bolts and carried on a horse that never tired.

Watie burst through their line and fired methodically, wounding two and frightening even more.

"Surrender!" he bellowed. "Surrender and live. If you choose to fight, prepare to die!"

As his words rolled along the battle line and distracted

the Federals, Tom Anderson and the others caught up. Their sudden appearance caused the Cherokee who had joined Opothleyahola to drop their weapons and jump to their feet, hands thrust high into the air.

"They're surrendering, Adjutant! Take their petition and get them back to camp immediately." Watie watched as a handful of his men rounded up a force easily three times his in strength—but not in determination. Watie was proud his soldiers had obeyed without question. They had followed him because he had taken command, and done the right thing.

"You," Watie barked to a Cherokee he recognized as having been a longtime Tahlequah resident. "Where are the rest?"

"Don't know," the man said, dazed. "We got separated back at the river. Some kept on, trying to get to the hills. The rest?" He shook his head, still dazed at the sudden capture.

"Everyone back to camp," ordered Watie. He motioned Tom Anderson to join him as they trotted briskly along, letting the sergeant tend to the prisoners. "The storm will slow anyone else. We need to find Colonel McIntosh."

"No need, Colonel." Riding through the gathering murk came an officer decked out in Confederate butternut. "You've found me. I've got three companies of men from my own 2nd Arkansas Mounted Rifles and two more from Captain Bennett's Lamar Cavalry."

"I can't rightly say how many of my regiment are here. I've got some guarding prisoners, and we just captured thirty more," Stand Watie said with some pride, probably exaggerating the number but coming close. He trusted his sergeant to have guessed accurately at the force they had just fought. "The rest of my men are out tracking down stragglers."

"We'll join forces, but from the look of the storm there's no reason to continue hunting this night," McIntosh said.

"We've already done a day's work. We killed more than two hundred fifty of Opothleyahola's followers and captured more goods than you can shake a stick at."

"What of your men, sir? What casualties?" asked Watie.

McIntosh laughed in delight. "Eight killed, thirty-two wounded. Hell, man, we captured more than that of Opothleyahola's force. We caught 'em with their pants down, and we whupped 'em good."

"Are you sure you want to break off the engagement for the night, sir? I can—"

"Let them struggle out in the inclement weather, Colonel. You've done well. Your son reported your regiment killed or captured a hundred without any losses to your own forces."

Stand Watie had not known this, but it pleased him.

"Rest tonight, Colonel, regroup. Get your scouts back. You deserve the respite. Colonel Cooper will arrive in the morning with his Indian Brigade. I want you and Cooper to chase down every last one of Opothleyahola's renegades, if it takes all winter."

"Very good, sir."

"And—Colonel Watie?"

McIntosh's tone put Watie on guard.

"Sir?"

"I've ordered Colonel Drew's regiment from Fort Gibson to reinforce you. Do you have a problem with that?"

"No, sir," Watie said, lying through his teeth.

"Good. I don't want anything to detract from this victory. We've finally stopped Opothleyahola! If this doesn't bring unity to Indian Territory, I don't know what will."

Stand Watie joined in the cheer that went up, but knew he would now have to fight with an eye on both the enemy and on his back, because that was where John Drew would be skulking.

A Nation Apart
January 1, 1862

"Fire!" Stand Watie thrust his pistol high in the air and ordered his soldiers to fire again and again. He turned his pistol toward the scrubby brush in the Patriot Hills where so many of Opothleyahola's followers had taken refuge. The weather was bitter, and the sleet storm that had started the day before refused to die—just like the Cherokee traitors Watie fought so hard against now.

"No quarter," he ordered. His men were hunched over, taking what cover they could. Already ice piled up on their backs, turning them into parts of the white landscape. Steam curled up from barrels hot after repeated firing. Stand Watie stood and shielded his eyes with his hand to see if the fusillade had any effect. He could not tell.

Unlike during his earlier exploits, he found no resolve to wildly attack. These fighters were dug in, and would cut his troops to bloody ribbons if he attempted an all-out frontal attack.

"Sir," called a corporal from along the line. "I think them's our men. We're firin' on our own troops."

"Impossible," Watie said. He had issued specific orders of patrol that morning and knew where his regiment was positioned.

" 'Fraid so, sir. Lookee yonder."

Stand Watie raised his pistol and almost fired when he saw the man in the Confederate uniform with colonel's insignia waving at him. His finger trembled, then he lowered his pistol. He took a deep breath to settle his nerves before giving the order to cease fire.

Watie stepped out into the snowy patch separating the two groups, wondering if the others would shoot him down as he had thought to do to their commander. John Drew came out and joined him in an dubious truce in the middle of the battlefield.

"What are you doing here?" Watie asked, barely containing his rage.

"Why are you shooting at us?" demanded John Drew. "We were following a trail made by some Union wagons. The sleet started filling in the ruts, but—"

"We are after some fleeing Union Cherokee," Watie said, rudely interrupting Drew. "You crossed their path without seeing it."

"You're trying to kill me!" accused John Drew. "You want me dead and—"

"Of course I do, but not as long as you're doing your duty—finally." Watie snorted in disgust. "Get your men back to Tulsey Town. You wouldn't want to get their fine parade ground uniforms dirty, would you?"

"You're in no position to order me to do anything. We're equals in the field." John Drew thrust out his chin belligerently, angered even more that Watie had the gall to issue orders when they were of equal rank.

"Very well, if that's the way you want it," Watie said testily. "I reserve the right to believe your force is turning traitor and fleeing northward. I've seen the trail of other bands near Walnut Creek, and it looks to me as if you're heading that way. Kansas? To join McDaniel and the other Keetoowahs with him?"

"Watie, my men are starved and half dead." Drew's belligerence turned to pleading. Watie thought that was even more reprehensible, and only cemented his opinion of his fellow officer.

"Everyone's starving. The difference is that my men have the will to keep fighting. Get off the field. Colonel Cooper's camped at Skiatooka's Settlement on the Arkansas River. He'll put your men to good use. As menials. He can use somebody to dig latrines for the real soldiers."

"He's by Keystone Lake?" asked John Drew, ignoring the jibe. The promise of getting out of the cold and not having the pro-Union Cherokee—or Stand Watie—shooting at him was a powerful lure.

"Colonel McIntosh said a supply train is on its way to Tulsey Town and ought to arrive in a few days. Get your men there. I don't think you'll run afoul of anything you'd try to shoot, especially since I'm remaining in the field."

John Drew held his breath and began to shake with rage. He spun about and stalked off, his boots crunching down on the dirty, icy crust on the prairie. He gave his orders and his men showed themselves, one by one, until his command backed away and went to fetch their horses.

"Ought to have sent a scout around to steal those nags," Watie grumbled. "Sergeant!" Watie shouted. "Get the troop mounted. We've got real enemy to hunt down." He glared at the other regiment of the Cherokee Mounted Rifles—the real enemy? He watched them leave and had done nothing to stop them. How many Southern Rights Party supporters would John Drew burn out or murder on his way to join Cooper?

Watie swung into his saddle and saw John Drew leading his dispirited men down a draw and back in the direction of Colonel Cooper's camp. Cooper had been hit hard and repeatedly by Opothleyahola's warriors. Watie guessed the colonel would retreat to Tulsey Town to regroup and get supplies from the wagon train out of Fort Gibson. Let John

Drew accompany him, even if Watie wished he had the man in his pistol sights just once more.

"Colonel, we got spoor. From the look of it, maybe twenty braves, all on foot and heading north." William Adair leaned forward in the saddle to ease the burden on his rear end. "It took some doing to find this trail, but my boys have the eyes of eagles."

"After them," Watie said, glad to be away from John Drew and his cowardly troopers. For days they had ridden down the escaping Creek and pro-Union Cherokee, dodging ambushes and trying not to freeze to death as one sleet storm after another blew through. The weather the day of the Battle of Patriot Hills had been the most favorable they had encountered. Watie was only sorry that McIntosh had not included them in his initial assault on Opothleyahola's camp. There would not have been any warriors escaping to the north.

As it was, they had found enough stragglers and their belongings to give determination to their forced marches. Over and over Watie had sent back huddled knots of prisoners to his camp on the Grand River, the ones who weren't killed outright. Where they went after that, he did not know. Let Will Ross deal with starving prisoners at Fort Gibson, although Watie saw this as putting the fox in charge of the henhouse. It still caught in his craw that John Ross had allowed traitors like James Vann to resign his commission without any penalty—and pardoning those who outright deserted sent the wrong message throughout the Cherokee Nation.

Watie knew it was up to him to show Colonel McIntosh and the other Confederate leaders that not all Cherokee were craven.

"There, Colonel, see it?" William pointed out the faint trail and how those escaping had tried to cover it. Not enough snow had fallen after they had left for the concealment to be effective.

"William, take half the men and swing out in a wide circle. I'll wait fifteen minutes, then attack. You scoop up what comes pouring out of that draw," Watie said. Wisps of smoke rose from a ravine, indicating a camp had been pitched. With his chief of scouts on the other side encircling the camp, he would have himself a modest catch to drag back to his own camp.

Watie rode among his men, quietly speaking with them, easing any tensions they might feel. All were hardened battle veterans now, and it was hunger rather than fear he dealt with. If the renegades in the draw fought, *then* there would be the eternally present gut-clenching fear of battle. He always felt it, and he knew the others did, too.

But it was his duty.

Watie opened his pocket watch and tried to estimate what William would consider to be fifteen minutes since he didn't carry a watch of his own. Watie knew he dared not postpone the attack too long or the men would get antsy and do something foolish. It was hard enough to keep them from slaughtering every pro-Union Indian, especially the Pins, that they came across.

He signaled his men forward in a long line, barely able to see who rode on either side in the storm. They entered the draw, and Watie drew his pistol. He heard the distinctive sound of cocking pistols and hammers pulling back on muskets as they advanced cautiously. An attack on foot was more prudent, but Watie wanted this over. Also, if Opothleyahola's followers tried to run Watie wanted his men already mounted to give pursuit. The strategy had changed from fighting to fleeing.

His men had fought well. His men had caught refugees trying to escape the Cherokee Nation for the safety of Jayhawker Kansas. And that was going to stop here and now. Stand Watie's Cherokee Mounted Rifles deserved a rest more than John Drew's craven traitors.

Watie was never sure who fired first. Perhaps it came

from his own men on the far side, or someone in the refugee camp spotted them coming through the storm. The bullet sailed past his hat. He returned fire immediately, and all hell broke loose. He kept his line advancing, aware of the tumult in the camp. Loud neighs from frightened horses and the mooing of panicked cattle greeted him, along with the whines and sobs of men being shot down.

"Surrender!" Watie called. "Throw down your arms!"

"It's Watie," went up the cry. "He's come to murder us all!"

Stand Watie did not hesitate to order a full assault. The sleet pelting down in icy dollops began to mingle with smoke from pistols and steam from the campsite fires.

From the opposite direction came the sound of thundering hooves as William Adair attacked. They caught the pro-Union Cherokee between the jaws of a nutcracker. The battle ended as quickly as it started.

Dazed by the sudden shifts in the fighting, Stand Watie rode about, seeing what had been accomplished. The fight could not have gone better if he had captured Opothleyahola himself.

"Report, William," he ordered.

"We got two wagons heapin' with supplies, Stand. Nabbed nearly sixty of the traitors, too, along with two hundred fifty head of horses. And I got three men who can count out taking inventory on what we captured in way of cattle. It's at least eight hundred head, and might be closer to nine hundred. Don't know where they stole them, because there was no track for a herd that size, not in the direction we came from."

"Good work, William. What of the soldiers?"

"Storm's on their side. We killed one, captured seven, and sent the rest scuttlin' north. When they recognized us, they lit out like their tails were on fire."

"Round up the cattle, use the fresh mounts, and head the regiment back to Grand River. I've got a report to make that will cause Colonel Cooper to smile from ear to ear."

Stand Watie didn't really care if Cooper was impressed with the victory over the renegades. *He* was. He was proud of his men and what they had captured.

"Let's see John Drew match this," Watie said, at the head of the column heading back to camp. It would be good to get out of the storm, and it would be even better seeing the expression on John Drew's face when he heard how successful Stand Watie's Cherokee Mounted Rifles had been after *he* had left the field.

Most of all, he couldn't wait to write his dear Sarah and let her know how accomplished her husband had become in the ways of war, albeit with the incomparable talents of men like William Penn Adair. It would not be long before this foolish war was over, and he could return to her.

Bitter Weather
January 4, 1862

"Colonel Cooper," Stand Watie said, startled at how gaunt his commanding officer was. Pale and drawn, Douglas Cooper looked as if he had one foot already in the grave.

"Watie, glad you made it," the ghost-white officer said. He tried to sit up straight and failed, slumping forward, both elbows on the shaky table supporting him. Watie saw bands of sweat on Cooper's forehead. In this frigid weather that could only mean fever.

"Are you all right, sir? Should I call your orderly? I know your doctor was killed, but someone must be able to help you."

"No, no, it's just that I am so . . . tired. We made a forced march from Hominy Creek back here. Tulsey Town is going to be a big city some day. Might be the size of St. Louis. You ever been there? I know you went back to Washington, years ago."

"Sir," Watie said, concerned. "You're all tuckered out. Rest. I can report when—"

"No, that's all right. My mind wanders a mite now and then. Not enough to eat. And this weather. So cold. Gets so I can't feel my toes at times."

"It has been cold, sir," Watie said, settling down on a stool across the table. Cooper's eyes were wide and bright, another sign of fever eating him up inside. It was a good thing Colonel McIntosh had come from Arkansas to rout Opothleyahola. In this condition, Cooper would fall from his saddle in the midst of battle. Watie had wondered why McIntosh had seen fit to launch the attack using only his own troops. Now he understood. Removing Cooper from his command would have caused a serious breach in authority, especially since Cooper had desertions of his own to cope with. His teamsters leaving at the moment he needed them most had rendered his troopers ineffectual. If they had plotted with Opothleyahola they could not have delivered a more telling blow.

"Good work, bringing in so many horses. And the cattle. Well, we'll all eat better now. That supply train from Fort Gibson helped us, it did, it did indeed, but fresh meat? Couldn't have come at a better time."

"The cattle are mighty scrawny and tough, but they cook up good in a stew," Watie allowed. He wondered what McIntosh would think if he assumed overall command of troops in Indian Territory. Douglas Cooper was in no condition to lead.

"Too bad John Drew missed them," Cooper said. Then he shook himself like a wet dog and grinned weakly. "Not really, is it? You want him to starve in the cold."

"He might be able to get that right," Watie said. "If so, that's about the limit of his talent."

"He had equally complimentary words about you, Stand." Cooper heaved a sigh that turned into a cough from deep in his chest. "I'm working to keep the two of you apart. No need to brew more bad blood. He's scared of you, Stand. You keepin' those ruffians of yours in check?"

"He has reason to be afraid of me, after all John Ross has done."

"Stand, Stand," chided Cooper. "Diplomacy. You're supposed to say we're all on the same side, or something equally banal."

"Are we? John Ross and John Drew and the others in the Keetoowah Society—where do their sympathies truly lie? With the Confederacy? I don't think so. John Ross manumitted his slaves, and he has been more than lenient with the men who deserted from Drew's regiment. The pair of them are doing all they can to keep us from winning."

"Winning," said Cooper, a distant look coming to his eyes. "We could all go home. That would be good, wouldn't it?" His mind began to drift again. Watie forced himself not to think of Sarah and his children, not at the moment. After they had pushed back the Federal forces and won their sovereignty, *then* he could think of home fires and the warmth of a bed with his wife beside him.

"Rumor has it Drew and his regiment were sent back to Tahlequah. Is that so?"

"Yes, I ordered them. We can use the field rations better than they can. We're soldiers, you and I, Stand. We know how to wage war, how to win battles. We're warriors in the truest sense."

"What are your orders, sir?" Watie asked, not wanting to hear but knowing he was still in this sick man's command.

"Rest up. Wait for the storm to die down, then return to the northern border. Patrol there and hunt down any of Opothleyahola's men trying to escape into Kansas."

"Where is Opothleyahola now, Colonel?"

"He's a slippery devil, but we have him on the run. The fight at Patriot Hills broke his back, so to speak. Scattered his forces, left him without supplies. In this weather, he won't be able to fight. You did good out there, Stand. Real good."

"Should I track him down? Opothleyahola?"

"No!" For a moment Cooper looked spooked. Sweat poured down his face, and his eyes grew round. "You don't have the troops for that. Colonel McIntosh and I agree. We'll hunt him down later—if there's anything of his force to hunt. If he escapes to Kansas, let him be a burden on the Federals."

"How many men does he have with him?" asked Watie.

"Might be as many as ten thousand warriors," Cooper said, "but they don't have anything to eat. McIntosh figures they will head north, maybe to Roe's Fort on the Verdigris up in Kansas. If they do, they'll be the Federals' concern. Let them feed the bastards. That's what we're thinking, yes." Cooper's voice trailed off, and Watie thought the colonel was going to fall asleep—or pass out.

"So the Cherokee Mounted Rifles are to patrol the border and prevent Opothleyahola from returning?"

Cooper jerked awake. "Stop any Indians from going north. Destroy what supplies you capture and cannot use immediately. Don't give them an instant of comfort, and the winter will do our work for us. No bullets, just snowstorms," Cooper said. He began to drift again, muttering to himself.

Stand Watie rose and beckoned to the colonel's orderly. The private shrugged.

"Get him a medic, man!" flared Watie. "He's out of his head with fever."

"Ain't been right since he took a wound at the beginning of the campaign," the orderly said. "But the colonel he don't want no one to know about it. Makes his men think he's made from steel."

"They'll see he's dying," snapped Watie. "Get him help. If the doctor is dead, find someone who knows *something* about medicine." The private grumbled as he shuffled off to obey.

Watie peered up at the cloud-shrouded sky above Tulsey Town. Cooper might be right. This place could be a big town some day—but not now, and not if Watie had to pull out his regiment to go hunting stragglers along the border.

He pulled up his collar and went to find his adjutant. Cooper had said they could rest a few days. Watie wanted his men to get the best food possible before heading out into the cold.

John Drew got to return to the comfort of Tahlequah. That, as much as anything else, rankled.

Deepening Wounds
February 19, 1862

"This is outrageous!" Stand Watie cried. He jumped to his feet and paced like a caged animal in the confines of the canvas tent. More than once, he straightened enough to bang his head on the sloping sides of the tent. Watie was so upset that he did not notice. "Colonel Cooper cannot think it was murder. My men are *not* murderers! He's still out of his head with fever."

"Well, Stand, you know and I know, and good ole Doug Cooper knows that's true," said Tom Anderson, "but none of us—or him—matter. Not this time. If John Ross says Arch Snail was murdered, then you know all the newspapers throughout the Cherokee Nation will say the same thing."

"This is a bald-faced lie!" raged Watie, trying to hold down his ire. It was unfair. He was exiled to the Kansas border, to skirmish with Jayhawkers and the occasional remnant of Opothleyahola's forces that continued to evade Cooper's regiment. Since the Battle of Patriot Hills there had not been a single significant engagement. All he and his cavalry regiment had done was run down men by ones and twos and dash about frantically, rattling sabers and trying to protect the settlers from the Federals.

Watie wasn't sure how effective they had been. The Northern guerrillas were growing bolder and more effective in the way they invaded Indian Territory. With so many Cherokee and Creek and other deserters from the Five Civilized Tribes—many from John Drew's regiment—it wasn't too far-fetched to believe they knew this land better than he did. The lack of support he got from Fort Gibson also rankled, but he understood that more than Cooper's accusation. As long as John Ross's nephew was in charge of supplies at the fort, Watie expected nothing but maggoty meat and no grain for his troops.

"The colonel wants a full report?" Stand Watie took a deep breath and tried to calm himself. Rage did nothing to solve the problems facing him. There had been instances of his men going wild, but they had only killed Keetoowahs or their families.

"Reckon that's so. We all know the details. Just write 'em down official-like, and I'll have a courier take it to the colonel." Tom Anderson looked put out at having to bother with such a menial chore.

"How's Cooper doing?"

"Shaky, but getting through his ague. Leastwise, that's what he's told his troops. Never saw a man so disinclined to fess up to a war injury. You'd think he got shot by some woman's husband as he was sneakin' out the window of her bedroom."

Watie rubbed his hands together to get circulation flowing. This was another argument against constant patrolling. He never felt warm any more. Every morning he checked his fingers and toes to be sure none had fallen off from frostbite. So far, none had. He couldn't say the same for all his soldiers.

"A report. He wants a report when my promise is not good enough." This rankled the most. Cooper ought to trust him more than John Drew—and John Ross.

"These are tense times, Stand," said Tom. "You know that."

"I'll write the report. Is there anything about Arch's death you're not telling me?" Watie eyed his adjutant closely. Tom shook his head.

"You know all I do, Stand. Maybe more, since you knew Isaac Hildebrand 'fore the war, and he's the one making the charge."

"I can't believe John Drew promoted Hildebrand to captain. What a waste of bars." Watie settled down at his writing desk and began drafting his reply to the district commander.

Arch Snail had been a soldier in Captain Hildebrand's Company D of Drew's regiment. Watie's scouts had found him and recognized him as a deserter during the Caving Banks fight. The scouts had arrested him and were bringing him to Watie's camp when two others from John Drew's regiment happened on them. They ambushed Watie's patrol.

"How does this sound?" Watie asked Tom, peering at what he had written. "Snail was killed with his own pistol. As to the other two assassins I know nothing of them, but presume they are safe in Colonel Drew's camps."

"That's laying it on the line, Stand," said Tom. "Are you sure you want to be that harsh?"

"Colonel Cooper has to know my true feelings, and this certifies to the facts as I know them. The two from John Drew's regiment are the ones to ask about Snail Arch's death, not my men."

"I'll send it by courier." Tom Anderson turned when the sound of feet breaking through icy crust and frozen mud drew his attention. A wild-eyed young private pushed into Watie's tent.

"Colonel, it's not his fault. He was drunk. I don't mean him, I mean *him*. He was—"

"Whoa, slow down," Watie said. He recognized the

young warrior as a friend of his son's. "What are you talking about?" Watie turned to Tom and shooed him from the tent, pointing to the letter intended for Colonel Cooper. The adjutant scowled, then left to send the missive on its way.

"Colonel, it's not like you think. He was drunk. Drunk out of his mind and mad and—"

"Quiet!" snapped Watie. "I have no idea what you are talking about."

"Chunstootie," the young man said. "He was drunk."

"I don't know who Chunstootie is."

"He's a deserter. From John Drew's regiment."

"Aren't they all?" Watie said in distaste. "And he was drunk? Not only does Drew condone cowardice and desertion, he also allows his men to get drunk."

"He come after Charles, and Charles didn't want no part of it. But he's a scrapper, Charles is."

"Charles?" Watie asked, trying to sort through the tangled strands of the story. Then he sat a little straighter and his surroundings sharpened, as if he'd gone into battle and all his senses magnified. His mind raced. There was no reason for a private, even a friend of his son's, to bring the tale of a drunk deserter to his attention unless it affected him directly. He maintained good enough discipline that a private would have taken this up with his sergeant or possibly his company lieutenant. Unless. . . .

"Do you mean my nephew?"

"Yes, yes, Charles Webber. Saladin's best friend. Chunstootie got to mean mouthin' everyone and everythin', and Charles, well, he don't put up with that from nobody, much less a deserter, and—"

"Is Chunstootie dead?"

"Dead and scalped. Charles flew into a rage, and there was no holding him back."

"Was Saladin there?"

"No, the captain's out on patrol. But I figgered you

needed to know, Charles being your son's best friend, and
Charles also bein' your nephew and—"

"Get him in here on the double," Watie said. "I'll get
to the bottom of this."

"Right away, Colonel," the young man said, starting to
salute with the wrong hand. He got confused, then resigned himself to simply leaving. He caught the handle of
his knife on the tent flap, took a second to disengage, then
rushed away, leaving Stand Watie to stew in his own juices.

It wasn't enough John Drew badgered him over Arch
Snail's death—Watie knew the source of Cooper's request
had come from Tahlequah and John Ross, passed along
the grapevine through Drew's cowardly hands—but this?
It sounded as if his own nephew had killed one of Drew's
deserters. From all he had gleaned from the confabulated
report, no ambush or patrol from John Drew's regiment
could be blamed for the death.

Watie looked up, grim-faced, when his nephew came in.
Blood stained the front of his jacket.

"You wanted to see me, Uncle?" Charles asked.

"The *colonel* wanted to see you," Watie said firmly, letting
his nephew know exactly how serious he considered the
matter. "Did you kill Chunstootie?"

"He attacked me, Unc—Colonel," Charles Webber said.
From the way he spoke, Watie thought he was telling the
truth. Charles was hardly older than Saladin. What was he?
Sixteen? Old enough to kill. Was he also old enough to
know when not to kill? Probably not, but he was no cold-
blooded murderer.

What was he going to tell the family if it turned out
Charles had murdered Chunstootie?

"Tell me all about it."

Watie listened intently as Charles Webber spun his tale.
Chunstootie had been drunk and offensive, but only when
he attacked Charles did the youth defend himself.

"I must file a report with Colonel Cooper on this matter," Watie said. He wished he had stayed Tom Anderson for just a few more minutes. Putting two such incidents in the same letter eased the impact. As it was, John Drew would make a mountain out of a molehill. If John Ross had not pardoned all the deserters, Chunstootie would have been in prison rather than getting drunk and into mischief.

"I'm sorry this happened, Colonel, but he said things about the Confederacy and you and everything else that couldn't go unanswered. And he bad-mouthed Saladin, and I couldn't tolerate that."

Watie took out another sheet of paper and started a new report. The cork was out of the jug now, so he saw no reason to temper his remarks.

"Chunstootie was beside himself with liquor," Watie wrote, "and proved himself hostile to Southern people and their institutions." He looked up. Charles watched over his shoulder.

"He also vowed to kill anybody who tried to raise a southern flag. He got downright mean about it," Charles said.

Watie put this down in his own words, then concluded, "Such insolence and traitorous, drunken behavior will not be tolerated in any army unit comprised of Cherokee."

"That's going to light the fire under Colonel Drew," Charles observed. "Thank you for believing me, Unc— Colonel," said the youth.

"Give this to Adjutant Anderson and have him send it right away to Colonel Cooper," Watie said. "And I know the truth when I hear it, Nephew."

He knew that John Drew would not see it that way. Stand Watie knew he had just earned two actively dangerous enemies now. North, and Drew's regiment. So be it.

Fear
March 3, 1862

"Do you have to go, Stand?" asked Sarah Watie. She clung to her husband. "It's been so good seeing you again."

"I wish Saladin could have come with me," Watie said, enjoying the feel of his wife's body pressed against his. "It would have been a real homecoming, then."

"He's such a fine man, isn't he?" Sarah asked. She did not expect an answer.

"All our children are good," he said, looking over his shoulder. Jacqueline and Ninnie stood on the porch of the two-story brick house, arms around one another as protection against the brisk, cold wind whipping across the hills behind the house outside Tahlequah.

"I wish this were all at an end," Sarah said softly.

"My R and R?" joked Watie.

"The war. The killing. This silly dispute with John Drew. You know how I worry." She laid her head on his shoulder, then moved a little to get a piece of braid off her cheek. A tear trickled down to dampen her husband's gray jacket.

"You needn't. I'm safe. I'm a colonel."

"But Saladin is on the front lines. And there is that nastiness about Charles." Sarah looked at her husband. "You weren't just defending him because he killed one of John Drew's men, were you?" The edge in her voice warned Watie not to cross her. Sarah's feelings toward Chief Ross and Colonel Drew were not his. She wanted an end to the feud, but as much as she desired its end Watie knew it could not stop. John Ross worked too industriously to betray the Confederacy, doing it in such a way that he could never be called a traitor.

Chunstootie had been a fool, whereas John Ross was a clever and able statesman—and that made him even more dangerous to the Cherokee Nation. Ross sold them all out in little ways, chewing away at Cherokee sovereignty by dealing with pro-Union Indians and trying to support John Drew's deserters however he could.

"Stop it, Stand," Sarah said angrily. "I can tell by the look in your eyes what you are thinking."

"I never could fool you, my dear," he said. Stand Watie looked up at the house and his young daughters. In the window was his youngest son, Watica, nose pressed against the cold glass and making funny faces to amuse him. Cumiskey was nowhere to be seen, the parting too much for the young boy to endure—again.

How he longed to return to the house and get on with his life. They were so young, so very young to endure all that tore at their nation. How he wanted to go back to be with them, to tend the businesses up on Cowskin Prairie he and Sarah's brother James Bell had started, to do a hundred and one things that had nothing to do with fighting and killing.

Yet he couldn't. He owed a debt to the Cherokee Nation, and to the Confederacy. In some ways he saw them as two different worlds, but he was bound to both.

"General Van Dorn is preparing a big attack that will drive the Federals out of Arkansas once and for all time," he said. "He needs me and my regiment to support him.

Colonel Cooper has recommended me highly, as has Colonel McIntosh."

"They need you, Stand. But your family needs you more."

He heaved a deep sigh and nodded. "You need me, and I need you," he said with feeling, "but I have a duty to perform. I was not made a colonel so I could turn and walk away whenever it suited me." He straightened, his broad, flat face firm with determination. "I am not like Drew or his men. Let them desert if someone shoots at them. Or just quit because it suits their mood. I cannot do that and live with myself."

"It is so hard without you, Stand. The crops aren't going to be planted unless Watica can somehow supervise it. That is a great deal to put on a ten-year-old boy. Cumiskey is sick so much of the time, it is not likely he will be able to help."

"I know," he said, clutching her tightly. "That's why this war must be put to an end quickly. If I can, I'll send for you to visit me in the field—after the coming battle. Until then, it will be too dangerous."

"I'll be waiting for your orders, my colonel," she said softly. He kissed her, then did the hardest thing he had done since the war began. Stand Watie mounted his horse and rode away.

"He didn't pay the Creek," John Ross said to Colonel Drew, who rode alongside his buggy. "That is wrong. Why did General Pike pay the Choctaw and the Chickasaw, but not the Creek troops?"

John Drew nervously chewed on his lower lip, eyes darting about the road leading from Evansville, Arkansas. He worried constantly about Stand Watie. Drew knew the orders he had received were duplicates of those sent to Watie. The backstabbing rebel would be somewhere out on the road, too, and that presented a real danger to Chief Ross. John Drew didn't even want to think what it meant to him personally, after he had so strongly protested Chunstootie's brutal murder by Watie's nephew.

Every step toward the front lines where Van Dorn assembled his forces for the campaign increased the danger to him and the Cherokee's principal chief.

"He spent too much paying off the Osage and Comanche," John Drew said bitterly. "Albert Pike seems to go out of his way to create problems for us. He knows the Creek will rally again to Opothleyahola if they are not wooed."

John Ross shook his head to brush away an annoying fly buzzing near his eyes. "Pike claimed he had five hundred thousand, but all for treaty money. He should never have paid the Choctaw and Chickasaw if he was going to deny the Creek. Better none get paid than only a few."

"I'm waiting for him to pay us," Drew complained. Small movement in bushes beside the road spooked him. His hand flew to his pistol, but he did not draw when two doves took wing.

"You are nervous, Colonel," John Ross said. "This battle will turn the tide and give us our freedom from the CSA. We can deal with the Union from a position of strength, deal with them as victor dictating to the conquered."

"It's Watie. He's on his way here, too."

"The Cane Road is wide, and the day is fine," John Ross said, but he began feeling some of the anxiety gnawing at John Drew. By all accounts, Earl Van Dorn was a decent general and used the terrain well for this major campaign. He headquartered in the Boston Mountains south of Fayetteville. From there he could sweep out of northwestern Arkansas and drive back the Federals.

"No day is a fine one to meet Watie unless it includes peering down the barrel of a musket at him," John Drew said harshly. "I am very upset over having so little equipment in our train."

John Ross shrugged, then shifted the buggy reins from his right hand to his left. His fingers cramped on him and reminded him that the spring showers had yet to start, giving him new pain in all his joints. "Major General Van Dorn said to travel at our own pace, and to let the regimental baggage train follow. We dare not tarry, or let the slower wagons hinder our progress."

"I wish you were not here, Chief," John Drew said. "The danger to you is extreme. Does it matter whether a Yankee bullet or one from Watie's rifle kills you? You must watch both front and rear at all times, as long as you remain in the field."

"I must speak with Van Dorn," John Ross said. "His use of Cherokee soldiers might be in violation of their treaty. I want to hear that he wants your regiment only as support. We agreed that Cherokee soldiers would not fight outside the boundaries of our nation." The brisk spring wind still carried memory of a particularly long, bitter winter, but the occasional blooms foretold that the summer would be a fecund one. His nose even twitched with the first grains of pollen on the breeze.

Or was the nose-wrinkling smell from Stand Watie moving upwind from him? John Ross sneezed. Flowers blooming with insane fury, or Watie? For a moment he visualized a fresh grave with daffodils poking up on it. Whose grave was it, though?

"Pike at least paid our soldiers who stayed behind," John Drew said. Then he snorted in disgust. "A dollar a day for enlisted men, and two for the officers? Hardly money to grow wealthy by."

John Ross said nothing. Few knew that Albert Pike had given $220,000 to the Cherokee Nation treasury to pay for soldiers, even if only $70,000 had been in gold. John Ross thought the Confederate scrip worthless, especially since the money was only an advance on the expected sale of the Cherokee Neutral Lands. Ross smiled a little. He and his family controlled most of those lands, and the money would flow through to him after the Union was brought to its knees. He only wished more than the twenty-two soldiers left behind to guard the money had been available. He made a mental note to disband the guards when John Drew's regiment returned to Tahlequah after this battle.

Still, only twenty-two men, and there was no assurance Watie's regiment was actually on the road to join Van Dorn. John Ross became increasingly uneasy. It had been wise not to let Drew or any of the men in his command know of Albert Pike's payment. He had let it out that the twenty-two soldiers were to be paid as John Drew said, but otherwise no mention of the money had leaked out.

John Drew saw how Ross squirmed on the hard buggy seat, misinterpreted it, and said, "Chief, there's no reason for you to speak personally with General Van Dorn. Write out your concerns, and I will deliver the message only to his hand."

"My presence is more commanding than any letter. He must know how upset I am over the possible use of Cherokee troopers outside our boundaries."

"Watie will insist on putting his men at the front lines," Drew said. "He violates the treaty if he volunteers his men for any mission other than support."

John Ross hardly heard the protest. It was ludicrous, because he expected Watie to do exactly as Colonel Drew intimated. If anything, Ross hoped Watie would dash forward at the head of his men, as it was rumored he often did. A Federal bullet would end so much bitterness and bring a real peace to the nation.

"Perhaps you are right, Colonel," John Ross said. He shifted on the buggy seat and wished he could ride a horse, as he once had. His old bones refused to endure more than a few yards of a horse's jolting gait, even the gentlest of mares. "My leadership is vital. Back at Park Hill."

"The battle will be over soon, and we can return to straighten everything out," John Drew said. "General Pike's Indian Brigade, along with the other units Van Dorn has assembled, will seize the field easily. Sterling Price, General McCulloch, and even Watie will be there to punish the Federals."

John Ross nodded. "Pea Ridge?"

"There," John Drew said.

John Ross drove along a few more minutes, then bade John Drew farewell, turned his buggy around, and headed back to Tahlequah. There was so much money in the treasury it *had* to be a lure for a rapscallion like Stand Watie. It required watching over, and John Ross was the man to do it.

Confusion
March 6, 1862

Stand Watie saw Brigadier General Albert Pike before any other officer in the chaos of the forming army. Pike was distinctive, sitting astride his big gray stallion, his huge bushy beard floating on the wind like a garrison banner. Unlike other Confederate officers, Pike was decked out in a gaudy Indian shirt and buckskins that had seen better days. Over the shirt he wore his officer's jacket, replete with gold braid. What Pike stared at so intently, Watie could not tell, but his commander was unwavering in his study.

Riding up, Watie saluted and said, "Reporting as ordered, sir."

"Stand, how the hell are you?" greeted Albert Pike. He grinned, saluted, and then thrust out his meaty hand for Watie to shake. Watie matched the powerful grip, but was glad when Pike finally released his hand. "This is going to be the big one for us. I feel it in my gut. You ever have that feeling?"

Watie nodded. He had known he was going to be successful in battle twice before, but mostly he felt misused and bored in what he counted as nothing more than garrison duty. His regiment had patrolled endlessly along the

Kansas border, but days went by when they saw no other humans, much less Jayhawkers trying to sneak into Indian Territory to do mischief or slaves attempting to escape north. Mostly the patrol had given him too much time to fret about John Ross and how Sarah and the children were getting along.

"Thought so. You have good instincts," Pike rambled on. "You have any problem being in my command . . . along with Colonel Drew?"

"The two of us have our differences," Watie said diplomatically. Pike laughed harshly.

"I heard about that dust-up where your nephew scalped one of Drew's men."

"Chunstootie was a deserter," Watie said coldly. "And drunk, and bad-mouthing—"

"No need to go into it, Stand. I'm on your side, you and the rest of the loyal Cherokee. But Ben McCulloch and on up the line all the way to General Van Dorn tell me I got to have John Drew riding alongside us for political reasons. Might be for the best, though."

"How's that?"

"I can keep my eye on him. After reading some of his reports, I might need to ride with a cocked pistol in hand, the muzzle aimed at the back of Drew's head. If I ever see the whites of his eyes, I can fire."

"That would happen too fast even for a man with your quick reflexes, General," Watie said, smiling crookedly. His slight of John Drew produced a deep-throated laugh from Albert Pike.

"A sense of humor, too. I like that, Stand, I do. Now get your boys ready. What's going to happen is this. General Price will attack southwest along Telegraph Road past Elkhorn Tavern, down there where the Butterfield Overland Mail Company runs their stagecoach now and then up to Saint Louis. McCulloch will drive east past Leetown and try to put Little Mountain on his left flank for protection."

Watie pictured the area in his mind, translating from the map he had to the actual terrain. This put Pea Ridge to Price's right flank, making counterattack from that protection unlikely. The Federals would have to gain the ridge to shoot down on either Price or Van Dorn. Directly ahead of their attacking force would be the Union Army, with Little Sugar Creek at their rear. With luck, the Federals would be taken by surprise and unable to get across the creek fast enough to keep from being slaughtered.

"Now, my Indian Brigade's going to support Price, and along with me rides John Drew. I want you and Colonel Sims, along with his two hundred breakneck, hellbent-for-leather Texans, to work together, on our right flank between John Drew and Pea Ridge."

"When do we move out?"

Albert Pike scratched himself, stared up at the sun, then spat a black gobbet of chewing tobacco. "Midnight," he said. "We're going to move at midnight to sneak up on those bastards to take them at first light tomorrow. And we're not going to give one inch anywhere along the way. Stand, we are going to win and win *big*."

"Yes, sir!" Watie said, saluting smartly. He had not minded serving under Douglas Cooper but the man's wounds kept him from being a vibrant, effective leader—unlike Albert Pike.

All of Albert Pike's command had painted themselves for war. John Drew looked uneasily at the men, gleaming in the faint moonlight like demons. He had ordered his men not to wear their war paint, and this made him aware how out of step he always was. His men were Cherokee and proud of it. Those with Pike were a mix from many of the Five Civilized Tribes, and wild as any prairie tornado. Drew was uneasy with the way Pike's soldiers whooped and hollered and danced through camp, rattling bells at their ankles and brilliant turkey feathers woven into their hair. He was no stickler for dress and military order, but they looked more like a band of renegades than soldiers.

"Ready to move on, Colonel?" asked General Pike. He peered at Drew and stroked his beard, as if emphasizing the difference between them. John Drew had never been able to grow a beard, much less one as bushy as Pike's.

"My scouts said there is movement on the road behind us, back along the Bentonville Detour."

"That's McCulloch's baggage train. Moving slower than we are. What the hell are you scouting behind us for, anyway? You thinking on retreat? We haven't even found the Yankees yet."

"I'm not familiar with the countryside and—"

"Forget it, Colonel. Get those men of yours moving. Watie's already on his way with Sims."

John Drew fumed at this. Pike always threw up to him how much better an officer Stand Watie was. Let them settle their differences face-to-face, then Pike and the others would see who the real hero was, and who turned tail and ran like a scalded dog.

Colonel Drew rode through the ranks of his cavalry, getting them to their horses and forming rank. Behind him they rode slowly in the cold night, following Pike's infantry and wishing he were with McCulloch's baggage train. Drew shivered and brushed ice from his nose as it formed, tickling and dripping. For an hour they rode until they came to a river south of Little Mountain where McCulloch struggled to fell trees and get his men across the frigid water.

"Getting them across is going to take time," Albert Pike observed. "Better to use foot bridges like he's doing, though, than to get his men across that dinky stream and find their toes frozen. Infantry don't move as fast without toes, you know."

John Drew didn't know if Pike joked or simply stated what he thought was the truth.

"There's more 'n that, General," came the report from Pike's scout. "The Federals have felled trees on the other side, blocking the road. No trouble getting the infantry by the blockades, but the wagons will have a devil of a time. You want we should clear the road south?"

Pike rubbed his hands together for the warmth it gave, then glanced at John Drew. He came to a quick decision.

"We backtrack," Pike said decisively. "We can get back to Pea Vine Ridge and follow Sims's 9th Texas Cavalry."

"Watie is with Sims," John Drew pointed out.

"I reckon, since we're all fighting on the same side, that's not a problem. Is it, Colonel?" Pike passed along orders for his brigade to retrace the route it had just taken, returning to Leetown. Drew grumbled as he turned his men around, but preferred going in this direction to crossing Little Sugar Creek and spending an endless night working around traps laid by the Union soldiers.

After an hour's ride, Pike asked of Drew, "You see the turnoff to Leetown?"

"No, General," John Drew said. "I figured you and your scouts were looking for it."

"Damnation," swore Pike. "I missed the road in the dark."

"McCulloch's baggage train is at least a half hour behind us, back in the direction of the creek," Drew said. "We could guard it and—"

"Those aren't my orders," Albert Pike said gruffly. "I will not waste any more time." He stood in his stirrups and swung around, peering into the gloom, as if his eyes could somehow penetrate the darkness of the woods to their left. "That way. Through the forest," he declared. "We'll keep going south until we get to the Bentonville Road, then we'll know where we are."

Less than twenty minutes into the woods, Pike held up his hand. Drew rode up and whispered, "What is it, General?"

"Listen, man. Listen! There's a whole damned army moving through the woods ahead of us."

John Drew heard the crunching and occasional cursing of the men hidden by trees and dark. His cavalry would be at a disadvantage in the woods, unable to mount a decent charge unless he ordered them to dismount and advance on foot.

"Scout ahead. Find out how many men are out there," ordered Pike. Two of his best scouts melted into the dark, returning in less than ten minutes.

"Well, what do we face?" demanded Pike.

"General," one drawled, turning the title into more than three syllables. From the look of his paint, he was Choctaw. "That's General McCulloch's infantry."

"He was crossing the creek, and ought to be south of here!" protested Drew.

"Seems he got the same bee in his bonnet about joining up with Van Dorn back in the direction of Elkhorn Tavern," the scout said. "Anyhow, he got orders from Van Dorn himself, and when I upped and introduced myself he told me to pass them along to you. The general's afraid the Federals under Curtis will cut the Bentonville Road around Elkhorn Tavern, so you and McCulloch are to capture Leetown and prevent the Yanks from flanking him on the west."

"Damnedest thing I ever heard," Albert Pike said, shaking his shaggy head. "You sure that's McCulloch's force ahead?"

"Got the orders from his hand, General," the scout said, irritated at the question. "I know which side I'm fightin' on."

"Lead me to McCulloch. I want to palaver with him directly. None of this makes a whit of sense. The enemy's to the south, not behind us at Pea Ridge. Come along, too, Colonel. You might as well deal yourself in on this sorry hand."

They made their way through the dark forest until they reached the leading edge of McCulloch's infantry. Drew couldn't help but laugh at the way the soldiers were scattered and almost helpless in the dark. At least none of his Cherokee would be so inept in the night.

"What's going on, Albert?" demanded Ben McCulloch. "You joinin' up with me or you goin' your own way?"

"General," greeted Pike. "From what my scout says, Van Dorn wants us together to take Leetown. Didn't even know it had fallen."

McCulloch shrugged. "Don't know one way or the other," he admitted, "but we can be sure it don't fall. If I was Curtis I'd have my men on the banks along Little Sugar Creek there south of Leetown. We come on them two miles up the creek to the west, we don't have to cross and we can take the land from them."

"If they are even there," grumbled John Drew.

"They must be or Van Dorn wouldn't send so much of his force ag'in 'em," said McCulloch. "We swing around, head in this direction," he said, drawing a map in the forest dirt and indicating a spot westward of their current position. "We kin be in place jist after sunrise."

"Take longer," Pike said. "We're so turned around we can't even find the Bentonville Road."

"Straight through the forest, in the direction my brigade's movin'," McCulloch said confidently. "You horsey boys just trot along behind us. My men don't cotton to walkin' in your horse shit."

"Sir," Albert Pike said, saluting.

John Drew saluted, also, then left with Pike.

"This is a complete fiasco," Drew complained. "We're lost in the forest, and he's talking about attacking at dawn?"

"McCulloch's a good general," Pike said, but he didn't sound too confident, and this worry was well-founded. When the combined Confederate force emerged from the woods to attack Leetown at 10:00 A.M. they found themselves facing an entrenched Union position.

"We took too long getting here," John Drew said.

"We're not retreating," Pike averred. "Listen up. Hear that? Gunfire." From the direction of Elkhorn Tavern to the east came sporadic fire. "That's where the real battle is, there and at Pea Ridge right behind the town. Let McCulloch deal with the Yankees at Leetown. We'll head for Elkhorn Tavern. Gallop your regiment, Colonel. We will prevail this day!"

John Drew assembled his men and rode off behind Pike's Indian Brigade. Drew knew that less than three miles down the road they would ride into the teeth of a storm so fierce there was no way out.

In the fields south and east of Leetown were Union batteries that opened fire when they spotted the galloping Confederate cavalry. John Drew got his men halted and studied the battlefield, definitely not of his choosing.

If they ran, they would be cut down by the artillery. No fewer than a half-dozen other regiments moved across the prairie toward them. There was only one hope for survival. Retreat. Retreat to the wooded area on the north side of the road.

"Bugler, sound retreat!" John Drew bellowed, his voice faint in the roar of musket and cannonade. His Cherokee Mounted Rifles readily obeyed, but Drew's heart leaped to his throat when he saw rank upon rank of men, both on foot and mounted, waiting in the trees where he had sought refuge.

Too late. It was too late to issue any other command that would not get all his men killed. They charged headlong into the woods along the north side of the Bentonville Road.

The Battle of Pea Ridge
March 7, 1862

"Hold your fire," Stand Watie shouted to his men. "Don't fire!" He had to use all his willpower to keep from remaining silent and letting his and Sims's men open fire on John Drew's regiment. The two regiments had come through the woods, seen the Union batteries forming in the field beyond, and had grouped for an attack. It came as a complete surprise when he recognized John Drew's unit riding down the road and past the deadly artillery.

"Watie!" cried Drew, recognizing whom he faced in the forest. From behind him sang deadly musket balls and occasional cannon fire. The Federals were as startled by John Drew's sudden appearance as Watie.

"Get to cover or they'll shoot you in the back!" came Albert Pike's insistent and accurate command. His brigade tramped past Watie's position, dropping to their bellies and getting ready to fire across the flat prairie where Watie had intended to launch his attack. The general joined Sims, Watie, and John Drew.

"What a complete disaster," Colonel Drew said. "We're lucky we didn't get killed."

"You are lucky," said Watie, glowering. How he had wanted to order his men to fire on Drew, but he could not after seeing Pike and his Indian Brigade still accompanying Drew.

"Enough chitchat," Pike said. "We weren't expecting Curtis and his men to be on our necks like this. What's out there, Stand?"

"A three-gun battery," Watie said quickly. "Colonel Sims and I were preparing an attack. We realized the road is a vital link. Cut it, and Van Dorn's force will be divided. We have to hold it."

"Too true. I wish the old boy were in better shape," Pike muttered.

"What do you mean?" demanded John Drew.

"Van Dorn's so sick he was going into battle in an ambulance," Pike said. "This is a critical battle, and cannot be put off."

"That's why nothing is going right," grumbled Drew. "Our commander's sick! He's in no condition to lead!"

Albert Pike slapped his hands against his arms to warm them as he stared off into the distance. "There's more 'n that going wrong, Colonel," he said. "What were you planning to do, Stand?" From the line of Pike's infantry came sporadic gunfire, men thinking they had good shots at bluecoats. From all Watie had seen, hitting a Federal at this distance would take more luck than skill.

"Colonel Sims and I were going to commit to a full frontal assault." Watie knew how foolish that sounded now, but Pike had asked. If they had gotten halfway across the open area near the road before the Federals opened up on them they would have been fortunate.

"Hold back. Let me see who else is in the field." Pike studied the length of road, rubbed his eyes, and then began scribbling orders. He whistled loudly and got a courier over to him. He thrust the tattered piece of paper into the boy's hands. "Give my regards to the brigade commander to our east. Have him charge the Federals as a diversion while we take the artillery battery."

The courier vanished like smoke in a high wind. Pike stroked his bushy beard as he thought and studied the daunting array of Union soldiers he faced.

"We'll take a thousand men straight away, along with all of Sims's men, and kick up a ruckus. Watie, you and Drew move your regiments forward and take that battery yonder. Capture it if you can, and turn the cannon back on the Union troopers down near Little Sugar Creek. If you can't do that, then blow the gun to hell and gone. I don't want any more southern blood shed because of a trio of three-pounders."

Albert Pike never looked to see if either of the Cherokee officers agreed with his scheme. He lifted his hand and gave the order for the attack, the diversion already moving into the field to the east.

Drew and Watie glared at one another, then went about getting their men ready. Stand Watie called, "Anderson, move 'em out now! For glory!"

His regiment galloped to the attack, leaving John Drew's more disorganized one behind. Watie immediately saw the trouble this posed. He had pulled the fire from the cannon down on his own men. Cannonballs slashing through his ranks, he found his attack blunted and drifting west, away from the support of Pike and the others in the brigade.

"Dismount! Take cover," Watie ordered when he saw his men being picked out of their saddles by Federal snipers. Individual rifle fire became more deadly through its accuracy than the thundering cannon. Watie jumped off his horse, stumbled along, and finally skidded to a halt on his belly, letting his horse run free. He might have to fetch it later—if there was a later. His breath came fast, and he wondered if his heart might explode in his chest.

Looking around, he saw many of his regiment had taken cover in the gully cut through the prairie. It was shallow groove, hardly more than surface erosion, but enough to provide some small cover. He drew his pistol and chanced a look over the rim of the gully.

Dead soldiers littered the way like some gory highway toward the Union artillery battery. Taking it would be almost impossible. Then Watie saw John Drew doing the worst thing possible. Drew launched his all-out attack, either not knowing or not caring that his support had evaporated due to the witheringly accurate fire from the Union position.

"Attack, men, attack! Give 'em what for!" shouted Watie, seeing that John Drew might succeed—if there were a diversion. It might be the only way any of them left the field alive that day. Whooping like a brave on the warpath, Stand Watie led his men forward on foot, firing the best they could at the fortified positions to the south.

Somehow, through the tumult, Watie realized his diversion had worked. John Drew's regiment, along with Sims's Texans, had swarmed over the Union battlements. Watie's attack faltered when they encountered an entire Federal company retreating across the battlefield. They sank down and picked off one Yankee soldier after another, routing the company and sending the enemy away in confusion as extreme as that which stalked the Confederate ranks.

"The cannon," Watie yelled. "General Pike wants those cannon, men!"

With dozens of his troopers at his side, Watie made it over the top of the log-and-dirt walls constructed by the Union sappers. John Drew's men had preceded him. Watie stopped and stared at the carnage. The Union artillery crew had been scalped.

A bullet sailed past his head and took off his tall hat. Watie ducked and swung around, no longer caring about what Drew's men had done to the artillerists. Drew's and Sims's men were being pushed back across the field by a Union counterattack of gigantic proportions. If Watie didn't order his men to retreat, the position would be overrun by the Federals in a few minutes.

"Swing the guns around!" Watie called. "Aim them right on down their throats!" He put his own back to swinging the field pieces around. He made sure to keep his hands on the carriage, because the metal barrels were still hot from rapid firing. As soon as the guns were aimed in the direction of the advancing Yankee infantry, Watie grabbed a swab and applied it to the barrel to cool the metal. As he worked, so did three others of his cavalry troop who had some knowledge of the firing sequence. Gunpowder and wadding and ball were rammed down the cannon barrel while another man prepared the lanyard that would fire the piece.

"Clear out," Watie yelled. He clapped his hands over his ears as the others turned from the cannon. The cord tautened and the cannon bucked hard like a bronco, spitting out its deadly load into the center of the Union infantry. "Keep firing!" he yelled, going to help others with the remaining two guns. How long could he keep this up?

Watie wanted to order his men out of the artillery nest, but if he did so Confederate soldiers would die by the scores. It was a dilemma. To stay courted death. To leave meant death for even more Southerners.

Watie kept his men at their post long enough for Sims and Drew to get off the field and give Watie a chance to see how disastrous this battle had been for the rest of the Confederate forces. Bodies were strewn everywhere—and blood-soaked gray predominated in uniform color. But the three guns turned on their former masters had created confusion in the Union ranks long enough to give Albert Pike the chance to regroup and retreat northeast toward Elkhorn Tavern.

Only when Watie saw that Pike was clear of the action, and that maintaining his own post would be suicidal, did he order the guns blown up with the remaining powder.

"Back to the woods!" he shouted. Some of his men had miraculously recaptured their horses and lent a hand so others could ride with them. Watie found himself and Tom Anderson trudging along side by side. Tom shot him a crooked grin.

"Can't be like old times, Stand, since we never got shot at like this. Don't remember any bear comin' at us with bayonets, either."

Watie had to laugh in spite of the debacle. So many of their men had fallen in the fight, but Tom knew just the right thing to keep him from despairing over much. They lowered their heads and picked up the pace, only occasionally dodging bullets from the Union soldiers. Both sides were demoralized by the slaughter.

Barely had Watie regained the dubious safety of the forest from where they had mounted their attack then John Drew rode over, furious.

"You fired into my men with those cannon!" he shouted. "You tried to kill me!"

"I was shooting to cover your retreat," Watie snapped. "Why'd your men have to scalp the bluecoats?"

"Enough of that, men," Albert Pike said, riding over. His jacket had been reduced to tatters, leaving him more like an Indian than many in Watie's Cherokee regiment. "Things have not gone well," he said, with a masterful understatement. "All the other senior officers are either dead or missing in action, leaving me in command."

John Drew snorted in disgust and sawed at the reins of his horse to return to his unit. Pike stared after him, frowning.

"What's got him all het up?"

"What are your orders, sir?" Watie asked. "I don't think any of us are up for another sally."

Albert Pike looked around. Watie's men were in the best condition—and that said little. They were not militarily trained. The organized fire from the Union soldiers had caused a fear to begin eating away at them, in spite of their long months in the Cherokee Mounted Rifles. They were used to more individual action, racing along and picking off small bands of renegades, not the intense hand-to-hand fighting and bombardment they had endured this day.

John Drew's regiment was in even greater disorder.

"My own brigade's not for it, either," Pike admitted. The smoke cleared from the field and showed the ruin left behind. "We need to send out runners to contact senior officers and find out what Van Dorn is planning. We sure as hell don't want to sit out here with our arses exposed to Gruesel's regiment." Pike pointed in the direction of the Union line. "Those men have seen battle back East, and aren't going to break and run. They're veterans of a dozen battles bloodier than this one."

Watie bristled at this, but Pike soothed him. "Not saying anything ag'in your braves, Stand. Just a fact of life. Different kind of fighting needed here." Pike turned and shouted to John Drew, "Get your men formed at the rear of the 6th Texas Cavalry Regiment, Colonel Drew. Follow them into battle and join the fight in your own fashion."

"Not even two P.M., and already I can taste defeat," muttered Pike. He turned to take messages from couriers looking both frightened and determined.

"What are our orders?" asked Watie, after Pike finished reading the messages.

"Seems things are worse than I thought. Jim McIntosh is dead."

"Colonel McIntosh? The one who ran down Opothleya-hola?"

"Got promoted to brigadier in time to get himself killed. Worse, General McCulloch is dead, too. And Colonel Hébert from Louisiana was captured. I knew I was top dog in this field. I didn't realize I would be in command of most of this damned army."

Watie let Pike stew for a few minutes and come to a decision.

"I don't know what McIntosh or McCulloch were supposed to do during battle, and I don't know where the rest of our forces are. Worst of all, I have no idea what we are facing." He stared across the body-strewn field. "Colonel Watie, prepare your men. We're moving out to rejoin General Van Dorn's main force at Elkhorn Tavern south of Pea Ridge. I want a scout out to Round Top, that little hill we passed on the road last night. Get to it, get to it!" he shouted.

Watie did the best he could to get his men into a semblance of order. He kept glancing over his shoulder in the direction of the Union troops. The only thing letting the Confederate forces escape was an equal disarray among the ranks of the bluecoats. They could not possibly know how many Confederate officers had been killed, and that Pike knew nothing of the overall battle plans.

If they had, they would have won the day before Watie got his men mounted, mostly on other troopers' horses. Whether the original riders were dead or had simply slunk off, he neither knew nor cared. Many of the mounts looked to be from John Drew's regiment. The thought of the other Cherokee leader made Watie seethe with anger. Scalping the Federals was one thing, denouncing him for firing on Drew's retreating men was something else.

Those in Watie's regiment might not be full-bloods, but they were Cherokee. They were *all* Cherokee.

Why didn't John Drew understand that?

"Move out!" Watie commanded, getting his men onto the road and heading toward Elkhorn Tavern. As he rode with his men in a ragged line down the road, Watie jumped. Pike lacked the caissons to haul along the artillery used by other Confederate regiments, so he was blowing up the field pieces to keep them from falling into Union hands. From all Watie could tell, the general wasn't doing too good a job of it. The barrels were intact.

He shrugged it off. He had not done a very good job destroying the three Union cannon he and his men had captured. It would take a spell for the artillerists to get wood together to rebuild the caissons. By then Pike ought to have rejoined Van Dorn's main force.

Watie wanted to think someone was in charge who had an idea where and how the battle was to proceed. Now, too many officers had been killed. As he rode, he realized the reason so many officers were dead was because their troops had been slaughtered, also. Never had he seen such heaps of bodies, slowly beginning to stink in the weak March sun.

"Stand. Stand!" came Albert Pike's gruff voice. "You get your regiment on down to Elkhorn Tavern. Take Drew's with you."

Stand Watie blinked in the sun and looked around. Then he said, "I don't know where Drew is."

"Wasn't he told to retreat with the rest of you?"

Watie said nothing. There was nothing to say. Colonel John Drew had been left in the woods with no support against the advancing tide of a powerful Union army. Not too strangely, Watie did not consider it much of a loss if the Confederates lost the services of Drew and his Kee-toowah-riddled regiment.

Deserted
March 8, 1862

"Colonel Drew, there's a powerful lot of Federals comin'
at us!" complained the corporal. "If you don't give no
orders, I'm gettin' out of here!"

John Drew made his way through the tangle of dead
undergrowth at the edge of the forest and saw what the
soldier meant. Line after line of advancing Union infantry
meant trouble. Big trouble.

"Get a message to General Pike," Drew ordered. "We
might be in position to attack." The Cherokee Mounted
Rifles formed the extreme flank of Albert Pike's forces—or
what remained of them. He could either attack in concert
with other units in the brigade, or he could tell his men
to hightail it through the forest.

"Colonel, there's nobody out there. They left us
hangin'!"

"Retreat," John Drew ordered, knowing he could never
get his men into a skirmish line to meet the approaching
soldiers. Even if it were possible, his regiment would be
outnumbered ten to one. Or more.

"Sir, most all the boys are already makin' tracks outta
here," the corporal said.

John Drew retraced his steps and mounted. He rode

about what remained of his command for a few minutes, urging his non-coms and the officers he could find to regroup after retreating toward Leetown southwest of their current position. Drew had no idea if he had told his men to walk into the bayonets of Union infantry or if there would be relative safety there. Camp Stephens, miles beyond Leetown, had provided temporary quarters for his regiment on the way north, and might again as they made their way back to Indian Territory.

A bullet sang past Drew's horse, spooking it. He regained control and decided it was time to exercise his leadership in the retreat.

He let out a whoop and took off through the woods, hoping others in the regiment would see him and know this was the way to safety. Drew wasn't sure how long he rode, but when his horse began stumbling from exhaustion he reined back and dismounted to walk the animal before it died under him.

To his surprise he had come out on a road. But what road? Drew signaled to others beating their retreat to assemble. A few resisted, preferring to go their own way, but a lieutenant and two sergeants obeyed and herded the soldiers toward their commander. As they worked to regroup, Drew studied the road. Crusts of ice remained in the deep ruts, but some had turned to mud, showing recent passage of heavily laden wagons.

"That way, Colonel," a sergeant said. "The wagons went that way."

"How can you tell?" John Drew was no tracker, and figuring out which way the wagons had gone with the mud so sloppy and not holding hoofprints was beyond him.

"I see one all broke down. It was pushed off the road into a ditch."

John Drew walked along the road until he saw what the sergeant already had from his higher vantage. He nodded. This was a Confederate baggage wagon. Whoever the supplies belonged to, they obviously needed protection. The wagon had been abandoned because, John Drew reasoned, there had not been enough soldiers to help repair it.

"Down the road. That way," he ordered, getting into the saddle again. His rump hurt, and the horse protested, but John Drew felt better now than he had since they had overridden the Federal artillery battery. Progress proved slow but sure, and stragglers joined the thin line until he had regained almost half his unit by the time he rode into Camp Stephens.

"Who goes there?" barked a sentry.

"Colonel John Drew's First Cherokee Mounted Rifles, come to rejoin General Van Dorn's forces," he reported. The sentry nervously fingered his rifle and then backed off.

"Just a minute, Colonel. Lemme report to the officer of the guard."

Drew ordered his men off their horses, those who still rode at all, and then dismounted, himself. It felt good not to be astride the stumbling monster. He wished he had a horse as strong and durable as the one Stand Watie rode.

"Colonel," greeted a brusque officer sporting similar rank on his shoulders. "I'm Stone, Sixth Texas Cavalry. Glad you made it. Were you with Pike?"

"I was. They retreated and we . . . got cut off from the rest," Drew said, not wanting to make the accusation of being deliberately abandoned because of Watie's perfidy.

"A real mess out there," Colonel Stone said, shaking his head sadly. "I was ordered to protect our main supply train by General Pike, but the attack never came."

"You outran them?"

"More 'n likely they're as discombobulated as we are. Not that that's any consolation. I lost damned near half my men. How about you?"

"Can't tell, not yet. Might be at least that, since we never got the retreat order in time."

"We're reforming a brigade," Stone said. "Colonel Cooper's supposed to be arriving from Indian Territory any time now with reinforcements. I reckon you know him?"

"I do, sir," John Drew said stiffly.

"Heard tell there was some disagreement in their rank over fighting in Arkansas. What's the word on that? You boys agreed not to fight 'cept in Indian Territory?"

"There is that part of the treaty Chief Ross was leery about," John Drew said. "There is also the fact our soldiers have not been paid."

Stone lifted his bushy eyebrows and said, "Not what I heard. Thought a heap of gold and scrip had gone your way. Leastwise, that's what I was told to explain why I couldn't get new uniforms and more rifles for *my* men."

"No one in *my* regiment is getting rich," John Drew said, suspecting Stand Watie had made some illicit arrangement with the higher-ups in the CSA to steal the lion's share of this money.

"Well, our artillery is low on ammunition, and it doesn't look like General Van Dorn or General Price is going to be around long enough to defend Elkhorn Tavern. Our supply train has food and muskets, but no powder or bullets."

"Are we to escort the train to Van Dorn?" asked John Drew, not wanting to involve his men in any more fighting. They had done well, and he was loath to engage the Union Army again. It was time his regiment returned to Indian Territory, where they were needed—and where they belonged. Drew was surprised John Ross had not insisted on following the letter of the treaty keeping all Cherokee soldiers within the boundaries of the Nation.

"You two, come here!" barked a one-star general from the back of a supply wagon rattling through the camp. Both Stone and Drew hurried over and saluted.

"Both of you, get your men ready and escort a supply train to Elkhorn Tavern for General Van Dorn's use."

"Sir, who are you?" asked Drew.

"Martin Green," the general said testily. "There's no time to quibble over chain of command. The general needs supplies in a hurry if he is to defend Pea Ridge. Union artillery is cutting his line to ribbons, and he has too little shell to reply in kind. If he doesn't get the ammunition and other supplies *now*, there is no way the line can be held."

Drew glanced at Stone, who was saluting briskly and saying, "Right away, sir!"

John Drew also saluted, and backed off as the wagon where General Green held court rattled on its way. Camp Stephens was bustling with activity. The best Drew could tell, it was all aimed at supporting the Confederate effort down the road.

"Lieutenant!" John Drew barked. "Get the men mounted. We're escorting that train." He pointed to a line of wagons already leaving the camp, heading down the road toward Elm Springs and eventually Elkhorn Tavern.

With the Texas cavalry leading and John Drew's trailing, they rode with the wagon train through the afternoon and into late evening. Drew saw how tired his men were, and came to a decision when the supply train came to a halt for a brief rest. He went to find Colonel Stone. The Texan looked peaked and hardly up for pressing on, as the wagonmaster intended.

"Colonel," said Drew. "I'm taking my men toward Cincinnati, Arkansas, with what baggage we can claim as our own."

"What? You can't! We have to get these supplies to Van Dorn."

"Colonel, we've done what we can, and fulfilled our mission. We are sorely needed back home, in the Cherokee Nation."

"You got other orders, then you must obey them," said Stone. "You'll be missed, but I wish you well."

"And I you, sir," John Drew said. He shook hands with the Texan, then returned to his tired men. It took the better part of an hour to get them turned and headed home, but there was a lighter attitude among them, and it seemed as if their horses understood they were going home and approved the change of destination.

John Drew was pleased. He had made the right decision. They were needed in Tahlequah.

Honor Amid Death
March 8, 1862

"You'd think there would be more to worry over than this," grumbled Watie's adjutant. Tom Anderson rested his hand on the butt of his pistol and looked disgusted. "In the middle of a real battle, Van Dorn issues a condemnation for scalpin' Union soldiers. Those are the same men that'd have killed us, given the chance. What's the difference if they went to the Happy Hunting Ground without their hair?"

"Drew's men did it, not ours," Stand Watie said. "I have a reply to the general stating our regiment did not lift any scalps, but I'm getting fed up with being accused of something none of my command's done."

"Well, Stand, you be careful how you say that. I think I saw one or two of ours doing a little hair cutting," Tom said. "Not many, but a few, in the heat of battle. The Yankees were comin' at us pretty strong, and tempers flared."

Watie heaved a deep sigh of resignation. It had been bad enough his messenger had been unable to find John Drew to inform him of the retreat. He wasn't sure if Albert Pike blamed him for the way the Cherokee regiments were divided in battle, but the general had a pile on his plate to worry about. He had been given command of a significant portion of the Confederate army, and didn't even know who had survived the first disastrous day of battle at Pea Ridge.

"Have any of our patrols reported back?" Watie asked, wanting to change the subject. The Confederate Army had taken severe casualties. From the incessant bombardment by the Union batteries, it seemed they might take even more if they didn't learn how and where the enemy was arrayed against them—and get some supplies.

General Pike had reached Elkhorn Tavern to find most of Van Dorn's supplies used up or destroyed. On his own initiative, he had sent word to General Green at Camp Stephens to re-supply as quickly as possible, but the baggage train was slow in coming since it had to swing north on the Bentonville Detour before curving around Pea Ridge and into Elkhorn Tavern. Watie wished the same could be said of the Federals. The Federals smelled victory, and were pressing in from three fronts. All that had saved Van Dorn's command so far was the holding of the higher elevation of Pea Ridge north of Elkhorn Tavern.

"Stand, come on over here," came Pike's gruff voice. Watie hurried to the general's side. With the bushy-bearded man were four colonels. Watie recognized one, but didn't know his name. The other three were so wounded by various degrees that they had difficulty moving. He had never set eyes on any of them before, and reckoned they might be from the Missouri volunteers or even the Louisiana detachment that had joined the battle.

"Men, we got our work cut out for us. It's not going to be pretty. The damn Yankees have us fenced off." Punctuating his words were loud belches from Federal artillery. "We can't do a flanking maneuver, since we don't have the men required. We're starving, and don't have much left in the way of ammunition. Martin Green's sent supplies, but there's no word of them gettin' farther than Elm Springs."

"Sir, from reconnaissance by my scouts, there's nothing

we can do except retreat," one of the more heavily wounded colonels said in a thick Southern accent. "I do not quit the field lightly, I assure you, sir, but we must preserve what we can to fight another day."

"General Van Dorn's in a sorry way," Albert Pike said, "but he wants to fight on. I need to know what strengths I can count on." Pike looked around the small, dispirited circle of faces. "It's not going to be pretty, gentlemen. I haven't commanded a unit this size since the Mexican War, and I don't rightly know what I've got to work with."

"Disheartened, wounded men," grumbled the colonel Watie thought he had seen before. "General, I won't lie to you. My men would follow me all the way to the U.S. Capitol, fighting every inch of the way, but there's no chance of surviving this. Pea Ridge has done us in."

"Colonel Watie?" Albert Pike looked to Stand Watie for support.

"They're right. My scouts tell me we might use what cannon we have to lay down covering fire, if we retreat to the west. There's some Federal infantry there, but they haven't been able to strengthen it sufficiently to stop us because of our own artillery fire."

Pike paced to and fro, chewed on his lower lip, and ran his tongue over his thick mustache as he worried over the problem. He came to attention.

"Gentlemen, I am not a quitter, and retreat is a disgraceful thing to do. However, it is more disgraceful to lose my entire command through bullheaded patriotism. My Indian Regiment has fought with the best the abolitionists can throw ag'in us, and we have triumphed. However, we have blundered too many times in troop movement and support to win this day. Prepare for retreat, fighting as you go, toward the west and Camp Stephen."

Stand Watie started to point out that Leetown was in Federal hands and going on the road would put them in danger, but he held his tongue. The others had to know this as well as he did. The other colonels left hastily, but Albert Pike motioned for Watie to remain.

"Stand, I'm going to catch holy hell for this when I tell Van Dorn what has to be done, but I want you with me as we protect the rear. I want the others to be sure to get away—and I want to be certain as I can be that my own men can get back to Indian Territory. You and your Cherokee Mounted Rifles are the best I have left to guarantee that. Can I count on you?"

"Yes, sir. All the way back to the Cherokee Nation!" Watie was proud that Pike thought so highly of him, even if it put him and his command in jeopardy.

"Good," Pike said, slapping Watie on the shoulder. "Now get your men fed and watered and as rested as possible. We are going to a picnic in hell 'fore this day's over."

Watie took time to write his Sarah a short letter, in case he was not among those who survived. Finishing his letter and stuffing it into the front of his uniform jacket, he walked among his camped men, talking with them about their families, their farms, their dreams. Then he got them in the saddle and ready for the retreat from Pea Ridge, knowing some of them would never see their families or farms again, much less dream of a future filled with brightness and peace.

The only comfort Stand Watie took was in knowing his son Saladin was safely back home.

The battle simply to escape was brutal. By the time Watie's regiment reached Cincinnati, Arkansas, guarding Albert Pike's rear the whole way, word came that Van Dorn's army had lost eleven hundred killed, twenty-five hundred wounded, and another sixteen hundred captured or missing.

But Stand Watie's First Cherokee Mounted Rifles had gotten away—if not intact, then with most of its men still in the saddle.

Furlough
March 22, 1862

"We're surrounded! They'll kill us all!" cried John Drew.

"Colonel, calm yourself," said John Ross. For all the soothing words from the Cherokee's principal chief, he shared his military commander's uneasiness. Nothing had been going well since the Battle of Pea Ridge. "We will see that Watie's men do not scalp us, as they seem to have done to those Union soldiers."

Spread on the desk in front of him were clippings from various Northern newspapers. John Ross closed his tired eyes and felt the weight of long, hard years on him. Always there was political conflict. That he was used to. The kind of war being waged in the news was something he could deal with. John Drew's concern went farther, though, than dealing with reporters and editors—Stand Watie's entire regiment had been given furlough in Tahlequah, giving rise to real fear that those wild savages might attack Rose Cottage. Park Hill was only a few miles from the center of the Cherokee Nation, and Ross valued this house highly.

He valued his life even more. It was good that he had moved—again—with the money given him for rent on the Neutral Lands and scrip for payment of the soldiers. If Watie came here, he would never capture the treasury.

"Watie's men have been paid, as have yours. That will keep them occupied for a spell," John Ross said.

"When Watie finds you paid my regiment in gold and his in that worthless Confederate paper, he is going to come after our scalps."

"He seems inclined to do that, doesn't he?" John Ross lifted the first of the clippings he had been sent and studied it. The *Boston Transcript* declared:

> The meanest, most rascally, the most malevolent of the rebels who are at war with the United States Government, are said to be recreant Yankees. Albert Pike is one of those.

John Drew smiled slightly when he read the rest of the article, comparing Pike with a poisonous reptile. He dropped the newspaper article and leafed through a pamphlet calling scalping of the artillerists an act of barbarism conducted by savages.

"Uncivilized is the thread running through this tapestry of disgrace," Ross said. "They blame Albert Pike for not keeping good order, and you, Colonel, are accusing Watie's men of perpetrating these horrors on captured Union soldiers."

"They did," John Drew said sullenly. John Ross fingered the papers and leaned back. He had seen much of the correspondence between Van Dorn and the Union commander Curtis. There had been atrocities on both sides.

Some of Van Dorn's men had been murdered after they surrendered—Germans, Van Dorn had said.

And the scalpings. Cherokee, Curtis had said.

"We need to let everyone know as soon as possible," John Drew said. "Albert Pike is riding around telling everyone how brave Watie and his men were. He's ignoring the role of my regiment!"

"I've noticed that," Ross said, still thinking hard. It was a difficult balance he had to maintain. Watie had to be cut down to size and saddled with the scalping charges levied by Benjamin Wade and his Committee on the Conduct of the Present War. Ross could deflect criticism of his own troops—John Drew's—if the northerner focused his attention solely on Watie's regiment. With Pike and Watie on the receiving end of the deadly propaganda bullets, he could weaken them politically and move to unify his slipping control over the Cherokee Nation.

It might mean a truce with Opothleyahola, although the Creek chief was no longer a power as long as he was in exile in Kansas. John Ross knew there were many things he could do to solidify his authority.

"We will make these newspaper reports available to our Cherokee language paper," Ross decided. "The full-bloods will become incensed at what the mixed-bloods are doing."

"The Keetoowah Society backs us fully now, Chief," John Drew said.

"We need more than the Pins to shore up our support," Ross said thoughtfully. "We need the ordinary settler, the citizen who plows his land and harvests his crop, coming to us to find what Watie is really doing. I fear it means abandoning Albert Pike as an ally, because he must be painted with the same brush as Watie."

"Watie will try to kill you. His men are rowdy. They'll ride here and string you up if they think you are plotting against them."

John Ross smiled wanly. "Colonel, Watie would string me up, as you put it, for no reason. Bring your regiment in and bivouac them around Park Hill. Let me know if General Pike protests the movement, and I shall tend to him."

"What of Watie?"

"What of him?" John Ross picked up a clipping from the *Chicago Tribune* and read with some distaste their story of scalping wounded and helpless soldiers. The *New York Tribune* called Pike a "ferocious fish." Soon enough the papers would know Stand Watie's name, and his part in the brutal slaughter at Pea Ridge.

Neosho, Missouri
April 26, 1862

"We are finally moving to engage the Federals," Watie said, looking over General Pike's orders. "I have been worried since Pea Ridge how vulnerable the Nation was to Union attack."

"Worry about more than that, Father," cautioned Saladin Watie, waving a thick sheaf of newspaper clippings around like a tomahawk. "John Ross attacks you at every turn."

"Pah, he's always done that."

"He is trying to saddle you with scalping the artillerists, when it was John Drew's men who did the crime."

"There were Texans with Drew," Watie said, his mind already across the border into Missouri on the raid Albert Pike had sanctioned. "They've done this before." He remembered the Battle of Wilson Creek and how overly enthusiastic the Texans had become at their victory. Watie smiled wryly, thinking none of the Texans would ever be welcomed into the Five Civilized Tribes.

"But Ross has others accuse you and our men so he doesn't sully his own hands," Saladin said, anger growing. His lips thinned to a line. "Think of how this affects Mother and my brothers and sisters."

"They might read the lies, but they know me. That means they know the truth. I have told every last soldier in my command that they will be up on charges if they scalp any enemy."

Watie listened to his son's protests with half an ear. It was time to move on from the defeat at Pea Ridge, and he was glad Albert Pike was doing it. After their retreat from the ridge to Camp Stephens, Watie had found John Drew had passed through already, stealing valuable supplies on his irresponsible retreat to Indian Territory. General Pike had ordered Watie back to Tahlequah for a furlough, then to Cowskin Prairie to be in position to protect the northern border again while he moved south with the main body of Indian soldiers to Choctaw country at Boggy Depot. Watie had heard John Drew had split his command, leaving some to protect John Ross at Park Hill and sending the rest to Webber's Falls on the Arkansas River. Such a scattering of Confederate forces left the Cherokee Nation open to immediate Union attack.

Luckily, Curtis had not followed through with his victory at Pea Ridge. If he had, all of Indian Territory might have fallen to the Federals.

"Father!"

"What? Oh, sorry, Saladin. I was thinking about going into Missouri. We have to do well, to erase any of John Ross's lies about us, and to show the Federals they dare not attack us."

"They will come through Kansas, Father. I've shown you how they can sweep through the middle of our nation and capture Tahlequah."

"Tahlequah? That's only the capital," Watie countered. "They will go to Park Hill and capture John Ross, because they think taking our principal chief will bring us to our knees." He laughed harshly. Watie wished the Federals would do just that. It might cement his own authority in the Cherokee Nation.

Besides, John Ross's sympathies lay more with the United States than with the Confederate States.

"Rider coming, sir!" called a sentry. "Looks to be a courier. No, not just a courier. It's Colonel Coffee himself come to visit."

"No, don't go, Saladin," Watie said when his son started to leave. "I want you to hear everything he has to say. It'll stand you in good stead when you have command of your own regiment."

"That's rushing things, Father," Saladin said, laughing. Watie looked at his son and glowed with pride. Then he had to turn to greet Colonel John T. Coffee.

"Colonel, welcome to my camp."

"I envy you, Colonel Watie. You have houses to quarter your men."

"We took over buildings abandoned when the Federals began their raids."

"I received orders from General Pike," Coffee said, launching into the heart of the matter. "We go against the Union First Missouri Cavalry Regiment. They have been raiding, but mostly Pike wants to prevent them from advancing south along the Mississippi and dividing Indian Territory from the rest of the South."

Watie nodded. He had considered this himself. Rumors abounded of imminent invasion from Kansas. If the Union 1st Cavalry held territory along the river, it prevented Earl Van Dorn from sending reinforcements from Arkansas—if Van Dorn remained in charge much longer. After Pea Ridge, Watie doubted it was possible for the general to keep his command.

"Are your men ready to fight, Colonel?" asked Coffee. He twirled his mustache and smiled, obviously ready for the attack himself.

"Race you there, Colonel," Watie said, returning the smile. This would be something to write home to Sarah and the younger children about.

* * *

"My company is in position for attack, Colonel," Saladin Watie reported. "We will take them unawares."

Watie nodded. Saladin wheeled his horse about and trotted off to prepare for the charge. Spread out in the hollow near Neosho lounged the Federal regiment, enjoying a spring afternoon's warm sun and not expecting anything more than an occasional bug bite.

They would be stung sorely. Watie drew his pistol and held it high. Looking along his line he saw Saladin was prepared, as were the other company commanders. On the far flank rode Tom Anderson, with William Penn Adair, back from scouting, at the other end of the line. At exactly 2:00 P.M. Stand Watie fired the pistol, giving the order for the Confederate force to attack.

With a loud whoop, he put his spurs to his horse and charged, the Cherokee Mounted Rifles in a long, thin, rippling line on either side. Out of the corner of his eye he saw Colonel Coffee's cavalry also advancing at a decent clip. They were moving more slowly, ready to support Watie's troops should it be necessary and to cut off any retreat by the Federals.

The attack went exactly as planned. Watie's men cut through the camp, scattering men and separating them from their ammo dump. Saladin Watie brought his company up to take possession of the arms and ammunition while the rest of the regiment swung back on the far side of the enemy camp, ready for another pass.

Stand Watie took some satisfaction in seeing how his regiment formed one side of the steel trap, and Colonel Coffee's the other. Watie again fired and set his men sweeping forward. This time the element of surprise was gone, and the fighting more intense, but having cut off the Federals from their ammunition made it a one-sided battle.

"Get 'em!" Watie cried. "Go after them. Capture them!"

"Colonel, wait!" Coffee yelled. "Destroy what you can and then retire."

"We have them!" protested Watie. "We shouldn't retreat!"

"This is only half their unit. The rest are coming double-time from the town."

The words hardly left Coffee's lips when withering fire cut through the camp from a rise to the east, overlooking Neosho. Watie worked to regroup his men and get them heading back south. He rode to where Saladin worked to lay powder trails to kegs.

"Destroy it. Fire the dump now!" ordered Watie. "We can't stay!"

He fired in the direction of a squad of bluecoats trying to regain their ammunition dump. He fired until his pistol came up empty. Watie saw Saladin light the fuse with a sputtering lucifer. It sizzled as it slowly crept toward the kegs of black powder.

"Come on."

Together, father and son rode from the Union camp. When they were less than halfway up the slope to the south where the bulk of their regiment had already retreated, a huge explosion slammed into them. Stand Watie slumped forward, got his horse trotting again, and then reached the rise. Saladin Watie struggled on foot to reach safety, his horse having been shot out from under him, but Watie saw his son was in no danger. The camp burned, blazing splinters from the exploded powder kegs setting fire to anything flammable.

"Report!" barked Watie. He looked left and right.

"How bad was it, Father?" asked Saladin. He swatted out smoldering spots on his uniform. He reached for his hat, but it lay halfway back down the hill. His curly hair fluttered on the hot wind blowing uphill from the camp.

"Two killed, five wounded. Some captured," Stand Watie said. "We killed at least thirty, and I see three captured Federals."

William Adair had been most active taking prisoners, and had three frightened bluecoats under the watchful eye of his scouts. Tom Anderson struggled to get his company assembled. They had been scattered during the retreat under fire from the Neosho reinforcements, but it was nothing the adjutant could not deal with.

"A good day," Saladin Watie declared.

"A good day," Watie agreed. He wished for many more. It was the only way he could prevent a Union invasion of his homeland.

Promote!
May 3, 1862

General Albert Pike dismounted and walked his horse into Fort Gibson. The fort was small but a vital one, providing much of the supplies for his army. He only wished John Ross had not insisted on putting his nephew in charge. Somehow, Pike felt uneasy every time he had to ask Lieutenant Colonel Will Ross for ammunition or uniforms, or anything else. It was as if the fort commander kept a list, and expected offsetting favors for what the Confederate command provided for its field soldiers.

"General, welcome to Fort Gibson," greeted Ross. He was tall, slender, and all too well-groomed for Pike's comfort. The general had ridden through mud and been bitten by mosquitoes and felt as if he had wallowed in a pig slop for the past three days as he traveled northward from Boggy Depot.

Pike took some pleasure in thrusting out his grimy hand. Will Ross tentatively shook it, as if he might get some odious disease from his commanding officer.

"This fort's surely a sight for sore eyes," he told Ross. "Not that my eyes are all that's sore." He rubbed his rump to indicate the long days in the saddle. "First of all, do you have any communiqués from General Beauregard?"

"In my office, sir," Ross said. They turned to their right and walked along the covered porch to the small office where Ross commanded the entire post. Ross scooped up a pile of letters and handed them to Pike, who pawed through them.

"Here it is," Pike said, opening an official envelope. He scanned the contents, then shrugged.

"Good news?" asked Will Ross.

"General Van Dorn has been replaced by Major General Thomas Hindmann as commander of the Trans-Mississippi District."

"Pea Ridge," muttered Ross.

"There is that, but the threat to the entire district is of some concern to General Beauregard. Union forces are massing along our borders. He fears invasion will come before the end of summer."

"I have heard that, sir," Ross said. Pike tensed at the tone the man used. Something was coming he had not anticipated. What?

"You see, General," Ross went on, "it would please my uncle greatly if I were promoted to general. With your good intervention, perhaps with Hindmann or even General Beauregard also recommending me, I am sure it would be easily accomplished."

"General?" Pike had expected many things, but not this.

"Chief Ross is a man who remembers good deeds—and always punishes those who do not have the best interests of the Cherokee Nation at heart."

Pike knew a threat when he heard one and bristled.

"I am sure the Confederate War Department would frown on promotion of an officer whose command has, in large part, deserted to the enemy."

"John Drew's problems are not mine."

"They are, since you are technically attached to his regiment. Moreover, you were his adjutant. And a two rank jump is most unusual, except in a field brevet. What field experience do you have, Lieutenant Colonel Ross?"

"There might be some, should I go to command the company guarding my uncle's home."

Pike snorted and shook his head. "In light of the publicity the two regiments of Cherokee Mounted Rifles have received over the unpleasantness at Pea Ridge, I doubt the War Department would look kindly on any of us being promoted."

Pike recoiled slightly when Ross slammed his hand on his desk, making the papers jump. If there had been any chance Ross would get a recommendation for promotion, this ended it. Pike knew if this undeserved promotion were ever pushed through political channels it would give Chief Ross a means of directly controlling Stand Watie. Albert Pike did not like the way he was being used as a pawn and placed between two groups vying for power within their tribe.

If he had to choose, he would prefer having Stand Watie riding at his shoulder to William Potter Ross.

Into Missouri Again
May 31, 1862

"Are the men ready, William?" Stand Watie asked his aide. William Penn Adair looked left and right, then nodded.

"All ready, Colonel. I got chewed out when I told one commander he was going to lead our reserve company. He didn't like the idea the head of the scouts was giving him orders like that."

"Tell him I'll see him court-martialed if he disobeys. We can't all be at the front when it comes to fighting. And it's nobody's fault Tom's laid up with the ague so bad he can't ride."

"He said," William went on, "that this was the first important thrust into enemy territory."

"We know the terrain," Watie agreed. The region around Neosho, Missouri, was familiar to him and his soldiers from their earlier victory. William had done a good job here before, and Watie wanted him in command with Tom sick. This time they rode alone, Colonel Coffee having been sent farther west to patrol the Kansas border. That was the chore Stand Watie had wanted, since reconnaissance bespoke of a major invasion soon. To blunt that attack or even turn it back would be a feather in any soldier's hat. For him to do it would erase General Beauregard's disdain for Indian soldiers. Watie had heard Pike's tale of how Will Ross had wanted a promotion to general, and how those back east were still dealing with the reports of Cherokee scalping Union soldiers.

A month earlier the Cherokee National Council had passed a resolution stating that the war be fought with dignity and mercy for the wounded and captured enemy. "No scalping" was the underlying, if unwritten, order. Watie had seen John Ross's hand in the decree, since it aimed only at Stand Watie's Cherokee Mounted Rifles, but such orders took on a double-edged utility. If John Drew or his soldiers scalped again, it would go harshly with him. All Watie had to do was be sure Colonel Drew did not falsely incriminate him. Given enough rope, John Drew would hang himself.

Watie hoped that the murdering John Ross was on the gallows with him when it happened.

"The captain was vehement about taking part, Colonel. He promised all manner of trouble if he wasn't up front during the battle." William Adair looked carefully at his commander. Watie turned and faced him squarely.

"I'll deal with this renegade later." Watie paused and smiled slowly. "Who *is* it? As if I didn't know already."

"You're right, Stand," William said, grinning crookedly. "But it's not because Saladin is your son that I put him in the reserve. It was his turn to provide support."

"Humility," Watie said. "It'll help him learn to do his duty and not look for the fancy medals." He had to walk a careful line with his son as a company commander. Too many privileges would destroy discipline in the ranks, but as a father he worried that his son would be injured. These were not easy raids they made.

"Regiment ready, sir," came the report from a junior lieutenant.

"At my command," Watie said, drawing his pistol. The

shallow depression where they had ambushed the Union 1st Calvary before was now devoid of soldiers, only the debris of the earlier battle left, but Watie knew that was not true of the area on the far side of the ridge. Rather than fire his pistol, Watie lowered it forcefully and pointed in the direction he wanted his regiment to advance. There would be time later for firing. Now stealth mattered more, if an entire regiment were to sneak up on the 10th Illinois Cavalry, supposedly encamped at Neosho.

Watie hoped his information was accurate. If he broke the back of the 10th Illinois, this would eliminate Neosho as a staging area for any attack into Indian Territory. The Cherokee Nation would be safe from yet another threat aimed directly at its heart.

Barely had the troopers ridden through the center of what had been the enemy campground when Watie swung about and looked to his right flank.

"William, what's going on over there?" Fear seized Watie, and he pushed it down. To panic now would jeopardize his entire command.

"I don't know, Colonel. Those aren't men from the Tenth," his head scout said, peering through binoculars. "From their insignia, it's another Missouri unit."

"How many?"

"It might be a scouting party heading south," William said. "Or it might be upward of five hundred men. That's a powerful scout, if that's what it is. They don't seem to think much of us, if they've even seen us."

Watie motioned to his bugler and ordered him to his side. "Son, sound a right wheel and charge."

"We're fightin' them boys?" the bugler asked, his eyes wide. "Thought we was goin' to be over the hill 'fore we saw 'em."

"You have your orders, Private!" snapped Watie. He saw that this improvised shift in attack had brought his son's company around and into action with the rest. There couldn't be any hesitation now, or Saladin would find himself in the middle of five hundred surprised and fighting mad Federals.

The bugle sounded its ragged call, and the charge began. Amid thundering hooves, Stand Watie caught the column from the 14th Missouri Cavalry by surprise. Rather than run, the Federals went to ground, falling on their bellies and returning fire. Watie's men galloped past, swung about, and attacked from the opposite direction, catching the Union cavalry between the front ranks and the reserve companies.

"Attack, attack, attack!" Watie screamed at the top of his lungs. The words were swallowed in the sharp crack of muskets and the frightened whinnies of horses, the always ear-shattering sounds of battle that he never got used to. As Watie's men charged again, new sounds were added to the cacophony: screams of wounded and dying men.

Watie kicked out as he rode past a sergeant struggling to fix his bayonet. The toe of his boot caught the Federal under the chin and snapped back his head. The bluecoat staggered into others, and fell heavily. Then Watie flashed past, worried about his lack of ammunition. He had emptied his pistol and needed to reload—as did the rest of his men. They had caught the Federal column by surprise, but that advantage was gone now.

"What do we do, Colonel?" asked William Adair. "They're digging in now. We got a few of them on the first attack, but we have to go to ground to fight them, if we stay."

Watie's mind raced. "Kill their horses," he ordered. "Run off the horses, and regroup in the valley where we began the attack."

He worked to reload his pistol, then began sending his orders to his company commanders. Watie did not want to stay and fight this column, but he could damage the

Federal command and put it out of future battles if he destroyed their mounts.

His troopers enjoyed the attack more than Watie would have liked them to. This was not brutal murder, but it came close. When he got his regiment regrouped, he saw they could slaughter the 14th Missouri because it was in such utter disarray.

"How many of them are wounded?" he asked.

A sergeant replied to his question. "We're all right, Colonel. They took one in ten or even one in five. We can wipe 'em off the face of the earth."

"Leave them be," Watie said decisively. "We were on our way to attack the Tenth Illinois in Neosho." Louder, he barked his orders to his company commanders. "Get into formation!"

It wasn't what he liked, but the Federal scouting column was in no position to attack his rear now. Watie had come to break the back of the 10th before they could launch their own strike into Indian Territory. If he didn't do that, the threat would remain.

The regiment crested the ridge and looked down on the far side of the rise. The echo of gunfire had alerted the 10th Illinois—but not enough. They stirred sluggishly in their camp, not sure what was going on.

Stand Watie showed them fear.

The Cherokee Mounted Rifles opened fire, reloaded, and then charged through the camp, setting fire to tents and blowing up the ammunition dump. Being situated at the outskirts of Neosho allowed many of the Federals to escape into the town. Watie considered putting the torch to the entire town, but saw too many military targets remaining in the campsite to divert his men. A few escaped soldiers meant less than destroying wagonloads of uniforms, blowing up powder dumps, and setting fire to the caissons carrying heavy field pieces.

The resistance faded fast as more and more of the 10th Illinois Cavalry sought refuge in the town.

"Horses, take the horses!" Watie ordered. He was pleased to see Saladin ride forward and do his duty. Saladin's company circled a corral and then freed the horses. They herded the remuda back through the camp, further destroying the Federals' equipment.

Watie considered riding down the road leading south out of Neosho and once more engaging the scout column. He might have regained some of the discipline lost during the attack. Then Stand Watie knew that going after the scouting column again was folly. He had accomplished all he had been ordered to do—and more. He had horses, he had sown the seeds of discord and fear among the Federals, and had taken few casualties in the attack.

A good day, and one which would protect the Cherokees against invasion for a long, long time—perhaps until the end of the war.

Cowskin Prairie
June 6, 1862

"You making any money off the sawmill, Stand?" asked William Adair. The lieutenant colonel in command of Watie's scouts took a handkerchief and wiped at late afternoon sweat on his broad forehead. It was dry again this year and hot, hotter than it had been last year.

"I'm thinking of shutting down my sawmill until after the war," Watie said. He sat in the shade afforded by his small but comfortable house. All around were men from his regiment, tinkering and doing camp chores and mostly relaxing after several months of hard fighting.

"That'll cut down on your cash flow," William said.

"You worrying more about my money, or the sawed boards I promised you for that new house of yours down in Tahlequah?"

"I don't know if I want to build there," William said, sitting beside Watie. "Webber's Falls is nice, if it wasn't for John Drew camping there so much. Maybe somewhere around Fort Gibson."

"John Ross's nephew has set himself up as fort sutler," Watie said. " 'That's got to be a rewarding position, him being in charge of supplies for the fort and selling them at the same time."

"You hear any more about the money Ross got from Albert Pike for rent on the Neutral Lands? More 'n seventy thousand in gold is the rumor I heard."

"It went into the tribe treasury," Watie said. "I saw the receipt, but what John Ross used it for after it got there I can't rightly say." He stretched and wished for a little wind to steal away the stifling heat. Bugs buzzed, and he needed to get a drink of water. The heat and lack of rain sucked the moisture right from his body. Stand Watie wouldn't have traded his house at Cowskin Prairie for the world though. When it was safe he was going to move Sarah and the children here, away from the tribal politics of Tahlequah. He wanted to spend time with his family again, free of machination and away from war.

Making a living had not been easy here, but he had always liked this country from the first time he laid eyes on it. The prairie was flat enough to plant in, if he chose. The hills in the distance and streams hidden there provided good fishing. The river gave power for his sawmill. There were even several lakes not far away where he enjoyed fishing on days like this. A swim or simply sitting in the shade of a tree and letting the world spin away on its own counted as much as bringing in a wide-mouthed bass.

Those pastimes seemed alien to him right now. When the war was over, he would make sure it became a daily occurrence. Cumiskey and Watica would appreciate the time he could spend with them, and Saladin would be old enough to run the family business. Then he could see to Minnehaha and Jacqueline finding decent husbands.

At this Watie sighed deeply. So many young men were dead, and the Cherokee were split down the middle, half siding with the Union or wanting neutrality as John Ross preached, and the rest in the Southern Rights Party camp. It wouldn't be easy for his daughters to find good men, but he felt confident they would do well because they were growing up into good, proper ladies. Sarah was seeing to that.

"You're mighty reflective today, Stand. Not worrying about rumors of Colonel Doubleday moving south on us, are you?"

"You sent out the scouts. If the Federals were invading, there would be plenty of warning from them."

William Adair wiped his face again. "We're surrounded by a powerful lot of hill country. You can't cover every route down into Cowskin Prairie."

"Don't have to. If the scouts miss any troop movement, General Pike's won't."

"You put too much faith in Albert Pike," William opined. "He's got troubles of his own, and has ever since Pea Ridge."

"He took the blame for the scalpings, and it wasn't even his Indian Brigade that was responsible," Watie said. "That makes him an honorable man, even if he did nothing about John Drew's regiment. Or John Ross."

"Politics," grumbled William. "There's not much a military man can do about it."

They fell silent, but Stand Watie grew increasingly uneasy. He got to his feet and brushed off his pants, looking around. The distance was purple with haze, and the buzz of biting flies covered anything but the most obvious sounds. Something was not right.

"Don't let me spook you, Stand," William said. "I was just thinking we ought to be more prepared. I know the men need a rest, and this is a good place. With the town only—"

"Assemble the men. Get the bugler to give the signal."

"What's wrong?" William Adair jumped to his feet, trying to understand what had alerted his friend.

"There, see? Out there by the lake?"

"Just a dust devil kicking up a fuss."

"It's not spinning, William. It's a cloud. Like it was kicked up by horses' hooves and wagons, maybe caissons."

"You got quite an imagination, Stand. I didn't mean—"

"Do it, Lieutenant Colonel," Watie said sharply. He ran into his house and began putting on his uniform, settling the pistol and gun belt around his waist. The hot wool jacket with its faded gold braid weighed him down, but Watie wanted the authority it lent to his orders. He rushed back outside.

Already men were assembling, bringing their muskets with them. Before he could say a word, a whistling sound brought him around. The explosion knocked him from his feet as the cannonball landed a dozen yards from him.

"Where's that coming from?" demanded William. He found out as more cannonballs hammered into the sawmill. One set the mill on fire.

"Get to defensive positions," ordered Stand Watie. "How many men are still in camp?" he asked of William.

"Five hundred."

"Get them mounted. We can't fight here." The heat from the burning mill caused him to avert his face. There wasn't water enough to put out the fire. Better to let it burn. He had thought of shutting down the mill because of lack of water in the stream running past it. Now he had an even better reason to abandon it.

It had already turned to charred ruins.

"You men know the lay of the land. That's got to be Federal artillery opening up on us. If it's Doubleday, as I fear, he has all his force to the east. Don't try running south. Go west or north and circle around."

"We can fight 'em off, Colonel," one lieutenant said. "We can—"

The words died in his throat as a bullet ripped away the side of his head. The man stood, not aware he had died. Like a screw slowly driving into wood, the man twisted about and collapsed bonelessly on the ground.

"They've moved into rifle range," Watie shouted. "If you see them, fire! Half of you return fire, the other half tend the livestock, get the horses, take what supplies you can!"

His words vanished once more in a new barrage. These shells went over the camp and landed far behind. Watie wasn't sure if this was meant to contain his men or was simply the product of miscalculation on the artillerist's part. If the field pieces were being brought up, they had to be sighted in every time. And if that were true, it meant an aggressive attack was being mounted.

"Keep firing," Watie ordered, going back and forth behind the men to encourage them. "We're retreating."

The men firing fell back and ran to fetch their horses. Watie saw he had not ordered the withdrawal fast enough. A cavalry detachment pounded toward them from the Federals' left flank, looking to sweep around and contain them at the sawmill.

Watie vaulted into the saddle and shouted encouragement to his men, ordering them to not engage. The artillery barrage continued, causing him to momentarily wonder at the bravery or foolishness of the Federal cavalry attacking him. They rode under their own cannon fire.

"To the hills," he shouted. Watie hated to leave the six hundred head of cattle to the Federals, but there was no chance of taking them with his men. They would be lucky to escape with their lives. If only he knew how many men Doubleday had!

Watie put his heels to his horse's flanks, then tried to turn and join the battle raging at the far edge of the sawmill. The Federal cavalry had arrived, and William Adair and a dozen others were fighting for their lives. As he watched, William went down, struck on the head by a pistol butt.

"Father!" came the cry from a man wearing captain's insignia. "There's nothing you can do for him. Come on!"

He hated leaving his lifelong friend to the Union soldiers, but Stand Watie obeyed the captain—his son, Saladin.

Invasion
June 28, 1862

Stand Watie huddled near the low fire cooking his supper in Round Grove. He said nothing, and those around him weren't inclined to speak, either. Since William Adair had been captured, Watie had withdrawn and was difficult to speak to.

"Father," said Saladin, settling beside Watie. "We can always trade prisoners for William."

"No, no we can't," Watie said grimly. "Colonel Doubleday was only the front of the invasion. The Federals are pouring over the border and into our homeland. All my scouts were captured."

"The Pins," Saladin said, his anger rising. He increasingly flew into rages. "I heard the head of the Keetoowahs promised the Union commander that John Ross will surrender if he enters Tahlequah."

"Salmon?" Watie spat. He and Salmon had their differences in the past, but this was treason of the worst order. The Pins ought to know what Federal occupation of the Cherokee Nation would mean. The slaughter would be horrendous.

"Salmon has promised two thousand men to aid in the overthrow of the Confederacy," Saladin went on. "Please,

Father, it is what I have heard." The young man touched the hilt of a knife thrust into a scabbard and fingered it. Watie did not ask how his son happened to "hear" this information. The smell of blood and torture of Union prisoners would be long in fading.

"Doubleday blazed the trail," Watie said, ignoring the news of the Pins' treachery. He had come to expect nothing less from them. "Colonel Weer is leading the real force from Kansas. Stopping him will be difficult."

"Impossible, Father," corrected Saladin. "Our regiment is scattered. Doubleday seized the mill. We hunker down out here on the prairie. There is no way we can be effective without regrouping and joining forces with General Pike or—"

"Or John Drew?" Watie spat. "How many Keetoowahs still collect Confederate pay while serving in Drew's ranks? Most, I would guess. He is a fool."

"Salmon might rely on some deserters from John Drew's regiment," Saladin Watie agreed, "but most who would desert already have after Caving Banks."

"Nothing was done to punish them," Watie said. "John Ross pardoned them. How many rejoined Drew's ranks?"

"What would you have us do in the face of Weer's attack? Six thousand men are under his command. How many are we now? Two hundred?"

Watie felt the sting of this simple truth. So many of his men had taken to the hills surrounding his sawmill, and all too few had found their way back to his command. How could he deny the need for those men to rush home to defend their families? If he had not felt his duty so acutely, he would have returned to Tahlequah to fight for his home and wife and children.

If only more of his soldiers had remained. In unity there was hope of victory. Individual fighting was proud and heroic, but foolish when facing six thousand Union soldiers and an unknown number of his neighbors who harbored Keetoowah sympathies.

"We must blunt his invasion. He thinks he can run straight through our belly to the heart and take Tahlequah. If the capital falls, what is left but retreat south into Texas?"

"Surrender," Saladin said softly.

"Never! I am sworn to uphold the treaty with the CSA. They will send troops to defend Indian Territory, and I will fight their enemies."

"*Our* enemies," Saladin said. "We fight among ourselves more than we do the blue-coated soldiers."

"That will change. Get the men mounted. We're returning to the sawmill, and we *will* drive out the Federals. That will force Weer to commit troops that otherwise would be thrown against Fort Gibson and Tahlequah."

Saladin Watie shook his head, but went to obey. His father was stubborn, and that made him a dedicated and fierce fighter. Within the hour what remained of Stand Watie's Cherokee Mounted Rifles rode hard toward the burned-out mill and a battle that might spell their end.

"Elks Grove," Watie said to his officers, "has been occupied by Weer. We dare not ride through without knowing the extent of the force there."

"I know something of the disposition," spoke up a man pushing his way through the ring of officers. The man wore a simple cotton shirt and store-bought pants with torn knees and dirty cuffs. Watie did not know him but thought he might be one of the locals.

"How can you help us?"

"I live in Elks Grove," the man said. A front tooth had been broken, and his lip bled sluggishly. From the way he limped, Watie thought he might have been shot, also. "When Weer rode into town, I fought. So did several others. They were killed. I got out and warned Colonel Clarkson, who was camped a half mile outside town."

"What happened?" Watie asked, knowing the answer from the man's condition and attitude.

"Colonel Clarkson was captured, along with all his supplies," the man said. "Weer is not missing a pocket of resistance. Fight and die, surrender and . . ." The man shrugged. "I don't know what the Union soldiers are doing to prisoners, except I doubt it's too smart to surrender. They have hundreds of pure-bloods with them."

"Cherokee?"

"Maybe from Opothleyahola's army, maybe those who left or were run out a year ago."

"A lot of our people went to Kansas," Watie said. "The winter starved many of them to death. Those coming back to the Cherokee Nation with an invading army might not cotton much to those of us fighting for the Confederacy."

The man wiped away blood from his mouth, then said, "I have told you all I know. I must find my family and try to avoid being scalped by the full-bloods." As quickly as he had entered the camp, he left. Stand Watie felt a hollowness inside that refused to go away. It was as if he grasped for a rope for support and found only air.

"What are we going to do, Colonel?" asked a captain. "If we head southwest we can reinforce the garrison at Fort Gibson."

"We need to slow Weer's advance. If he has Clarkson's supplies, he is that much stronger and bolder," Watie said. "We must attack from a place we know best."

"The sawmill?" asked Saladin Watie.

"Mount the regiment. We ride for the mill," Watie said. "Or what is left of it."

"All the livestock has been run off. We have what horses we could take with us. And the Federals would not have left anything useful, Father. Why go there?" Saladin shifted uneasily in his saddle as they studied the smoking ruin that had been the sawmill on Spavinaw Creek.

"We need a rallying point. Everyone on Cowskin Prairie knows this is *my* mill. If we can recruit from men like the one who told us of Clarkson's capture, we stand a better chance."

"We have none, Father," Saladin Watie said coldly. "We must think of protecting Tahlequah, not stopping Weer out here, alone, with no reserves."

"I've sent word to General Pike telling him what we have learned," Watie said. "We can use this as a base when he arrives from Boggy Depot."

"If he's smart he'll go to Fort Gibson, throw out Lieutenant Colonel Ross, and defend the territory from there."

Stand Watie thought a moment, then smiled wanly. "You are right, Son. And General Pike *is* smart. But this isn't his country. It's ours, and we have to fight for every inch of it. Do we let Weer ride through, hoping he will be too tired to fight when he reaches our capital, or do we dog his steps and make him wish he had never come into the Cherokee Nation?"

"We fight," Saladin Watie said in resignation.

"Let's make what we can of the mill and use it as our fort," Watie said, heading the column snaking down the side of the hill in the direction of the gutted buildings. He rode through the ruins, the acrid smell of burnt wood causing his nose to twitch. How he had worked to make this mill with his brothers and uncles. He and Elias Cornelius Boudinot had thought to make this a major business before the war.

Now? Dreams and burned-out buildings, all smoldering on the ground.

"Fan out. Retrieve what matériel you can, men," Watie ordered. His men dismounted and began poking around, finding rifles and pouches of lead shot. He rode to the creek, now more mud than water. If it had not dried up, the mill would have produced sawed planks all summer long.

If. . . .

Stand Watie jerked about when the gunshot sounded. He worried one of his men had accidentally discharged his weapon. Then came another shot, and another, and a veritable thunderclap of gunshots. Pushing his tired horse, he galloped back to the mill and saw that two lines of his men had taken cover and fired in the direction Colonel Doubleday had attacked.

"A big force, Colonel," Saladin Watie reported, all business. "I think it might be Colonel Weer's commander of cavalry out there."

"Lieutenant Colonel Jewell?" Watie knew nothing of the man but his name. How he wished they had better intelligence about those they faced. Before the war, men like Van Dorn and Albert Pike had gone to school with the Union officers and knew their quirks and preferences, how to fight them, how to win in battle.

He knew their names, and nothing else.

"Mount, retreat," Watie ordered. Under his breath he added, "Again."

This time it was more a rout than a retreat.

Knife Through
the Heart
July 6, 1862

"More men, I want more men guarding me!" shouted John Ross, turning angrier by the second. He stood on the front porch of Rose Cottage and stared wide-eyed in horror at the two companies of John Drew's regiment scattered around the grounds. "That's not enough men if Watie tries to capture or kill me. You've heard the rumors. He's moving south to capture me because he thinks I'm dealing with pro-Union Creek."

"If Watie hadn't caved in so fast, there'd have been time to get more men from Fort Gibson," John Drew said, struggling to find an excuse for the few men he had patrolling Park Hill. "And there have been some defections from my best company, too."

"Defections? You mean desertions!" raged John Ross. The old man felt his joints snapping and popping as he paced nervously. It was *all* Stand Watie's fault. If he had presented a decent defense north on Cowskin Prairie, the Union army would not have made such quick progress through the Cherokee Nation. Colonel Weer and his men camped outside Fort Gibson, cutting off reinforcement from there. And John Drew's men slipped away like sand from a fist. One day there were dozens, the next only a few clinging fearfully, unsure where they would be even the next day.

"That was Salmon's doing. He sold us out to the Federals," complained John Drew.

"How many of your soldiers have deserted?" John Ross asked pointblank.

"Six hundred," Drew said in a choked voice.

"Six hundred?" John Ross could hardly believe the number. This wasn't a tiny cut. It was an arterial wound.

"I've heard rumors most joined Colonel John Ritchie's Second Kansas Indian Home Guard. Some—many—of the refugees from Opothleyahola's army retreated north and either joined the Union army or starved during the winter."

"That's not the worst of it," Ross said, his rage turning into exhaustion. He had run on nervous energy for too many days. Tahlequah was almost entirely evacuated, the loyal citizens hiding in the hills should Watie come tearing through, killing anyone he found. Park Hill was only a few miles from the capital. If Ritchie or Weer or whoever the North sent entered the town, they would find it easy pickings. John Ross closed his eyes and tried to imagine his capital in flames.

He shook hard to rid himself of the pernicious image. There had to be a way out, one he had not explored yet. Negotiation. Weer would talk to the principal chief of the Cherokee Nation. That would give time to contact the Confederate War Department to see what deal could be reached.

Play one off against the other. Get rid of Watie, hold the Federals at bay with his words. That was the only way John Ross saw that the Cherokee could survive this disaster.

Damn Stand Watie!

"What is the worst?"

"What is the worst?" John Drew foolishly asked.

"The slaves. The slaves we're fighting with the United States about. When they heard Colonel Weer was on the way, they revolted. Some killed their masters, others just ran away. We might be facing full-bloods who have starved all winter in Kansas, runaway slaves, *and* the Union army."

"I had not heard that," Drew said weakly.

"You were too busy trying to hold your forces together," John Ross said, giving the imprudent officer an excuse. "How well can you defend Park Hill?"

"I need more men. If Watie comes, we'll be outnumbered."

"Yes, yes, Watie will try to do that. He knows the national treasury is here, and will want to loot it. More than that, he needs to kill me to regain any reputation he had before his defeat."

"How much money is there?" asked Drew.

John Ross chose not to answer. He had gotten rid of as much of the Confederate scrip as possible, considering it worthless paper. He still had a hoard of gold, possibly $50,000 worth, given him by Albert Pike and intended to pay the Nation's bills. With the approaching tide of blue-coats, many who would have been hounding him for payment on supplies and services had chosen to leave town, giving him a grace period. Many would never be paid, if they were killed. And if the United States won, those debts would be declared void, leaving that much more gold in the tribal treasury.

How many wagons would it take to move $50,000 in gold? Not many. Perhaps only one sturdy wagon, John Ross decided. There had to be other supplies loaded along with the gold, if they were to get very far. He needed to secure the treasury to be sure Stand Watie was not able to capture it.

"Where is he? Watie?" asked John Drew.

"Since he was routed at his sawmill, no one is sure. I wish he was burning in hell, but no word of his death has reached me," Ross said. He would have paid well for such information, and everyone around Tahlequah knew it. That no one had boasted of having Watie's scalp in his hand told John Ross that the leader of the Southern Rights Party was still at large—and still a danger.

"Colonel Drew! Colonel!" came the call from a courier riding a lathered horse. The man jumped from the staggering animal and then stumbled himself, regained his feet, and hurried up the steps of Rose Cottage. He saluted. "I have a report, sir."

"Yes, yes," Drew said, not wanting to hear it. He was pushed aside by John Ross.

"Tell me, son. What is it?" Ross asked.

"It's for you, sir. From Colonel Weer." The man fished out a crumpled, sweat-stained envelope and handed it to John Ross, who opened and read the letter inside.

"He wants to know where I stand, now that so many of my followers have switched their loyalties. What can I say?" Ross asked aloud.

"Sir, there's something more," the courier said. He looked anxiously from John Drew and back to Ross. "The chaplain, sir—the chaplain of Colonel Drew's regiment."

"Go on, spit it out," John Ross said irritably. None of this had an easy solution and that annoyed him worse than a splinter just under the skin.

"Reverend Downing, sir, and two hundred men from the regiment joined Ritchie's forces this morning."

John Ross had expected no less, but it still shocked him. For all purposes, the only soldiers left in John Drew's Cherokee Mounted Rifles were the two undermanned companies camped on the grounds of Rose Cottage.

John Drew's command was gone, deserted or turned coat. That left only Stand Watie's regiment to uphold the sovereignty of the Cherokee Nation. And they were brutal savages intent on murder and pillaging those who opposed them.

Fire
July 12, 1862

"What do you mean, Ross isn't with his command?" Albert Pike's eyes narrowed as he studied the courier who had brought even more bad news about the Union invasion.

"Lieutenant Colonel Ross is in Arkansas, petitioning the Commander of the Trans-Mississippi District for a promotion," the messenger said, eyes darting about as if he wanted to cut and run. Pike did not say a word about that nervousness. He felt it himself.

"Who's in command at Fort Gibson?"

The courier shrugged. "All I know is that Colonel Weer has the fort surrounded. Heard tell he's going to attack soon."

Pike muttered to himself, stroking his dirty beard and wondering what could be done. John Drew's regiment was a regrettable ruin, most of the men gone over to the enemy. The Keetoowah Society ran wild through Tahlequah, burning and killing any Cherokee they considered to have Confederate leanings—which were many. The slaves rode with the Pins, adding their knives and torches to the punishment.

And Watie? Pike had no idea what had happened to Stand Watie and his regiment. The last information from the north told of a rout at Cowskin Prairie and complete elimination of the Second Cherokee Mounted Rifles. What men Pike had remaining in his Indian Brigade were loyal, but there were so few of them. He needed reinforcements.

From where? If he had known William Potter Ross was going to Arkansas to talk to General Beauregard, he would have sent along a request for supplies and men. Hell, he would have gone himself to plead the case for the Cherokee. Pike doubted Ross was presenting any realistic picture of the danger facing Indian Territory after Weer's invasion had driven all the way to Fort Gibson.

"Been dry this year, hasn't it?" Pike wondered aloud. The courier rubbed his nose and continued to look around like a trapped rat. He didn't know how to answer. "Get back to your unit and tell your officers to set fire to the prairie. Drive out Weer. Make him retreat."

"If the grass is fired, there's no stopping it," the messenger protested, outraged at the idea. "It might even burn down the fort!"

"What good is the fort if it's surrounded, and we have no way of lifting the siege? Better to burn it to the ground than let Weer occupy it and use it against us." Pike knew Fort Gibson was a major supply point. With it in Federal hands, all of Indian Territory would be doomed.

The courier rubbed his nose again, then left without another word. Pike watched the man go, wondering if he would return to his unit as ordered or was deserting, as most of John Drew's men had done.

"Orderly!" Pike bellowed. "Get me a messenger in here on the double." He would send a duplicate order, to be sure those Confederate officers still in the field and still loyal would set the fires. This ploy wasn't much. It was damned little, in truth, but Pike had to do something. The situation was perilous, and all too soon would be lost.

* * *

"Colonel Drew went to Webber's Falls?" John Ross asked of his son Allen.

"Reckon so," Allen said. He had been promoted to captain, and had already shucked off the wool jacket in favor of a ruffled white shirt and broadcloth coat. Being the principal chief's son carried many burdens not felt by others, not the least of which was the need to deal with both Union and Confederate officers, trying to walk a narrow line of diplomacy. Worst of all was wearing the uniform of a cause he did not believe in.

"Send Colonel Weer my reply, then," John Ross said.

"Father, I don't understand why you refuse to meet with him. So many of our party are openly favoring surrender and treaty with the United States that it is nothing less than an affront to him."

"We need to bargain from a position of strength, Allen," the elder Ross said. "Consider. Weer sends repeated requests. Only when he stops trying to palaver are we in danger of losing out. We hold enough cards to make us a player in this game." John Ross paced behind his desk, occasionally looking out the open window at the dry grass stretching to the distance. Park Hill was usually a lovely place in the summer, but lack of rain had turned the grass sere this year. It was as if Ross had lost some of his sight, and colors were being stolen away one by one.

He shook himself to focus better on the game he played. Poker, yes. Bluffing. He had to win the whole pot, or the Cherokee Nation would cease to exist.

"Do the Confederates offer any help?" demanded Allen. "Your own physician has gone over to the Federals. Doctor Gilpatrick is an honorable man. Listen to him. Meet with Weer and lift the siege on Fort Gibson. We need food, Father."

"You were not here four days ago when more than three hundred of our people and thirty Negroes stopped out there. They were on their way to join Colonel Weer's force.

It won't be long until Weer abolishes slavery and those slaves remaining will either revolt or be manumitted."

Outside came the pounding of hooves. John Ross looked out and smiled when he saw his nephew.

"William!" he called, waving to him.

"Uncle John." Will Ross dismounted and hurried into the small office. He nodded toward his cousin, then said to his uncle, "General Beauregard has refused my promotion, but I have learned he is not favorably inclined toward Albert Pike, either. If Pike is removed, there is a chance I might move into his post, commanding all Confederate forces in Indian Territory."

"Will, there is much you have not heard," John Ross said. He settled in his chair. "Allen, tell your cousin what has happened while he was gone."

As Allen told Will of Weer's attack on Fort Gibson, John Ross sat and thought. If what Will said was true, Beauregard would remove Pike before much longer. That presented opportunity, but there was so much dissent in the Confederate high command that any brevet promotion for his nephew might be meaningless. When was the proper time to deal with Weer?

And how could he preserve the Cherokee Nation treasury? Everything seemed to be sliced so thin. John Ross felt time would run away from him, unless he made exactly the right decisions now.

Surrender
July 15, 1862

"They are in Tahlequah," Allen Ross reported breathlessly. He threw down his Confederate officer's jacket and worked to put on his broadcloth coat. Sweat stuck his shirt to his body. He forced the reluctant cloth across his sleeves. The coat clung to him as he continued to sweat, both from the sultry day and the fear that mounted in his gut.

"Who?" asked his father. John Ross sat in the chair in the front room of his house, looking through the lace curtains. His wife had already left for Philadelphia to seek refuge with her people, taking with her a goodly portion of the Cherokee Nation's treasury for safekeeping. "Not that it matters."

"Captain Greeno," said Allen. "He circled Tahlequah, but only four men remained in town. The rest have left."

"Some time ago," John Ross said, very tired. How the weight of the years pressed down on him! He had not heard from the Confederate high command, and now it was too late to negotiate with the Union commander. The day before, Colonel Weer had sent out a major with a small force that took Fort Gibson with scarcely a shot being fired.

"This captain, he's a physician, and a clever man from all accounts," Allen went on. He sat beside his father. Allen poured himself a glass of water and drank it rapidly, then refilled and drank another.

"Not so fast, Allen," cautioned John Ross. "It will cause you to bloat like a horse." He silently stared at the brown grass outside and at the men remaining in John Drew's regiment that patrolled Park Hill. His precious Rose Cottage was at risk now. He stood to lose everything. The only consolation John Ross had was that Stand Watie had already seen his businesses and houses go up in smoke already.

It was cold comfort.

"He will arrive. What are your orders for your guards? Should they fight, or do you want to follow Mama north?"

"Does it matter? You should go soon," John Ross said. "Send for Will."

Allen stiffened. "You think more of him than you do me," Allen accused. "Because he graduated first in his class at Princeton? Because he has a head for business?"

"Does it matter whom I chose for principal chief, Allen? I think not. What must I do to keep the Cherokee Nation intact? *That* is a more pressing issue than who I groom to succeed me."

"There is dissension in the Union ranks," Allen said. "I was told that Weer might be relieved of his command."

"Whatever for? The man has won. He's captured Fort Gibson, and took our capital without firing a shot. It is only a matter of time before he forces my surrender, and that of the entire Cherokee Nation."

"There is another officer, a Colonel Frederick Salomon, who is jealous of Weer's position. He has the ear of their commander."

"How should I use this?" John Ross wondered aloud. "Especially now that the Federals are riding into my front yard?" John Ross shoved himself to his feet and shuffled out to the front porch of Rose Cottage, leaning heavily against the whitewashed railing, ready to greet Captain Greeno and tender his surrender.

Some shred of sovereignty might be salvaged. John Ross had to see what that might be.

Anarchy
July 18, 1862

"Are you certain?" asked Stand Watie. The young lieutenant looked frightened, as if Watie would take him to task for the information he brought. "Calm yourself," Watie said. "I need to be certain you heard right."

"General Pike's resigned his commission," the lieutenant said. "I heard that from two or three men runnin' away from Fort Gibson."

"I know Fort Gibson has fallen," Watie said in disgust. Lieutenant Colonel Ross had been elsewhere, and the captain in charge of the fort had not been up to the task of fighting off the Union invasion. Someone—Watie could hardly believe it was Pike, though rumor held that it was he—had foolishly set fire to the prairie, burning the dry grass and making worse an already intolerable situation.

After he had run from Cowskin Prairie, Stand Watie had tried to regroup his men and fight a guerrilla war. Too few of his men had survived, and he could not blame many of them for wanting to return home. He himself felt the need to see to Sarah and his children. In spite of this soul-searing need, he had sent Saladin south to be sure they were moved into Texas, where relatives could put them up until after the war.

How he missed William Adair—spirited away to some Northern prison camp—and how he missed his earlier optimism about an early end to the war. The flood of information coming to him was a torrential outpouring that threatened to drown him. John Ross had surrendered without a shot being fired. Watie believed that. Fort Gibson surrendered with little more. That, too, was within his capacity to understand.

But Albert Pike resigning his commission? Who else in the Trans-Mississippi District knew the Indian Territory half as well? General Thomas Hindmann might command the Arkansas district and General Beauregard the entire western district, but who were they to understand the needs of the Cherokee and others of the Five Civilized Tribes?

Least believable was the report that Colonel Weer had been replaced by Frederick Salomon for jeopardizing his soldiers. Watie tried to think of a single engagement—from Colonel Doubleday's thrust to Jewell's fight to Ritchie's sweep through the middle of Indian Territory—where anything more than the threat of dehydration had faced the Federals. Weer had done well—too well, by Watie's standards. And John Ross and his lap-dog John Drew had done too little.

"What of their supply trains?" he asked the lieutenant.

"Heavily protected, sir," the lieutenant said. "They move more and more gear and ammunition south from Kansas, as if they intend being at Fort Gibson for some time. Don't know if they are going to supply the fort using the river."

"Occupation," Watie mused. "If there is trouble between Weer and this Salomon, perhaps we can add to the problems." He held a grudging admiration for Colonel Weer, and wished he could meet him, talk with him, find out the man's secrets of command and strategy, but he was the enemy. Any respect Watie held for the other commander had to be pushed under by the need to destroy him.

"Sir, what are your orders?"

"Lieutenant, get a company together. We're going hunting. We don't have the firepower for a real fight, so we'll do what the Jayhawkers did to us earlier. Be sure to take along enough flammable material for torches—and all the ammunition each man can carry. We are going to kill anything that moves. And if it doesn't move, we'll burn it!"

"Most have two or three pistols now," the lieutenant said, almost guiltily. They had an oversupply of weapons, taken from fallen comrades, but they needed ammunition and gunpowder.

"Have them all loaded and ready for a skirmish in fifteen minutes," Watie said, coming to a decision. He could retreat or he could attack. Taking a few minutes, he started a letter to his Sarah, then folded it and put it into his saddlebags, knowing there might not be a chance to finish it later.

There might not be a later for the Cherokee Nation.

The raid went well, and what supplies weren't stolen were destroyed. Stand Watie knew he had discovered an effective way to fight the Federals, even if its waging seemed underhanded to him. He had let his men run wild, giving no quarter even to men wanting to surrender. Worse than that, he had felt no guilt at it. Kill them, kill them all, Union soldier and John Ross follower alike, before they got the chance to do it to Stand Watie's followers.

Retreat

July 19, 1862

"Shoot only the officers," Stand Watie ordered his trio of snipers. "We don't have enough ammunition to shoot the rest." He vaulted into the saddle and rode fast down the road to where a small squad had split into equal parts and huddled on either side of the road.

The raid the day before had been more successful than Watie could have believed. He had even captured a sergeant who seemed hardly dry behind the ears and let the man overhear a fake discussion of a twelve hundred man army double-timing it in from Arkansas to reinforce Watie's Cherokee Mounted Rifles. Then the sergeant had "escaped," with the help of two Cherokee claiming they were Pins out to aid the Union.

Watie had congratulated both the men on their acting ability and had relished the idea that the sergeant would run straight back to his command with the false information. Sow discord. Shoot and run. It was all that was left to Watie. That, and this ambush he plotted.

"They're coming fast, Colonel," came the word from his scout down the road.

"Ready, men. Get ready. This is going to be the fight of your lives!"

Watie dismounted and tethered his horse behind a tree. He clutched the butt of his pistol until sweat turned the handle slippery. Then all nervousness vanished. The lead element of the Union patrol passed by, riding hard. Watie was proud of the restraint shown by his snipers. They did not open fire until the last of the soldiers came even with them. When those closer to Watie's position reined back to see what happened to their officers, the rest of the Confederates opened fire.

Watie stepped out, aimed, and fired. He saw a surviving officer clutch his chest and look down stupidly. The man looked up from the wound, surprise now on his face. Their eyes locked for a moment, then the Federal lieutenant slipped from the saddle and fell heavily. Stand Watie was already firing at another soldier. This man he missed. And the next and the next. He finally shot a horse out from under another Federal. Only then did Watie give the orders to retreat.

"Ride hard, men," he ordered. "We've got five miles to cover." Head low and pushing his horse to the limit, galloping a mile, walking another, trotting and then changing gait again, Watie got his mounted guerrillas across the countryside to the Fort Scott-Fort Gibson Military Road.

He had no time to deploy his men for a proper attack. They all went to the ground in a ditch alongside the road, and had less than ten minutes to prepare before another patrol rode past. This patrol lost three men wounded. The others turned and fled.

"Get their horses. Take what equipment you can," Watie said. He made sure he spoke to his young, puppy-dog-eager lieutenant within earshot of a wounded Federal soldier.

"This is going to be a good week, with the reinforcements arriving so soon," Watie said. From the corner of his eye he saw the fallen Union soldier tense and feign death. Watie motioned to the lieutenant to play along.

"Uh, yes sir, they'll be here by nightfall. How many again? Enough to retake Fort Gibson?"

"Easily. They'll be moving to the east side of the Grand River to cut off the Union supplies. Weer can't hold the fort longer than a day or two. I reckon we can trade him for John Ross."

"What of Lieutenant Colonel Will Ross?" asked the lieutenant.

Watie would have let William Potter Ross rot in hell, but he had a tale to spin. "He might be a prisoner of war, but we can ransom him with Weer and his entire staff. By keeping Ross a prisoner, our treaty says the War Department *has* to send even more troopers. Now come on. We've got to get out of here."

This time Watie and his men did not ride far. Their exhausted horses would have collapsed under them if they had attempted a long ride. Rather, they camped in a hollow so that Watie and two scouts could get to the top of a rise and watch the road. He saw the wounded Union soldier struggling down the road in the direction of Fort Gibson.

Sitting and waiting was a chore, but Watie took the time to reflect on his life. It seemed such a long time since moving from New Echota—and it was. He had a good family, one he would die to protect. His land and home were all forfeit to the war, but his family was intact south of the Red River in Texas, and would remain that way if Watie had to kill every bluecoat soldier with his bare hands.

"There, there, Colonel!" cried a scout.

"Get down there. Find out what they're saying," Watie ordered. The Cherokee stripped off what little Confederate gear he wore and hurried down, slipping on a captured Union uniform jacket showing he was a corporal. If the man were caught, he would be executed as a spy but he had volunteered, and Watie needed to know if the discord he had sown had taken root.

Two hours later, the scout returned, dirty and tired.

However, a broad smile split his face, showing a broken tooth and another one that had turned black when he gave his report.

"Went better 'n you thought it might, Colonel," the spy reported. "Colonel Salomon arrested Weer a couple hours 'fore I got into their camp and is sure we've got reinforcements enough moving in to pry 'em loose from Fort Gibson. They're abandoning the fort! Without firin' a single shot, they're runnin' from us!"

As the words came from the man's mouth, Watie looked past him to the heavily traveled road. He hardly believed his eyes. Taking a spyglass from one of his men, he lifted it to his right eye and began counting, studying the formation, calculating the full size of the force moving on the road.

Colonel Salomon led his column north toward the Verdigris River—and from the number of regimental banners flying, Stand Watie knew it was a complete retreat.

With only a handful of men, he had driven the Federals from the Cherokee Nation!

Two Battles
July 27, 1862

"No more looting," Stand Watie said firmly. "I will not tolerate it. Tell anyone you come across that burning and looting are crimes, no matter who is being burned out." He glared at the tight ring of officers. They were all that remained of an entire regiment. Four officers, including his son Saladin.

"But Colonel," protested a young lieutenant named Bushyhead, "the pro-Union Pins burned out *our* homes. It's only fair we do the same to them now that Salomon has retreated."

"It's *not* fair," Watie insisted. "They are all Cherokee. I do not care for the Pins and their ilk any more than you, but they are our brothers. You will uphold the law and protect them from the same crimes you would any of your family or the Southern Rights Party." He paused, reflecting on the hatred growing in the ranks of his soldiers for all the Keetoowahs had done. "Tell your men to defend themselves and their families the best they can, but no more burning."

He saw Bushyhead was not satisfied with this. Neither were the others, including his own son. They had fought hard and long these past weeks, and victories had been few.

Colonel Salomon had retreated, leaving behind only a few units that had to be flushed out and destroyed. Tending civil disorder distracted Watie from this mission.

"Declare martial law, Colonel," Saladin suggested. "Then you'll be the commander of the entire nation."

"I refuse to believe General Pike is no longer in command," he said testily. "When I hear it from his own lips, then I will consider declaring myself military commander—and not one second earlier." He clapped his hands together and rubbed them. His palms sweat profusely, and he knew why. He was nervous at the notion he would be responsible for the entire Cherokee Nation. He had just given an order that was sure to be twisted around into killing every Pin his men found. Somehow that no longer seemed such a vile thing to him.

How could he bring peace to the Cherokee Nation, though, if he allowed insurgents to survive?

If rumors were accurate, John Ross had left with Captain Greeno for Fort Baxter, Kansas, taking the entire Cherokee Nation treasury with him. Only Lieutenant Colonel Will Ross remained, and Watie was not certain where Ross's nephew had gone. He must have resigned his commission and given his parole to the Federals, but where had the son of a bitch gone to ground? Watie would gladly kill the man, since his uncle had turned tail and run.

Principal Chief Stand Watie. The words caused him to quiver just a little. The power in that title affected him greatly. Power had to go along with authority and responsibility, however.

"Now," Watie said brusquely, "it is not good military strategy to divide such a small force as ours, but I think we can make two strikes and do a great deal in driving out the remaining Federals."

He pulled a map from his jacket pocket and unfolded it. The sluggish summer breeze tried to fitfully wrinkle the paper. Watie held it down and motioned his officers closer.

"Captain Saladin Watie and I will ride the twenty miles west and attack Major Foreman's company of Union Creeks where he is camped at the crossing on the Grand and Arkansas Rivers. Lieutenant Bushyhead, you and the rest of the regiment will patrol the Park Hill Fork. A scout thinks the Third Kansas Indian Home Guard will be somewhere between Fort Gibson and Tahlequah. Attack them. You'll have almost four hundred men, the bulk of our force, at your command."

"Most of the men don't have horses, Colonel," the lieutenant protested.

"That's why you aren't riding the twenty miles to go after Foreman," Watie said, irritated. He wished he had more horses, but too many had been captured or killed. As it was, putting a hundred men on horseback was a major chore. What good was a cavalry without horses? With surprise on their side, Watie hoped to capture enough horses to put his entire regiment back in the saddle, even if they were the accursed McClellan saddles favored by the Union.

Bushyhead looked sullen, but said nothing. Watie studied the expression of the other lieutenant who would be riding with Bushyhead, and saw nothing but confusion on the young man's face. For a moment, Watie considered exchanging the young lieutenant with Saladin. Then he decided his first instincts had been right. Give Lieutenant Bushyhead the chance to prove himself. With so many men and the slight chance of meeting an overpowering force along the Fork, he would gain confidence and give his men the opportunity to see he was an able commander. Watie needed as many officers capable of independent action as he could get, and Bushyhead looked to be a good officer, if lacking in confidence at the moment.

"Let's move out," Watie said.

In an hour, his force was halfway to Foreman's bivouac. In three, he had his force spread out in a half circle around the unsuspecting Union officer's camp. Watie studied the camp and the war paint worn by many of the Indians in it—all Creek. He suspected many had ridden with Opothleyahola until the old Creek chief had been driven from the territory and into Kansas exile. Now they pranced about and pretended they were Union soldiers. Some even wore parts of Federal uniforms. As many wore Confederate jackets and pants taken from wounded and dead in battle.

Watie caught sight of a double flash of light off a signaling mirror. Saladin was in position. He drew his pistol and let out a wild yell as he spurred his horse onward. The sight of their colonel in the forefront carried the rest of the company into battle. It was a short, fierce fight. Stand Watie captured four Creek and routed Major Foreman, sending him running like a scalded dog.

It was a good day.

"My feet hurt," complained a soldier near Lieutenant Bushyhead. "How long we got to walk?"

Bushyhead looked down the winding road in the direction of Fort Gibson. All he saw was heat haze like a dancing mirror in the distance, flying insects, and hills covered with sparse vegetation. The road was singularly empty, not even carrying the usual commerce for a hot, dusty summer afternoon.

"How far is it into Tahlequah?" Bushyhead asked.

"Why are we goin' there?" asked a sergeant who had just signed on. "The colonel said to—"

"I'm in command. I heard what the colonel said. I was standin' there, and you weren't," the lieutenant said brusquely. His jaw set, and he bared his teeth in a silent snarl.

Not relaxing his fierce demeanor, the lieutenant said, "Let's go find ourselves some of them damned traitorous Pins. And there are plenty others who sympathize with the Union. And John Ross. Let's go find 'em all and burn 'em out!"

With a loud whoop, the men set off at a brisk pace, swapping improbable stories about what they would do when they found any pro-Union Cherokee.

What they actually did was worse, far worse.

Repudiation
March 1863

Cowskin Prairie looked little different from the time Stand Watie had made a small home there, along with several businesses. He avoided Spavinaw Creek and the burned-out sawmill, to keep from thinking on earlier times. The past months had been both hectic and productive.

He had rejuvenated his regiment, recruiting from the many families whose homes and property had been taken by the so-called Loyal Cherokee led by the Pins. Many recruits to his rank were out to avenge deaths—and Watie found himself less and less willing to argue with them if they wanted to take a life here and there, no matter if it was prisoner or some pro-Union Cherokee shooting at them.

If anything, he had become as brutal as any in his band. Seeing how his land had been torn apart drove him to scrub the Cherokee Nation free of Union soldiers, but supplies from the South were scarce and the normally cruel winter had been harsher than usual, following the especially dry summer and fall. Growing crops was out of the question, since pro-Union Cherokee were likely to burn out anyone they did not approve of.

Watie snorted and rubbed his nose. He had begun the slow expulsion of the Federals long months ago—and young Lieutenant Bushyhead, now long dead, had gone on the warpath against the Pins. The pro-union Cherokee had fought back, in the night, from ambush, any way they could.

The two factions would never weld into a full partnership again, and the past six months had been terrible in terms of lost life.

"He opposes you with all his heart and soul," Saladin Watie said in a soft voice. He pointed across the meadow in the direction of the camp where John Ross's followers assembled. Ross remained, wisely Watie thought, in Washington, spewing forth his poison while he let his aides try to wrest control of the Cherokee Council from the Southern Party.

"Traitor," spat Watie.

"That he may be, but he still has a following, especially among the full-bloods," his son warned him.

"We'll vote on a new principal chief. That will settle the matter once and for all."

"He still has the treasury."

"The Federals do," Watie corrected. "Who knows what they do with it, though I fear the worst. They are probably buying weapons and matériel that kill *our* people. That makes John Ross doubly a traitor."

"He still speaks well," Saladin said. "From what Elias says, John Ross holds them captivated in Washington with his fiery speeches and flowery compliments."

"He only gives them what they want to hear—as he has done with the Cherokee for so many years. It is time someone told our people the truth rather than silken lies." Watie grumbled, but he knew Saladin was right. John Ross's power extended deep into the very soul of the Cherokee Nation, and pulling it loose would be a monumental task.

Together they crossed the meadow, and as if by some strange alchemy the crowd separated into two factions, one wearing mostly gray and the other blue.

"The South has broken the treaty," Thomas Pegg raged, banging his bony hand against the makeshift lectern. His sparse hair was in wild disarray, and he appeared to have lost ten pounds from the last time Watie had seen him at John Ross's side, turning him into a walking skeleton. Watie thought he couldn't die soon enough, because he had ridden as a major with John Drew. And Watie wished nothing but the worst for John Ross, too.

"They promised never to use our soldiers in their battles. Pea Ridge broke that promise. They promised to defend us. Colonel Salomon broke the back of our proud nation, and the CSA never came to our aid. Worse, General Pike was relieved of his command, leaving our gentle people at the mercy of guerrillas and brigands and looters."

As those words slipped from Pegg's mouth, he stared straight at Stand Watie.

"The treaty is no more. It is shattered—by *their* action. I urge you to renew our treaty with the United States. Let them show more than the empty promises—and bellies— we have gotten at the hands of the Confederacy."

Half the crowd applauded. Other speakers supported the Ross position—that the Cherokee ought to repudiate their Southern ties, and once more align with the North.

A hush fell on the crowd when Stand Watie climbed to the stage. Pegg, although he was second chief, backed away as if he feared Watie would strike him. Watie paid him no attention. He turned and looked at the faces of his people, some smiling, others frowning. So it had been since the Treaty of New Echota. Never was more than a fraction happy.

"My people," Watie said in a low, booming voice that carried across Cowskin Prairie and seemed to vanish in the hills on the horizon. "I will not ask our second chief what has been done with the Cherokee Nation treasury, because John Ross might not have told him. I will not ask what he has done at Fort Baxter with John Ross these past months while *our* nation has been torn apart from inside. I will not ask any of these questions, because I do not care."

He paused. A ripple of uneasiness passed through the crowd, both those of Southern and Northern leaning.

"John Ross has divorced himself from the problems of our people—*my* people. Does he know the terror of pounding hooves, and a midnight visit by a masked mob? Has he struggled to push the Federals back after they invaded our land? You know the answers. You know I have not turned and run, but have stayed to fight for you. The dead Union soldiers and those who support them answer any question you might put to me."

"You're a bloody handed butcher, Watie!" someone shouted.

"I have tried to keep down the looting and murder of Keetoowah Society members, and others who are pro-Union. I also have tried to protect those who are Confederate from those who would kill them. In one thing John Ross is right—the Confederacy has not sent us soldiers or supplies—and there is a good reason."

Watie felt himself flushing, hot, sweating. His heart hammered, and he knew he was winning over many in the crowd. He felt it in his gut, as he did when a raid went well.

"John Ross," he said, as if the name burned his tongue. "He is the reason the Confederacy has ignored us. Who can trust a man dealing with your enemy for his own ends while prattling on about obeying signed treaties?"

"Not so!" bellowed Thomas Pegg. He pushed forward to the edge of the platform. "John Ross is a loyal Cherokee, and has only all our best interests at heart." Another delegate shouted Pegg down, and soon the speeches turned into a shouting match. Stand Watie held his tongue for a few minutes, then drowned out the others with a deep, booming voice.

"A vote. I call for a vote for principal chief of all Cherokee."

"No," Pegg said. "That is not possible. Like the United States, our nation is too deeply divided. I call for a vote, but one of division into north and south."

"Chief Ross approves of such a division!" cried some.

"Chief Watie!" cried others.

And so it went, the Cherokee Nation splitting in the same fashion as the United States itself.

Stand Watie had become principal chief—of the Southern Nation, just as John Ross was principal chief of the Northern. The Loyal Cherokee passed a resolution freeing the slaves, one that the Southern Party refused to acknowledge. Two nations, two leaders, two sets of law.

Even as the vote ended Watie knew it was a solution that was no solution at all.

Lost Again
May 1863

"We caught a half dozen Pins," Saladin Watie reported to his father. "They were executed." A feral gleam came to the young man's eyes. Watie wondered if the prisoners had been executed or tortured to death—not that it mattered a whit to him. He had seen too many of his loyal soldiers slaughtered in brutal ways by the Keetoowahs to care. What did matter to him was the effect all this bloodshed had on his son.

Saladin Watie was coming to like it—as much as his father. That sickened Watie more than words could tell, even when he revealed his innermost thoughts to his wife hiding down in Texas.

Stand Watie closed his eyes and let out a deep sigh. He did not want Cherokee killing Cherokee, but what other course was there? He had no reason to doubt his son, but whether the Keetoowahs went down fighting or were strung up like a Christmas goose made little difference. The Pins burned out pro-CSA Cherokee and, unfortunately, Watie could do nothing to prevent retaliation.

"He took ninety thousand," Watie said obliquely.

"What's that?" Saladin frowned, trying to follow his father's line of thinking.

"John Ross. I heard that the treasury was ninety thousand. He impoverished us and turned over the gold to the Federals, then left Fort Baxter and went to Philadelphia to stay with his in-laws."

"You are principal chief," Saladin said. "Since Ross has abandoned even the Northern Cherokee that makes you chief of the entire tribe."

"They don't believe it. Ask any of the Pins if they would follow me, other than to shoot me in the back."

"We face other problems, Father," Saladin said. "More pressing ones."

"I know, I know. What word of Colonel Phillips and his brigade?" Watie asked. He was not sure having a nation divided by such hatred *was* secondary to anything else, but it often seemed that way. Finish the war between North and South, and the Cherokee problems would be over. It sounded so simple—and he knew it was a lie even as he fought harder to make it so.

"He began moving his troops into Indian Territory and might make a two-pronged attack, one striking at Fort Gibson and the other at Tahlequah."

Watie thought hard. Which was more important, the main supply point for his army or the Cherokee capital? One provided food and sanctuary, but the other carried great emotional attachment. Lose your capital, lose your soul? It had taken months for people to trickle slowly back to Tahlequah after Captain Greeno had marched through there on his way to Park Hill to accept John Ross's all-too-easy surrender. Keetoowahs had killed any Southern sympathizers. Then the tide had turned after Salomon had retreated so suddenly.

Watie wished he had more control over his own troops. He spat in disgust. While he was wishing, he might as well ask for more soldiers. There had been scant support from Missouri or Arkansas in way of supplies or reinforcements in months. Victory after victory had done nothing to win more backing from the Trans-Mississippi District, to the point that Watie considered severing ties with the Confederacy and declaring the Cherokee Nation sovereign of both North and South.

But John Ross had tried that, and Stand Watie was no John Ross.

"Where is John Drew?"

"Cantonment Davis," Saladin reported. "He's at the salt works, but he's complaining that he's not being paid well enough and is threatening to cut off our salt rations."

"What is he being paid?"

"Four hundred a month."

"He should be filled with salt and his mouth sewed shut," grumbled Watie. "But he no longer commands a regiment. That is a bright spot on an otherwise dark cloth."

"What are we to do about Phillips?"

"Fight. We fight every step of the way, but if he has supplies and enough men, there is no way we can hold both Fort Gibson and Tahlequah."

"Which do we defend?"

Stand Watie shrugged, smiled wanly, and gave the only possible answer: "Both."

Cabin Springs Ambush
July 1, 1863

"We recruit more men every day," Saladin Watie said. "We might have enough to wrest the fort from Phillips if . . ." The young man's words trailed off when he saw his father wasn't listening. Stand Watie poured over a letter—yet another to his wife, in refuge down in Texas.

"Father," Saladin said gently, putting his hand on the older man's shoulder. "What are we to do? Colonel Phillips marched on Tahlequah and has taken it, too. We've lost both Fort Gibson and our capital."

"Yes, I know, I know," Watie said irritably. He threw down his pen and looked up, his face lined with worry. "There is nothing we can do about it."

"There is one bright spot," Saladin said.

"Douglas Cooper being promoted to general? Yes, that is good," Watie admitted. He still felt the loss of Albert Pike deeply. Nothing that had happened to Pike had been his fault. If he had to pick a commander for the troops in the Indian Territory, though, he could not do better than Colonel Cooper. The man was mule-headed at times, but he understood their problems as well as any man not a Cherokee could. *General Cooper,* he mentally corrected.

"It's been a long, hard campaign. I wish I could have

stopped Phillips from retaking Fort Gibson," he said, desolation in his voice.

"We have done the best we could with what we have at hand," his son comforted. "At least the District has a wagonload of powder on its way to us from Mexico. We're almost out of gunpowder."

"We are almost out of everything," Watie said. The summer had not been as dry as the prior one, but no farms produced food. Those of the pro-Union Cherokee were destroyed by his own men, whether he approved or not. And the Confederate-leaning Cherokee were ambushed and lynched by the Keetoowahs. No one was safe in the Cherokee Nation. Watie had not bothered to count, but felt he had lost more of his men to snipers and ambushes set by the Pins than to outright military action against the Federals.

He had certainly lost more supplies to the pro-Union Cherokee than to Colonel Phillips and his soldiers.

"Supplies," he mused. "Phillips is using Fort Gibson as a supply base again. That's going to do us in, unless we can retake the fort."

"Of course he is," snorted Saladin. "Will Ross is post sutler." This angered Stand Watie, but he pushed down the fury he felt toward any of the Ross family. It was as if Will Ross went out of his way to aid and abet the enemy.

"Supplies. Cut them off and *they* starve. They can no more live off the land here than we can."

"Their supply trains are well guarded. Tom Anderson reports some have more soldiers riding along than we have in the entire regiment."

Stand Watie fell silent for a moment. What would he do without Tom or Saladin, or so many of the others? With luck, and if rumors were right, William Penn Adair would soon be returned from imprisonment as part of a prisoner exchange. He could use William's skills as scout and return Tom to his post as adjutant.

"We cannot take the fort," Watie said, "not by attacking directly. But if we strike their supply wagons at Cabin Springs, we can make a few blue bellies grumble with hunger in coming weeks."

"We have the men for such a raid. We captured more than fifty head of horses in the past week, and all our troopers are mounted again."

"To Cabin Springs, Captain, to Cabin Springs!" Watie felt a surge of energy at the idea of squeezing the Union from the Cherokee Nation once again. It wouldn't be easy, but it had to be done.

Saladin Watie hurried off to mount the regiment. Watie looked at the letter he had been writing to Sarah. How he longed to see her again. The best he could hope for was decent mail service between Indian Territory and Texas, down on the Brazos, where she, Cumiskey, Watica, and the two girls stayed. Sarah tried to sound cheerful, but Watie knew her too well. She hated the separation, and from the subtle hints in her words he knew they suffered from lack of supplies, too.

"Supplies," he said. "That's the key to this war." He put away the letter and went to prepare his horse for battle. Today would see the beginning of yet another attempt to defeat the Federals and drive them out of the Cherokee Nation.

Watie hoped it would be successful.

"That's a powerful long baggage train," opined the scout. "Too many guards for it to be anything usual."

Watie studied the road and the long line of soldiers tramping along, as well as the wagons creaking under the heavy weight of their load. He had more than four-hundred men ready for the ambush, but they would be outnumbered if he attacked this train.

"Why so many men guarding this supply train?" he wondered aloud.

"Colonel, take a look at the pennon flyin' on the staff halfway back in the train. That there's a gen'ral's flag." The scout passed him a pair of field binoculars.

Watie frowned. A general coming in to Fort Gibson? He wondered if Colonel Phillips knew it. Nothing suggested unusual activity at Fort Gibson, as if they prepared for an inspection.

"I'll go see what I kin figger out," the scout said. Before Watie could tell him to stop, the man shucked off his Confederate uniform coat and walked boldly down the hill, looking like nothing more than an unsuccessful farmer on the same road as the military convoy.

"We have some brave men in the regiment," Watie said, as much to himself as to the handful of officers crowded near him. "Pull back. We're not attacking this train. There might be one following we can go after."

"I'll see to it," offered a corporal nearby. He set off at a run, not bothering to take his horse. Watie knew the man could run farther, faster, on foot than he could on horseback, and guards on a wagon train were less likely to put much store in a solitary man afoot than one mounted.

Watie led the way down the hill and along the winding Cabin Springs to a small glade. He let his men water their horses and take a short break. In less than an hour the man who had gone to spy on the long wagon train came trotting up.

"The men in Fort Gibson are in for a big surprise. That there's General Blunt ridin' in to take command. Nobody's told Colonel Phillips."

"Why would a general come in like that?" wondered Watie. He made a quick note and vowed to dispatch other information to General Cooper when he learned more.

"Somebody don't like the way Phillips commands, is my guess," the scout said. "Not aggressive enough."

"He's taken both Fort Gibson and Tahlequah!" Watie said, but realized his scout's opinion was probably true. Phillips had recaptured both with little effort, but had done nothing more since then. An aggressive commander ought to have spread out across the countryside to stamp out all resistance in the Cherokee Nation.

It took two more hours before the second scout returned, grinning from ear to ear. "Colonel, you're going to love this. A big, long train with danged few guards on it is trailin' along not ten miles down the road. I spied 'em from the top of Gooseneck Ridge, 'bout where they'd stop for watering."

"Cabin Springs feeds that stream," Watie said. He passed along the orders to mount. The entire regiment rode along the stream until they reached the point where the wagons would pause to water their teams. It took almost twenty minutes getting his men hidden and spread out in a semi-circle around the springs.

Then he took a company and rode up the ridge and waited. The battle was over almost before it began. Watie was startled to see Tom Anderson riding hellbent for leather, waving his hat and shouting for him to retreat. Watie hesitated, and then it was too late for him to change his mind about the assault. The wagons pulled up, and Watie's company charged down.

The Union soldiers were a wary lot, and none of Watie's troopers got very close before they opened up with devastating fire from their Springfield repeating rifles. The leading element of Watie's regiment hit what seemed an invisible barrier of deadly lead and bounced back in confusion. Saladin regrouped his men and got a little closer before being driven off.

"Retreat!" cried Watie. He rode to his bugler and shook the young man. "Sound retreat. Now, do it now!"

The weak notes conveyed more about the tide of battle than anything else could have. Watie got his surviving troopers back by the time Tom Anderson trotted up, out of breath.

"Stand, get the boys outta there," his adjutant turned chief of scouts gasped out. "That's not just any unit. They're a crack infantry regiment, Blunt's private guard. They got supplies, they got ammo, they got everything they need to hold you off."

Watie saw that, and reluctantly signaled that his men slip off into the countryside. They had instructions on where to regroup later that night.

When they did, even the small, crackling fires and sparse food did nothing to restore their spirits.

They had been defeated—and had a glimpse of the future riding into their nation in the person of General James G. Blunt.

Battle of Honey Springs
July 17, 1863

"We can do it, Stand," Douglas Cooper insisted, the elaborate gold stars on his jacket epaulets shining like miniature suns as they reflected the light from the sunrise. "The War Department finally realized the opportunities in Indian Territory. Everything's been set in motion."

"We did get the gunpowder and ammunition shipment." Watie hesitated, then plunged into what he considered a matter of some importance. "The lead bullets aren't well formed. My men worry the egg-shaped slugs will jam in their rifle barrels."

In truth, he worried about more than this. Since his defeat at Cabin Springs, the Federals had been increasingly aggressive about cutting off Confederate supplies. General Blunt had sent his men out with the intent of doing nothing more than starving the soldiers opposing him. Not once since Cabin Springs had Watie engaged any of Blunt's men in more than brief, inconclusive skirmishes. If he had to have supplies in a hurry, he would rather steal them from the Union army than buy them from crooked Mexican agents intent on nothing more than rooking the Confederates.

"It's all Mexican, but it's better than nothing," Cooper insisted. "We will be in a good position, and can drive Phillips from the field. When this is over, I'll be placed in command of the entire district, wait and see."

"Blunt," Watie corrected, hardly noticing Cooper's vision of the future—*his* future. "General Blunt is in command now, Fort Scott his command post. I'm not even sure Colonel Phillips is still at Fort Gibson."

"It doesn't matter who's commanding the Federals. Blunt, if it is his doing, made a big mistake scattering his forces the way he did. He's ranging throughout the countryside, spreading himself too thin. We can concentrate our forces at Fort Gibson and take advantage of that."

"You'll be in the Creek Nation, on Fort Gibson's doorstep?"

"We will attack in concert with Cabell, but even so the fort might be too well-guarded to seize. What I intend to do is prevent Blunt's forces from returning to the fort. Keep them outside, and we can pick them off unit by unit."

"What do you know of this Major Cabell?" asked Watie.

Cooper stroked his mustache, then said, "Only that he is bringing four thousand men with him. We need them desperately, Stand, if we are to drive Blunt from Indian Territory. I've heard Cabell is with the quartermaster's corps, but other than this I have no knowledge of his combat record."

"A quartermaster?" Stand Watie felt a sinking sensation. It was good that four thousand men were on their way from Arkansas—it was what the CSA had promised so long ago in the treaty John Ross had signed. But he felt as if he would be saddled with four thousand raw recruits rather than the seasoned battle veterans needed to turn the tide.

"What are the plans?" Watie asked, not sure he wanted to know. He thought his regiment could be more effective staying mobile in the field, sniping at the Federals and trying to cut *their* supplies again. Every victory, no matter how minor, brought in new recruits. The loss of both Fort Gibson and Tahlequah, though, robbed him of a lever to gain even more.

And all that had to be asked was where his family stayed. Watie felt a lump in his throat as he thought of his wife and children, eking out a meager existence down in Lamar, Texas. They were among friends, and safe from both John Ross and the Federals, but he missed them and agonized over their trials.

"Cabell is supposed to arrive any time now. We will hit Fort Gibson from two directions," General Cooper said, energized by the notion they might actually wrest Fort Gibson from Union hands again. "I have barges made to cross the Arkansas River near Honey Springs that will put us less than fifteen miles from the fort. With almost six thousand men pitted against Blunt's three thousand, we cannot fail. And when Cabell arrives, we will outnumber the Federals more than three-to-one."

"Cabell's not here yet," Watie pointed out. "If he is marching straight through from Arkansas on the Texas Road, will his troops be fresh enough to enter the fight?"

"They are regular army," Cooper said, dismissing such concerns as foolishness, although he did not come right out and say as much. "They'll be ready for hard fighting. Taking Fort Gibson is not going to be easily done."

"I know," Stand Watie said, and he did. "I'll bring my First and Second Cherokee Mounted Rifles behind your soldiers as support. We can cross Honey Springs, though it is swollen now, and be at the fort gates within a few hours."

"Do so, Stand. And thank you. I don't know what I'd do without you and your men. The Union would have overrun the Cherokee Nation long ago without you."

"Thank you," Watie said, shaking the general's hand. He was touched. "I won't fail you."

* * *

"Where's Cabell?" Stand Watie asked. "He's supposed to be here by now."

"He might still be on the road from Fort Smith," Tom Anderson said, "but there's no trace of him. But there is of General Blunt. He's cut through Cooper's men and divided our attacking force already. If he keeps going, he will force us back across the Canadian River."

"I was afraid of that. He knew our plans." Watie turned sullen. The damned Keetoowahs! Even in his own regiment there were Pin spies. He did not doubt Cooper had them among his troops—and every solitary figure sitting on a hill as they marched past might be eyes and ears for Blunt. It was hard to know when the onlookers were supporters or enemies, since they were all Cherokee.

"It looks that way, Colonel," Tom said. "What are your orders?"

"We can retreat east to the Canadian River, making it look as if we're waiting for Cabell to arrive," Watie said. "That would leave Cooper in a perilous spot, though."

"There are reports of too many desertions," Tom said in a low voice, not wanting to arouse others standing nearby.

"What of the Federal artillery?" asked Watie. "Are the cannon going to be a factor?"

"That's what cut Cooper's force. When he tried to return fire, something went wrong. His men tried to fight, then scattered. He has done well reforming them, but this has given Blunt time to move forward, pushing Cooper back to Honey Springs."

"The powder," Watie said. "The Mexican gunpowder is no good." He vented a deep sigh. "We must advance. If we don't, Cooper will fall and so will the entire Indian Territory."

"At least we're fighting on Creek land," Tom said, no humor in his words.

"Mount the men. Check the gunpowder with a few rounds, but not too many. We don't want to advertise our presence—as if Blunt doesn't know where we are."

Stand Watie mounted and touched the butt of his pistol, wondering for the first time if it would misfire when he needed it most. He had gone through the boxes of bullets hunting for only the best formed, and had insisted his men dispose of the others. More than half the bullets had been left in a ditch.

And where was Cabell?

"Forward!" Watie cried. Several miles separated his regiment from Cooper's, but he heard the heavy roar of Blunt's cannon and the duller, flat snaps of Confederate muskets firing. Before he reached Cooper's right flank, he met sharp resistance from the direction of a wooded area.

"Dismount, fight on foot," Watie ordered when he saw the ambush would decimate his regiment if they kept riding. His men slid from their saddles and fell belly down to return fire. The dull *snap!* sounds of the Confederate fire told him of the danger to his men. He emptied his pistol in the direction of the nearest Federal soldier, driving the young man back, then took time to reload. Watie worried every chamber might be a dud, but he had no other choice.

The skirmish line advanced slowly, pushing the Union soldiers around, folding them in on themselves. It would have been a decent victory had Watie not felt the urgency of reinforcing General Cooper's forces.

"Let 'em run!" he ordered when the Union line finally broke. The dozens of his soldiers, many of them Choctaw and Osage and Chickasaw and Creek and even Cherokee, reluctantly obeyed. It had been too long since they had felt the sweetness of victory.

"Mount. We have to keep going."

And Watie did, arriving on Cooper's flank in time to support the 1st Cherokee Home Guard against a frontal assault from the Union soldiers.

Watie's men acquitted themselves well, but Cooper had to retreat slowly until he reached the Canadian River. As Cooper slipped away from the punishing Federal fire, so did Watie. The enemy's artillery was devastating, and turned a numerical superiority in troops to a hindrance. Watie could not get out of the way fast enough, and lost men who should have been saved.

Worst of all, Stand Watie saw that he faced not white soldiers but other Indians. Creek made up most of the regiment Blunt threw against him, but he also recognized Seminole and Cherokee.

Cherokee. His brothers fought ferociously, and this was as disheartening as the realization his men were almost out of gunpowder. The Mexican powder had proven itself of such poor quality that even a drop of water in it rendered it worthless. He had always cringed at the stark noise of battle. Now he flinched for other reasons. Too many dull *pop!* noises marked the failure of one Cherokee musket after another to fire properly.

Watie wanted to talk with Cooper, to find if there was something to do other than turn and run. Then he saw how the battle went against the Confederates, and knew there was nothing. Cooper had crossed the Canadian River on his barges, and now struggled to regain the far side with far fewer men than he had arrived with.

"Charge!" Watie called to his men. His bugler sounded the command, and he stormed forward against the Federal flank. His first assault was turned back, and the second and the third. By the time Watie regrouped for a fourth charge, he saw the Union artillerists turning their cannon in his direction now that they had routed Cooper's main force.

"Retreat," he called. Watie had done all he could. Breaking the Union line had proven impossible, but he had drawn fire away from Cooper's retreating forces. It was time for him to get away with as many of his men alive as possible.

He swung his force around, only to find himself caught in a crossfire. The company he had set to running had not fled mindlessly, but had regrouped and then followed him. There weren't many of them, but there were enough to slow him so the artillery could drop shells on his head. Watie considered crossing the river and joining Cooper's men on the far side, where they might be able to fortify the banks and hold the line to do what he had considered earlier—riding east and waiting for Cabell.

Right now an extra four thousand men would turn the tide, even if they had punk gunpowder like Watie and Cooper. It would be difficult attacking across the Canadian into the mouth of the Federal cannon, but with Cabell's reinforcements it could be done. It *had* to be done if they wanted to recapture Fort Gibson.

The Federal commander couldn't have fielded more than three thousand men, but they were well-entrenched, thanks to spies warning Blunt of where the Confederates would attack at Honey Springs.

"We can't stay here. Forward," Watie ordered. He felt like a rat trapped in a deadly maze. There seemed nowhere to turn, to run, to survive. "Forward, and through their line!" Watie led the charge back down the road in the direction they had come. The snipers potshotted one after another of his men, taking them from horseback, but the majority of the Cherokee Mounted Rifles broke through the thin line and kept riding.

Watie wasn't sure how many men he had lost, but that hardly mattered. Most of his regiment was intact, even if they lacked decent firepower. The real defeat had come when Cooper had crossed the river, unable to fight.

Cabell arrived the next day too late to support any Confederate unit, Cooper's command retreated south into Texas along the Red River, and Stand Watie remained in Indian Territory to press the war as best he could against increasing forces and diminishing support from the Five Civilized Tribes, including those of the Cherokee Nation.

William Potter Ross
Fall 1863

"Blunt is ranging over into Arkansas," Saladin Watie reported to his father. "Cabell is constantly retreating, and Fort Smith might fall at any moment."

Fort Gibson, Fort Smith, when will it end? wondered Stand Watie. He lay back, the cold ground hard and lumpy under him as he stared into the clear blue sky. A few clouds tinted with darkness floated on the horizon. How like his life they seemed, those clouds. His wife and family had moved deeper into Texas, and were no longer among relatives, much less friends. Too many from the Cherokee Nation had scattered throughout Texas south of the Red River after the disaster at Honey Springs. The loss had snapped the back of the Confederate in Indian Territory, reducing the Cherokee Mounted Rifles to nothing more than guerrilla activity. Gone were the days when Watie expected to join with others in a unified assault.

If Cooper had not been betrayed by spies in his own rank, if the weather had not been wet and the Mexican gunpowder bad, if—it never ended. There were too many "might have beens" for Watie to tolerate. He had attacked Federal supply lines, capturing a baggage train here and burning an ammo dump there, but he had been robbed of any effective forays by Cooper's stunning loss. Blunt had forced the battle and stolen away any advantage Cooper might have had.

"Honey Springs might be the turning point for us," he muttered, more to himself than to his son. It was difficult to see how the CSA could recover. With Fort Smith also in Federal hands, the Trans-Mississippi District was lost. General Grant had been sent back East after taking Vicksburg, giving the Union the ability to concentrate its forces against Lee and ignore Confederate action anywhere else.

Stand Watie vowed to make them regret that hubris. But how?

"We can attack Fort Gibson," Watie said suddenly.

"Father, please," scoffed Saladin. "We have the chance to ride up to Cowskin Prairie and join forces with a guerrilla unit from Kansas."

"Quantrill?" Watie shook his head. He had heard nothing good about those brigands. They were bloody handed murderers, nothing more. They used the war as an excuse to rob and rape. Not that Watie's men had not engaged in those actions themselves—after Honey Springs he had found his command threatened by hints of desertion, and he had allowed more outlaw activity than he had previously, even if it hurt his sense of honor.

What appalled him was how little it damaged his pride knowing his men were little more than outlaws.

This had turned into a war of extinction. The Federals had shown that repeatedly when they burned pro-Confederate Indians' houses and crops; the atrocities committed on them by Creek and Cherokee returned from Kansas haunted his nightmares. When his own men reciprocated out of hurt and need for revenge, how could he deny them?

But Quantrill? He would not stay in the same camp with that man.

"He strikes fear in the hearts of the Union commanders throughout Missouri and Kansas," Saladin Watie said. "He's retreating into Texas for a rest."

"He's been chased out," Watie said coldly. "A man like that would never consider R&R if there was a chance to spill more blood."

"Riding with him seems more logical than attacking Fort Gibson," his son said.

"That's why it is such a good idea. I don't believe we could capture Fort Gibson, not with only a few hundred warriors, but we can bottle them up and destroy everything surrounding the fort. This will send a message to Blunt that he dare not sally too far from his base or he might return and find it captured."

"You have something more in mind, don't you, Father?"

"John Ross has been making speeches in Washington again, trying to establish himself as the only legitimate government for the Cherokee Nation. He calls himself the principal chief of the 'Loyal Cherokee.' Imagine that. I have more than three hundred men who are far more loyal riding at my back," Watie said. "It is time for Ross to understand what honor and loyalty to one's own people means."

"This isn't as much about Blunt as it is about John Ross," observed Saladin. "What are your intentions, Father? Really?"

"Will Ross runs the sutlership outside Fort Gibson when he isn't engaged as a colonel at the fort. If my scout is right, he has just received a big shipment intended to support General Blunt. It would be a shame if he lost all that profit, and Blunt also had to resupply. We can be waiting for that wagon train, too."

"Ambitious plans, Father," Saladin said. "What if there are more soldiers at Fort Gibson than you think?"

"We burn out Will Ross's store, then ride away, not fighting. But I know Blunt has grown overconfident, especially after Honey Springs. Why else would he venture into Arkansas?"

"Because he could capture Fort Smith," said Saladin. "He has all the cards in his hand."

"Then let's take a few of them off the table and force him to ante up for another round," Stand Watie said decisively. He shouted for his striker to pack his gear, then went to assemble his other officers. There was a mission to plan.

"How soon will their sentries spot us?" wondered Saladin Watie.

"They might be in town getting drunk. Blunt does nothing to control his troopers." Watie silently pointed to the west, indicating the two-story hospital at the easternmost edge of Fort Gibson outlined by the afternoon sun. A few horses in front showed the doctors were busy that day. Watie indicated his column should head south, circling away from both the hospital and the rows of officers' houses. Although they rode in the light of day, making no effort to hide their identity or otherwise draw attention to themselves, no one paid them any heed.

It was as Watie had hoped. The Federals had grown complacent, thinking they had won the war. His heart beat a little faster as he neared the southern side of the fort. A quarter-mile from the main gate were row upon row of one-story wood buildings holding the services needed to keep the fort functioning.

The fort stood with its gates open. Watie peered directly into the parade ground—and at the three field pieces there. He hesitated as he considered his chances, then knew it would be a slaughter if he ordered his men inside. Along the walls patrolled soldiers, not too alert but in position to deliver withering fire from all sides to anyone venturing inside uninvited. And the blockhouses on the southern corners might have more than a few men in them—disaster waiting to be delivered to anyone foolish enough to rush the fort.

"The businesses," Watie said to his officers. "The ones supplying the fort. Take what you can carry easily, destroy the rest."

His men scattered, knowing what to do. Saladin Watie remained by his father's side.

"Father, you aren't going to do anything against your promises to Mother, are you?"

"There's Ross's store," he said, trying to put his son's words from his mind. He drew his pistol and dismounted, dropping the reins to the ground. His horse snorted and backed off, as if realizing how close death stalked.

Watie kicked in the door, then burst into the store, pistol leveled at a startled William Potter Ross. John Ross's nephew, colonel in the Union army, let out a tiny yelp and held his hands in front of him, as if trying to push Watie from the store.

"We're seizing everything in this store as spoils of war," Watie said. "And I ought to execute you as a traitor." He cocked his pistol and aimed it at Ross's face.

"Watie, you can't—"

"For all you and your uncle have done, I can do anything I want. I was elected principal chief."

"Only of the Southern Nation, not of all the Cherokee," protested Ross. His hands shook, and he edged along the counter, as if heading for the door. Watie's muzzle followed him.

"You sold us all out, and for what? This? The chance to profit by selling flour and blankets to our enemies?"

"Your enemies, not those of the Cherokee," Ross said, some courage returning.

"Your uncle groomed you to take over from him," Watie said. "You were supposed to become principal chief. Instead you sell supplies to the Federals." His finger tightened on the trigger. Will Ross closed his eyes and muttered a prayer, waiting to die.

Stand Watie heard movement in the doorway behind him, but he did not turn. His finger relaxed on the trigger. He had promised Sarah not to harm Will Ross, should he have the chance of capturing him. She worried about Ross's mother, for whom she had great affection, and Stand Watie was not one to go against his wife's wishes. He could do so little for her, anyway, and news of him murdering Will Ross would devastate her.

"I place you under arrest for treason," he said. "You abandoned your command, and are giving aid and comfort to the enemy. I'll see if General Cooper can convene a court-martial later." Over his shoulder, Watie said, "Captain, take Mr. Ross into custody."

Saladin Watie let out the breath he had been holding. He pushed past his father and took William Potter Ross by the arm, herding the sutler from the store.

Watie lowered his pistol and then let the shakes come. He had been so close to killing Ross, just to take revenge on his uncle. Watie cared nothing for Will Ross, but he was a nothing compared to John Ross.

A nothing.

Watie made a circuit of the store, cramming small items into a burlap bag-to send to his wife and children in Texas. Another opportunity to loot like this would be rare—and he wasn't even certain he could send what he took to his family. Food, items small and valuable, all went into his bag. Then he cracked open a tin container of kerosene and sloshed the volatile contents over the store.

He stepped to the door and heard the uproar coming from Fort Gibson. The soldiers had finally decided something untoward was going on under their noses. Watie fired his pistol into the puddle of kerosene and immediately threw up his arms to protect his face from the sudden hot rush of flames.

Stand Watie raced into the street, aware of bullets kicking up dust all around him. The guards in the southwestern blockhouse at the fort shoved their rifles through a dozen loopholes and fired fast and hard at him.

Dodging, he got to his horse and slung his booty behind the saddle, securing it with two quick turns of a rawhide strip. He let out a rebel yell and started shooting into the other businesses along the street. The fire from Ross's store spread quickly and provided a towering wall of flame to cover his men's retreat from the town. Past the saloons, past the cribs now emptying as their half-dressed women began to panic, past the fringes of town and into the countryside south of Fort Gibson raced Stand Watie's Cherokee Mounted Rifles.

It had been a good raid—and he had captured the nephew of his bitterest enemy. It wasn't as good as victory at Honey Springs would have been, but it felt *good,* nonetheless.

Camp Starvation
Winter 1863-64

"Their wagon trains are fewer now that the snows have come," Saladin Watie observed. "Why not go south into Texas so we can be with the family?"

Stand Watie shook his head. It was cold again, but not as cold as some winters. "There is too much to do. If we let up for even a week, the Federals will take that as a sign of weakness. We must continue to harass them however we can."

"I don't like Choctaw Country," Saladin said.

"Neither do I," Watie admitted to his son. "I miss Tahlequah, I miss Cowskin Prairie. I even miss going to Fort Gibson." He settled back, folded his hands over his belly, and closed his eyes. His wool uniform kept him warm, and he felt almost comfortable at the moment as his recollections of the super returned. William Potter Ross had been captured, and his store burned. That raid had upset the Union commanders greatly, but the aftermath had not been good from Watie's view.

Will Ross had been ransomed quickly enough, through the efforts of his uncle in Washington. John Ross was an old man, but one who never stopped his politicking. Watie tensed at the thought of Ross working tirelessly to overthrow all that had been done in the Cherokee Nation, then pushed it from his mind. The Confederacy was losing the West, through lack of will and having no idea how best to use the native soldiers once at its disposal.

"The next time, I kill him, no matter what promise I made your mother," Watie said.

Saladin looked up, startled. He had not followed his father's line of thought.

"Will Ross," Stand Watie explained, seeing the confusion. "When I track him down next time, I will kill him. A bullet would be nice, but a noose after a legal court-martial would be even better."

"We cannot get within five miles of Fort Gibson without being seen now," Saladin said. "That raid might have temporarily deterred the Federals, but it worked against us ever retaking the fort."

"Wars aren't won by defense," Watie said. "We must attack, always attack. The weather is worsening. That means more supply trains from the north. We destroy them, we put many soldiers out of action through starvation."

"We must avoid that ourselves," Saladin cautioned.

Watie's own belly grumbled a little, but his men still had enough food. If their raiding went well throughout the winter, no one would suffer unduly.

If. . . .

"Four wagons?" asked Stand Watie. "That's all there is?"

"We scouted up and down the Fort Smith road hunting for others. That's the lot of 'em," the scout confirmed.

Watie pulled his threadbare jacket tighter around his heavyset frame to rob the wind of its teeth. He failed. The Federal wagon train had better have enough uniforms and blankets for all his men, or there would be serious threat of frostbite in the coming weeks. It was hardly Christmas and the weather had turned unrelentingly bitter, never letting up for even a day. One norther after another whipped down out of Kansas to bedevil his regiment, making it difficult to ride or camp.

It was becoming even more difficult to keep the men mounted. They were beginning to eat their horses. Watie wasn't sure some even hesitated at killing the animals rather than letting them die a natural death from freezing or starvation.

He lifted his pistol, then realized it was useless. To save powder, he had not loaded it. In the cold, the mechanism had a tendency to seize up, also. If they were lucky on this raid, there would be no shooting. The Federal guards on the wagons might be as miserable as Watie's soldiers. If so, they would surrender quickly.

"Charge!"

Watie and two score of his cavalry rode down the hill. When they began their descent, Saladin and his company on the far side of the road started his attack, catching the wagons between the two elements. The condition of the road made escape improbable, the deep ruts filled with ice and frozen mud.

Almost on top of the supply wagons, Stand Watie got a cold shiver down his spine that had nothing to do with the sharp wind blowing across the prairie. Something was wrong, desperately wrong. He holstered his pistol and struggled to pull out his cavalry saber, a weapon he never used because of its cumbersome bulk and awkwardness in battle. He felt he had to have some dependable weapon in hand.

And he was right.

The tarps over the back of the lead wagon flew up, caught the wind, and went sailing away. The canvas cover had hidden a dozen snipers, who leveled their rifles and opened fire on Watie's attacking men. A bullet whizzed past his head, but Watie hunkered down and kept riding. He refused to die on the snow-packed road in this clumsy ambush.

A second bullet nicked his arm. A third took his horse out from under him. Watie hit the ground, tumbling like dice. He rolled in the muck and came to his feet next to a wagon wheel. Using his saber, he hacked at one sniper's arm. Grabbing the Springfield rifle from the man's nerveless fingers, Watie turned it on another Federal in the wagon and fired at pointblank range.

The sharp recoil sent him staggering. He tripped and sat down heavily in the road, icy water oozing around his legs and chilling his body even more.

He used the rifle as a crutch to pry himself loose from the sucking mud and started to renew his attack. The fight was over. His men had overrun the wagons, and had fought fearlessly until the last Federal was dead.

"The other wagons!" he shouted. "Be careful!" He need not have worried—the three remaining wagons were loaded with blankets and much needed powder.

His belly grumbled from lack of food, but what they took from the teamsters would keep them going until they got back to their camp.

Watie unhitched one of the horses from the first wagon and mounted it. The horse balked—it had not carried a solitary rider on its back before, from the way it bucked and tried to turn in sharp circles to throw him—but Watie was too cold to walk. He gentled the horse and walked it around the wagon train, seeing his men stripping what they could from the wagons. He wished they could have taken the entire wagon train, but where they rode there were no roads.

Still, it had not been a bad day—except for the three of his men killed during the attack, and the six who deserted on the way back to camp.

Camp Starvation, his men called it. With good reason. It was a very long and terrible winter, and it got worse when he received news of his son Cumiskey's death.

Recognition
May 10, 1864

"We had to burn most of the supplies, Colonel," advised a new lieutenant. Watie struggled to remember his name. He had been taken ill with the ague, and only that morning had his fever broken. Ever since learning of his son's death in the winter Stand Watie had fought depression and sickness. The weather was fine, now, and the days pleasant, yet he shivered and coughed and sweated as if it were the middle of another sultry summer.

Threekiller. The name came to him through a haze. Watie nodded and said, "Good work, Lieutenant Threekiller. We must try to strangle the Federals, starve them as we have been starved."

"Yes, sir," the lieutenant said, not sure what to say next.

"Dismissed."

"Uh, Colonel, is there anything to the rumor that General Steele is coming to inspect our camp?"

Watie sighed. No matter how he tried to keep quiet the official visits, word always got out. How could his men know the intimate details of Confederate officers' comings and goings but not know equally well what the enemy did? For just one man capable of tapping into *that* intelligence he would have given anything.

"Later, later in the week. That's why we must do what we can to contain the shipments to Fort Gibson."

"A spring offensive against the fort?" Lieutenant Threekiller said, hope in his voice and on his face.

"We would need a considerable number of troops—"

"From Texas, sir? I've heard that."

"Keep it to yourself. We don't want idle speculation getting out, now do we?" Watie had no idea where that rumor had started. He had wanted to visit his family in Texas to see how Sarah and the children—the surviving children—were getting on. It had been so long—too long—but he had remained with his troops because he knew that if he left, even for a few days, there would be no command to return to. Saladin was a capable young man, but did not yet have the authority or force of will to hold together a regiment struggling simply to survive. Tom Anderson might be adjutant, but he was also a white man. Among the others Watie counted competent officers, but none he thought able to hold together his command. Gunter and Brewer were good men, but lacked the spark to inspire men.

Heaven knew that the Cherokee Mounted Rifles had needed constant inspiration this last winter, even from a commander riddled with sickness and self-doubt.

Camp Starvation. It had been aptly named. No one ever had enough to eat. Stolen blankets and Union uniforms had made the camp look more like a Federal bivouac than a Confederate one, but no one cared. They had to stay warm against one of the coldest winters Watie could remember. Mostly they had garnered their strength—hoarded it—for the raids on wagon trains and Federal outposts. They had even successfully raided within a few miles of Fort Gibson, stealing cattle that had fed the entire regiment for almost two weeks.

Spring wound warm fingers around the land, caressed

the soil, and coaxed edible plants to grow in the hills. The countryside was devastated by the war.

Here and there were a few farmers willing to share what they had with him and his men.

More often than not, however, his soldiers were taunted and shot at. Those farms were burned to the ground, and the occupants killed or driven away. Little in the way of bounty came from such places, and Watie knew that tactic only built a reservoir of ill feeling that would have to dealt with when the war ended.

If it ever ended. His nightmares—his fever dreams—were of a war that lasted forever.

Watie sat in the warm sun and let the rays renew his strength and chase away the sickness, if not his depression. Many of his men had deserted or died during the winter, but he still commanded more than John Drew had after his disastrous showing at Caving Banks. More than two hundred men still looked to Stand Watie as their colonel.

They were ready to embark on a new season of warfare against a seemingly inexorable blue tide washing over their land. He had been elected principal chief, but of a diminishing number of Cherokee. Watie was not even sure who the pro-Union Cherokee Council had chosen as their representative, with John Ross still in Philadelphia. It did not matter.

He felt warm and content enough to drift off to sleep, only to be awakened by the blaring of a bugle. Watie's hand went to his pistol, but he did not draw when he saw the banners flapping in the breeze at the head of a long column of men.

Many wore Union pants and jackets, but few men wore both. Still others chose the more traditional buckskins or even ratty, worn pants and coats that looked at odds with the crisp Confederate uniform on the man at the head of the column.

Watie got shakily to his feet and smoothed out his own

tattered uniform. The once proud gold braid had turned black, and his insignia, despite his and his orderlies' best efforts, had permanently lost its luster. He stepped up to greet the general making this surprise visit to his camp.

"At least no one calls it Camp Starvation now," Watie said under his breath.

"Sir," cried Lieutenant Threekiller, running up. "It's General Steele himself!"

"I can see that," Watie said drily. "He's early. I wasn't expecting him till later in the week." Watie had hoped to have one or two more successful raids under his belt before the general came. It was too much to think Steele had any plans for real military action, so Watie wanted to show him what the Cherokee Mounted Rifles could do as guerrillas and strike-and-run cavalry. Steele had repeatedly derided any warfare other than unit against unit, but Watie could not see that happening any more out West. The Confederate forces were too weak for a concerted battle.

To Steele, he was little more than a renegade out savaging an already ripped apart land.

"Sir, welcome," Stand Watie greeted, giving the general the best salute he could. His joints ached, and his elbow balked at bending. Steele returned the salute, then dismounted.

"You are a wonder, Colonel Watie," Steele greeted him. "All winter you held your men together as a fighting unit. You look fit enough to take on any challenge."

"What are your orders, sir?" Watie wished he could sleep, and felt anything but fit, but he wasn't going to argue with a general, especially one as contentious as William Steele.

Steele laughed harshly. "If we'd had a dozen officers of your caliber, Colonel, we'd be sitting in Washington right now, drinking brandy, smoking cigars, and singing 'Dixie.' " The general looked around the camp with some contempt. "I'm afraid there isn't anything important brewing at the moment either of us can sink our teeth into. There is so much political fighting going on, it is increasingly hard even to get acknowledgment from the War Department for my requests for payrolls."

"My own requests fall on deaf ears, too," Watie said. The Cherokee delegate to the Confederate Congress, Watie's nephew Elias Cornelius Boudinot, had been ineffective, and his decreasing authority in that body and with Confederate politicians irked Watie.

"Unlike you, I spend most of my non-paperwork time finding military targets worthy of attacking rather than trying to cut off supply lines, destroying ordinance." Steele looked as if he had bitten into a persimmon. "Three days ago my men blew up seven field pieces. How I wish you'd had those at Honey Springs!"

"Blunt would never have won, sir," Watie lied. It would have taken more than a few cannon to turn the tide at Honey Springs. They had needed decent gunpowder and the element of surprise, which had been surrendered by any number of spies in Cooper's ranks.

For all he knew, Watie might have contributed more than a few spies to that dismal effort, also. After they had crossed the Canadian River, many of his men were simply . . . gone. They might have died, they might have deserted, or they might have been turncoats reporting to Curtis and Campbell and the other Federal commanders.

Steele hesitated, as if good sense had prevailed and he was going to tell Watie what he really thought of the Battle of Honey Springs and their chances of winning, given any number of other conditions—and that he considered Watie an outlaw on a par with William Quantrill—but he held his tongue.

"Your men worry I am here to conduct an inspection. I am not, Colonel." Steele cleared his throat. "In fact, the reason I am here at all is to say"—his words boomed out now across the camp, drawing men from every corner—

"that you shall no longer be entitled to call yourself Colonel Stand Watie."

Watie's eyes widened. He wobbled a little, as much from shock at what the general said as from the ague. After all he had done, Steele's dislike for him had finally prevailed. After all the battles and death, they were relieving him of command.

General Steele turned so that he faced the assembled Cherokee Mounted Rifles. "It is my duty to inform you all, at the recommendation of General Cooper, that your commander has been promoted, by order of the War Department and President Jefferson Davis, to the rank of Brigadier General." Steele turned as his aide handed him a small wooden box which he opened to show two shining gold stars inside.

Steele stepped up and worked a moment to unfasten Watie's colonel insignia, then fastened on the stars.

"Be it known, General Stand Watie, that you are the first Cherokee to reach the rank of brigadier general in the Army of the Confederate States of America." Steele's demeanor was completely formal, stiff, military—and he made no effort to hide how distasteful this duty was for him. Military action, to him, came from troop movement and engagement, not from guerrilla fighting.

A cheer went up. Watie shook Steele's hand, not sure what to say, not sure he could even speak.

"Thank you," he croaked out. Turning to his men, he added, "And thank all of *you.*"

He wished Sarah and the children could have been here for this moment but, like so many others' families, they were hundreds of miles away. At least he could share the honor with Saladin, who watched from the edge of the mass of soldiers. Watie saluted General Steele, then turned and saluted his son—and his loyal soldiers.

Steamboat Fight
June 15, 1864

"It's good to see you again, old friend," Stand Watie said to William Penn Adair. Adair was thin as a rail and had a pallor more appropriate to a dead man, but he was back, bartered like a slave with the Union. Watie didn't know how many officers had been traded for William, but if it had been left to him he would have emptied Confederate prisons for this one man.

"It's good to see they appreciate you, Stand," William Adair said, touching the stars on Watie's shoulders.

"I need you as commander of my scouts. No one knows this land better than you. And we must catch up on all that has happened."

"I've heard about your adventures, Stand," William said. He laughed. "Word filtered into the Detroit prison, and I was proud every time they cursed you."

"I burned down Rose Cottage," Watie said. He wasn't sure if this was a thing to be proud of, but it had felt good seeing John Ross's precious house reduced to cinders. It had been good killing the Union soldiers guarding it, both black and white, and it had seemed right that John Ross had no more claim on the Cherokee Nation with this simple act. Destruction ought not to be a reason to feel good. But he did.

"I know. Since being returned, everyone has besieged me with the stories." He settled down. "So you need a commander of scouts? That means you have something in mind."

"It would not please General Steele, but nothing I have done pleases him."

"Heard tell you've let the Cherokee Mounted Rifles run a little wild," William said, no hint of criticism in his words. If anything, Watie read the longing at having missed so much rapine and pillage. "I've got a military attack in mind that would please even Steele," Watie said. "I tried to contact General Cooper to coordinate our troop movements, but he is off in Choctaw country talking with Chief Garland."

"This isn't big enough to include General Maxey?" William asked, mentioning the man recently placed in command of the District of Arkansas. "He's a strong supporter of yours."

"General Maxey has sent a few complimentary letters," Watie said modestly. He touched his jacket and heard the crinkle of a letter Maxey had sent him only a week earlier, praising him for his daring in attacking Federal supply wagons. General Steele had never considered this good use of military personnel, more intent on finding "proper" military ventures for his own soldiers. The time for that had passed at Honey Springs.

"Tell me what you need from me, Stand, and I'll do it," William said. Watie knew he could trust his old friend. He began outlining his plan for the attack. As it unfolded, William smiled. He almost laughed aloud in sheer glee when Watie finished.

They stood in the rim of Pheasant Bluff looking down on the Arkansas River, just upriver from the mouth of the

Canadian. Since Vicksburg fell, the Union moved supplies more freely by water than land—Stand Watie had made sure this was true in Indian Territory. Colonel Phillips had ordered a barge pulled by the steamboat *Williams* sent up the river to Fort Gibson.

"There it is," Watie said, pointing. From their vantage point they saw the bend in the Arkansas where the steamboat had to slow as it navigated past dangerous sandbars. "Ours for the taking."

"What other cavalry regiment has ever captured a riverboat?" William Adair wondered aloud. "You have a fine mind, Stand. You ought to be in charge of the Indian District, not William Steele."

"I'll second that," Tom Anderson said, a touch of bitterness in his voice. He had been passed over for promotion by Steele and was out to prove himself anew.

"One battle at a time," cautioned Watie, pleased at the support of his friends and fellow officers. The confederate high command might not see in them general officer ability, but he did. Either of them was as capable, if not more so, than he was at command; although Tom would be better off in Texas with a white brigade.

The *Williams* puffed and chugged and spewed black smoke as the engines reversed. On deck Watie saw the men working to reverse the pistons in order to work the boat free from a sandbar. They might have fastened a rope to a tree on the bank and used their steam capstan to pull the boat free. But the captain, for whatever reason, chose to warp off, reversing the direction of the sternwheel so it caused water to rush under the boat and lift it free.

"We have time," Watie said. "Saladin is bringing around a new company we just recruited. I think they will do well. Get on down and take command, Tom." Watie took some pride in the composition of that company. Osage, Choctaw, Chickasaw and even Creek were proud members. Watie had heard even a few Pawnee from the western plains had joined, and all were willing to be led by a white man. It made him feel that after the war some peace might be worked out.

"Count on us, Stand," Tom said, turning his horse down the steep trail to the riverbank where the company mustered.

"The steamboat is going to put in to the dock just below us to take on more wood," Watie said, watching his adjutant ride away from the river, along a trail winding around out of sight. "That is the vulnerable point. Tom's company will remove the guards, and the rest of the regiment will take the boat."

"I'm proud to be back, Stand, and even prouder having you as my commander," said William. They shook hands again and then William turned his attention to the area below.

"We should get down to the river," Watie said. Leading their horses, the two followed a narrow, meandering trail down to the river level. Already assembled and ready, the remainder of the Cherokee Mounted Rifles waited impatiently.

"No scalping," Watie warned them. "Don't take any risks, but don't take any prisoners, either."

William's eyebrows rose at such callousness, but he said nothing. He strapped on a gun belt and checked the pistol handed him by a corporal. Then he shrugged into a tattered jacket that should have carried a lieutenant colonel insignia but instead showed William to be only a captain.

"Sorry," Watie said, looking at his friend's shoulders. "We'll barter for proper uniforms using the supplies we're going to capture today."

"Wagons?" asked William, looking back up the red-rocked bluff.

"Saladin has six ready to be loaded. The rest of the booty will go to each soldier," Watie said, nervously rubbing his fingers across his gun. He jumped when the *Williams* blew its steam whistle, marking its docking.

The Union guards on the dock had been replaced. More

men from Watie's regiment hid behind the long rows of cut wood, out of sight of anyone on the Texas deck. The pilot would be busy matching steamboat speed with the current flowing against the bow. The captain was already out of the pilot house. He was on deck, getting his deckhands ready to load the wood for the final leg of the trip up the river to Fort Gibson.

"Ready, men. Get ready but don't attack until the order is given," warned Watie. He glanced over his shoulder. William Adair stood ready. It felt good having his friend back and willing to be chief of scouts. Scouting information would be even more important after today, because the Federals would not make the same mistake with their river traffic again. The next steamboat might have a company or more of armed guards on it.

But now? No one expected a cavalry unit to attack a steamboat on the river.

"Now. Go. Attack!" shouted Watie. His men swarmed forward as soon as the heavy hawsers fastened the *Williams* to the dock. Watie saw the shock and surprise on the faces of the rivermen before they died. The Confederate Indians poured onto the boat and raced from deck to deck. Most of the fancy iron and glasswork on the statehouse deck had been ripped out to make room for troops. If the vessel had been filled to the gunwales with Federals it would not have mattered.

There were too many from Watie's regiment with blood in their eyes. It took less than fifteen minutes for the crew to be killed or for them to escape overboard into the churning river. Both Watie's adjutant, Tom Anderson, and William Adair had to order the Indians back to keep them from diving overboard into the water and following their quarry.

"Take everything you can carry," Watie ordered. "Then load everything else onto the wagons!"

No other Confederate cavalry unit had ever captured a steamboat and its cargo. Saladin brought up the wagons so the cargo could be loaded and distributed later throughout the Cherokee Nation. It took the better part of two hours for them to wrestle off the cargo and get rattling along the riverbank with it.

Watie looked on with pride as his men scuttled the *Williams* at the dock. It was a fitting testimony to a change in power in Indian Territory.

"My present to you," he said softly. "From *General* Stand Watie!" With a whoop he joined William Adair and rode after his soldiers.

Reenlistment
June 27, 1864

"John Ross wants to disband all Indian units in the Union Army," Stand Watie said, speaking to the crowd assembled at Limestone Prairie. For days they had come, in twos and threes, sometimes in ragged companies wearing even more ragged Confederate uniforms. More carried tomahawks and knives than pistols and muskets. "He wants to leave the fighting to the white man." Watie paused, then went on. "He does not consider us worthy of combat. He thinks we are incompetent, inept, men of no merit, honor or bravery."

This produced an angry buzz.

"The leaders of the Confederacy know better. What regiment has fought better, more loyally, with greater efficiency than the First Cherokee Mounted Rifles? None!"

This brought a cheer. To his left stood General Cooper, a wide grin on his face. To Watie's left were his officers, the ones he trusted most—William Penn Adair, Tom Anderson, and his own son, Saladin. For a moment, Watie felt a gnawing doubt. He was no speaker, yet he held the assembled crowd using the power of his words.

Words. The words that haunted him were from his wife in a recent letter. He did not know what Saladin had writ-

ten her, but she had the idea their son had become a
hardened murderer, one who enjoyed the war and killing.
The words stuck in his craw because Stand Watie wasn't
sure that Sarah wasn't right. She saw more clearly from
five hundred miles away than he did at inches.

He wasn't even sure if *he* didn't enjoy the killing now.
There had been so much death and destruction meted
out to the Cherokee—and it had come from men who had
pledged their loyalty to the tribe—John Ross, his nephew,
John Drew, so many in the Keetoowah Society. They had
delivered death and misery to their own people, and it
seemed he could do little enough to balance the scales of
justice.

Kill them? Gladly! If John Ross, as old as he was, were
here now, Watie would have killed him with his bare hands.
The man had done so much, too much, to tear apart the
Cherokee Nation that it might never be pieced together
again.

A sour taste rose in his craw and fixed itself at the back
of Watie's throat. He had pledged his support for the CSA
because of all the broken promises made by the United
States. Money, supplies, it had all been promised and never
given. Watie saw the same patterns forming with the Confederacy, as if they also coveted Cherokee land. He made
excuses and what he did today flew in the face of good
sense, but his nephew Elias Boudinot had been unable to
wrest the most minimal support from the Confederate
Congress for them. If the Cherokee could aid the greater
war effort, fine. If they could not, forget them!

It rankled, yet Stand Watie saw no way out other than
to continue with the devils he knew.

"We have met and talked and made our decision," Watie
went on. "I hereby reenlist in the army of the Confederate
States of America, proudly, freely, and with all my heart
and soul. I urge you all to do likewise!"

The cheer deafened him. His own regiment had already

pledged reenlistment to show support. Many of the other regiments came to the end of their service, though. It pleased Watie when the First Choctaw not only reenlisted en masse, but also penned a plea to Chief Garland that all males fit for military service be sworn in to service of the Confederacy.

"You've done a good job, Stand," congratulated Douglas Cooper. "I worried that, when so many of their terms were up, we would lose soldiers. Getting them to reenlist has ensured that Indian Territory will remain a potent force fighting the Federals. This is going to look real good back in the Congress."

"Thank you, sir," Watie said. He had spent days talking to leaders and ordinary soldiers to bring this about.

"You won't be left hanging, I assure you. I've written to General Maxey for a special reenlistment payment, in addition to a full year's salary for all those gathered here today."

"The money will be appreciated, if only as a gesture," Watie said. Cooper tensed, and looked at him. Watie went on. "We need arms, uniforms, we need artillery, if we are to drive out the Union soldiers. Fort Gibson is a festering sore, and we cannot pry them loose from it. They use the fort to supply their raiders, and we cannot stop the supplies they receive from the North."

"Taking Fort Gibson is everyone's goal," Cooper said, "but we lack the manpower to do it, Stand. You know that. Even with all the men here today going up against the fort, they would not succeed."

"We'll continue to raid," Watie said, ire rising. "Like savages." He hated himself for saying it. He sounded like General Steele, and it startled him to realize he wanted to fling army against army rather than continuing the trivial, if effective, raids. Taking the steamboat with its barges of supplies had sorely damaged morale at Fort Gibson, but that had not won a victory. It had not driven out the Federals from their secure post at Fort Gibson.

"We continue destroying enemy supplies to make their lives harder," Cooper corrected. "You are doing a good job, General. The Confederacy owes you a great debt, one that might never be repaid. That is the sorry lot of soldiers—and true patriots."

"Do you approve the reorganization I have outlined, General?"

Cooper nodded. "I have already written to Commissioner Scott voicing my support. It will be a good way to recruit even more soldiers."

"Three brigades," Watie said, "the Cherokee, the Choctaw, and the Creek. In the Cherokee Brigade will be Cherokee, Chickasaw, and Osage."

"The Creek Brigade," Cooper cut in. "I worry about that after all the trouble we had with Opothleyahola. We don't want any desertions to reflect badly on me—on us. You are, after all, the only Indian general."

"There will be no trouble with the Creek soldiers. Creek and Seminole have long fought side by side." Watie's mind ranged back to the days of the Red Stick War. Yes, they had fought well as allies. "The Choctaw Brigade will give us the most trouble."

"Do what you can to see to recruitment, General," Cooper said. "I need to go to Fort Towson, and must get on the road."

"Give my regards to General Maxey," Watie said, knowing why Cooper returned to Fort Towson, and how much Maxey had done to support the Indians. Without him, they would not have received even the trickle of supplies they got from back east. Maxey might not have been an outstanding soldier, but he had won Watie's support as an honorable man who kept his promises.

In part, at least, Maxey was the reason Stand Watie had

organized this mass reenlistment to show support for the CSA.

And it had worked. All around the newly re-upped soldiers congratulated one another. Stand Watie and his officers went to mingle with them, to listen and argue and cement the relationship of individual soldiers to the cause of the South. The days of John Drew and mass desertion were past . . . thanks to General Stand Watie.

Cabin Creek Again
September 18, 1864

"Raids, nothing but piddling little raids," grumbled Stand Watie.

"We've done well, General," Tom Anderson said. "Our brigade's got the most supplies of any Confederate unit in Indian Territory."

"Look at them," Watie said angrily, pointing to his troopers lounging around their camp. "Shoes with holes in the soles. Uniforms that look like a moth has feasted. The fabric is so thin I can see skin through the places where there *aren't* holes. Rifles? Many can't fire because we need parts. Others won't because we don't have enough powder and shot." Watie stomped around, his ire growing. "And food? When was the last *good* meal you ate, Tom?"

"Same as you, General. This morning's breakfast was—"

"As tasty as shoe leather, which we don't have enough of!"

"What are you saying?"

"Saladin's been down in Lamar County to see his mother, brother, and sisters," Watie said. "On the way back he rode a spell with General Gano."

"Richard Gano? Heard tell of him being something of

a firebrand. Just the kind of man your son would take to," spoke up William Adair.

"General Gano's got information. Don't know how he got it, don't care. I am sick of burning houses, even if they do belong to Pins and other pro-Union dolts. They've about freed every slave in the territory, and nothing is being grown, nothing is being repaired. The entire land looks as if it is some vast desolate wasteland."

"A big cemetery," Tom Anderson said under his breath.

"I want more 'n that. I don't want to burn out another Cherokee's home and chalk up a victory that will make the High Command back in Arkansas think I'm a great soldier."

"What do you hear about this General Kirby Smith?" asked William. "Taking over the entire Trans-Mississippi District is a big chore for a man I've not heard of before. The way they change commanders, it's a wonder any of them understand our problems."

"He's fought Canby before. That's why he was put in charge," Watie said, distracted. His vision would not be so easily sidetracked.

"What can we get from General Smith we haven't from all the others?" asked Tom.

"Forget who is in charge," Watie said angrily. "Forget that the War Department has ignored us. Forget it all. Concentrate on what we can do to supply our own people. Our soldiers need food and clothing. So do our families."

"You thinkin' on a big enough raid to get clothing to send south into Texas?" asked William. "We can't get close enough to Fort Smith or Fort Gibson to take what we need. The Federals are too strong, and getting stronger every day now that the war is going their way back East." William coughed and shook his head sadly. "Remember the raid on Fort Smith?"

"That was the problem," Watie said. "It was only a raid. I hate saying it, but General Steele was right. This is not a way to wage war. We needed artillery, and enough troops to overwhelm the garrison. Stealing a few mouthfuls to keep us in the saddle was wrong because it left the Federals in power."

"What's Gano's proposal?" asked Tom. "You know we'll follow you anywhere, Stand, but we don't rightly know this Texan." The way he said "Texan" carried more than a little disdain with it.

"Well, son, let me *tell* you what *my* proposal is," came a booming voice. Richard Gano strutted up, proud as a banty rooster and looking even finer. His uniform, for all the time he had spent on the trail from Texas, was impeccable. Gold braid shone brightly, and he had a flashy silver buckle holding his gun belt that had been hammered out of a Texas Ranger's badge. Behind him stood Saladin Watie and a half dozen others, all looking superior.

Seeing his son and Gano with his staff almost made Watie change his mind. Almost. If what Saladin said was true, Gano offered more than a quick, limited raid.

"Go right on, General," said William. "Let's hear your proposition. We're all spoilin' for a good fight."

Before Gano finished, not only Watie but this small circle of officers were eagerly asking questions about what might break the back of Colonel Phillips and everyone in Fort Gibson.

Cabin Creek, mused Watie as he studied both road and the hills surrounding the prairie where a sluggish stream flowed over smooth rocks and around lazy bends. "The last time we were here was something of a disaster." July 1863 had been a notable failure for him. The stream had been swollen and almost impassable then. But not now, not this time. He felt in his bones there would be Confederate victory today.

"I got my entire Texas Brigade hidden yonder in that

canebrake. Some strung out into the trees, others back a ways to give depth in case they got scouts workin' the area."

"My brigade will take them once we sight the last wagon." Watie's heart beat faster. "How many wagons are likely to be in the supply train?"

"A hundred," Gano said easily. "More. My information says it'll be worth more than a million, five hundred thousand in supplies, enough to keep us all going through the winter."

"Someone at Fort Scott give you the word?" asked William Adair.

"Now, that'd be tellin' stories out of school, Colonel," Gano said, smirking. "I might need to ask for more favors later on. Wouldn't do havin' everyone know where I find these things out. After all, you can't go to the well too often or you'll find it's gone dry on you."

"Understood, sir," William said. To Stand Watie he said, "General, let me get out with my scouts. A supply train this big is sure to be well guarded."

"I'm counting on it," Watie said. "Get out there and let us know in time to position our men properly, Colonel Adair."

William saluted and hurried off, taking two score of scouts with him. This left Watie to the hardest part of any battle: anticipation with no chance for action. He wanted to ride among his brigade and be sure they were prepared, but if he did, it would stir them up unnecessarily.

"The sergeants know their job, Stand," Tom Anderson said. "If you like, I can see if there's anything more to be done."

"That's all right, Tom," Watie said. "Patience used to be one of my virtues. That's long gone, along with most of the others." He heaved a big sigh, wondering when the necessities of war ever called for abandonment of integrity. In another hour, his moral shortcomings would no longer matter. Only his ability to command in the heat of battle would count.

"Hot damn, Stand," said Tom Anderson. "There's more wagons there than Gano thought. And fewer soldiers guarding them than there ought to be."

"Are the men ready?" Stand Watie asked needlessly. He had seen his adjutant mustering the forces and getting them to their horses. They lined the road for almost a mile, just out of sight of the long supply train.

"William's found the end of the train damned near two miles down the road. He counted two hundred fifty wagons! There're no more than five hundred guards for the entire supply train, Stand!" Tom Anderson shifted in the saddle, drew his pistol, and looked to his commanding officer for the sign that they were to attack.

Watie marveled at everything he had learned. There was hardly any need for the Texas Brigade. His own Cherokee Brigade could capture the entire train without their help. That made him feel good. Then time for reflection passed, and time for action beckoned.

"Charge!" Watie cried. The bugler picked up the command, and pistols fired sporadically along his attacking line. His mare stumbled in soft dirt, then got her feet under her, rocketing him into the midst of the pitched battle.

There were fewer than five hundred Federals guarding the long wagon train, but they put up a spirited battle. Watie's brigade had taken them by surprise, and they valued their lives more than the supplies bound for Fort Gibson. Many turned and fled, heading directly into the leveled guns of the Texas Brigade. Watie did nothing to stop them. He rejoiced in the smell of gunpowder, the crash of muskets, and the cries of wounded men—wounded Federals.

By the time his entire force had circled the wagon train,

the drivers realized their guards were gone and they had no choice. Watie ended up with more than three hundred prisoners that day—and 750 mules and all the supplies meant to get the Fort Gibson garrison through a very long, cold winter.

"Take what you will need this winter, men," Watie ordered. "Let General Gano take the balance back to Texas." He eyed the strutting little Texas general, who saluted him. Watie knew the supplies, at least some of them, would go to Cherokee families down south—and in Lamar County, where his own family stayed.

In one afternoon, he had dealt a severe blow to the Fort Gibson garrison and seen to provisioning his own men through the entire winter. This time Cabin Creek spelled victory. It felt good.

Boggy Depot
Winter 1864

"The men're gettin' mighty hungry, Stand," Tom Anderson said. "Can't say I don't agree." Stand Watie's adjutant rubbed his belly. It growled loud enough to be heard.

"We shouldn't have let so much of the Cabin Creek supply train go south," Watie said. "Even if it did end up with our families."

"You say it did. I don't hear that. The Texans kept most of it."

"Sarah got some." Watie smiled. "A recent letter said she had been making me new shirts, and was glad I had taken the matter into my own hands." He rubbed the shirt she had made for him. He had given the one he had taken from the supply train to a private whose entire family had been killed by the Pins. Watie figured he needed help more than a shirt, but it was all that could be offered.

"Glad to hear it," Tom said, "but the winter's too cold for us to ride out. Boggy Depot's a terrible spot to camp."

"Malaria," Watie said, agreeing. It usually hit in the summer, but Boggy Depot lived up to its name and his troops came down with malaria no matter what season. "Where else can we go? The Federals have us boxed in, unless we go south to Texas."

"That's a thought," Tom allowed. "We're not doin' much to further our cause sittin' around small fires and freezin' our fingers off."

"That's not all we're freezing off," Watie said, grinning a little bit. He rubbed himself, although the wind had stopped. It was always the restless whip of the wind that sucked the heat from his body. He didn't know what it was now in the still cold that bothered him so. A quick swipe across his forehead came away without the telltale sweat that betrayed malaria.

He was healthy enough, but the weather still wore on him.

"Might be we could do better if we had food, medicine, more blankets."

"Might be we could win the damn war if we had a big enough cannon," Tom said. "That's not going to happen, either."

"Might," Watie said. "Tom, I want you to get on across the Mississippi and see if you can shake loose supplies. Tell General Smith of our plight. Go right to the top. Don't bother with underlings. We need someone to speak with a booming voice to the War Department, if we are going to get the supplies we need just to stay alive."

"I'm not much of a talker, Stand. I'm not much of a soldier, either, but I'll do what I'm told." Tom Anderson brushed the front of his dirty uniform and tried to look military. Watie wasn't sure the man succeeded, but other than his son and William Penn Adair, Tom Anderson was the man he trusted most. With his life, with anything having to do with the brigade, Stand Watie trusted his adjutant. More than this, he was the only white man in the brigade. If the War Department did not listen to him, they would never listen to a Cherokee.

"If you can, tell General Maxey about our situation, but insist on talking to Kirby Smith."

"Grass surely is thin this year," Tom said, staring out at the poor grazing. He shivered. "And the malaria is killing more of us than gunfire from the Federals."

"I wish Elias had been more successful. He spoke so earnestly in council, but in front of the Confederate Congress in Richmond he gets nowhere."

"There might not be anywhere to go, Stand," Tom said honestly. "There have been too many losses out West. Back East doesn't sound any better for our cause. Elias can't squeeze blood out of a rock."

"There must be something more he could have done. I am disappointed in my nephew." Stand Watie paced around in little circles, hands clasped behind his back. "If I thought my presence would sway them, I would go, but I am needed here with my brigade. General Cooper has said there might be action later."

"Stand," Tom said tiredly, "there won't be any campaign until spring. Maybe not then. What kind of fight could any of these men put up?"

"A good one!" Watie flared. "They will do as they are ordered because they are good soldiers, loyal and not inclined to desert like John Drew's regiment."

"Granted," Tom said. "When do you want me to leave?"

"Right away," Watie said. "I have heard that attempts to get cotton to Mexican ports for sale in Europe have failed because of the Union blockade."

Tom sucked in his breath. He exhaled slowly. "Stand, if you're not looking at this clearly, you'll never see the real problems."

"You're right, Tom, as always. Being the optimist is my way of getting through these hard times. I *have* to believe conditions will improve. What's the only other way it might end?"

"The Mexican cotton brokers have stolen damn near

every strand of cotton. What few bales made it through to Europe fetched low prices because of the poor quality. No matter what I get out of the War Department, don't expect Mexican cotton sales to help us."

"It is going to be a very long winter, Tom. Very long."

Tom Anderson saluted, and left to cross the Mississippi on a futile mission.

Unraveling Fortune
May 26, 1865

Stand Watie read his wife's letter slowly, savoring every word. He ran his fingers over the paper, knowing she had touched it. He wished her perfume lingered on the paper, but knew it did not. Sarah had long since been without such a luxury. He would have settled for the smell of her cooking, of her apple cobbler, of her.

"What's she got to say, Father?" asked Saladin, coming up and squatting down next to the low stool where Watie worked.

"She worries about us," he said. "Especially about me. Rumor of the Union bounty on my head has reached Texas," he said, grinning without any hint of humor. "There are also stories of my death and my capture. It seems I am the sole topic of conversation down south."

"She worries because you are in danger so much."

"Aren't we all?" Stand Watie looked around the bivouac and saw not a brigade ready to fight but a gang of men in tattered clothing, still mostly starving, and unable to accomplish more than a quick raid. If they had to fight a pitched battle, Watie knew they would lose, and that tore at him. The First Cherokee Mounted Rifles once had been a force to be reckoned with. John Drew's regiment had never come close to this one in terms of determination, loyalty, patriotism, sheer courage. Honey Springs had sapped so much of their strength and will.

The winter had been brutal, and no supplies had come from Tom Anderson's trip to palaver with General Smith. If anything, the rebuff had been worse than an outright denial. Smith had sounded more like Steele, castigating the Cherokee for not fighting hard enough.

It had been a long trip from the treaty John Ross had negotiated—saying Cherokee soldiers would be used only on Indian land, and that the Confederacy would provide supplies and support—to this sorry turn of events. Watie felt as if it were yet another nail driven deep into a Cherokee coffin.

"What does she have to say of the others?" asked Saladin. "I miss them all, but especially Ninnie."

"Minnehaha is doing well with her studies. Your mother is responsible for a small school, and your Uncle James is helping her."

"It's a good thing he resigned his commission and went to be with Mother," Saladin said. "I have nothing against Uncle James, but he was no fighter."

"I valued his counsel," Watie said, and he had. James Bell had always seen clearly, presenting facts in such a way Watie could more easily sort them and come to his decision. James had always realized who the principal chief of the Cherokee Nation was and had advised, not pushed, in the times he offered his help.

"I spoke with Colonel Adair's aide a few minutes ago, Father," Saladin said. "A courier is riding for our camp."

Watie looked into the Oklahoma sky. Heavy leaden clouds grew into fluffy mountains to the east, and he thought he saw cloud to cloud lightning strikes, not a good omen. To the north he saw puffy white clouds, but many rushed upward into anvil-headed monoliths that were more threatening than those to the east. Watie felt as if he had been put on such an anvil and hammered flat. Nothing remained in him but a small, hard core of determination. He would continue fighting as long as there was life in his body. How could he inspire his men to follow him on a road that was rapidly drawing to a dead end?

How he missed Sarah.

"Stand," came William Adair's call. "We got a rider coming fast from across the river."

"The Mississippi, or somewhere closer?"

"This is a courier from General Smith's headquarters. I recognize him as one of the best. The general uses him for only the most important missions."

Watie folded his wife's letter and tucked it away. He had nothing more to do than wait. Perhaps Kirby Smith sent orders for a new spring offensive. Watie wasn't sure where Douglas Cooper raided, but he had not heard of the man's activities in more than a month. For all that, he had not been privy to even rumors of other units fighting in Indian Territory. His officers closed ranks with him, and he appreciated it. By the time Smith's messenger arrived, Tom Anderson, William, Saladin, and a half-dozen others, mostly junior officers recently promoted to fill positions created by malaria and other ugly deaths, waited impatiently. They knew that whatever attack Kirby Smith ordered had to be made fast, while their rifles and powder—and the men— were in condition for it.

"Sir, compliments from General Smith," the courier sergeant said, hitting the ground running.

"And mine to him," Watie said, patiently letting the courier get past the pleasantries to the real message. Perhaps it would be an all-out attack on Fort Gibson. That fort was the key to taking back the Cherokee Nation. Without it providing safety and supplies to Federal troops, the Union would have to retreat. The bluecoats could be swept from the territory by the end of summer, given enough determination.

The sergeant swallowed hard, then straightened. "Here, sir. It is my sad duty to deliver this information to you." He pulled an envelope from inside his wool jacket. From where he stood Watie could see the ornate wax seal showing this had truly come from General Smith's hand.

He took the envelope and broke open the seal. He read the terse letter inside.

"Thank you, Sergeant."

"Your reply, sir?"

Watie's anger boiled up deep within, but the words, though laced with his wrath, were level enough.

"Tell General Smith that he might surrender the entire Trans-Mississippi District to the Union commander, but that I will not, I *cannot*, betray my people in such a fashion. I will not surrender until it is impossible for my brigade to fight on!"

The sergeant blinked, licked his lips, then said, "But it's over, sir. The general's surrendered to Canby."

"For General Smith the war is over. As principal chief of the Cherokee, as a general in the army of the Confederacy, it is my right and duty to decide when to surrender."

Stand Watie stood a little straighter and said in a firm voice, "I will not surrender."

Silence met his decision.

The Grand Council
June 10, 1865

Stand Watie sat on the dais at Camp Napoleon and watched as the delegates from the other tribes entered and sat silently. To his right sat General Cooper, who had requested this meeting. Since a trip to Richmond and the removal of General Steele, Cooper had done all he could to establish a new command in Indian Territory. Watie wished Cooper had been more decisive and open in his movements. It seemed as if the general had simply vanished from the face of the earth.

"Are you ready, Stand?" asked Cooper.

"I don't like it," Watie replied, but he rose and stepped forward. He faced the silent, crowded room and struggled to find the right words.

"We have called this Grand Council to discuss our future, the future of all tribes in the territory, both civilized and savage." Watie saw no reaction in the delegates, nor had he expected any. They all knew of General Smith's surrender the prior month. They all knew Lee had surrendered at Appomattox on April ninth. Everyone in the hot, close room realized they had signed a treaty with the wrong side.

"We have many among us who are capable of negotiat-

ing terms of an armistice with the United States," Watie
said. "My nephew, Elias Cornelius Boudinot, is such a
man." He turned and indicated the elegantly dressed man
at the side of the dais. Watie was not completely pleased
with the way Elias had dealt with the Confederate Congress, but that was a different war, now. This war, the one
after the surrender, depended on words, not force of arms,
and in that Elias was good, very good.

"What we need is to present a united front for the armistice talks. We must develop a plan, make our demands,
show that we will not be treated as the vanquished."

"Have you surrendered your troops yet, Stand?" called
someone in the middle of the Creek delegation.

"No, I have not. I will not surrender until the Five Civilized Tribes have worked out a new treaty with the United
States that will not leave us as impoverished as before. The
Federals did not pay the rents on the Neutral Lands. They
never honored the old treaty, including the Treaty of New
Echota." Watie knew that among his own people he tread
on dangerous ground by even mentioning the old treaty
and the loss of their Georgia lands. The full-bloods had
never accepted that treaty, unlike the mixed-bloods. Signatures on that treaty had led to the feud between the
Ridge Party and the Ross Party.

As he thought of John Ross, he wanted to spit. The old
man worked ceaselessly to further his own ambitions. Ross
wanted to hold a peace conference at Fort Smith, but Watie
was adamant that all the tribes in Indian Territory be agreed
before sending any delegates to such a conference.

"Are you going to keep fighting? Your men have run
wild. You even tryin' to maintain discipline?" The accusation came from halfway back in the crowd. Watie could
not tell who spoke, and it hardly mattered. The question
was foremost on all their minds.

"Gentlemen," said Douglas Cooper, rising. "I am sure
General Watie will surrender his command when it is most

advantageous to the Five Civilized Tribes, and not one minute before. I have given over my command to Colonel Phillips, the Union commander at Fort Gibson, and am here only as an adviser. However, please know I have only the best interests of your people in mind." Cooper smiled crookedly. "My home at Washita is open to any who wish to take council with me. And I am sure Albert Pike will be glad to lend what authority he can to any decision you reach at this Grand Council." Cooper saluted Watie and said, "I take my leave, sir, so you may discuss freely the concerns of your tribes."

"Sir," Watie said, returning the salute and suddenly feeling very alone. For months Cooper might as well have been dead, the way he had cut himself off from Watie and the other field commanders, but Watie felt Cooper spoke truthfully when he said he wanted only the best for the tribes.

Douglas Cooper walked out of the hall, leaving Watie completely in charge.

"We need to make our demands on the United States forceful. We must remain as one, or we will all lose our property. We have seen how the Jayhawkers operated. Do we want them stealing our lands and keeping *us* as slaves, no matter how they decry the institution of slavery?"

Watie allowed the meeting to break apart. He and Elias went from group to group, soothing old hatreds and forging new alliances and friendships among the delegates of the Five Civilized Tribes. It was a chore as demanding as any attack he had led in the field.

Only when all had agreed on the need to maintain a separate peace and to ignore that any of them had fought for the South did Stand Watie feel more confident.

Thirteen days later Stand Watie surrendered his command, the last Confederate general to do so.

The Peace Council
September 1865

Stand Watie was tired, both in body and spirit. He and the rest of the Cherokee delegation had ridden directly from Armstrong Academy, the capital of the Choctaw Nation. Along the way he had received a mixture of greetings, ranging from quiet support in his own nation from the mixed-bloods to outright animosity from bluecoat soldiers and those Cherokee who had only recently returned from their exile in Kansas. From them, many of them Keetoowah Society members and full-bloods, he got only derision.

He was principal chief, no matter what claims John Ross made.

"He'll be there, you know," Elias Boudinot said.

"Ross? Yes, I suppose so. He's been in Washington all this time trying to regain his place as principal chief."

"Uncle, he has always claimed to be principal chief," Elias said in exasperation. "The Northern Cherokee claim him as their leader. Now he wants the United States to declare him chief of all Cherokee."

Watie shrugged this off. He had spent a lifetime wrangling politically with John Ross. If the Federals stripped him of his due as principal chief, there would be more trouble than they cared to deal with. He had more important matters to deal with, such as forcing the United States to let the Cherokee keep their land—and their nation.

"We will face not their politicians, Uncle, but their military leaders," Elias went on. "They will try to cow us into yielding our sovereignty. We—"

"I understand all this, Elias," Watie said in exasperation. He had no time for double-dealing. If President Johnson sent only military officers to this peace conference, good. He was used to dealing with such direct men. Moreover, he might have fought against some of them. Watie appreciated a good opponent.

"Commissioner of Indian Affairs Dennis Cooley will be elected president of the meeting," Elias said, "but he has his orders already for dividing our land."

"What orders?" asked Watie. His nephew had not told him this before. "How do you know?"

"Senate bill #459, the Harlan Bill, is at the center of their plan. It was voted into law the day Cooley left Washington."

"We are not here for a fight over our land," Watie said. "They called this meeting only to sign the peace treaty. The matter of our land will be dealt with later."

"Uncle Stand, they have decided it. All they want from you is to surrender to their terms."

Watie and the others entered the meeting hall. He spent several minutes speaking with the delegates from the Five Civilized Tribes, and was only a little surprised to see representatives from other tribes living west of the Mississippi. The United States had wanted a comprehensive meeting of tribes, and was mostly successful.

"That's Cooley," Elias said, whispering in his uncle's ear.

"Gentlemen, welcome," Cooley said. "I see there are far too many of you to accommodate in these facilities. Therefore, you shall adjourn and form delegations of five only. Present your credentials this afternoon, and we shall continue." Cooley rapped his gavel, rose and left.

Watie frowned. He turned to Elias. "What does he mean?"

"They're already at work to limit our vote," Elias said. "Five from each tribe?"

"But they wanted representatives to sign the peace treaty."

"There is more to be done here," Elias said grimly. "We must fight it at every turn, but this is not the place. We should choose our delegates, as Cooley asked."

"Then let's speak with the other chiefs," Watie said. Dealing with the United States was as tiresome as dealing with John Ross, but he would do it because his people required his strength now.

"Do I understand this a'right?" Stand Watie asked, looking up at Elias Boudinot. "They want all tribes to forfeit all rights to our land, and we have lost all annuities and other payments due us—which they had never paid *before* the war?"

"Cooley wants nothing more than a signature on what seems an innocent enough document," Elias said, running his finger down the long list of things to be forfeited by the Five Civilized Tribes, along with the Comanche, Osage, Quapaw, Seneca, and Shawnee. "They seek to divide us, Uncle Stand, and make each tribe negotiate separately."

Watie looked around the room at the other chiefs assembled for this so-called peace conference. What the United States wanted was nothing less than total impoverishment of the tribes. No Southern state was being given such harsh terms, and he saw no reason why any Indian tribe should agree. Divide and conquer. Watie knew the result of that tactic, should the United States succeed.

The Cherokee Nation would be most brutally dealt with, because he had been the last Southern general to surrender and the North wanted to punish him and his tribe.

"They said they fought to eliminate slavery. This will reduce us to less than slaves. Slaves have masters to feed, clothe, and shelter them. This will make us even less. What do we do, eat dirt to stay alive?"

"Anger will get us nowhere," Elias cautioned. "You must never lose your temper when dealing with bureaucrats, Uncle. That means they win."

"They will establish tribal land, but only for those Cherokee who ran to Kansas—the Keetoowahs, and the others who preyed on their own people."

"Uncle," Elias said more sharply.

Stand Watie fell silent, his mind racing to find other solutions. He left Elias and went to talk with Clermont, the chief of the Osage, and Samuel Checote, principal chief of the Creek. Slowly, the other chiefs came to listen and add their wisdom. It became obvious to Watie there could be no unity among them because of the seeds of discord already sown by Cooley. He had promised bits and pieces to each, and nothing significant to any of them.

Watie turned to see Elias speaking earnestly with Commissioner Cooley. The two left together, speaking with great animation. What did his nephew brew? He had become too embroiled in the affairs of the political animals for Watie's comfort, but alone of those representing the tribes, Elias Boudinot seemed to know how to get what they wanted.

Sitting impatiently, Watie passed more than an hour before his nephew returned. Elias was flushed, and spoke in low, conspiratorial tones.

"Uncle, things begin to work themselves out. Cooley will castigate John Ross as the one responsible for the treaty presented to the tribe by Albert Pike. Ross did, after all, sign it, and you did not."

"I would have, except John Ross—"

"Hush. There is no need to even say you supported it.

The Loyal Cherokee, as the Federals call the Ross faction, later repudiated the treaty."

"Just before Ross was captured by the Federals," Watie pointed out.

"That does not matter. John Ross's part in that repudiation need not be mentioned. Ross is old, seventy-seven now, and only his representatives are here because he is so frail. They do not carry the force of his conviction, and I have convinced Cooley to deal with us instead of them."

"What does he want in exchange for us returning to our own land?" Watie asked sarcastically. Elias ignored the tone.

"We must allow Negroes to settle on our land."

"What! They don't permit that anywhere else in the United States. They think to create a colony for the freed slaves on *our* land."

"Uncle, these are their terms. We will be free of intervention by the white man, but we must give much of our land to those who fled to Kansas during the war."

"The Pins."

"Yes," Elias said.

"They still work to destroy us as a tribe. We dare not agree to this, or they will ravage us far worse than any cannon or musket did during the war."

"The Creek seem to agree. They insist on branding Opothleyahola a traitor when Cooley wants him lauded."

"Let the Creek fight their own battles. This is for the life of the Cherokee!" Watie was outraged at how little they were being given in return for complete surrender. "Better to pick up arms again than to bow to such demands."

"You should talk to the Chickasaw and Choctaw. They are shouldering the full blame themselves, when they might have put some off on Cooper or Pike. This is not the time to stand on principle, Uncle. We must deal the best we can."

Elias rushed off to again speak with Cooley and other commissioners. Watie watched as his nephew was greeted cordially by the others, and wondered what other deals were being made . . . at the expense of the Cherokee Nation.

"He is destroying us," protested William Penn Adair. "He sold us out to the Confederate Congress, and now Elias does the same thing to the United States!"

Stand Watie said nothing. He listened to the obsequious words his nephew spouted and tried to hold down his ire. Elias had insisted this was the only way the Cherokee could ever escape total annihilation, and Watie had agreed—a little.

"He's throwing away any chance of clemency," William whispered. "Stop him, Stand. You are principal chief, not that popinjay!"

"The organization of the Indian Territory," Elias Boudinot said, striking a pose in front of the assembled commissioners, "is one of the grandest and noblest schemes ever devised for the red men, and entitles the author"—Elias bowed in the direction of Commissioner Cooley—"to the lasting gratitude of every Indian."

"Hogwash," raged William. Watie put a hand on his friend's arm and shook his head.

"Elias is the last to speak, and we are the last to sign."

"You'll sign away everything!"

"No," Stand Watie said, the taste on his tongue metallic and bitter. "All we are doing is signing a peace treaty, and one promising amnesty. Nothing else will be settled today. If the United States wants more, and they do, old friend, they do, then they must come to the Cherokee Nation for it. We will deal on our home land, not here in Arkansas."

Elias continued his speech and, with a flourish, drew a pen and held it out for his uncle. Stand Watie made his way forward and with all the dignity he could muster, signed the treaty giving away nothing to the United States. He smiled crookedly as he signed. As far as he was concerned, this peace treaty was as empty as the promises made by the men in Washington. The war of bullets might be over, but there was still the war of words to win.

And he was the man to do it.

Exile
Winter 1865-66

"Elias sold us out," William Penn Adair declared. He warmed his hands from the wan heat emanating from the iron Franklin stove in the middle of the room. He hunched over, and Stand Watie wondered if his friend was sick. So many of them were.

His dear Sarah was here with him at last, as were the children. Saladin was sick again with the flu and Jacqueline sneezed and sniffled, but Ninnie was hale and hearty, helping her mother. Watie missed his other son, Watica, who was off to school. And he would always miss Cumiskey, with his quick smile and shy sidelong look, dead these two years.

"Elias did what he could to keep the nation together," Watie said. "It is not his fault the commissioners intended to split the tribes and seize all our land." It galled Watie that John Ross had done more to preserve the integrity of the nation than Elias, though. Ross maneuvered to be named principal chief over the new Cherokee Nation, but Watie retained the title, empty of authority though it was.

He snorted in disgust, causing a small trail of condensation to form a feathery trail. He was recognized as principal chief by Washington, but over what? The Cherokee Nation barely existed, more a hope than a reality.

The winter was bitter, and they imposed on the hospitality of the Choctaws. Not agreeing to the conditions of surrender had infuriated Cooley and the others, in spite of their amiability toward Elias. The soldiers at Fort Gibson, under a new commander, had driven all mixed-blood Cherokee from the land, letting only the full-bloods settle, but this was a hollow victory, and all knew it. The whites wanted the land. Titles became confused, and needed to be litigated in white court at Fort Smith. The tribal courts had always settled such disputes, but no longer. Washington had disbanded all judicial bodies, demanding a hand in decisions made concerning the Five Civilized Tribes.

In spite of the white man's insistence on running the territory entirely, some came to Watie for resolution of old disputes, but not many. Some still saw him as a military leader. The only Indian general in the Confederate Army had long since laid aside his weapons, but he continued to fight.

"Elias has conveyed our ill feelings toward the treaty," Watie said, "and John Ross might forge a single nation for us with all his devious politicking. It is my job to retain control, no matter who prevails."

Outside the simple house whined bitter, vicious wind. A tiny pile of hard white pellets worked higher as the snow was blown past the doorjamb. Ninnie quietly swept it away and hunted for a cloth to force into the crack to keep it from leaking more snow. No matter what, Watie and his family were together again. That mattered to him as much as it did to Sarah.

She sat in a corner of the room doing her sewing, humming softly to herself. For her sake, he would never give in. For his children, and all the others entrusted to his care as principal chief, he could never yield.

"Elias is not our only ally in Washington," Watie said. "Douglas Cooper pleads our case."

"He has not even been granted amnesty. In their eyes,

he is a war criminal, a traitor!" William moved his chair a little closer to the stove. Watie opened the iron door using a set of tongs to keep from burning himself, and heaved in a few more twigs. They sizzled and crackled, then grudgingly yielded their heat. He needed to chop more wood, since Saladin was bedridden. Jacqueline could help him carry it in.

"Cooper is well enough received," Watie said. William had turned into such a pessimist. "Cooley summoned Albert Pike to negotiate on our behalf, also. Pike is an honorable man."

"Another one for whom amnesty has not been granted."

"That does not bother the government agents," Watie pointed out. He settled back, thinking on what to do after the treaty being negotiated established the Cherokee Nation once more. The railroads moving in at the edges of the territory had to be stopped, or at least slowed. With them would come floods of white settlers. Watie did not quite understand the Homestead Act, but knew it would permit Cherokee land to be given over to white settlers without compensation for the tribe.

So many things to worry about. He realized the war was still being fought, while William thought only in terms of what had been. For now, moving back into position was good enough—even if they froze slowly on Choctaw land.

With spring would come the thaw, and with the thaw a renewal of both crops and the Cherokee Nation. Stand Watie had faith.

Changes
August 10, 1866

Crops were adequate, but Stand Watie took scant pleasure in the accomplishment of growing them. He held the telegram sent him by Elias Boudinot from Washington as he stared out over the farmland. Drought had given spotty crops this year, but nothing as severe as that during the war had stalked the land this year. He sank down and put a gum tree to his back. Insects buzzed around his face, and he idly swatted at them.

Then he opened the flimsy telegram again and read the message for the tenth time.

"What is it, Father?" asked Saladin. The young man crouched down and dusted off his calloused hands. He had been weeding, a neverending chore in spite of the scant rain. Weeds always grew, even if crops did not.

"John Ross died nine days ago," he said.

"Good! The old—"

"Saladin," Watie said sharply. "I take no pleasure in his death."

"Why not? He killed your nephews and brother and—"

"So long ago. John Ross did so much worse after that, always conniving to gain the upper hand. Even when the

United States declared me principal chief he refused to quit."

"He wanted only what was best for himself, not our people," Saladin said. "Didn't he make off with the treasury and turn it over to the United States so they could make war against us? He betrayed his own people!"

"Yes, that is probably so. He signed the treaty last month."

"What treaty?"

"It grants us a whole nation once more." Stand Watie smiled a little. "He fought to disband the Southern Cherokee and reinstate himself as chief, but it didn't work. He accomplished what I wanted. That is the ultimate joke on him, but it is no revenge I can truly enjoy."

"I would have killed him using a knife, so he would have died slowly!"

So cruel, his son. The war had so hardened him. Watie hoped Saladin would learn more of diplomacy. He would need it when he became principal chief—of the Cherokee Nation.

It was ironic that John Ross had completed the work they had all started at the Fort Smith peace conference, and then died. Ironic, and unsatisfying for Stand Watie. An old enemy had vanished from his life, leaving a void. How he might have felt better about Ross's death, he could not say. John Ross had been an old man, one ravaged by sickness in the past few years. Watie considered what his son had said about killing Ross with his own hands.

That would not have satisfied him. Stand Watie had to admit he was unsure what would have erased the anger and hatred forged over the years by one duplicitous act after another. Perhaps outliving his ancient enemy was enough. Perhaps nothing was.

"Mother has supper ready," Saladin said, standing. Watie looked up at his son—a young man, strong and good, and the kind needed to make the Cherokee great again.

"Then let's not keep her waiting, as we have so much during the past few years." Stand Watie tucked the telegram into his pocket and walked beside his son to the simple house that showed his first steps toward regained prosperity.

Epilogue

Following John Ross's death, the Cherokee National Council convened in November at Tahlequah and elected William Potter Ross principal chief, emphasizing the sharp division between the Northern and Southern Cherokee.

Stand Watie and Elias Cornelius Boudinot continued to fight against both the poverty of their people and Chief Will Ross until August 1867. Election of Lewis Downing at that time lured many Southern Cherokee back into the Nation, where they settled in the Canadian District, still wary of the Pins. Stand Watie and his family settled near Elias Boudinot at Webbers Falls, poor but proud.

John Ross's remains were returned to the Cherokee Nation and placed near the former site of his beloved Rose Cottage at Park Hill.

In 1868, Saladin Watie died at the age of twenty-one. Watica died in 1869, leaving Stand Watie with only his two daughters. Watie died suddenly on September 9, 1871. His two daughters, Jacqueline and Minnehaha (Ninnie), died in 1873. None of Stand Watie's children had married or had any children.

When Oklahoma became a state in 1907, the Cherokee dominated a significant part of the state through education, determination, and the courage of its tribal members.

The Wingman Series
By Mack Maloney

__#1 Wingman	0-7860-0310-3	$4.99US/$6.50CAN
__#2 The Circle War	0-7860-0346-4	$4.99US/$6.50CAN
__#3 The Lucifer Crusade	0-7860-0388-X	$4.99US/$6.50CAN
__#4 Thunder in the East	0-7860-0428-2	$4.99US/$6.50CAN
__#5 The Twisted Cross	0-7860-0467-3	$4.99US/$6.50CAN
__#6 The Final Storm	0-7860-0505-X	$4.99US/$6.50CAN
__#7 Freedom Express	0-7860-0548-3	$4.99US/$6.50CAN
__#8 Skyfire	0-7860-0605-6	$4.99US/$6.50CAN
__#9 Return from the Inferno	0-7860-0645-5	$4.99US/$6.50CAN
__#12 Target: Point Zero	0-7860-0299-9	$4.99US/$6.50CAN
__#13 Death Orbit	0-7860-0357-X	$4.99US/$6.50CAN
__#15 Return of the Sky Ghost	0-7860-0510-6	$4.99US/$6.50CAN

Call toll free **1-888-345-BOOK** to order by phone or use this coupon to order by mail.

Name _____

Address _____

City _____ State _____ Zip _____

Please send me the books I have checked above.

I am enclosing $_____

Plus postage and handling* $_____

Sales tax (in New York and Tennessee only) $_____

Total amount enclosed $_____

*Add $2.50 for the first book and $.50 for each additional book.

Send check or Money order (no cash or CODs) to:

Kensington Publishing Corp., 850 Third Avenue, New York, NY 10022

Prices and Numbers subject to change without notice.

All orders subject to availability.

Check out our website at **www.kensingtonbooks.com**

A World of Eerie Suspense
Awaits in Novels by Noel Hynd